Division One:
A Small Medium
At Large

by Stephanie Osborn

Chromosphere Press

Huntsville, AL

Chromosphere Press
P.O. Box 3412
Huntsville, AL 35810
www.chromospherepress.com

Table of Contents

Chapter 1

As soon as the Alpha One team entered the Core that morning, the flooring around their feet reacted, glowing an urgent, deep red between the matte black tiles, and flashing gently in a pattern—three beats on, one beat off. The walls near them also developed the same color scheme and urgent flashing pattern.

"Whu-oh," Echo noted, seeing the color change, "Fox wants us, right now."

"Yeah, I see it. I wonder what's up?" Omega wondered.

"Dunno. We'll find out soon enough. Let's go."

"Right beside ya, Ace."

The tall, cool blonde woman with the Celtic complexion and the even taller, dark-haired man with the broad cheekbones that bespoke Native American in his ancestry picked up the pace, aiming for the office of the Director of Division One of the Pan-Galactic Law Enforcement and Immigration Administration, headquartered in New York City on Earth, Sol System. They were headed across the Core, which was, effectively, a huge spaceport concourse, hidden—via a space warp—in the very same building which housed a modest Jewish center and school in Brooklyn, on Division Avenue, just off the East River. It was, however, well connected to landing sites nearby—and other Agency Offices all over the world—via an extensive and highly sophisticated underground maglev tube train system, whose Headquarters sub-basement terminus was affectionately dubbed by the agents, 'Grand Central Station.'

This pair of Agents was the top team of the very same Agency about which so many urban legends had sprung, the lead team of the Alpha Line special forces department, the Agency's version of the Texas Rangers. Echo was the department's chief, and Omega was his recently-trained partner and newly-minted executive assistant, but they were both excellent—and feared—field agents. As Alpha One progressed at speed, aliens and other agents alike respectfully moved out of their path, their reputations preceding them.

They took the curving ramp up to Fox's office without slowing down. Echo knocked, and from within emerged a muffled, "Come in."

* * *

Fox sat at his desk, typing something into the virtual keyboard embedded in his desktop, and looked up as they entered. He appeared to be a couple of decades older than the thirtysomethings that comprised Alpha One, but with just as athletic a physique; he was, in fact, some five decades older than his premier team. His rugged, moderately lined face was clean-shaven; his hair was salt-and-pepper, rather heavily weighted toward salt. It lent him a distinguished air, especially when clad with the black Suits which all Agents wore when on duty.

"What's up, Fox?" Echo wondered as soon as he and Omega got in the door.

"Close the door, Echo, and take seats, both of you," Fox ordered. As the dexter side of Alpha One complied with the command, Fox turned his attention briefly to the sinister side. "Omega, how are you doing? Feeling a little more relaxed about things, now you've come back to us? It's been a month or so for you to settle back in..."

"Yeah, Fox, I'd say I'm doin' pretty good," Omega replied softly, offering a slight smile, her gentle Southern dialect in evidence. "I'm a lot less afraid of any missed 'programming' showing up, I think."

"Excellent. I'm glad to hear it, young lady."

"Yeah," Echo agreed, his own Texan accent only slightly diluted after years of living in New York—though he could, and did, adapt and modify it at will as the need arose. "And what passes for Alpha Line was glad to hear she was back, too. Which makes me think. I wanted to thank you, Fox, for the loan of the conference room off the Core for our odd department meeting now and then."

"Not a problem, Echo," Fox noted. "I'm inclined to expect those meetings to become more frequent in future, as the department really gets rolling. In fact, I've decided to designate that particular conference room for Alpha Line, and dedicate it exclusively to your department's use."

"Really? That's cool," Omega said, eyebrows rising.

"Yeah, Fox, thanks. That's a great idea. It worked really good for our last department meeting," Echo averred. "We aren't big enough, by a long shot, to fill it up yet, but judging by the number of applications that have been coming in—"

"Especially that stack that came in this morning," Omega interjected, and Echo quirked his face in acknowledgement.

"—That's gonna change soon, and we'll NEED a room that big."

"Exactly. And that's why I chose it for you." Fox nodded.

"The preliminary department logo design that Duff came up with went over well, too...along with certain other announcements." Echo shot a mischievous glance at his partner.

"I gathered," Fox replied with dry amusement. Omega flushed.

"Well, but I really didn't expect the, uh, I guess it was sorta kinda a promotion...let alone the enthusiasm the other agents seemed to give to it," she admitted. "Especially when...well, after everything that's happened. You know."

"I know, but it only makes sense, Meg," Echo said. "If I'm gonna be the department chief, but still go into the field, there's gonna be times I'm gonna need to delegate responsibilities. And I'm gonna need help keeping up with everything. I needed an assistant. The logical person for that position is my partner. And you're already handling setting up all the qualifications testing and training for the new department members, anyhow."

"Yeah, but I was barely past my...'rookie-hood,' if that's even a word! I mean, what about Romeo, or India, or..."

"We—Fox and I—actually did discuss it with both of 'em, individually," Echo said, voice quiet. "We didn't tell 'em you were at the top of our candidate list, or even on it, but we DID tell 'em that both of them were on it, which was true. Believe it or not, not only did they both turn it down, each one—independently—nominated you for the assistant slot."

"They didn't want it?" she asked, amazed.

"No, they didn't, and that didn't surprise either one of us," Echo said. "They're happy as Alpha Two, backing up you and me, baby. It's the paperwork and junk, I think. The bureaucratic side of things. Remember, you're my assistant—I mean, after all, Fox has TWO workin' for him—but it isn't the same as if you were the department assistant LEAD."

"Yeah, I know. And that's okay by me. I think that'd be way too much right now," Omega considered. "Besides, nobody's gonna wanna follow orders from a junior Agent."

"Don't be too sure about that," Echo replied, raising a skeptical eyebrow. "You're getting a reputation as somebody who can keep up with me. That isn't easy to do. And the whole damn Agency knows it."

"Agreed. Don't think that it didn't get around about all you've done, Omega," Fox noted. "When Supplies released that notice about ensuring full-year wardrobes for rookies, it got out among the agents about your Antarctic mission, and how you stuck with Echo despite the frostbite and hypothermia. And when Slug attacked, we called in every available hand we had, from every Office on the planet, to help sweep the city looking for him. Half the Agency saw what you were going through, and the other half heard about it from them."

"And when you had the integrity to try to leave the Agency after discovering Slug's mental programming, in order to protect me and the others," Echo murmured, "well..."

"He's right," Fox affirmed. "In as far as I can tell, you're VERY well respected in the Agency, Omega. Oh, there's probably a handful of agents that are so paranoid, they still aren't certain of you, given the whole programming thing. But they're a distinct minority, and so far, they've had the very good sense to keep their mouths shut. You've gotten favorable attention in the Pan-Galactic Council, too. I had no problems getting you approved in the Ennead as Echo's assistant."

She tucked her head, trying to hide the blush she felt heating her face. Seeing it anyway, Echo grinned.

"I think it was the cheer that went up in the Core when you made the official announcement, Fox, that threw her," he said. "It fairly rattled the building, and she wasn't expecting it."

"For that matter, neither was I," Fox admitted, "but I wasn't particularly surprised. Now, let's get down to today's business."

* * *

"Right," Echo said, and he and Omega drew their chairs over to Fox's desk. "What's goin' on?"

"You know what today is, right?"

"Umm..." Omega murmured, glancing at her wrist chronograph. "Agency time or New York time?"

"New York time."

Omega pressed a couple of buttons.

"October 30th," she read the display.

"Right. So tomorrow is—"

"Halloween," Echo groaned. "Oh, great."

"Why?" Omega wondered, becoming anxious. "What's wrong?"

"That's right, you haven't experienced it yet," Echo realized. "Well, it's like this, Meg. Halloween is a big deal for the Agency, and especially for the Earthside alien population. It's the one day a year that they can actually walk around normally, without disguises, and get away with it."

"At least in some places," Fox amended. "Other parts of the world, not so much; it depends on where you are. But the U.S. and Mexico, and to a lesser extent, the British Isles, western Europe, Canada, Australia and New Zealand, the Philippines, and Latin America, all go for it, with the costumes and all, and so the aliens just blend right in. The Middle East, Africa and Asia, not so much, but hey. It's a big festival, and Earth gets a lot of interstellar tourism out of it. But it's being complicated by a launch of NASA's new space plane the day after. I mean, it's only a test in low Earth orbit, but it's still getting a lot of attention."

"Great," Echo grumbled. "Right on top of the whole Halloween tourist season."

"Exactly."

A wide-eyed Omega snorted, then started to giggle. Within seconds she was doubled over in her chair.

"I'm sorry, guys," she gasped around spasms of laughter. "I dunno what I expected, but that wasn't it. So you're tellin' me we gotta get ready for trick-or-treatin' aliens tomorrow night?"

"That's exactly what we're telling you, Meg," Echo said, frowning slightly. "And it isn't as funny as you seem to think it is."

"I know, I know," she said, struggling to sober...and failing. "But look at it from my point of view. I was expectin' another interstellar terrorist, or maybe an invasion attempt, or sabotage of the space plane or something. And you give me trick-or-treatin' aliens." A guffaw escaped her, and she clapped both hands over her mouth and nose. This was followed by a muffled, "Sorry."

* * *

There was a silent pause, as Fox and Echo exchanged bemused glances, then looked at Omega. Abruptly Echo let out a loud snort of his own, then a chuckle.

"I guess she's right," he decided. "If that's what she was expecting, we didn't give it to her."

"Except that this time, she might have been closer to right than you think, Echo," Fox said, brow creasing. Omega blinked in surprise and began to settle, as Echo sat up straight, on alert.

"Wait, what? What else is going on?" Echo asked, intent.

"Do either of you know who died on Halloween in 1926?"

Omega frowned, thinking, but Echo responded immediately and without the slightest hesitation.

"Harry Houdini."

Omega stared; Fox raised an impressed eyebrow. Echo felt himself flush.

"I had an uncle on Dad's side who was an amateur magician," he explained. "He was pretty good, too. Even won a couple of awards. When I was a kid, he used to teach me stuff whenever he'd visit. I thought it was cool. Still do."

* * *

"Now THAT explains a few things," Omega muttered, considering some of her partner's more unusual fighting moves, along with his ability to produce weapons and tools seemingly from thin air, and Echo grinned at her remark. "Where is he?"

"Oh, he died in an oil field accident when I was, mm...around eleven or twelve, I guess."

"Aw. I'm sorry."

"No big deal. Long time ago." Echo shrugged. "But it's where I learned, uh, a few tricks, let's say."

"Very good, Echo. But did you know that Houdini was NOT from Earth?" Fox wanted to know.

"What?! But that was way before...there wasn't even a pre-Agency back then..."

"No, there wasn't. And that was actually why he and his family came here. They were Glu'gu'ik from Va'du'sha'ā, the ninth planet of Zeta Reticuli A. Omega might know 'em as Grays in the urban legend vernacular."

"Whoa," she whispered, surprised and intrigued. "In disguise, I assume."

"You assume correctly, as usual," Fox continued. "They took the Earth surname Weisz, but Houdini is an Anglicization of their native name, Ho'd'ni, or Hou'd'ni, plural, for the entire clan—just like the word Glu'g'ik is singular in their language, and Glu'gu'ik is plural," he added for Omega's benefit. "His birth name on his homeworld was Ari Ho'd'ni. They were political refugees, narrowly escaping a...well, on Earth the Russian Jews called it a pogrom. That's apparently why they chose a Jewish background cover; they could relate. But that's also why the whole Hungarian-birth thing is so confused, and he supposedly covered it up, and all that—they were only in Hungary for a little while after arriving on Earth. They thought it might be easier to establish themselves there, then move to the States, and then more or less 'lose' the whole history, that way."

* * *

"Okay, I can see it," Echo decided. "His small stature, his stage abilities, all of it. So how much of what Houdini did on stage was standard Glu'gu'ik quantum foam manipulation?"

"That, I couldn't tell you," Fox admitted. "The Glu'gu'ik race could do most of that without much difficulty. But probably some of it was easy enough for Ho'd'ni that he didn't need to. Especially when you consider that Glu'gu'ik are smaller than humans, so all he really had to do was slip out of his disguise, exchange it for a different one, and presto."

"Wait," Echo interrupted. "Are you saying his wife Bess..."

"He didn't have a wife named Bess. Humans and Grays aren't compatible sexually; I thought you knew that, Echo."

"I do," a slightly sheepish Echo admitted. "I'm just still trying to wrap my mind around the notion he was a Glu'g'ik."

"Ah, all right. Well, 'Bess' was most likely a different disguise, something ginned up with his brother to enhance their cover—and then they realized the potential use onstage."

"Sonuva—" Echo began, stunned.

"But how does that have to do with things now?" Omega wondered. "Surely any direct descendants of his family are long dead by this time."

"Well, there are a few still around, actually. Some of Houdini's brothers were already married before they left Va'du'sha'ā, and had children once they got to Earth, and there are grandkids and great-grandkids out there, scattered around. Most don't really know about the connection, as the family chose to go underground—changing surnames, and whatnot; it seems it was safer that way. But that doesn't mean there isn't kin back on Va'du'sha'ā, who know where the family went," Fox pointed out. "In fact, there's a cousin, and she's coming here today, with the intent to hold a séance tomorrow night."

Alpha One pondered that for a few moments.

"I'm still not seein' it," Omega admitted.

"Yeah," Echo agreed. "Holding séances for Houdini on Halloween is just what you do, in some circles."

"Except that Glu'gu'ik can manipulate—" Fox began.

"The quantum foam, yeah, I know," Echo finished for him. "So theoretically, this cousin could actually contact Houdini."

"You're kidding," Omega said, staring at him.

"No, he's not," Fox averred.

"But so how is that important to us?"

"Because the reason they fled their home world was due to massive civil unrest. According to their historians, the entire planet was in a huge civil war. Think of it like a massive, planetary War of the Roses—their history indicates something like half a dozen or better claimants to the throne, with the Hou'd'ni clan right in the middle—they were special stewards to the throne. What sort of special, I don't know. There were skirmishes, and hundreds, probably thousands, of people were killed, but there wasn't an outright war...yet. What I do know is that, right on the brink of a planetary war—which would likely have involved a nuclear exchange—was when the Hou'd'ni family came to Earth...and the whole civil unrest thing fell apart," Fox explained, "apparently due to something that they brought with them."

"What?" Echo asked. "What did they bring, and how did it relate to the civil unrest?"

"That, we also don't know. Because the family patriarch, and Houdini's siblings, all conspired to bury the matter so deeply that not even their descendants—here OR on Va'du'sha'ā—know about it. But the cousin from Va'du'sha'ā may. According to my intel, the cousin wants to get back at the 'other side,' and thinks that she may be able to find out where this... kheyfets...is, if she contacts Ari Ho'd'ni. More, GALINT indicates that the group with which she's aligned is one of the more powerful—and brutally ruthless—factions that existed then."

"But I thought they were a democratic republic now," Omega protested.

"They are; it kind of fell out in the aftermath of the Hou'd'ni flight. And the majority of the population is happy about it—but not everyone agrees," Fox explained. "And evidently there is a big enough faction— or factions, GALINT suspects more than one—who want to go back to the rule of royalty, that they're willing to risk another full-out civil war to do it." He paused. "But since then, the Zeta Reticuli system has joined PGLEIA and added a LOT of offworld connections and treaties. So then you have to start factoring in who's allied with whom, from what system, and how many of them aren't as stable as we'd like them to be...and the whole mess just grew exponentially."

"Crap," Omega grumbled.

"Exactly," Fox agreed. "And—"

"And Zeta Reticuli is now in Division One," Echo realized, finishing for him.

"Oh, damn," Omega murmured, a look of comprehension spreading over her face. "So the Zeta Reticuli problem is..."

"Ours," Fox finished. "Right."

"Well...shit," Echo said, with feeling.

* * *

"So the first thing we need to know is, when is this cousin coming in?" Echo noted. "Closely followed by what's her name, what does she look like, and where does she intend to hold the séance?"

"Her name is Ke'ri Gla'd's," Fox answered, handing over a file folder. "It's a family name. Here's an image; she arrives at the Trenton Terminal in about four hours on a Tentesse Spacelines flight and will be coming through here roughly an hour later for processing. And we don't know where she intends to hold the séance."

"Does it matter where she holds it?" Omega wondered. "I mean, if you're manipulating quantum foam..."

"Yeah, it matters, baby," Echo explained. "Because, while the Glu'gu'ik can manipulate the quantum foam to contact their dead, they can only do so on the anniversary of the deceased's death, and in or very near the location of that death, OR in or near where the body was placed. And they have to be blood kin of the deceased. Really advanced practitioners can sometimes do it on the person's birthday, too."

"Right," Fox confirmed. "It's a kind of odd spacetime proximity sort of thing. So whatever planet the death...or birth...happened on, you use the anniversary, because the planet is more or less in the same space. It works best when there's also been a complete cycle of apsidal precession, but in a pinch, reasonably nearby. Of course, if the body is there, it's easier. But given the timing, I'd say the faction wanted to be as sure as they could of the contact..."

"Yeah," Echo agreed. "So that means she has to come to Earth and hold a 'séance' on Halloween, either in the cemetery or in the hospital where Ari died."

"Which means," Omega said, pulling her cell phone from her pocket, "we need to find out where he died and where he's buried."

"Oh, I can tell you that," Echo said, a hint of a grin on his face. "He died in Grace Hospital in Detroit, but he's buried over in Queens, in the Machpelah Cemetery."

"What we DON'T know," Fox added, "is where said hospital is now, and which one she's planning to use."

* * *

"Mm...okay...Grace Hospital..." Omega muttered, pulling up various files and internet searches on her phone. "Grace Hos...no, DETROIT... uhh...okay, here we go...lessee..."

"I love having a trained researcher on the team," Echo told Fox, his expression morphing into a full grin.

"No joke," Fox agreed, impressed. "She's actually faster than MY assistants, and they're no slouches. I'm a little jealous, Echo."

"No poaching! You can't have her," Echo declared, still grinning. "She's mine."

Fox raised an eyebrow. Echo saw it, blinked in surprise, and mentally played back what he'd said.

Oh shit, he thought, dismayed. *THAT was a double entendre I didn't mean to make. And right in front of the boss, too. Hell—I made it TO the boss! Damn. I hope he doesn't take it the wrong way. I didn't mean it the way it sounded. We're just friends, Meg and I.* But in the back of his mind, he wondered why he found the notion of a purely platonic relationship with his partner vaguely...disappointing.

"HUSH, y'all," a preoccupied Omega declared. "And behave. I gotta figure this out."

"Figure what out?" Echo wondered, glad of the diversion.

"Yes, Omega, what have you found?" Fox joined in, shooting a thoughtful glance at the chief of Alpha Line; Echo tried to ignore it.

"Okay, I found the history of this Grace Hospital in Detroit," Omega noted, "but it merged with another hospital quite a ways on back, an' now it's called Sinai-Grace Hospital. What I can't figure out is if it's the SAME hospital. Well, I mean," she amended, glancing up, "it's the same organization, but I'm still tryin' to figure out if it's in the same PLACE. 'Cause it sounds like THAT'S the pertinent thing."

"It is," Echo confirmed.

"Oh, here it is!" Omega said, stabbing something on her phone's screen with her index finger, then making a pinching-and-pulling motion to enlarge whatever she'd found. "Um, lessee. Oh, wow. Okay. No, it's NOT

11

the same place. Looks like they moved after the merger, into a bigger and better facility...mmm..." The two men watched as blue eyes scanned the small display, waiting patiently for her to determine the information. "No, it's definitely not the same place. The OLD hospital building..." blue eyes darted to and fro, "got bulldozed back in...1979, I think," she said, looking up. "It's a parking lot now. Could they hold a séance in a parking lot?"

"I doubt it," Fox considered. "I mean, they COULD, but more than likely he'd have died in a room on an upper story, which means that unless they wanted to get on an antigrav platform and try to figure out where, in the space ABOVE the parking lot..."

"Yeah, no," Echo agreed. "That's an awful lotta work to go through, when you can just come to the cemetery here in New York. Not to mention, it'd attract a helluva lot of unwanted attention, floating through a parking lot."

"Exactly," Fox agreed. "Thank you, Omega. I believe you have just narrowed our search for us. We're down to the Machpelah Cemetery now, and you did it within moments, at that."

"Hey, not a problem, guys. Google-fu always was my specialty," she murmured, shooting them an unassuming smile. "I was the go-to gal in the astronaut office for stuff like this. Saves us having to head all the way over to Detroit, when it sounds like you'd need us here for the tourists, anyway."

"True," Fox agreed. "But I think I'll notify the Chicago office to pop a few agents over there and stand guard, just the same."

"Can't hurt," Echo agreed. "Meanwhile, Meg, let's you and me go off and study this file Fox gave us. I'll see about getting you more up to speed on the Glu'gu'ik and their abilities, and we'll start trying to work out the best way, not only of preventing the séance to begin with, but of discrediting it, in case we can't stop it."

"Why shouldn't we be able to stop it?" Omega wondered, shoving her phone back into her pocket and standing with Echo. "Just take her into custody. And why bother with a plan to discredit?"

"You've never seen what happens at Houdini's gravesite on Halloween, have you?" Echo wondered in amusement.

"Um, no," she admitted.

"You're in for a shock. C'mon. We've got prep work to do."

"Wait, Echo," Fox called, as they reached the door. Alpha One turned and gave him their attention; Echo pulled the door closed behind himself to maintain confidentiality. "I've been giving this—what Omega asked— some consideration already..."

"And?" Echo filled in. "You got something else you want us to do, Fox?"

"Yes, I think I do," Fox said, contemplative. "Rather than...stop...the séance...perhaps we should let it go on, find out what it is the cousin is looking for, THEN take her into custody...and find it ourselves. It might be worth confiscating it for safekeeping, and putting it in The Vault. And the Ennead agrees with me."

"Wow. The Galactic Council approved the plan?" Echo verified.

"Yep. Provided Alpha Line was willing and able to execute it."

"We'll do our best, then," Echo said.

"The Vault?" a curious Omega queried. "What's that?"

"Remember that film from a couple decades back about the archaeologist who found the Ark of the Covenant?" Echo reminded her.

"Uh-huh. We watched part of it last week, after we got off shift from training the new department members, remember?"

"Oh yeah, we did, didn't we? Okay, remember that big storage warehouse at the very end?"

"Ooo. Yeah."

"Kinda like that. Only more hidden. A LOT more hidden. And...more complicated."

"Right," Fox agreed. "Some parts of it look a lot like that. But other areas...well, let's just say there are areas of special high security inside it, for the things we really want to keep under wraps."

"Oooh-kaaay..." Omega fell silent, eyes going distant in thought. Echo turned his attention back to Fox.

"All right, while the hamsters are spinning up the wheel to juice her circuits, Fox, what's your rationale? Just to have it in our own grubby little mitts in case somebody ELSE comes looking?"

"Precisely, old friend." Fox sighed. "I know it makes things more difficult on you and Omega..."

"But a galactic civil war is several orders of magnitude worse than that," Echo noted. "Okay, Fox, we'll see what we can do for you. If nothing else, maybe we can nab her, then go chasing it ourselves at our leisure... more or less."

"Excellent. Good hunting, Echo, Omega," Fox said, as they left his office. "Use as many resources as you need, but find this thing."

* * *

When they'd finished reviewing the files that Fox had provided, sitting at the table in the conference room the Director had likewise assigned for the budding department's use, they brainstormed together for a few moments. Finally Echo leaned back in his chair, laced his fingers and put his hands behind his head, thinking.

"...So how do you wanna play this?" Omega asked her department lead and partner, flipping through another folder full of department applications. "It isn't like we really have more than a couple of teams, at least not officially. There's just us—Alpha One; and Romeo and India—Alpha Two. We got Kilo and Gustav, that we've already told we're gonna bring on as the Enigma Team and designate as Alpha Three, but they're not really so much trained in field work, at least not yet..."

"Who else do we have who are high-likelihood candidates?"

"Um, lessee. There's Golf and Easy, from Headquarters; Love and Uniform, from the L.A. Office; Paris and How, Geneva Office; and Jack and Nuts from the Chicago Office, though Nuts isn't quite as good a candidate as Jack is...still, they're partners, and work well together..."

"And none of 'em have been through the Alpha Line training you set up yet."

"Nope. Because none of 'em are officially Alpha Line yet."

"Damn."

"Yeah."

"And most of the teams are from other Offices."

"Yup."

"Are they still at Headquarters after the testing, the other day?"

"So far, yeah. Nobody was slated to leave for a couple days yet, while you decided who you wanted."

Echo pushed upright.

"Okay, here's the way I think I wanna play it," he said. "You and I are gonna take the point on this. But we're gonna bring in Alpha Two to assist in direct surveillance, particularly today and tomorrow, and to help us make the bust. Once we have this Ke'ri Gla'd's person in custody after the 'séance,' Alpha Two will bring her back here to Headquarters and put her in the hoosegow until Fox is ready to handle her. Then you and I will set out to find this...thingamajig, and bring IT back to Fox, too. While we have her under surveillance, I want the other candidate teams on alert and assisting us in that surveillance. We four—you, me, India, and Romeo—will serve as surveillance leads, each of us at a different location. We'll split up the candidates among us, so we have additional eyes and ears on things. It'll also give us a feel for how good the candidates are in the real world, as opposed to test-taking."

"This works. Want me to call 'em in for a departmental-type meeting?"

"Do it. Meeting to commence in five minutes. We gotta get moving on this. I want us organized and in place at least half an hour before her flight is supposed to arrive. And that's not far off."

"Consider it done," Omega said, reaching for her cell phone.

* * *

"...And that's the situation, and how we intend to handle it," Echo finished briefing the teams. "You will all be expected to function as if you were an Alpha Line team, and cooperate with all other such teams."

Paris raised his hand.

"Yes, Paris?"

"Is this another test, sir?"

"No, this is a real mission," Echo averred. "The potential here is for the outbreak of interstellar war. Translated: It's SERIOUS. So we need extra eyes and ears on the perp; we HAVE to stop her before she accomplishes her objective—but at the same time, we need to find out what her objective IS. I think some of you are too new to the Agency to remember the Klydonian invasion a few years back, but trust me—an interstellar war would be

WORSE. We want to stop it before it starts."

"Will it be part of our Alpha Line qualifications evaluation?"

"It will be taken into account when decisions are made about who makes it into the department, yes," Echo confirmed. "By looking around the room, you'll note that certain decisions have already been made." He paused and watched as the candidates glanced about the conference room, realizing that most of the applicants that had been in the room mere days before were not in this departmental meeting. "All right. Each candidate team will be assigned to one actual department team member; you will answer to that member, report back to him or her, and follow orders issued by that department member. In turn, that department member reports to me, follows my orders, and passes down information and orders to you as necessary. The assignments are as follows: Enigma Team, you will remain at Headquarters and provide any code-breaking or translation needed by other teams."

"Yes, sir," Kilo and Gustav chorused.

"Golf and Easy, you will be with Alpha Two Romeo."

The candidate pair nodded at Romeo, who nodded back.

"Love and Uniform, you are assigned to Alpha Two India."

India turned and smiled; Love, the female of the candidate team, smiled back. Uniform, the male, nodded affably.

"Paris and How, you will be reporting to Alpha One Omega."

The two agents sat back in some surprise as Omega nodded and smiled at them. They glanced at each other, then at Omega, but did not acknowledge her friendly greeting.

"Jack, Nuts, you're with me," Echo determined. The pair nodded.

* * *

"All right, then, those are the assignments. Omega, India, Romeo, here's how we're gonna break it out," Echo explained. "Candidate teams, listen up: You're gonna be following your respective lead on this. We want eyes on the perp from arrival at the gate until departure from Headquarters. Romeo!"

"Yeah, man!"

"You and your team will stake out the arrival gate. India?"

"Yes, Echo?"

"You've got Grand Central Station, downstairs. Meg?"

"Yeah, Ace?"

"You and your team, cover the Core. My team and I will hit up the spacecraft rental area and watch to see what she gets. With any luck, we can get a tracer on whatever she rents, and keep tabs on her constantly."

How raised her hand. Echo waved his hand at her.

"Yes, How."

"Agent Echo, sir, we respectfully request the craft rental assignment."

Echo, who had been pacing at the head of the conference table, paused and turned toward his partner.

"Meg? You okay with a switch in venue?"

"Um, excuse me, sir," Paris said. "We're asking to be assigned to you."

"What?" Echo said, deadpan. The room stopped dead, and everyone gaped at the pair. "On what grounds?"

"We're experienced agents, sir," Paris noted. "We'd prefer not to be assigned to a rookie, even if she is in Alpha Line."

Omega blanched, then looked down, into her lap, saying nothing. India and Romeo exchanged glances, then turned expressionless gazes upon Paris and How.

* * *

For a split-second, Echo saw red.

But he managed to master his anger response, as befitted a department head, and addressed the two candidates.

"Paris, How, let me ask you a few things..."

"Of course, sir," How murmured.

"Have either of you done an extended Antarctic mission?"

"I've been to the McMurdo office," How volunteered.

"But have you performed a mission there?"

"Uh...no."

"Were you wearing a polar-weight Suit at the time?"

"Well, of course."

"How many interstellar terrorists have you captured or taken out?"

"Um, well," Paris hedged, "we were in on arresting a rogue Kochavi who set up a brothel on the Lower East Side, about a year ago..."

"That's not what I asked. How many interstellar TERRORISTS have you captured or taken out?"

"Er...none," Paris admitted.

"How many Agency days have you gone without sleep in a row? While still maintaining high function, on duty?"

"Uh...three?" How looked at Paris for confirmation. "As a team, that is."

"Individually," Echo pressed. The pair glanced at each other and frowned.

"Just two," How confessed.

"Two," Paris agreed.

"Can either of you erect a telepathic block?"

"No," came the answer in unison. "No human can," Paris added, missing Omega's wince. "You know that, sir."

"On the contrary," Echo corrected. "The very Agent you just denigrated can erect a telepathic block strong enough to hold off a rogue gastropoid. She's run through McMurdo Office on a dangerous extended mission wearing nothing but summer-weight clothing. She's functioned—AROUND THE CLOCK—for nearly a full Division week. And she's taken out TWO interstellar terrorists, PERSONALLY, one of which was taken out after said week around the clock, and assisted me in taking out a third. This is in addition to helping to capture a stowaway on a space probe, nabbing a saucer jacking ring, and retrieving a lost, newly-landed Dendroid child. Oh, and she also rescued the crew and passengers of a crashed saucer before the power plant blew...SINGLE-HANDEDLY."

Echo paused, spread his feet, and folded his arms, staring down the two agents, before continuing.

"So, tell me...does that sound like a ROOKIE to you?"

Neither How nor Paris had an answer to that.

"Good," Echo declared, brown eyes hard, voice firm. "Then you won't mind being assigned to AGENT Omega—who, I might add, is long past her rookie status, per my own paperwork—and obeying her instructions in providing surveillance in the Core, will you?"

"But we—" Paris began.

"Request denied," Echo barked. "Meeting adjourned. Candidates, study the mission briefing material. Alpha Two, Alpha One, with me. Alpha Three, you're welcome to join us; we're going for coffee in the break room."

* * *

Alpha One and Two left the conference room, headed for the break room and some coffee; the newly-minted Alpha Three politely declined, in favor of further study of the briefing packet. The candidate agents were also left in the conference room, to study the information Echo had provided, and get ready for their surveillance assignment.

"That...was not good," India decided as they walked through the Core; she glanced at Omega, offering a sympathetic frown. "Honey, I'm really sorry about that."

"It ain't gonna end well," Romeo noted. "Echo, m' man, I dunno but what you oughta have swapped on 'em, then rode hell on 'em."

"Meg can ride hell on 'em as well as I can," Echo pointed out. "I get your point, and I kinda hate to put Meg through this, but if I caved and switched the assignments, they'd never respect Meg like she deserves."

"You're not seriously considering them for the department, are you?" India demanded. "After that little scene?"

"Truthfully? No. They just scratched themselves," Echo said with a shrug. "But we still need 'em for the surveillance duty. Meg? Baby, you okay with this, or had you rather I did switch?"

The others had noticed that Omega had said nothing since the incident. Now their attention turned to her; she was somewhat pink in the face and her brows were furrowed. But she didn't answer Echo.

"Meg?" he tried again, elbowing her lightly. "Baby? Are you okay?"

"Huh?" She jerked to alertness. "Wha? Echo, did you say something to me?"

"Yeah, baby. Are you okay?"

Omega ran a slightly distracted hand over her braid.

"I suppose," she grumbled.

"What's wrong? That whole little scene?"

"Yeah. It made me madder than hell." She shrugged. "But like I told you in Fox's office, that's why I said I didn't think anybody would follow me."

"That's gonna change," Echo promised. "I'll see to that. Personally. But given their attitude and your mood, do you want to still go through with them on your team, or do you wanna swap with one of us?"

"That depends," Omega considered.

"On what?"

"On how much leeway you're willing to give me in handling 'em."

"I trust you, Meg. Handle them as you see fit."

"Whoa, Meg! You gonna haze 'em a little?" Romeo wondered, grinning. "They earned it."

"No," Omega said, raising an eyebrow. "I'll be nice. But if they cross me, they're gonna wish they hadn't." She turned to her partner. "Mind if I pass on the coffee, and run back to my quarters for something? I won't be long."

Echo raised an eyebrow, a hint of a grin forming at the corners of his mouth.

"You got something in mind."

"Yeah, I do."

"Sure, go for it. Want me to have a coffee waiting for you when you get back?"

"No...I really don't think I need the additional buzz right now."

"Fair 'nuff. See you shortly."

Echo, Romeo, and India entered the break room, as Omega peeled off, headed toward the agents' quarters.

* * *

In the conference room, the new Alpha Three Enigma Team moved into a corner in order to study the parts of the mission that might pertain to them.

Deciding that, after all, they were a team even if none of them was officially Alpha Line as yet, Golf, Easy, Jack, Nuts, Love, and Uniform put their heads together over the files, as well, looking for weaknesses and

20

specific identifying characteristics.

"Ooo, look at this," Love noted, tapping a photographic image of their quarry.

"Oh, nice snag," Golf decided. "She's got a little scar, there. Let's make sure to tell Echo when he gets back."

"All our leads," Easy added.

"Yeah," the others agreed.

* * *

But Paris and How remained stand-offish, at the far end of the conference table. However, this was a matter that did not much trouble the other agents, who were offended on behalf of the department's administrative assistant.

"Hmph," How muttered, watching the others. "What a bunch of suck-ups."

"In all fairness, isn't that what we just did, try to suck up to the boss?" Paris wondered.

"No," How disagreed. "We've got as much seniority as anyone here. More than some. What makes them think they even need to put us through this whole screening process? We've earned a promotion into this department."

"Well, you're preaching to the choir, but I'm just sayin', that may be how some of the others see it."

"It's an outrage, to assign a team as experienced as ours to a rookie agent. We've been agents for nearly ten years, between the both of us."

"If half the stuff Echo said about his partner is true, though, I'm not sure if she's still ranked as a rookie. In fact, didn't he indicate he filed the paperwork to take her off that status?"

"It doesn't matter," How insisted. "We're still way the hell more experienced than she is. She hasn't even been here a year yet!"

"Yeah, I know. And I'm still not entirely sure about some of the rumors I've been hearing."

"You're talking about the gossip that she's an alien?"

"Yeah. Echo all but confirmed it, when he claimed she could put up a telepathic block that strong. Humans just can't DO that."

"I guess they could be doing some sort of clandestine exchange program..."

"Yeah, but why keep it a secret? I mean, damn, we got aliens roaming around all over here. We got HOW many embassies upstairs?"

"I dunno. A bunch." How broke off, thinking. Finally she added, "Look, Paris. If she gives us a direct order, are YOU gonna obey it?"

"Huh. It depends, I guess."

"On what?"

"If I think it's a smart move, yeah, I'd probably do it—but only if it was something I was gonna do anyway. If it seems like a dumb rookie mistake, hell no."

"Okay, that makes sense to me. If she pulls a dumb rookie move, we report it, right?"

"Of course. Stupidity can get agents killed. And if Alpha Line is ever gonna be anything close to what they're advertising, stupid rookie mistakes have no place in it. Deal?"

"Deal."

* * *

An hour later, the ersatz Alpha Line department reconvened in the conference room. Love informed them all of the distinguishing scar she had spotted on Ke'ri Gla'd's' left temple—an important point when a ship laden with Grays would be arriving from their homeworld.

"Excellent catch, Love," Echo praised. "Everybody, take note."

From there, they split up, each team heading for its assigned location to find likely—and inconspicuous—places to conduct their vigils.

"And remember," Echo reminded, "use the earbuds and subvocal microphones, and put your cell phones in surveillance mode. They'll keep us in constant communication, that way."

* * *

Omega took Paris and How out into the Core proper, and looked around, surveying the area for likely cover.

"Okay, How, I want you to get out your cell phone and go over there to the electronics farm in the corner. You're gonna sit there and pretend that you're charging your phone while hooking it into the wifi LAN—you don't have to really do either, just make it look like it. Choose a seat deep into the corner, facing out; that way, you can keep an eye on most of this part of the Core. I want you especially to focus on the corridor coming in from the escalators down to Grand Central, until such time as you hear otherwise—from any member of Alpha Line. Only if you hear a direct order to shift position, however, will you do so; otherwise, simply direct your attention where it's needed."

How turned and surveyed the area being referenced, then cast a subtle glance at her partner Paris. Paris met her gaze with a dispassionate expression. She considered for a moment, then glanced at Omega.

"How, did you hear me?" Omega wondered.

"I heard you," she replied, and turned toward the electronics farm. "I'm going."

"What about me?" Paris asked.

"I want you on the opposite side of the Core, near the elevators—take the diagonal from your partner. Park yourself on one of the concourse benches over there, preferably with this," Omega said, handing him a white take-out bag that she'd been carrying since the department meeting reconvened; the bright red and yellow logo on the bag was readily recognizable. "It's a selection of fast food I had someone bring in from the local Mickey D's. Most of it's reasonably healthy," she grinned, "and I double-checked your files for any food sensitivities and junk, just to make sure."

"So this is my cover? I'm taking a meal break?"

"Exactly."

"Don't you think it should be...a little more, I dunno...um, sophisticated, than that?"

"No, I don't," Omega replied, smile fading a bit. "The simplest covers are usually the best."

"I really think we should—"

"Take the bag and do as I said," Omega ordered, smile disappearing altogether, jaw hardening, eyes becoming cool. "Go find a seat that commands a good view of the area, especially the elevators, just in case she comes up from Grand Central that way, instead of via the escalators near How."

"What are you going to be doing?"

"Watching over all of it."

"What?" Paris responded, surprised. "The whole Core? How are you going to do that?"

"I have my ways," Omega replied. "Now go."

A sullen Paris turned to make his way to the elevators. Halfway there, he paused to glance back...

...But Omega was gone.

"Hmph," he grumbled to himself. "If she's skipped out, there WILL be a report. And it won't be pretty."

* * *

Omega had not skipped out; she was now high above the main floor of the Core, on one of the balcony walkways, strolling casually along it, looking down at the ebb and flow of people coming and going on the main floor.

From time to time she stepped onto one of the antigrav platforms and let it carry her across the open space to a different level, always watching without seeming to do so.

Just then, a familiar voice came in on her nearly-invisible earbud.

"This is Alpha Line Chief Echo. Give me a go/no-go call. Team Romeo, report."

"Easy here. In position at the adjacent gate."

"Golf here. In position at the carry-on pick-up."

"Romeo here. In position at the people-mover. Team Romeo reports go."

"Team India, report."

"Love here. In position at the food court."

"Uniform here. In position by the escalators."

"India here. In position at the first-aid station. Team India reports go."

"Team Omega, report."

Both candidate agents tried to answer at once.

"How her—"

"Pari—"

Omega shook her head, trying not to roll her eyes. Then, without saying anything aloud, she thought the words, and the subvocal mic tucked into her collar picked up the instinctive movements of her jaw, lips, and tongue, translating them to speech.

"Break, break. One at a time, guys," she told them. "How, report."

"How here. In position in the electronics farm."

"Paris, report," Omega continued.

"Paris here. In position near the elevators, eating my chicken nuggets."

"What?!" Echo exclaimed over the comm. "Oh, never mind. Color commentary is not required, Agent Paris. Please keep communications strictly to necessary information. Is that understood?"

"Yes, sir."

"Omega here, Echo," Omega tried not to sigh. "In position overlooking the Core, ready to move at a moment's notice. Team Omega is go."

"Team Echo, report."

"Jack here. In position near the elevator banks."

"Nuts here. In position near the baggage claim."

"And I'm in position behind one of the rental kiosks," Echo added. "Team Echo is go. This surveillance operation is officially under way. Current schedules indicate her ship will be landing in twelve minutes. Repeat, ship will land in twelve minutes. Confirm."

"Twelve minutes; Romeo confirms."

"Twelve minutes. Golf confirms."

"Easy confirms twelve minutes to landing."

"India confirms twelve minutes."

"Uniform copies. Twelve minutes."

"Love confirms twelve minutes."

"Omega copies. Twelve minutes and counting."

Silence.

"Omega team, do you read?" Echo said. "Omega, is your team in place?"

"Affirmative, Echo," Omega said, looking down at the two agents on the main floor. "I think they're waiting for each other, after the last comm snafu. Paris, go."

"Um, Paris affirms twelve minutes."

"How, go."

"How confirms twelve minutes."

"Nuts copies. Twelve minutes to ship landing."

"Jack also copies twelve minutes."

"Good. Team Romeo, eyes and ears out. We wait for your verification of eyes on the target."

"Roger that, Echo," Romeo responded. "Hear that, guys? Heads up. The ball's in our court."

"Golf is go."

"Easy is go."

"All right, team," Echo added, "radio silence from here on out, until target acquired. All comm henceforward will be ONLY notification of target position and movement, and orders as needed from the team leads."

There were a few murmured acknowledgements, then Omega's earbud fell silent.

Time to wait, she thought.

* * *

Precisely thirteen minutes and twelve seconds later, the comm became active again.

"This is Easy, at the adjacent gate," came the communique. "I have bogey in sight. Appearance is per files. Wearing a matte black close-fitting jumpsuit with long, dark gray jacket or cardigan, and black boots with silver trim. Some sort of skullcap with decoration; it's black and has...looks like red flowers on it. Headed your way, Golf."

"I see her," Golf reported. "She's coming by to pick up a carry-on bag. Yeah, that looks like some sort of red flower ornamentation, but it isn't Earth flowers."

"Copy that," Echo said. "Good eye. Either she's trying to blend in, or she's meeting an accomplice and that's her identifying signal."

"It seems to be just a fashion, Echo," Golf noted. "There's a lot of the female Grays wearing variations of that sort of headgear. Most of 'em are blue or purple or green, though. She's the only one I see in red. Oh, no, there's an orange one. So be aware—she's in what I'd call a candy-apple red and black hat-thing."

"Blending in, then. Anybody on the team colorblind, just in case?"

Silence.

"Good, then," Echo added. "Romeo, do you have eyes on the target?"

"Affirmative, Echo," Romeo replied. "I just helped 'er on th' people-mover with 'er bag. I'm following at a distance, walking alongside th' people-mover, but deliberately lagging behind, so's she won't notice." There was a long pause, then Romeo added, "Heads up, Team India. She's on the escalator."

Seconds later, Uniform responded, "I got her. She just arrived in Grand Central Station...aaand she's hungry. Headed your way, Love."

"Yup, got her, Uniform. Looks like she's going for the grblch teriyaki."

"Blargh," someone said, then added, "Oops." Someone else snorted. Echo could be heard chuckling.

"Under the circumstances, accidental editorial remarks are not off-limits, guys," he said.

"Thanks," Nuts murmured. "Sorry, Boss."

"No problem. I'm not fond of the stuff, either, but it's popular with most of the off-worlders. When they decided to put in a food court for the tourists last month, that junk was a logical menu item." There was a fractional pause, then Echo added, "Eyes on our quarry?"

"Yes, I see her," India responded. "She got the grblch as rat-on-a-stick and she's eating it as she goes. Headed for— heads up, Team Omega! She's headed for the elevator banks, not the escalator up!"

"On it!" Omega responded, moving quickly to a position where she could see the elevator banks. "Paris, keep your eyes peeled!"

"Of course," came the slightly smug answer.

"Moving to assist!" How added.

"Negative!" Omega ordered. "Stay where you are, How! You'll attract too much attention if you're over there, too!"

But it was too late; Omega watched as How ran across the Core toward her partner—

—Just as Ke'ri Gla'd's emerged from the elevator.

Spotting How and Paris, who had jumped up to meet his partner,

Gla'd's smoothly stepped back into the elevator car, even as the other pas-sengers exited, and hit the <door close> button before either agent could reach the elevator. The car closed, and the indicator showed it moving in the proper direction for the rental craft floor. Paris and How promptly spun, and sprinted for the stairwell door.

"DAMN!" Omega exclaimed, leaning over the railing. "PARIS! HOW! *STOP!*"

But the pair slammed through the doorway into the stairwell and dis-appeared.

"What happened, Meg?" Echo demanded.

"How blew the surveillance. Gla'd's is now aware she's being watched. She stepped back into the elevator! She's probably headed your way, but so are those two, down the stairs!"

"Shit!" Echo exclaimed. "Jack, keep your eye on the elevators. Nuts, hit the stairs before the target gets here and try to head 'em off if you can. We might still be able to pull this operation out of the fire. Fox, do you copy?"

"Yes, Echo, I've been listening in. Looks like we have a problem."

"Meg, how fast can you get to the street, just in case?"

"Plenty fast, Ace," Omega said, unbuttoning her Suit jacket. "I came prepared."

With that, she vaulted over the railing, free-falling through the mul-tiple-floor volume of space above the Core...and hit a button on her belt buckle.

The antigrav unit kicked in then, and a tiny pair of jets emerged from the sides of her belt and roared to life. The airborne Agent swooped through the Core, out a corridor, and up an escalator shaft to the street level exit down Kent Avenue from the Headquarters building proper, landing just in time to see an elderly human woman—in the same outfit that Team Romeo had described—getting into one of the 'special' cabs that tended to be wait-ing for off-world visitors.

"Shit shit shit," she whispered, grabbing her goggle glasses, donning them hastily, and using them to take several quick images of the rear of the departing cab from multiple angles. "Okay, got it."

"She's gone, then, Omega?" Fox asked.

"That's an affirm, Fox. Left in a taxi," Omega answered. "But I got some shots of the license plate and cab ID, so we should be able to trace it, or at least hit up the driver and find out where he took his fare."

"Good girl," Echo praised. "All teams, report back to the Alpha Line briefing room immediately."

"Team Romeo headed in."

"Team India inbound."

"This is Omega," she responded, letting her voice express weariness and disgust. "I have no idea where the rest of my team is at this point, but I'm headed your way."

"I've got 'em, Meg," Echo said in a grim tone. "I'm bringing 'em with my team."

"I'll stand by for a debrief and consultation after you're done," Fox noted.

"Good plan, Fox," Echo said, and Omega could hear the irritation in her partner's tone.

"Oh, I definitely think it is," Fox added, his own tone less than pleased.

Chapter 2

"...But she had us on opposite ends of the Core!" How protested.

"Which is where you should have been," Echo pointed out. "One to watch the escalators, the other to watch the elevators. And you should have STAYED there."

"But how are we supposed to apprehend, if we can't back each other up?" Paris complained.

"Who said ANYTHING about apprehending?!" Omega wanted to know. "Where in the briefing packet did it say anything other than 'surveillance'? I told you where I wanted you, and that you were not to leave that position unless otherwise ordered! Instead you both jumped up and converged on the target, spooking her and sending her into an immediate retreat out of the facility! We were NOT planning to take her into immediate custody. We were hoping that she would lead us to this thing she's after!"

"We weren't talking to you," How remarked, more than a little sullen.

"Excuse me?" Fox interrupted, raising an eyebrow at the agent's cheek. "SHE was your TEAM LEAD."

"She is a rookie," Paris said with emphasis, "and it showed. She had me pretending to eat lunch, of all things."

"That was a suggestion she ran by me during our prep for the department meeting, and which I approved, because it was a GOOD COVER," Echo noted. "Simple is always best for cover. It was HER idea to actually see to it you HAD food to EAT, and that it was decently human-palatable, in order to make it as realistic as possible. I'll also have you know that I filed all of the formal paperwork over THREE MONTHS ago, to remove her rookie status and make her full, active Agent with complete access."

* * *

"And her probationary period ended prior to her Antarctic mission, back in the summer," Fox added. "Your team lead is also the departmental chief's assistant, and the head of departmental training. She planned the training programs that all Alpha Line Agents follow. And let me add, with Director approval, it's a damn good program. Her workout system is the one I now follow when I'm in the gym, by the way."

"Well," Omega murmured, "that one is partly based on the workouts that Echo and I ginned up to do together."

"No matter. It was your idea to include them as part of the training program, and I repeat, it's a damn fine system," Fox noted.

"Besides," Echo pointed out, "I think I already told you two that Omega's paperwork designated her as past rookie status, as well as pointing out her extensive experience in the field, back when you protested your assignment to her team in the pre-briefing."

"They did, eh?" Fox confirmed. He turned to the two agents, who sat, dour and silent, in visitor chairs in Fox's office; Alpha One was standing. "Is that true?"

The two candidate agents said nothing.

"I SAID, is that true?"

"Yes, sir," they finally murmured, more or less in unison.

"And how did Echo respond to your protest?"

"I gave them a rundown of Meg's qualifications, then I refused their request to swap assignments," Echo noted.

"So you knew Omega's qualifications, and her position in the department. And you were directly assigned to her as your lead," Fox observed. "And yet you still saw fit to disobey direct orders from Omega?"

"Sir, her time with the Agency is—" Paris began.

"Immaterial, in the circumstances," a stern Fox finished the agent's statement. "Omega has done more in her months with us than many agents do in several years. And she does it well, and without regard for personal outcome. Mission success and team coordination is her primary focus. Her secondary focus is team safety. Personal safety is well down the list of her priorities...as you'd have known, if you saw her fly through the Core like I did, just a bit ago. The woman vaulted over the railing on the FIFTH FLOOR, and THEN activated the antigrav and jet units...as she passed the SECOND floor."

* * *

31

"What?!" a shocked Echo said, turning to look at his partner. "You could've—!"

"It was faster," Omega explained, shrugging. "Build up some speed in the free-fall, then kick in the afterburners, as it were. Once we lost sight of the mark, we could have lost her altogether. I didn't want that to happen."

"It was impressive," Fox admitted. "And plenty fast. But you nearly gave an old man a coronary, in the process."

"Sorry," Omega said, offering the Director a sheepish grin.

"But we've got way more experience!" How protested, interrupting the discussion. "We've been here for—I've been here five years, and How four! We shouldn't even have to go through all this screening!"

"Is that the way you see it?" Echo wondered. "Because if so, your view of Alpha Line is greatly skewed. I need the cream of the crop...and then I need them to get even BETTER. I need agents who don't let ego or sense of self get in the way of the job at hand. I need agents who can take initiative, but who can also follow orders. I need agents who can pay attention, and understand what the mission needs from them, not what they intend to do. I need team players. I don't need egotists and grandstanders."

* * *

"Paris, How," Fox explained, "you DO understand that, per regulations, an Alpha Line Agent on a mission, no matter the level of experience, is ALWAYS the ranking Agent? They take charge in any given situation— they are EXPECTED to. Alpha Line is my worst-case, last-ditch-scenario right arm, acting with my full authority. Not infrequently, they will be acting with full Ennead authority, as well. And in the event of multiple Alpha Line Agents, such as we had today, the departmental ranking determines the senior Agent. In this case, you two—who are NOT Alpha Line—were instructed BY THE ALPHA LINE CHIEF to report to Omega, who is currently the closest thing that department has to a second. She was your lead, and Echo was her lead. SHE was the superior agent, and you were to report to her, even as she reported to Echo. It was NOT the other way around."

The pair blinked. Shocked expressions formed on their faces.

"Did you, or did you not, understand this?" Fox demanded.

* * *

"...I...we," Paris began, seeming to search for words, "we...were told... but we thought it...I mean..."

"We thought it was just a way to show off the importance of the new department," a pale How murmured. "That's...I mean, that's what our supervisor at the Geneva Office thought, too, when we discussed it with her. We didn't realize it was an actual reg." She looked at her partner, and her face crumpled into an unhappy frown. "We screwed up, Par."

"Yeah, we did."

"Did you read any of the material that was presented to you about the department, when you applied?" Omega asked, wry. "The stuff in the applications packet? The material I spent hours putting together and writing up?"

"And that I helped her organize and gather, developing and outlining the department's priorities, as I envisioned it?" Echo added.

"Um, just the basic stuff, about what the department was supposed to do, to be," How said, now shamefaced. "And the instructions for applying, of course."

Frustrated, and not a little disgusted, Echo spun on his heel, throwing his hand in the air. "Why do we even bother, Meg?"

"I dunno, Ace," Omega sighed, slumping and leaning back against the wall. "Maybe 'cause we believe it's gonna amount to something, one of these days?"

* * *

"I'd say it already has," Fox consoled his lead team. "Just because not all of your applicants fully realize it yet, doesn't mean it hasn't. After all, you've already taken out—what? Three interstellar...no, make that FOUR interstellar terrorists and assassins. Just the two of you. In the last four months. All four of whom had infiltrated Agency facilities, one of which was Headquarters." He sat back in his chair, as Paris and How goggled at Fox's enumeration.

"Well, Alpha Two helped on that one," Omega reminded him. "Lotsa people helped."

"But we took the lead, Meg," Echo pointed out. "And in the end, it was you and me who took Slug out. Well, truthfully...it was you. I just held the gun for you, 'cause you were too weak to do it yourself. But you aimed it."

"So. Alpha One, have you reached a decision regarding this candidate team?" Fox leaned his elbows on the desk and steepled his fingers.

"Meg?" Echo turned to his partner.

Paris and How gaped. "She gets a say?!" Paris gasped.

"She's the training lead, and my executive assistant," Echo pointed out in intense annoyance. "Of course she gets a say. What have we been trying to tell you for the last, oh, hour?"

"I really think I should recuse myself, Echo," Omega said.

"And I get why, and I respect that notion, but I still want your opinion on training 'em."

"So I can't recuse myself. You're not gonna let me."

"Nope." He offered her a tired grin.

"Okay. Let me just say it like this, then," she tried. "Unless their attitude changes significantly, I wouldn't want the training of 'em."

"Training?" Paris whispered. "You mean what we already have isn't sufficient?"

"Nope," Fox answered, though he suspected the comment was intended to go unnoticed. "Not for this department. Not by a long shot. Weren't you listening to them earlier? Weren't you listening to ME?"

"...That confirms my assessment, Meg," Echo decided, as if the interjectory remarks had never been made. "They were unable to work with the larger team, and were too convinced of their own abilities and seniority to listen to anyone else...including the department chief. How, Paris, you are officially washed out of the Alpha Line application system. You may apply again, one Earth calendar year from today, if you so choose. This application—and all records associated with it, including a report on today's events—will remain on file for future reference, however."

How and Paris paled even more.

"And a black mark is going into your personnel records because of today's events," Fox added. The rejected agents winced. "That said," the Director continued, gentling his voice slightly, "since there does seem to be some misunderstanding about the nature of Alpha Line Agents in the hierarchy, said black marks will not be as serious as they might otherwise have been. I saw a learning process begin with you both, once you fully understood that hierarchy, just a few minutes ago. It may be that I need to put out a few bulletins, Agency-wide, to emphasize the regulations regarding our newest department. And Echo, Omega, I intend to get right on that. Meanwhile, I assume the rest of your team, and those agents whose candidacies are still open, are working on tracking down that taxi?"

"They are, sir," Omega said. "I passed on the images from my goggle-glasses in our quick little debrief, and they're on it now. By this time, they may already have a lead on where it went."

"Good. Let's get some eyes back on our quarry, and quickly, before we lose her and have an interstellar war on our hands. Alpha One is dismissed. I'd like to talk to How and Paris, here, a while longer, and try to get down to the source of the misunderstanding regarding the regs."

"Okay, Boss," Echo said, swiping a finger past his brow in salute. "We'll keep you apprised of the situation."

"Please do."

* * *

"So, what have y'all got?" Echo demanded as soon as he and Omega walked back into the conference room. Both members of Alpha One noted the eyes scanning them and looking behind them to see if Paris and How were with them. They also noted the covert glances between the various agents, and knew the others had recognized the significance in the fact that Alpha One was alone.

"We got her pegged, Echo," Romeo reported. "I took half the team and coordinated the search for the taxi, an' India took the other half and ginned up the right questions to ask the cab driver. So when we finally found 'im—he was already two more fares along—we got the exact location."

"The cabbie recognized her, then?" Omega asked.

"Oh yeah," India affirmed. "We got positive ID. It helps that this is one of the, uh, 'special' drivers that's used to handling our particular varieties of tourist. And he's experienced, so he's learned to get a really good look at the fares he takes from here, just in case. He remembered her."

"Good. Where is she?" Echo asked.

"She's staying at that boutique hotel that specializes in alien tourists, over on Meeker," Romeo declared. "Had a reservation under the name Chu'b Har'd'n—same name she used for her spaceline tickets. Want us to get some eyes on 'er?"

"Let's get a room number for her, first."

"We got it already, no prob, man."

"Really?" Omega asked, surprised. "That's good work. Fast, too."

The others all smiled, pleased.

"Okay," Echo responded, thinking. "In that case, I want some volunteers to go undercover in the hotel. I'd like to get an audiovis bug into her room, if we can. I wanna know it any time ANYone comes or goes from that hotel room. And I wanna know when, who, why, how, and what transpired inside."

"Sir, we'd like to try," Love said, raising her hand. "Uniform and I have done something like this before, over on the West Coast, out of the Los Angeles Office."

"We got our volunteers, then," Echo said, smiling at the pair. "India, I want you to stay here with the other candidates, and keep an eye on things as best you can with remote observing; try to find out if this Gla'd's makes any moves before we can get Uniform and Love in position. Romeo, you handle helping 'em get set up and infiltrated. Don't forget to get your hands on several audiovis bugs from Special Supplies. Alpha Three, I need you to make sure the bugs are properly ciphered before they leave, and that we can decrypt on this end."

"Roger that, m' man. I'm all over it," Romeo said, and Kilo and Gustav, the Alpha Three Enigma Team, nodded agreement.

Romeo, Alpha Three, and the candidate team gathered up their equipment—their phones and electronic tablets were scattered across the table, from where everyone had been coordinating tracing their perp—and headed for the door.

"Wait," Echo said, and everyone in the room stopped, focusing their attention on the Alpha Line chief. He ran his hand through his hair, then caught Omega's eye; her concerned expression and raised eyebrow told him that he'd inadvertently telegraphed his abstraction to her. "Meg, are you good with this lot? Training, I mean. You know what I'm referring to."

"Yeah, I am," she said, voice and expression frank and open. "Huge contrast, there."

He paused, and dropped into their unspoken codes. *You think they'd make good new members?*

Given the way they've coordinated everything so far, and understand the importance of the mission, and their place in it? Oh hell yes, she told him. *I mean, I really didn't expect them to have her location yet, let alone a room number.*

Me either. That was some good teamwork, while we were gone.

Exactly. So...what? You want to go ahead and make the call, so they know they're part of the team?

Yeah. I think it will improve morale all around, especially after that little debacle we just finished off in Fox's office. I'm sure you saw that they noticed we came back alone.

Yeah. Omega shrugged. *I think that's a good idea, actually. Go for it.*

Echo turned back to the rest of the room.

"Sorry about that," he told them. "I needed a private word with my executive assistant for a second, to make sure we were on the same page before I formalized this."

"What's up, Echo?" India wondered.

"Well, we currently have three candidate teams that have survived the tough applications process for Alpha Line," Echo noted, "and I wanted to inform you all that those three teams have officially passed all requirements. As of right now, I'm making the following assignments: Golf and Easy, you will be Alpha Four. Love and Uniform, you are officially Alpha Five. And Jack and Nuts, you're Alpha Six. Meg and I'll enter the new assignments into the system here in a little bit. That's the sum total of new members of Alpha Line for this round of applications. Congratulations, guys."

Soft exclamations of happiness and compliments were made, and smiles went around the room.

"When this mission is over, we'll see about getting Alpha Five and Alpha Six moved into housing in Headquarters," Echo added. "Alpha Four, y'all are already here, right?"

"Yes sir," Golf confirmed. "Easy and I are already assigned to HQ, so it shouldn't be a problem. It's just a lateral in-house transfer, for us."

"Good. Okay, guys. Back to work," Echo said then, and the department members split up.

* * *

It turned out to be relatively easy to get one of the newly-designed audiovisual bugs into Gla'd's' hotel room. Even though judging by subsequent video, Gla'd's used a bug detector on her room roughly every hour, the new bug was designed to remain undetected...and it lived up to expectations. The alien woman was also, apparently, something of a gourmand, and very curious about typical Earth foods. Consequently, it was a simple matter to get both Love AND Uniform into her hotel room, alternating several deliveries of room service.

"Lord have mercy," Omega murmured, watching the transmitted video as Uniform left with the fourth set of empty trays, even as Gla'd's phoned in a fifth room service order. "Do Glu'gu'ik normally eat that much?! What kind of metabolism do they have?"

"No, they don't, and not THAT high," Echo said, shaking his head. "I'm not sure what she thinks she's doing, but that's gonna catch up to her, sooner or later." He rubbed his chin with his hand, thoughtful. "Hm. Maybe we can make it work to our advantage, somehow."

"Could be," Omega agreed. "But at this rate, I'm thinking you and I can go scope out the cemetery in advance, and leave the rest of the team here to keep watch. 'Cause I don't think she's goin' anywhere tonight. She's just gonna eat herself into oblivion and crash early—probably in several senses of the word. We've got the rest of the day and all night, to get things ready for tomorrow night."

"Good plan. I'll set up shifts, so nobody gets tired and misses anything," Echo decided. "Then we'll set up our cells with alerts if something comes up, and maybe we can even get some sleep. The séance won't be until tomorrow night, anyway."

* * *

Gla'd's ate to her heart's content, and in fact did go to bed early, already suffering from a mild carbohydrate hangover. Alpha One scoped out the Machpelah Cemetery, and got a good—if brief, compared to their usual shift—night's sleep while their newest recruits kept a watchful eye on Gla'd's.

The next morning, they began serious preparations for a Halloween séance that night.

* * *

"All right, you two," Fox said, late that morning in his office. "I have something I need for you to do for me."

"Fox, we already kinda got our hands full with this Glu'gu'ik situation," Echo pointed out.

"Don't worry. I got us some help."

"What sort of help?" Echo wondered, raising a skeptical eyebrow.

"Aside from the fact that Alpha Two is going to be tailing our perp directly, and the rest of Alpha Line is converging on the cemetery, even as we speak, to get into position and blend into the crowd," Fox explained, "I called in a little additional help. I contacted all of the off-worlder-run taxi-cab companies in the area and asked for their cooperation."

"Aw, man," Omega murmured.

"What she said," Echo agreed. "Are you sure you can trust 'em, Boss? Some of those guys are on the shady side, to put it mildly."

"Well, under normal circumstances, you'd be right," Fox said. "But what I did was to preface the specific request with what would happen if this Ke'ri Gla'd's managed to succeed."

"Ooo," Omega hummed, brows drawn together. "I assume you painted a VERY vivid picture of interstellar war..."

"I did," Fox averred. "And I may have embellished it a bit with my own World War II experiences. Just a tad." He shrugged, a crooked grin on his rugged face. "Even the shadiest of them had to admit that it wouldn't be good for business. Any kind of business. So they agreed to cooperate."

"What, exactly, are they gonna do?" Echo wondered.

"They're going to see to it that one of their number picks up the Gla'd's fare—I gave them imagery to identify her—and whoever gets her will notify us in a coded, encrypted signal as soon as she's picked up. We'll

39

also get notification if she deviates from the expected route, and when she reaches her destination. We have her thoroughly nailed down."

"Okay, that sounds good," Echo decided. "So what do you need Alpha One to do, other than coordinate our department at the designated target site?"

"Well, it's like this," Fox said, wry expression telling them it was more complicated than they wanted to hear. "Omega won't know, but Echo, you should remember the little, ah, incident we had over in Bayside last year with the, um, 'inexperienced' trick-or-treaters..."

"Aw hell," Echo grumbled. "You mean old Mrs. Lucchese?"

"That's the one."

"Lucchese?" a surprised Omega piped up. "Like the crime family?"

"Precisely," Fox confirmed. "The current borough president, who just so happens NOT to be from 'around here,' contacted me this morning and asked me to have someone swing through her neighborhood in Bayside, to make sure none of the newbies frighten the old matriarch. He said that the experienced off-worlders have been working hard to educate all the newbies, but he's still pretty worried, especially after the near-debacle they had last year. And the last thing we need is the Lucchese family getting pissed at some of the people under our jurisdiction."

"Well, that's true enough," Echo decided. "Mafia turf wars on our own turf, we don't need. And I suppose that's serious enough to warrant an Alpha Line look-see."

"Right. And with your diplomatic experience, and Omega's naturally genteel disposition, I thought you two were the most likely candidates. If you have to intervene—and I'm not saying you will, note—the two of you are, in my mind, the ones most likely to smooth things over without any unfortunate incidents." Fox shrugged. "I know it's out of the way; the Machpelah Cemetery isn't too far off as the crow flies, but the matriarch's house in Bayside is almost on the far side of Queens. But it really needs to be done."

"Okay," Echo capitulated with a sigh. "Meg, are you up for a first-hand view of your 'trick-or-treating aliens,' baby?"

"Oh, I think I could be talked into it, Ace," Omega answered with a grin.

"All right. Fox, unless you have anything else for us, I want to get back across to our department meeting room and make sure everyone's on the same page with this."

"No, zun, that's about the size of it. Alpha One is dismissed if you need to go."

"Thanks, Boss. C'mon, Meg, we got more work to do."

"Right beside ya, Ace."

* * *

Back in the Alpha Line meeting room, Echo called everyone together for a quick briefing of the new addition to the mission profile, and a quick brainstorming session.

It turned out that, relative to what the others had planned and coordinated, the detour had little effect; Romeo—by dint of his extensive experience as a former Navy SEAL—had been given the task of strategically placing the Alpha teams, and all it really meant was that Alpha One would need to leave at least an hour earlier than they'd planned, in order to make the detour and still be in position on time at the cemetery. Everything else would fall into place as it was projected.

"Well...good," Echo decided, pleased. "This is shaping up damn well."

"Aw man," Romeo protested, "don't jinx it like that."

"Huh?"

"When I was in th' SEAL team, we had this one C.O. would always get t' this point in th' mission planning," Romeo explained, "an' then he'd make a comment like that. Every. Damn. Time. And every damn time, when we got t' th' point in th' mission where he made that comment in th' planning, all hell would break loose."

"Aw, quit bellyachin', Romeo," Omega grinned. "Echo isn't that C.O., and this isn't the SEALs."

"Yes, sweetheart," India murmured. "You're worrying too much again."

"Yeah, well, I got friends here now," Romeo fussed. "An' I done lost one buddy in th' SEALs. I don't wanna lose any more, thank you."

"It's okay, pal," Echo offered, gentling his voice. "I know how it feels.

41

We'll be careful."

"Yeah! Damn straight," the comments went around the room.

"Y'all better be," was Romeo's answer. "Don't, I'mma be pissed."

* * *

Echo drove the Corvette slowly and carefully through Bayside late that evening; the sun was just before setting, and the trick-or-treaters were out in force. Omega, in the passenger seat, scanned the area with a sharp eye as they drove.

Abruptly she espied a trio of children—two older, one younger in between. The two older boys were dressed as zombies, but the young child was costumed as a ghost, with a sheet over its...rather large head, and draping down to its equally-large feet. The child waddled along, one hand held in each boy's grasp, seeming happy and content, if decidedly curious about the evening's proceedings.

Just then, another child wandered by. Its costume was recognizable from a popular film franchise, and consisted of a coarse brown robe, a green, full-head mask with large eyes and pointed ears, and a face that, to Omega, generally resembled a small, wizened Einstein. A cylindrical silver toy device hung from its belt.

The child in the sheet suddenly jerked away from the older boys, oddly-misshapen hands outstretched as it waddled quickly toward the child in the film costume, enthusiastically crying, "OoooOOOOooo!"

The two boys quickly diverted after the small fry, retrieving their 'ghost' and continuing on their way.

Omega blinked several times, then turned and faced forward in the car, processing what she'd just seen.

"What?" Echo asked, having noticed her abstraction.

"Um, nothing," she murmured, shaking her head. "Just a little case of, uh, déjà vu, I guess."

"Oh yeah," Echo nodded sagely. "Those happen a lot on Halloween night around here."

"I'll bet..."

* * *

"Heads up, Meg, we're about to turn down the street that Old Lady

Lucchese lives on. The street is just up ahead."

"Okay, but..." Omega broke off.

"But what?"

"That mode of address just seems...kinda disrespectful," Omega admitted, trying to find a delicate way to put it, "and I've never heard you be disrespectful before."

"You have, when I'm referencing perps."

"Well, yeah, but this is an elderly woman."

"What, you think she had no clue what her husband did, what her sons do?" Echo asked, tone sharp. "You think she wasn't involved, wasn't right in there with 'em, back in the day? Oh HELL no, Meg. Everybody around here knows she was in it up to her nose; they saw her involved, way back when. I have no respect for her, because she hasn't earned it." He shook his head. "She's somewhere around 90, with a bad case of senility, possibly approaching dementia, but the kids won't put her in a nursing home or assisted living facility because they're afraid of what she can say, when she's in one of her 'moods.' They don't come around her themselves, because they aren't comfortable seeing her like that, and wondering if it's gonna be them in twenty years. So they keep her confined to the house, with guards from among their hand-picked people, and a few hired nurses to stay with her and make sure she gets her medications and doesn't burn the place down or something."

"That's a horrible way to live," Omega murmured, shocked.

* * *

"Yeah," Echo agreed. "It's a kind of prison, but it's still better than the prison she deserves. She has the run of the house, access to the back yard, nice soft beds, gourmet meals cooked for her, servants at her beck and call. She just can't ever leave."

"You sound like you've been inside."

"I have. Who do you think was sent there to investigate after last year's incident?"

"Oh." She paused. "So...that's how you know about her history, too, I guess."

"Hell yeah. I quietly talked to some of the old-timers in the area during my investigations. Damn, Meg, the stories I heard! Do you know, she killed at least three people, her own self? There's witnesses and evidence to prove it."

"Ugh. But she's not in jail."

"Nope. Never been convicted, never even been arrested."

"Damn. I never have really understood why..."

"Why the crime dynasties continue? Pretty much for the same reason dictatorships do, baby. If you have enough people with a vested interest in enforcing your regime, everybody else is too scared to talk."

"I think I'd talk, even if they killed me for it."

"I'm sure you would. But would it make you think twice if, say, they'd managed to kidnap India? Or Romeo? Or even me? And you were told that, if you talked, whoever they had in their control would be killed, nice and slow?"

Omega stared at him, mouth open, expression blank.

"Oh, shit," she whispered.

"Yeah. Now you're getting it." Echo nodded, grim. But something inside warmed at the notion that his partner would be so affected, were something bad to happen to him. *For that matter, I would too, if the situation were reversed,* he fully realized. *Meg is somebody special, and I love having her for a partner. She's a great friend, and somebody I trust to have my back. And she always does.*

"Okay, here we go," he said, turning onto the designated street. "I'm gonna take it slow, and we'll scope things out this way. Given the kids, I have to go slow anyway, and it'll give us time to look without looking like we're looking, if you get me."

"Yeah, I do."

"Good."

They eased down the street, which had an unusually high population of pedestrians going house to house, most of whom were costumed. Quite a few appeared to be costumed, but in fact were not, and these were the ones under Alpha One's jurisdiction.

"That's the house over there," Echo said, nodding, and Omega paid attention.

"There's an awful lotta trick-or-treaters going up there," she noted.

"Yeah, in years past, they were known as a great place to get candy on Halloween, but after last year when the old lady freaked, I thought the aliens were supposed to stay away," Echo said.

"Are those the guards, standing on the front porch?"

Echo, who was wearing his goggle-glasses for reasons that Omega had been unable to figure out, tapped a point along the earpiece. "There," he murmured, letting his foot off the accelerator and turning to stare at the porch. "I got the binocular function activated. Yeah, that's one of her guards. Oh shit," he muttered, as the front door opened and someone came out.

"What?"

"Old Lady Lucchese just came out, and she's carrying something."

Within moments a disturbance broke out around the porch, with children and aliens alike throwing down their candy containers in disgust. Some flung them at the porch. Others simply stalked off, dumping their buckets and pails and bags on the sidewalk next to the trash bins.

"Oh man. What did she do?!" Omega wondered, shocked.

"Hold on, Meg, I'm going to head down the street, find a place to park, and then we're gonna try to intercept some of the aliens and find out what's going on, and put a stop to it, before we end up with a riot," Echo declared.

"Do it, Ace."

Echo hit the accelerator.

* * *

"She did what?!" Echo exclaimed, as he and Omega stood on the sidewalk, talking to one of his acquaintances.

"Aw, the old lady is batty," Garg, a Gurguv from Dekken, told him. "You guys really need to do something about her. Give her a brain transplant or something."

"Lemme get this straight," Omega said, astounded. "Old Mrs. Lucchese came out with a POT OF MEATBALLS? Then started ladling them into the trick-or-treaters' candy pails?"

"You got it," Garg said with a shrug. "Piping hot, and just loaded with garlic. I'm surprised you couldn't smell the reek inside your car."

"But aren't easily half of all the off-worlders reactive to garlic?" Omega wondered.

"At least," Echo confirmed. "One way or another, anyhow."

"Oh hell, yeah," Garg verified. "There's plenty of vomit on their lawn, and a few of the guys left the place breaking out in hives. You might want to call HQ and give Zarnix a heads-up that he's probably gonna have some patients tonight." Garg glanced at his wristwatch. "Like, in about half an hour or so."

"Shit," Omega murmured, reaching for her phone and swiping off a quick text message to Fox. "Okay, got it."

"Not to mention, if the meatballs and sauce were that hot, it would have melted all the candy y'all had already managed to collect," Echo pointed out.

"Exactly," Garg agreed. "So...yeah, we were pissed. But what're ya gonna do? This house used to be the best in the neighborhood for good treats on Halloween. I guess the lady's just got too old, and finally gone off the deep end." He shook his head. "It's kinda sad, really. You humans have such a short lifespan, and once you start to go, you deteriorate so fast."

"Well, that's the way we're built," Echo sighed. "Medics are working on it, but there's only so much you can do. Listen, do we need to go keep the peace?"

"Nah, I don't think so," Garg said with a shake of the head. "The guards at the door were tryin' to stop her, soon's they saw what she did. One even went in and was tryin' to find her nurse. Chances are, by the time you could get there, they'll have her back inside and sedated." He threw them a wry Gurgevan smile, which on a human would have looked like a scowl. "That'll settle things pretty fast, once she's outta the way. The guards have a reputation for a liberal hand with the candy. After all, it's comin' from the Lucchese money, not their pockets."

"I still wonder if we should check it out," Echo considered.

"Sure, it ain't gonna hurt," Garg agreed. "Just do it kinda subtle, and don't go up there if you don't have to. Those guards—they got a good memory for faces, 'cause they ain't lettin' any of us come back for seconds.

They'll remember you, unless you brain-bleach 'em."

"Good point," Echo decided.

"How do you know that?" Omega wondered.

"Well, the guards are supposed to vet anyone approaching the house, see, but they were complaining about 'how these weird looking kids keep appearing at the door as if by magic.' I think Eddie and his gang were tryin' to score extra candy by teleportation, only they kept getting caught whenever they'd 'land' to grab a handful."

"Eddie and his gang?" Omega queried, confused.

"Zardrans, right?" Echo verified.

"Yup," Garg said with a smirk.

"Okay, Garg, thanks for the information; we'll take your advice."

"No problem, Echo. See ya around. I need to go get me a new candy bucket, then try to scrounge up some more candy, before it gets too late. Pleased to meet ya, Omega. I heard you were a nice lady, and the rumors were right." Garg waved, and headed down the street.

* * *

Alpha One watched the Gurgev go, then Omega turned to her partner.

"So, what's the plan? Do we just move on to the cemetery?"

"Not quite," Echo said. "I'm not completely comfortable leaving here just yet, and we've got time. The 'Vette is out of sight of the house, so what I think I wanna do is loop the block on foot, observing everything, then walk by the front of the house and make sure everything is okay and the old lady is back in the house."

"Fair enough," Omega decided. "C'mon, Ace, let's go."

They set off in the opposite direction from Lucchese House.

* * *

As they strolled casually down the street, Echo kept a weather eye out for any aliens he knew. Whenever he spotted one—which Omega was willing to swear was about every ten yards—he paused to chat, and find out if they had been to Lucchese House yet, and if so, what they had encountered.

Several had been there at the same time that Garg had, but one, Wakang of K'hardugsin, had been there only minutes later.

"Yeah, she was still out there," Wakang related, "but I guess they took

47

the meatballs away from her. You could still smell the garlic, though. I'm really glad K'hardugs don't react to that stuff."

"I bet," Omega murmured, and the alien woman smiled.

"Mrs. Lucchese was really confused, though, and kinda upset," Wakang continued. "Several of us felt sorry for her. But Erul said she was a bad woman in her young years, and amrak does tend to come back around."

Echo glanced at Omega, evoking the memory of their previous conversation.

"So what happened then?" he asked.

"One of the Kinti—I think his name was Ruga—gave her a healing touch, when the guards weren't looking," Wakang shrugged. "I'm not sure it really helped all that much, though."

"Why not?" Echo wondered. "Surely having some of that dementia healed would have helped."

"Well, 'cause it didn't work quite the way he expected, I think," Wakang explained. "It was more like a, like some kind of, of forward—AND reverse—brain bleach. All at once, it was like she thought she was... how old is she?"

"She's around 90," Echo supplied.

"And what is considered a young adult human?"

"Twenties, thirties?" Omega suggested.

"Yes." Wakang nodded. "Which would be the 1950s, yes?"

"Oh, you mean when she would have been that old? Yeah, that's about right," Omega agreed. "Oh no. You don't mean to say..."

"Yes." Wakang nodded again. "She started mincing around, flirting with the guards, and asking where her husband was, because they were going to go to the Cub Room at the Stork Club that night, and he was late..."

"Holy shit," Echo grumbled. "Frying pan, meet fire."

"Maybe," Wakang said. "All I know is, when they finally got her inside with her nurse, she was smiling and happy again, instead of confused and unhappy."

"Yeah, but look for the crime rate in New York to increase in the next few months," Echo said.

"Yuk," Omega opined.

"So things were settling down when you left the place?" Echo followed up.

"Yeah. They got Mrs. Lucchese back inside—I heard the nurse say she was gonna sedate her—and then the guards went to handing out candy again."

"That's something, I suppose," Echo decided.

"Well, look, Echo," Omega pointed out. "Sometimes those kinds of senility and dementia can manifest like the person thinks they're in their youth again. So it might just be that the Lucchese family will assume this is the next stage of the disease, and treat her accordingly."

Echo's eyebrows went up as he considered his partner's statement.

"You're right," he concluded. "Maybe they'll take care of the situation for the rest of us."

"Probably," Wakang agreed. "I heard the nurse saying something similar to the main guard."

"Great," Echo said, obviously relieved. "Thanks, Wakang, you've been a big help. Happy Halloween, and safe trick-or-treating!"

"And to the both of you," Wakang added with a smile, and they went their separate ways.

* * *

The Lucchese matriarch's house was a well-maintained, large, Tudor style dating from around the late 40s or early 50s, and Omega suspected it had been built for Mrs. Lucchese by her husband when they were newlyweds. It was set back some distance from the street in a sprawling, landscaped yard, but only far enough to get it out of reach of anything that might be thrown from a passing car. A fence ran around the perimeter, composed of a stone-and-mortar base with heavy iron bars embedded in it. Heavy evergreen shrubs screened the thick windows, which were also heavily barred; the door was recessed from the front porch in a little stoop, and was itself also heavily reinforced. Security cameras dotted the façade, and no less than three sentries stood guard near the front entrance. Omega fully expected others dotted the grounds, out of sight.

A steady stream of costumed children, some with parents, and uncostumed aliens led up the walkway from the street to the front porch. There, the bodyguards doled out candy rather liberally from several huge mixing bowls on a folding table; sometimes the guards even smiled.

But, while there was a lingering reek of garlic, and here and there the acrid, pungent smell of vomitus, there was no sign of a disturbance at the Lucchese residence.

"Well, that's something," Echo murmured without moving his lips, in a tone barely loud enough for his partner to overhear. "Looks like they all handled things among themselves."

"Looks like it," Omega replied in kind.

"Good. We can head for the cemetery, and get into position. Maybe even get there a bit early."

"Back to the 'Vette, then?"

"Yep. Let's go, baby."

They headed down the street, past Lucchese House, toward the Corvette, parked in the next block.

Just then, Omega's attention was attracted by a couple of trick-or-treaters as they passed; her eye was becoming more experienced, and she readily recognized them as extraterrestrials, deep in a discussion of their 'stash.'

* * *

"Uh-oh, I got a bunch of chocolate in here, an' I can't eat chocolate or I'll be callin' Zarnix in the medlab, for sure." The alien in question was fairly hopping up and down, popping candies in his mouth as fast as he could stuff them, while peering into his jack o' lantern plastic bucket.

"That's okay," the other one said, all but dancing in place from the sugar rush, holding a pillowcase and rummaging in it. "I got a handful of peppermints, and they make me nauseous. I'll trade ya the mints for the chocolates. I can eat 'em, even if you can't."

"Done."

"At least we didn't get everything ruined by that crazy old lady and her meatballs."

"No shit, dude. Garlic makes me break out in hives. And you could smell it clear out to the street! Good thing Lukas didn't come with us this year."

"A lycanoid? With all that garlic? Oh grablap, no!"

"You know we're gonna be eighteen kinds of hung over tomorrow from all this sugar."

"Oh dingor, yes, but it's SO worth it."

* * *

As they moved past the pair of trick-or-treaters, Echo noticed Omega biting her lip. Then she pressed them together for several moments. She drew in a deep breath and did not let it out, and he realized she was holding her breath...and turning increasingly red in the face. Mildly alarmed, he poked her sharply in the side with his elbow.

"Breathe," he hissed.

Omega snorted...loudly. An abrupt explosion of sound came from his partner, as pent-up laughter spilled over.

"No, no, no," Echo grumbled. "Not now. We're still too close."

"Hey! HEY!" one of the guards called, taking several large steps toward them across the lawn. "Youse got a problem, deah?"

"Huh-wha?" Omega looked up, as if she were unaware of the big, threatening man who was now just on the other side of the fence. "Oh, no suh, Ah'm all right," she added, laying on her richest, thickest-syrup-sweet Southern dialect. "Nah, Ah'm not from aroun' heah, see; we're up heah visitin' fam'ly, an' me an' mah husband," she grasped Echo's elbow in both hands, "were jus' havin' some fun explorin', this bein' Halloween an' all. Ennyhow, Ah just overheard those kids strikin' deals over their candy, is all, an' Ah thought it was funny as hell."

"Oh," the bodyguard said, starting to grin. "You mean all, 'I don't like this shit, I'll trade ya for that shit' kinda thing?"

"Exactly," Omega said, giving him her biggest smile. "They 'uz so SERIOUS about it! Ah wuz tryin' not ta laugh in their faces, though, but Ah guess Ah was turnin' red, 'cause Alex heah goes an' pokes me in the ribs, an' Ah just busted out laughin'! Ah couldn't help mahself."

"Well, Ah was worried 'boutcha, darlin'," Echo allowed, laying on his own native Texan accent as thick as it would go...which was plenty thick, if he tried. "Ah don't reckon Ah ever seen you turn that red before."

"Ha!" the guard exclaimed. "Well, they can be pretty funny sometimes. An' the little ones..." he glanced around to make sure no one else could hear, "the little ones 're kinda kyoot, ya know?"

"Yeah, they are," Omega agreed, giving him a conspiratorial smile. "But Ah bet a big ol' strong guy like you, nobody expects ya to say a thing like 'at."

"Nope," the guard agreed. "So's I'd 'preciate it iffen youse guys didn't repeat it. Here. Have some candy. Happy Halloween." He pulled a couple of foil-wrapped chocolates from his jacket pocket and tossed them at the couple, who caught them nimbly.

"Thanks! An' don't worry. Mah lips are sealed," Omega grinned, unwrapping the chocolate and popping it in her mouth. "Alex, honey, you won't say nothin', will ya, sugar?"

"Not a word," Echo averred, and grabbed Omega's arm, escorting her—a closer observer than the guard might have decided he 'hustled' her—down the street, unswerving, toward the waiting Corvette.

Chapter 3

When Ke'ri Gla'd's caught a cab at her hotel to head for the Machpelah Cemetery late on Halloween, she was unaware that a certain black Lexus, some distance behind, was following her to that same destination.

"Not too near, not too far," Romeo said to India, as he drove down the street, following the yellow taxi, several cars in front.

"Here's hoping she doesn't catch on, and that she doesn't make too many detours," India agreed.

"Well, I wouldn't mind a drive-thru, which she might do, given how much she been eatin'," Romeo decided.

"You've got no room to talk, honey!" India exclaimed with a laugh. "I swear, both your legs are hollow. I don't know where you put it all!"

"An' there she goes, into th' coffee shop drive-thru," Romeo said in satisfaction. "I'mma get me a big ol' café breve, like Meg likes, an' a Danish. You want an espresso, or one 'a them frozen, blended things?"

"Get me a frozen mocha, I think," India said. "But nothing else for me."

In moments Alpha Two were in and out, slurping drinks and sharing the Danish, while never losing sight of their target.

* * *

In short order, the Lexus drove past as the taxi let out an older woman, short and slightly stocky, dressed in a form-fitting black jumpsuit, almost a catsuit, with a black-and-scarlet drape cardigan over that. Tall black boots with silver trim shod her feet; long white hair cascaded down her back.

"That's her," India said. "It matches the description of her disguise we had from Alpha Four."

"Good," Romeo said. "Then we'll park on the side street, head in, an' mingle with th' professional magicians."

"On it."

* * *

By the time Alpha One arrived at the cemetery at last, full night had fallen. Street lights illumined the sidewalk along the street, but within the cemetery itself lay mostly darkness, only broken by a few flashlights carried by the few foresighted individuals in attendance.

There was a large crowd already there, numbering several hundred; in fact, the crowd was so large that it spilled out of the small, cramped graveyard and into the surrounding streets. Some were in costume, some in formal dress, but most were in street clothes. They milled about, watching; some were anxious, but most were bored or amused. Several people, two of whom were in tuxedos, three of whom were in more...esoteric...clothing, took turns attempting to raise the spirit of Harry Houdini. As Alpha One insinuated themselves into the crowd, Ke'ri Gla'd's, in what was apparently another human disguise—a short, red-headed, middle-aged female in silken caftan and robes—eased into this smaller group.

"Watch, Meg," Echo murmured, lips barely moving. "You can tell who's who by how they're dressed, and how they conduct their séance. The guys in tuxes will be really formal and kind of rote, and they'll have a real stage presence. Those are the professional magicians, and they're just here to honor Houdini's memory; they don't believe his spirit will return. But the ones who are wearing the robes and buckskins and shit are the spiritualists who really believe the stuff. And they're halfway expecting something to really happen."

"I have the feeling they're the ones who will be right, tonight," Omega replied in kind. "But I sorta don't expect any of 'em are necessarily gonna be happy about it."

"And I expect you're right," Echo agreed. "Aha. Look, across on the other side of the family plot."

"Alpha Two," Omega murmured. "But not sticking close together. Good. Oh, and there's Alpha Six, and Four. Is Five still extracting from the hotel?"

"Actually, Five wasn't scheduled to get here until after us," Echo told her. "They were working with the hotel's offworld management, and extracted as soon as she set foot in the taxi. They should be...glance casually over your right shoulder."

"Aha. Got 'em."

"Yeah. And we blend in rather nicely with the magicians' societies here, too."

"Yup, I noticed that."

"Heads up," Echo warned. "She's decided to take her turn. Wow. Classic Glu'gu'ik quantum spirit contact ritual."

"Ooo," Omega hummed, intent on the scene.

* * *

Ke'ri Gla'd's stepped forward, threw her head back, and raised both hands toward the night sky.

"Spirit of the great Hou'd'ni, hear me; for I am Carrie Gladys Hardin! I beseech you, I who am your kindred, of your blood and kind, come to me now," Gla'd's invoked. "Pa Da'ko ta Gra'ko On'de, de b'oo!" She paused.

"'In the Name of the First Creator, it is time,'" Echo whispered the translation in his partner's ear. Just then, Gla'd's flung her arms wide.

"Ari Ho'd'ni, ne ko'ko'be, la'la'da ge nu!" she cried.

"'Harry Houdini, I command you, come to me!'" Echo translated again.

"Well, it's dramatic enough," Omega decided, sotto voce. "And the language makes it sound like a magical incantation."

"Shush—something's happening," Echo hissed.

* * *

Before the alien medium, faint colors began to swirl in the darkness. Within moments the colors thickened, darkened, as the very fabric of space-time itself seemed to distort. A bipedal, humanoid form began to take shape, hovering several feet off the ground. It was a man, some five and a half feet tall, with curly black hair, a high forehead over vivid blue eyes, and handsome, chiseled features. The crowd sucked in a collective breath of shocked excitement.

But as the 'apparition' of Houdini materialized, its appearance changed from the traditional aspect known from photographs, into the classic short-bodied, egg-headed look of a typical Zeta Reticulan Gray, complete with bulbous head, flattened nose, huge black eyes, and lipless mouth. The crowd surrounding the 'medium' shrieked in fear and drew back as far as they could. Many of those farthest from the gravesite found themselves pressed against the fence surrounding the cemetery.

* * *

Echo and Omega exchanged meaningful, mildly disturbed glances, then looked across the crowd, where Alpha Two was embedded. Omega rubbed her chin, glanced at her watch, then shook her head. *It's cool. Wait. Don't take her yet.*

Got it. Romeo nodded slightly. He made a subtle hand gesture, and he and India both sent the hand signals that forwarded the order to the other Alpha Line teams.

Meanwhile, Echo reached into his pocket, palming his cell phone. His thumb tapped several places along its screen and cover, activating the audio recording app.

'Carrie Gladys Hardin' held up a staying hand to the unnerved crowd.

"Hold!" she cried in English. "The spirits of the dead do not always appear as we would. Harry Houdini, I address you."

"I...hear..." came a quavering, eerie voice, sounding almost like a distant echo.

"You know who I am."

"I...do..."

"You know what I seek."

"Yesss..."

"Where is it?"

Houdini's alien shade was silent.

"I adjure you, Harry Houdini, answer me! Where is it?"

What came from the extraterrestrial spirit's lips next was in no wise English.

"On'de, oo de n ko'te a tw'a, n do'ok a ko'a'du'ne ba'wa'ne. Tor'ko kl'ee, bo kwa'ta'do! To'de, n do'ok la on'wa ne la'la'du wo'of. D'an, der klo'vi't do'n. K'oi'du de we. Nda'da'be. Tra'de, ba on'de, n do'ok la on'de ne k'ap wi'if'de'z, n fes'nus pe'dun ge'da n nu'ke'ke. Ka'de, n do'ok la ne du ka'ka'du b'an dan kre. Gun'gun oi'ko's'un, wo ga lo om, qu'a'du bre. Kin'de, n do'ok k'en'ti'do, der ne wo ku. Wo'pe'wo'be p'op n b'oo! Bu'ke n dwa'z, der or'k lu'ke n kwa'z!"

And with that, the ghostly apparition faded into nothingness.

The frightened crowd bolted.

* * *

"Alpha Line—GO!" Echo shouted, and five teams, two elite and three in training, moved toward Ke'ri Gla'd's, weapons out.

"Ke'ri Gla'd's, you are under arrest, on charges of sedition and conspiracy in two Division One systems!" Omega called, advancing beside her partner, one blaster out and trained on the alien subversive agent.

Staring into no less than ten blasters, with no obvious way out, Gla'd's put her hands in the air.

"It appears you have me," she murmured.

* * *

In the streets surrounding the cemetery, Fox had coordinated to have other agents ready, intercepting the frightened crowd, wielding brain bleachers and calming them, pointing out the 'fraudulent techniques' the 'fake medium' had used.

Soon the matter had been contained, and Alpha Line, their prisoner in custody, was headed back to Headquarters.

* * *

"...That's right," Fox said. "We aren't sure yet; we're still trying to get an eye on him. But there may be another kinsman coming in on the next flight. It's possible she was able, somehow, to get off a signal to him— maybe some kind of quantum entanglement thing—or it may be that it was planned like that all along, and he was coming in to help her, once she had the location of our mysterious thingamajig from Ho'd'ni. I'm trying to make contact with the government on Va'du'sha'ā to verify; perhaps they can stop him before he boards the spacecraft. But let's not assume they can."

"Okay. Then Meg and I better get with it," Echo said, as Alpha One stood with the Director in the door of their departmental meeting room.

"That would be advisable, yes," Fox agreed. "Omega, are you game for heading out as soon as you can?"

"Yes sir," a cheerful Omega agreed.

"We just have to figure out where we're going, first," Echo said, waving his cell phone.

* * *

"Y'all got this?" Romeo asked, as Alpha Five and Alpha Six escorted Ke'ri Gla'd's to the Security holding area; Alpha Four had been allowed to go off duty upon arrival back at Headquarters, given their undercover work. Alpha Two was going off duty momentarily, leaving the two remaining new teams to stand watch...and begin coming up to speed on departmental protocols and procedures.

"Yeah, I think so," Nuts decided. "She hasn't given us any trouble, after all."

"Okay," Romeo said, then tapped the other Agent on the shoulder. "Tag, you're it!"

"Thanks, man," Nuts said with a grin. "Go get some rest."

"We are all about that," India decided.

Alpha Two turned and headed for the agents' quarters, and Alpha Five and Six escorted Gla'd's, wrists and ankles firmly fixed in force cuffs, into the elevator to head for Security.

* * *

But as soon as the elevator doors closed, and the four relaxed their guard, Gla'd's smiled.

"Gentlebeings, it has been...interesting," she told them...

...And faded away.

The force cuffs deactivated and clattered to the floor of the elevator car.

"SHIT!" Easy cursed. "What the hell did she just do?!"

"I dunno," Jack grumbled. "But we messed up, guys, somehow. And we better call...is Alpha One on duty, or off duty?"

"I got no idea on any of it," Golf said. "Call Fox."

"More shit, piled higher and deeper," Nuts sighed.

* * *

"...So that's why you recorded it on your phone," Omega said, watching as Echo played back the recording on it, transcribing the response Ho'd'ni had given his distant cousin Gla'd's. "You figured Houdini would give clues or somethin', and you wanted to get an accurate rendition of it, then use that fancy linguistics degree of yours to translate it!"

"Pretty much," Echo confirmed, glancing up with a slight grin from his seat at the conference table in the Alpha Line meeting room. "You get to show off the edumacation from all your degrees all the time. I figured it was high time I got to show off my degrees, for a change."

"Degrees, plural?" she pressed. "I knew I shoulda looked closer at your files, that night after the Antarctic mission when you showed 'em to me."

"Well, it isn't like I'm keeping 'em locked away from you," he pointed out. "You can look at 'em any time you want to, now. You got the password...don't you?"

"Yeah, I do," Omega admitted. "And once in a while, I've consulted it, you know, for like making sure I didn't miss your birthday or something. I just hadn't thought about looking at THAT. I mean, it's patently obvious that you're competent at everything you do, so it just hadn't occurred to me to check."

Echo flushed at the blatant compliment.

"Oh. Well, yeah. I have bachelor's degrees in linguistics and diplomacy, and a masters in linguistics," he said, glancing down and correcting a grammatical point in his transcription. "Damn, I wish this was a desk, not a table. The height isn't quite right, and I can't adjust it, or the chair, or anything."

"Hey, lemme shut up and let you concentrate, then. This is something I definitely can't do, and I can't even help you with. So have at it."

"Thanks, baby. This shouldn't take long," he told her.

* * *

Echo bent over his notepad, scribbling away, working to translate the recording he had made of Ho'd'ni's clues from the graveyard. Finally he sighed and sat back.

"You get it, Ace?" Omega wondered, looking up from her study of their case file.

"Yeah, I do, but I gotta admit, I still don't understand it all," Echo answered. "Come here and look."

Omega moved to her partner's side and looked over his shoulder. There, she saw alternating lines of Glu'gu'ik and their literal English translations, all in Echo's firm, bold handwriting. The Glu'gu'ik was in script, but the English translation was written in block Roman letters.

* * *

On'de, oo de n ko'te a tw'a, n do'ok a ko'a'du'ne ba'wa'ne. Tor'ko kl'ee, bo kwa'ta'do!

First, as is the right of it, the place of my challenge my greatest. (You) face front, and escape!

To'de, n do'ok la on'wa ne la'la'du wo'of. D'an, der klo'vi't do'n. K'oi'du de we. Nda'da'be.

Second, the place where once I flew high. Lost, yet (s/he/it) remains still. Timing is all. (You) remember.

Tra'de, ba on'de, n do'ok la on'de ne k'ap wi'if'de'z, n fes'nus pe'dun ge'da n nu'ke'ke.

Third yet first, the place where first I won my wings, the fastness foundation toward the morn.

Ka'de, n do'ok la ne du ka'ka'du b'an dan kre. Gun'gun oi'ko's'un, wo ga lo om, qu'a'du bre.

Fourth, the place where I was writ(ten) larger than life. Ominous framework, no fun at all, (s/he/it) happened here.

Kin'de, n do'ok k'en'ti'do, der ne wo ku. Wo'pe'wo'be p'op n b'oo! Bu'ke n dwa'z, der or'k lu'ke n kwa'z!

Fifth, the place (they) purport, yet I did not. (You) watch well the time! Bright the days, yet/but how light the nights!

* * *

"I'm havin' a hard time getting that," Omega admitted.

"Well, what I have here is a literal translation," Echo pointed out. "I think it's something of a poem in blank verse. I expect it would translate better as, 'First, as is the right of it, the place of my greatest challenge. Face front, and escape! Second, the place where I once flew high. Lost, yet it still remains. Timing is all. Remember! Third yet first, the place where first I won my wings, the fastness foundation toward the morn. Fourth, the place where I was writ larger than life. Ominous framework, no fun at all, it happened here. Fifth, the place they purport, yet I did not. Watch well the time! Bright the days, but how light the nights!' Some of the pronouns

I'm making a guess at, because they're not specified; I've just got the verb conjugations to go on."

"Oh-kaaaay," Omega murmured. "I apologize for my stupidity, Ace, but it still doesn't make sense to me."

"Sorry, baby. It isn't because you're stupid, of all people. I think that's just because you're not a Houdini buff, like I am. Or, like I sorta am; I don't claim expertise on his life. But I think I have some of the general locations on this, at least."

"All right. I'm listening."

"Okay, the first one references 'the place of my greatest challenge.' Houdini used to say that his greatest challenge was escaping from a pair of handcuffs especially made to hold him. I'm not sure why it was so hard for a Glu'g'ik, unless maybe the guy who made the cuffs wasn't human either, and had figured out Houdini's secret and had access to offworld tech. Anyway, it took him hours to get out, but he did get out. And it was at the Hippodrome Theatre, in London, England."

"So it sounds like that's our first stop."

"Yeah."

"Can you figure out the rest of 'em like that?"

"Most of 'em, yeah. I'm not getting the third clue, or the fifth clue. At least, not yet. But the second one is in Australia, and the fourth one is in the States." He shrugged. "I figure I probably just need to think about the other two for a little while."

"It sounds like a world-wide treasure hunt, of sorts."

"Looks like it's shaping up that way, yep."

"So we need to get moving."

"Yeah. Grab a couple of spectral imaging scanners and let's go check in with Fox before we head out."

"On it."

* * *

"You're kidding," Omega said, jaw slack. "She got free?"

"Evidently," Fox noted. "We're still trying to figure out exactly how. It seems she somehow...dematerialized...right through the force cuffs, and vanished, right there in front of your teams."

"Damn!" Echo cursed. "Since when do Glu'gu'ik do THAT?"

"I'm not sure," Fox said, shrugging. "Back when I was working for Pul, I heard some rumors, but...that's ALL they were. Rumors. I'm going to put out some feelers among the other Divisions and see what I can find out. Maybe even ping Pul, if I can locate him anymore, since he retired from the Ennead. If I get anything, I'll let you know right off."

"Please do," Omega agreed. "Meanwhile, I guess we'd better get our asses in high gear, 'cause she's probably after this whosiwhatsis already."

"She has to get transportation first," Echo noted. "Even if she did dematerialize or something, she has to know where to go first. And her best bet is to get hold of some travel info, and that's at the very least going to take her to the spacecraft rental agencies."

"I thought about that, and got with the people in our concourse," Fox said, "but they haven't seen anyone remotely fitting any of her descriptions. I'm betting that she won't dare reveal herself in our own headquarters after escaping from us, so she'll go for one of the off-site operations, maybe one of the shadier ones, for a craft. And I'm betting you're right, Echo; even if she can 'teleport' planet-wide, it's gotta wear her out after a while. So I put out a whole network of agents on the street, watching the off-site spacecraft rental agencies, legit and not. If we're lucky, maybe one of 'em can get a tracer on the ship she rents. I'm not holding my breath, but it would be good."

"Agreed," Echo said. "Near as I can make it, our first stop is across the Pond, so Meg, you and I need to figure out what transport we're gonna use."

"World-wide, huh?" Fox queried.

"Oh, hell yeah. One damn big treasure hunt, all over the blasted planet," Echo said.

"All right, I've got something for you to use on that world-wide treasure hunt, then," Fox declared. "The first in a batch of airskimmers."

"What are airskimmers?" Omega wondered.

"An aircraft based on spacecraft technology," Fox explained. "They aren't designed for exo, but they're reasonably fast and they're long-range. They'll beat the Corvette for speed and range, though the Corvette would probably be a little more comfortable; and they'll even fly a LOT farther than the T-bird before needing to refuel, though they aren't nearly as fast."

"I appreciate the new equipment, Fox, but is there a reason we can't take a saucer?" Echo asked. "That's what I was leaning toward."

"Yes, there is—that space plane test run. Launch is tomorrow, down at the Cape. Everybody and his dog is watching for stuff in the sky."

"Well, shit. A saucer would be a lot faster."

"I know, but it can't be helped," Fox said. "Anyway, I'm giving Alpha One the very first airskimmer in Division One. Alpha Two will get the next one."

"Cool!" Omega declared, and Echo grinned.

"Glad you like the idea, baby," Echo noted.

"Echo, would you be offended if I assigned it to Omega, rather than you?" Fox queried. "You already have the Corvette AND the T-bird. I thought it would be fair to give Omega her own craft for the partnership to use. Though you'll have to teach her how to fly it."

"Yeah, Fox, I'm cool with that," Echo said, shooting his partner another grin. "And I'll be happy to teach her how to fly it...which I'd do anyway. If she can handle the T-bird—and she can—she can handle this thing. Remind me what model spacecraft it's based on, again?"

"It's based loosely on a Ladaten XB22 Comet," Fox said. "The body is completely different, of course, because it's a LOT more aerodynamic, but the controls and handling are essentially the same."

"That's the two-to-four-crew spacecraft with the supercharged interplanetary ion drive, right?" Omega asked.

"Aha! Someone is becoming a buff, eh?" Fox wondered with a laugh.

"Oh hell yeah, Fox," Echo said, chuckling. "And yes, Meg, that's the one."

"You sound pretty...knowledgeable...yourself, Fox," Omega observed, curious.

"Well, yes," Fox admitted. "I've been known to 'hot rod' my vehicles. I'm the one that taught Echo how to modify most of his vehicles, over the years, to have the latest and greatest tech on 'em. It's been a while since I've had time to dabble in it, but once you get a feel for the airskimmer, I'll be happy to teach you what I know, as well—if Echo hasn't already done so."

"I've started on it, at least on other craft," Echo confirmed. "But I sure wouldn't object to the Director himself, my mentor on that sorta thing, helping out."

"All right," Fox agreed with a smile. "It should be fun, at that. We'll work something out the next time our days off coincide."

"Terrific!" Omega exclaimed, and all three shared a grin.

"Not that you ever really get a day off," Echo observed.

"True. I'll still be on call," Fox conceded. "But I can always leave orders not to disturb me unless the situation gets past a certain level."

"That'll work," Echo decided.

"Now, do you know what you want to name the airskimmer?" Fox asked Omega.

"Not yet," Omega decided. "Lemme see it and fly in it, and I'll see if it has a 'personality.' Then I'll have a better idea."

"Okay. For now it will just be 'Alpha One Omega One,' then," Fox informed her. "You can name it later." He tossed a couple of key chain controllers to Alpha One. "It's waiting in the new wing of the vehicle hangar, in the slot corresponding to its designation. That's its assigned parking space."

"Right. Let's go, Meg," Echo said. "We got work to do."

"All over it, Ace," Omega vouched, as they left Fox's office at speed.

* * *

Half a step behind and on her partner's right, Omega watched somewhat absently as Echo strode through the Core en route to the vehicle hangar, broad shoulders squared, body language confident, stride quick and sure.

Now there's my Agent, she thought to herself, proud of her partner. She smiled slightly, studying his handsome features, noting the way those strong shoulders tapered to a trim waist, with powerful, swift legs below that.

She remembered brushing a stray wisp of hair out of his eyes first thing that morning, when he had run a distracted hand through it after being presented with yet another new batch of Alpha Line applications; the feel of it had been silky-smooth.

Then he had come up with a positively brilliant method of wading—

64

and weeding—through the stack of applications, to be initiated once they finished the current assignment, and she had been delighted...and relieved... by his idea.

Yup. My guy has it all, she thought. *Brains, brawn, AND looks.*

That was when the wording of her mental statements hit home.

Whoa, whoa, whoa! she told herself. *Echo's my PARTNER, not 'my guy,' or 'my Agent.' I got no business thinking of him any other way.*

'Oh, don't you?' a little mental voice asked. *'As much time as you spend together, as much as you enjoy his company?'*

He's my best friend, she rejoined to what she deduced was her own subconscious. *Of course I enjoy his company. And I don't even have the right to call him 'my guy' even if he IS my best bud.*

'Oh, come on now. You spend all your waking hours in his company, by choice as much as duty.'

Yeah, but does HE enjoy MY company as much? she asked in return.

'Wasn't HE the one who wanted to go to the movie with you the other night, when several of the other—MALE—agents invited him to join 'em at that pub, instead?'

Well, yeah, but...partners.

'It could be...MORE. You know you want that.'

What the hell are you talking about?! Omega demanded of that little voice. *I haven't...oh damn.* She stopped dead, right where she stood in the corridor off the Core. *I have.*

* * *

"Meg?" Echo had realized she was no longer at his side, and stopped in some annoyance, turning to his right to see where she'd gotten off to. Finally he spotted her, over his shoulder. "Come on, Meg, we've—" He took one look at her face, then spun toward her and practically leaped the couple of steps between them, grabbing her by the shoulders. "Baby?! What's wrong?"

"Huh?" she said, looking up at him. *Uh-oh. Think fast, girl. You can't possibly tell him you just realized you're nuts about him.*

"What's wrong? Are you okay?"

"Um, y-yeah, I'm okay," she tried not to stammer. "I'm just, um. You ever sorta have a brain fart? You know, where you're going, 'Did I do that or not?'" *There,* she thought. *At least it isn't a lie.* She watched as he relaxed and started to grin.

"What did you forget?" he asked then. "Do we need to double back and get something?"

"No—no, we don't need to go back," she said, making excuse. "It's... have you ever gotten so used to a certain thing that you forget if you even have it?"

"What, like one of your weapons?"

"Exactly," she jumped on the offering. "Like, sometimes for a split second, I can't tell if I'm wearing all three holsters or not, let alone if I got my pieces in 'em..."

"Yeah," Echo agreed, the grin still there. "An' then you're like, 'Aw shit, I can't do that, not goin' into a mission,' and then you gotta look around to make sure nobody's watching, then you poke under your arm, or mash your arm into your side, to feel if it's still there."

"You HAVE done it!"

"Well, not in recent years, but I remember doin' it a few times when I was still only a couple years into this job, yeah. One time X-ray caught me doin' the check on myself and stared at me like I'd grown an eye-stalk or something...'til he figured out what I was doing. Then he laughed himself silly, and carried me high about it for days."

"Aw! You're not gonna...I mean, at least not in front of..."

"Nah," he said, sobering. "I won't do that to ya at all, baby. I swear I won't. I get it, and I would never embarrass you like that. X-ray never teased me in front of anybody, either, just so you know. It was all just between us, an' mostly guy stuff, at that. You know, relating our weapons to, uh, certain parts of the male anatomy, shit like that—stuff that you CAN'T go off and forget, because it's attached. Only he was teasing me about going off and leaving it."

"Oh!" Omega struggled to avoid the blush at his anatomical reference. "No wonder he didn't tease you in front of anybody."

"Yeah, it woulda embarrassed him at least as bad as me! So, do you have 'em all? Two blasters, one Winchester & Tesla?"

"Two under the arms, one in the back," Omega said, nodding, letting her face adopt a wry expression. "But...well, let's just say I feel kinda silly at the moment." *And that's no lie, either,* she decided. *Damn, girl, what the hell do you think you're doing, developing a crush on your partner like this? He's your boss, too, remember. This ain't good.*

"Good, then," Echo said, in seeming contradiction to her thoughts, turning back around. "C'mon, baby, and let's go see about this little problem with a medium."

"Ha!" Omega said at that, as a random mental reconstruction of her partner's comment generated a pun for her.

"What?"

"For a perp, we've got a small medium...at large."

"Ohh," Echo groaned. "Baby?"

"Yeah?"

"PLEASE, stay away from Romeo!"

Omega laughed.

* * *

Well, here's a right fine mess, a worried Omega thought, sobering herself, as she paced Echo through Headquarters toward the vehicle hangar. *If Echo finds out how I feel, we'll both be embarrassed...maybe enough that he won't want me as a partner any more. And if anybody else finds out, never mind getting carried high. The other agents will never let us hear the end of it, and that won't be good for Alpha One's reputation, together or individually. Especially after all we found out about how Alpha Line is generally viewed, from that little debacle with Paris and How. And while I'm still developing said reputation, Echo's got a really powerful one...that this would just ruin. Not to mention if it came across as nepotism or something, to the other agents. So under NO circumstances can I let anyone find out I've developed a crush on him.*

Just then, that little inner voice of her subconscious showed up again.

'A crush? Like some silly little schoolgirl? Honey, you know better than THAT. You're in love with him.'

No no no, Omega protested. *I am NOT.* She paused mentally, considering. *Dammit. I am. He's everything I could ever want in a man, in a mate, and I've managed to faceplant over him. Hard.*

The inner voice was now annoyingly quiet, apparently satisfied in having brought to the surface matters that had been manifesting subconsciously for some time. She shot a surreptitious glance at her partner, then hastily stifled a sigh.

I gotta figure out what to do about this. Do I get him aside at some point...probably after the mission...and admit it to him, give him a chance to decide in private what he wants to do about it? I mean, it's working for Romeo and India, and they're Alpha Two, and a damn good team. It might work for us, too. IF he's interested. Of course, it could also break up the team if he's NOT interested, and isn't comfortable with the idea. Dammit.

Then a thought hit her with the suddenness of a thunderclap, and threw her into an emotional flat spin re-entry.

I was intended to be Echo's assassin, she realized. *I'm not really human any more, when you get down to it. I've been tinkered with, I've been modified, and I've been programmed. And it almost worked; I still remember his face, after Romeo tackled him and he looked up, to see me training my blaster back on his head. It's as clear now as it was in those moments, and I don't think it'll ever fade. Dear God, I wish the brain bleacher worked on me, if for no other reason than to forget the image of Echo's head in my gun sights.*

She stopped herself before she shook her own head; Echo would notice that motion, without doubt, and ask what she was thinking.

At any rate, she decided, heart sinking as hope faded, *the chances of him being interested in ME after seeing me...like that...are probably slim and none. I never yet have figured out why on Earth—or any other planet, for that matter—he still wants me as his partner. Then factor in all the genetic manipulation? I dunno what I am any more, but 'likely romantic partner' ain't in the list. Especially, I expect, for HIM.*

* * *

She shot another look at Echo, as they arrived in front of the airskimmer. Echo stopped, turned, and waved her forward; she pulled out the keychain fob, pointed it at the hatch and pressed the unlock button. It beeped once, and the hatch popped open.

"Enter, mademoiselle," Echo said, sweeping a hand toward the hatch, "and prepare to learn how to fly this thing. And do it in a hurry; we've got a perp to catch...again."

Which means, Omega realized, as she entered the small aircraft, *I better put the little conundrum of my feelings aside and activate the gray matter, or I really WILL be in deep shit.*

* * *

"I said you needed to hurry up and learn how to fly it, and that's true, but I was mostly teasing. It's really not gonna be that hard for you, baby," Echo said, strapping into the pilot's seat, as Omega strapped into the co-pilot's chair. "Note the yoke instead of a control stick, but it works exactly the same way as the T-bird's stick, only your hands won't get tired as fast. A lot of it is like the T-bird, and what there is of the rest has been simplified. And the spacecraft it was based on had one of the simpler control interfaces, anyway."

"Okay, that sounds good," Omega decided. "The learning curve should be nice and steep, then."

"Oh yeah. I fully expect you to have mastered this thing well before we finish this mission. Probably by the time we can even reach our first destination. Now, let me get this thing in the air and headed for London, set the auto-pilot, and we'll have a few lessons. Pay attention to what I'm doing, though; you'll probably catch on before I can even finish that."

"All right, Ace."

* * *

Omega did, in fact, catch on to a great deal just in the first five minutes. By that time, they were well out over the North Atlantic, so Echo temporarily switched off the auto-pilot and put the craft in trainer mode, allowing the co-pilot's control yoke to function, but maintaining override capability from the pilot's console.

Within minutes, she had the hang of controlling the craft—mischievously putting it through a quick barrel roll, somewhat to his surprise, though fortunately, he was still strapped in—and Echo returned the airskimmer to control of the auto-pilot, while he taught her some of the other ship's functions. This included explaining the hover and VTOL function, an ability that the T-bird didn't have, but which could be useful for landing in tight areas...such as the middle of large, congested cities like London.

Other features included passive metamaterial cloaking, solid holo-gram camouflage, holographic vid-comm ability, universal translation run straight through the communications system, a sensor suite that, while not full-up, still included most of the essentials, and various heads-up display modes.

He also took her on a quick tour of the small craft—which was nev-ertheless bigger than either the Corvette or the T-bird—and which included a flight deck some seven feet in diameter, very limited stowage for mostly-standard equipment and supplies in the rear of said flight deck, a minuscule kitchenette that largely consisted of a pod brewer, microwave, and dorm-room-sized fridge/freezer combo, and a tiny head in the very aft.

By the time they crossed the western coast of Ireland, over seven and a half hours later, Echo had decided to hand over the landing in London to his partner. All he had to do was sit back and watch, and tell her where to put down.

* * *

Omega set the passively-cloaked airskimmer down where Echo di-rected: in a hidden back mews in a little wedge of a block between Bear and Cranbourn Streets in Westminster, off Charing Cross Road. It was nestled in what apparently had once been an alley between those two streets, but the alleyway had been blocked off as a thoroughfare by a tiny little box of-fice constructed on one end, and a minute tattoo parlor on the other. It was currently empty of any potential onlookers.

"That was a good landing, baby," he praised her. "Nice and smooth, even as tight as it is in this back alley."

"Thanks," Omega murmured, offering him an appreciative smile. "It's a little like the Corvette, in that respect."

"Yeah, it is, and that's good. Now for some disguise."

He waved a hand at his partner, and in response, Omega leaned over his shoulder. He gestured at the display he had pulled up. It held several rows of thumbnail images of various brick designs and hues.

"You've got a good eye for matching colors and patterns. Which one do you think?" he asked. "I think it's between these two, maybe three... see here?" He gestured between thumbnails. "But I'm not quite decided which."

"Um..." Omega murmured, considering. "Yeah. That one, I think. Matches the brickwork best." She pointed to the second thumbnail he had indicated.

"Done." Echo tapped the small thumbnail image, and outside the skimmer, a large solid hologram formed, engulfing it. It made the now-hidden skimmer look like a small wing of the adjacent building, blending nearly perfectly with the old red brick. "There's a back door to the box office on Cranbourn; we can get out of the alley through there. Then we head across the street, up the court in the rear, and in through the stage door."

"Won't there be anybody in the theatre?" Omega wondered. "No, wait. What time is it, London time...?"

"Right. There would have been performances late last night, and it's still fairly early in the morning. The theatre should be pretty deserted. And in our Suits, we ought to blend in with any legitimate businesspeople in the area."

"Let's go, then."

* * *

In only a few minutes, Alpha One was prowling around backstage at the empty theatre.

"Damn, Ace, you really know your way around this part of London," Omega decided. "How did that happen?"

"Remember about that Klydonian invasion, a few years back?"

"Yeah. Oh, was this one of the resistance staging areas?"

"Yeah, all of Westminster, pretty much—because government and all. Fox sent me over to help out the London Office, just long enough to help 'em get organized. I got assigned a big chunk of central London, from Regents Park across the Thames down to the A3, and from Hyde Park over to the A10. I got to know the area really well, really fast." Echo surveyed the dark backstage area. "All right. Now, the trick here is, this whole theatre has been rebuilt multiple times since Houdini was here. So we have to find the old parts, then scan 'em to try to find any hidden Glu'gu'ik artifacts an'

71

shit. And hope that whatever it is we're looking for wasn't destroyed in one of the remodels."

"What do you think we'll find?"

"I'm expecting some sort of hidden compartment with..." Echo broke off, considering. "Something in it. I don't know what, yet."

"Okay. Then probably we need to be checking the structural walls and all, don't you expect?"

"Most likely, yeah. I'm thinking..." He turned in a circle. "Let's hit the back wall, the wall into the dressing rooms—I know the actual dressing rooms are new, or I'd head right for them—and maybe the sections of wall that support the, uh, the whatchamacallit...oh yeah, the proscenium."

"Okay, I can see that. What about the audience? The house, as it were?"

"Oh, that's been completely redone," Echo told her. "It's maybe a tenth the size it was when Houdini performed here. They gutted all that and redid it. There's nothing left of the original audience area."

"Oh, okay. How do you know all this?"

"I, uh," Echo flushed, "when I was helping out during the invasion... well, Houdini performed here and all..."

"Aha. Fanboy came by to check it out?"

"Well, it was part of the assignment," Echo made excuse. "I was supposed to hit up all of the historical sites and see what could be done to protect 'em. I just happened to be pretty interested in THIS one...so I asked a bunch of questions." He shrugged. "To tell the truth, I was kind of disappointed to find out just how much renovation had gone on, and how different the place is now from how it was then."

"Yeah, I hear ya. I saw some historical stuff get changed during my time at NASA that I was kinda offended at, too. Oh well. Time to scan?"

"Yup. Break out the spectral imaging scanners, and let's start sweeping."

"Okay. I'll take stage left, you take stage right."

"Uhh..." Echo began, and Omega glanced at him, to see a puzzled expression. "I'm not up on my theater terminology. I never did any, uh..."

"Oh. Um, okay, well, stage directions are opposite audience directions, Ace. So if the audience is facing the stage, but the actor is looking out at the audience, the audience's left is stage right, and vice versa."

"Ah!" Echo exclaimed, understanding, then brought up short. "Wait, what?"

"Huh? What do you mean?" Omega wondered. She moved to the center of the stage, facing the empty house. Holding up her right arm from the shoulder, she pointed with her index finger. "Stage right." She let that hand drop, and held up her other hand in similar fashion. "Stage left."

"Hold on, baby, I get that. It's something else it made me remember," Echo said, reaching inside his jacket to remove a certain small notebook from the inner breast pocket. He flipped open a few pages, then read, "'First, as is the right of it, the place of my greatest challenge. Face front, and escape!' is the first line of the Houdini ghost's clue. Well, this is the place of his greatest challenge, by his own testimony...'"

"Oh! I get it now!" Omega exclaimed. "'Face front' must be a veiled reference to stage directions!"

"Exactly!" Echo agreed. "But listen to this: 'First, AS IS THE RIGHT OF IT, the place of my greatest challenge.' That's how he worded it. He means stage right! Whatever we're hunting for, it'll be on this side!'"

And they headed for the stage-right wing of the theatre.

* * *

Hidden in the shadows behind the current show's set pieces, which were stored in the wings between the curtain legs, two dark eyes narrowed, scrutinizing the pair's systematic search.

A bulbous, gray, translucent head nodded to itself, pleased, and continued to watch...

And wait.

* * *

They scanned the rear wall, the walls in the wing, and even the stage itself, though Echo thought it was highly unlikely that much of the wood flooring was authentic to the original structure. They found nothing.

Until Echo reached the proscenium arch and began working his way along it.

His scanner abruptly let out a loud bleat, showing a schematic of the wall containing a small, hollow sphere; a tiny object was within it. Omega came running at the alert noise.

"You got something?" she wondered, excited.

"Looks like it," Echo decided, studying the scanner display. "And the scanner says the signature is Glu'gu'ik. So, by the shape of this compartment—I mean, it looks to be a perfect sphere, in a load-bearing wall constructed of pretty much solid brick, and it's showing the bricks just sort of...truncate...at the sphere's surface—I'd say Houdini did a little quantum foam manipulation to make a place to hide...whatever the scanner is showing to be inside it."

"How do we get it out?" Omega wondered.

"The hard way," he said, pulling a device out of one of his pockets. "But it won't be THAT hard."

The mechanism he held was roughly square, about six inches on a side but less than one inch thick, with claw-like metallic appendages along one large, blank face, and several dials and gauges on the opposite face; one toggle switch lay along the bottom of the dial face. The external surface was composed of some dull gray metallic alloy.

"What the hell is that, Ace?" Omega wondered, curious.

"It's a hurgir," Echo explained. "That's Deltiri for 'excavator.' I had a feeling we might have to go through some hunks of building to get to some of this stuff. So I brought along one designed to do more delicate work. The Deltiri have 'em big enough to hollow out mountains. Okay, lemme see here..."

He used the claws to clamp the hurgir onto the brick wall, as nearly in front of the hidden chamber as he could make it, getting Omega to pull readings off the imaging scanner, then entering them into the settings on the hurgir. Finally he drew a deep breath and turned to his partner.

"Here goes," he told her.

"Do it," she said.

He hit the toggle switch.

The hurgir scuttled, spider-like, a few fractions of an inch across the brick surface, locating the exact position determined by the scanner, then there was a small crunching sound as its claws dug in, and it settled down and set to work. A low, ululating hum sounded in the quiet of the empty theatre, and the small space between the wall and the hurgir glowed a soft blue. This went on for a couple of minutes, then the sound and the blue light ceased. Echo removed the hurgir, returning it to his pocket.

A neat square hole—nearly the same size as the hurgir—now reached into the wall. He pulled his cell phone and activated the flashlight app, shining it into the maw of the dark hole. It opened upon a small, perfectly round chamber, situated over a foot deep in the thick wall.

Inside that chamber was a little object, perhaps as much as two inches on a side, but irregular in shape. It looked for all the world like a three-dimensional jigsaw puzzle piece, save that instead of an image on any of its surfaces, it had an odd, satiny, silvery-white metallic finish.

"Huh. There it is. That wasn't nearly as bad a hunt as I thought it was gonna be," Omega decided. "Any sign of booby traps, Ace?"

Echo double-checked the scanner display. "Negative. Go ahead and grab it, but be careful. The thing itself could be designed to react in a hostile fashion."

"So don't let it zap me or nothin' like that."

"Right."

"Then let's do it like this." Omega drew out a set of heavy gloves, made of multiple layers of on-and off-world insulating materials, from an inside jacket pocket. She donned them, and then reached for the object.

Just before she grasped it, however, a voice sounded behind Alpha One.

"Oh, I believe that is mine," said a voice from behind them. "F'al on'cik, la'la'da ge nu!"

Before they could react, the device became translucent, and faded away.

Alpha One spun.

A certain familiar Glu'g'ik faced them, a smirk on her face. Her hand was outstretched.

The device lay in it.

* * *

"Thank you both so much for the assistance," Ke'ri Gla'd's said,

75

smirk growing broader. "You made it vastly easier for me. Well, I must be off. Ta!"

"Oh, no! I don't think you're goin' anywhere," Omega said, lunging forward and grabbing Gla'd's' near arm in her right hand as she reached for her force cuffs with her left.

"Oh, really, gr'ub?" Gla'd's said, scornful, then issued a command. "F'al on'cik, kwa'tan'da glub."

The small device in her palm faded out...just as Gla'd's grabbed Omega's forearm with both hands.

"STOP!" Echo cried—even as Omega screamed in pain.

"AaaaAAAHHH!" Omega shrieked, and started shoving at the Glu'g'ik. "Leggo leggo LEGGO! Leggo my arm! NOW!"

"What?! Why are you not...?" Gla'd's wondered, seeming angry and irritated. "We should be gone by now."

Both of Echo's blasters came up as Omega struggled to free herself from the Glu'g'ik's tight grip.

"Let go of her NOW," the male Agent growled, the slow, low voice threatening in the extreme, "or, I swear to you, you won't live two more seconds. A blaster beam travels faster than you can possibly phase, or whatever it is you do."

Gla'd's grumbled something in Glu'gu'ik and released Omega's forearm. Immediately the alien faded, and fractions of a second later, vanished...along with the artifact she had come to collect.

* * *

A pale Omega dropped to her knees, and Echo holstered his blasters and ran to her side, bending over her.

"Are you okay, baby?" he asked, deep concern obvious. "What did she do??"

"I...dunno, an'...I dunno, Ace," Omega murmured, panting and holding her aching arm tight against her belly, shielding it with her other arm. "All I know is that, when she grabbed my arm, it felt like she was trying to rip me apart at the seams."

"Here, let me have a look at it," Echo said, kneeling beside her. Omega gingerly held out her arm, and both Agents let out shocked cries.

"Ohmigosh!" Omega exclaimed.

"DAMN, baby!" Echo blurted. "Can you SEE that?!"

"Oh HELL yeah!"

* * *

Omega's hand and forearm—including her glove and jacket sleeve, nearly all the way to the elbow—appeared...translucent. Echo could actually see the flooring of the stage through it. As he watched, however, it darkened and became opaque once more. Echo put out both hands and gently, even tentatively, grasped her fingers in a light hold, afraid of hurting her.

When nothing happened, and she didn't react, he gingerly peeled off the glove, spread her fingers across his palm and turned her hand this way and that to survey it from all sides, then shoved her sleeves up to view as much of her forearm as he could easily uncover. It now looked normal, though the skin appeared somewhat mottled and pink to him, rather than its regular smooth, pale coloration.

"Can you feel that? Does it hurt?" he asked, looking up at her face. But her gaze was focused on her hand, an expression nigh akin to horror in her eyes; she stared at her hand like she had never seen it before. "Baby? Meg?"

"Uh. Huh? What did you say, Ace?" Omega wondered, finally coming up for air.

"Can you feel this?" He gently squeezed her fingertips.

"Yeah. I can feel it."

"Does it hurt?"

"No, nothing hurts, now."

"Okay, grab on and let's clean up here and get after her," he decided after a moment, grasping her hand firmly and standing. As he pulled her to her feet, he said, "But pay attention, and if you start not feeling good, tel—"

"Uhn," Omega grunted, and swayed. Echo jumped to grab her shoulders and steady her. "Hang on a second, there, Echo, literally," she whispered. "I'm...a little dizzy."

An obliging—and not a little concerned—Echo stood and held his partner's shoulders, steadying her until Omega met his eyes and nodded.

"I'm not gonna fall over now," she told him.

"All right. Let me do one thing, here. Just stay put right where you are, while I fill in that hole we made," Echo said.

"I'm not goin' anywhere just yet," Omega determined.

Echo swiftly produced another one of his seemingly-endless gizmos; it looked not unlike the hurgir, except that it produced a green light. He placed this one over the hole in the wall and initiated it. And when he removed it, the hole had been filled in, and the surface made to look like the surrounding brick.

"There," Echo said. "We've done as much as we can, here. Let's get out of here before someone shows up."

"I'm with you, Ace," Omega said. "Just...don't go very fast. Not yet."

"It's okay, Meg. I'm right beside you. Let's go."

Echo walked slowly beside his partner, his hand subtly cupping her elbow, until they reached the airskimmer. A quick tap to an app on his phone deactivated the solid hologram hiding it, though the passive cloaking was still active; but Alpha One knew what they were seeing anyway. He took her elbow in a firmer grip and walked with her up the boarding ramp, allowing her to do it herself, but providing a steady hand in case the incline threw off her equilibrium, or otherwise caused problems.

* * *

Once inside, he sealed the hatch, then turned to her. But before he could say anything, she spoke.

"I think maybe you better drive, Ace," she told him. "I expect I'm all right, but I still feel kinda funny. So it's probably not a good idea for me to be in the pilot's seat, especially when I'm still learning the aircraft."

"I was about to make the same suggestion," Echo said, with a slight smile. "Okay. Have a seat in the copilot's chair and strap in, then."

* * *

But as soon as Echo lifted the craft off the ground, Omega's head spun. Fractions of a second later, her stomach lurched.

"Oh boy," she muttered, grabbing the straps and fumbling frantically with them until they unbuckled. Then she lunged out of the seat and ran aft, aiming for the skimmer's tiny head.

* * *

"Meg?!" Echo exclaimed, seeing her run past. "What—?"

His answer came with the sounds of retching floating forward from the head. This was immediately followed by splattering sounds in the toilet.

Quickly Echo put the airskimmer back on the ground, then unstrapped himself and hurried aft.

Omega was kneeling in front of the toilet, continuing to throw up into it. Echo bent and pulled her braid onto her back from where it had fallen over her shoulder, moving it out of the way of potential splatter. Then, as she practically convulsed with the force of her retching, he caught her forehead and held it in his palm, slipping the other arm around her waist, providing firm bulwarks for her to stabilize against another round of violent vomiting.

When the purging slowed, he eased her back against the wall and flushed the toilet. Then he went to stowage and fetched a bottle of water from the cooling unit there, and brought it to her.

"Here," he said, keeping his voice soft. "Rinse your mouth out good and spit into the toilet, then sip on that."

Omega obeyed in silence, and while she did, Echo pulled his cell phone.

"Fox, Echo. I'm gonna call an Alpha One Orange. Yeah, the Glu'g'ik attacked Meg...somehow...when she tried to take her into custody. Uh-huh; it's hard to explain. We're still not sure what the Glu'g'ik did, but while it was happening, Meg was yelling her head off, in a lotta pain. And it took a couple minutes for things to, um, get back to normal after. So now she's really dizzy, and when we tried to lift off in the airskimmer just a little bit ago, evidently her head took off first. She's been throwing up pretty bad for the last, oh, five or ten minutes, for no good reason I can see other than the attack. Can you notify the medlab at the London Office that we're coming in? I think we need to make sure Meg's okay before we go after the damn Glu'g'ik again. Yeah, she got away after the attack on Meg. And she got the first whatsis away from us in the process of the attack. Yeah, that'll be good. No, it might be as long as fifteen or twenty minutes; I don't know if she can handle an emergency-speed arrival, and I'd rather not put Meg through another vomiting bout like she just had, if I can avoid it, so maybe we oughta move slow. Well, yeah, that's a good point. Yeah, I hate to admit it, but maybe you're right. Okay, yeah, we'll take it at speed, then. Echo out."

He put his cell phone back in his pocket, then crouched down beside his partner.

"All right, baby," he said, maintaining a low, quiet tone. "Fox wants you at the medlab five minutes ago, so I'm going into emergency evac mode. You sit tight, hang your head over the john, and barf if you need to. We'll be at the London Office in a couple minutes. Hopefully before you can throw up your pancreas."

A pale, slightly greenish Omega simply nodded. Echo rose and headed forward to the flight deck.

* * *

When they arrived in the vehicle hangar only a couple of minutes later, Echo unstrapped and returned to the head. Omega had thrown up again when the airskimmer had lifted off, but then gradually gotten control of matters. Even so, Echo decided he didn't like the looks of her. She appeared weak and was still very pale. *It's not surprising, after throwing up most of what she's eaten in the last couple of meals—what we got the chance to eat, anyway,* he thought. *And she's definitely green around the mouth and nose.*

"How are you doing, baby?" he wondered, crouching down as she looked up at him.

"Kinda wobbly," Omega admitted. "Some of that is from losing my lunch, though."

"First lunch, second lunch, breakfast, snacks...yeah. Low blood sugar. All right," Echo decided, "I saw the emergency medic team waiting on the tarmac nearby; let's get you out there to 'em and seen to."

"I...I dunno if...gimme a minute..."

"No, let's get you there as soon as possible, baby," Echo disagreed. "Hang on."

He slipped one arm under her knees, and wrapped his other arm around her shoulders, then got his feet squarely underneath himself.

"Oh, Ace," Omega murmured, "don't do this."

"Why not?"

"For one thing, you don't need to be lugging me around. I'm not light."

"You're solid muscle, but you're not THAT heavy, baby. I can get this."

"Besides, what if I throw up all over you?"

"What if you do? I get you to the medlab and seen to, then I strip, shower, and put on clean clothes. No big deal. Besides," he added, "it wouldn't be the first time."

"Huh?"

"That's a story for when your stomach is a little stronger, Meg," Echo said with a slight grin. "Now try to relax. Lean your head against my shoulder, and just rest. That's good. Deep breath...and...up."

Echo's arms tightened around his partner, then he performed a reverse squat, pressing upward into a standing position, Omega cradled against his chest. Then he stood still, giving her a chance to regain her equilibrium after the movement.

* * *

Omega felt her partner's arms go around her, gathering her close, and lifting her very gently. She stifled a sigh, enjoying the feel of it; she rested her head on his shoulder in gratitude, turned her head into his chest, and suddenly it hit her just how worn and tired she was.

This time, she didn't stifle the sigh —of weariness. Echo heard it.

"You okay, baby?" he wondered, voice soft, a kind of concerned gentleness in it.

"I dunno, I'm just really, really tired, I think," she murmured into his shirt. "I hope I don't barf all over you, Ace."

"And I already told you, it's all right if you do," Echo demurred. "Are you ready to go?"

"I hope so."

"Still dizzy?"

"A little."

"I'll make this as smooth as I can, then."

Echo turned slowly, and bore Omega toward the hatch, his stride careful and even.

* * *

Echo reached the airlock hatch, Omega in his arms. He nudged the hatch's standard release with an elbow, and waited while it opened. Then he carried his weak, ill partner down the ramp that extended to the tarmac.

She simply rested against him, her face tucked against his chest, breathing slowly and deeply; he knew she was concentrating on keeping herself calm and relaxed, in the hope of avoiding additional vertigo and nausea.

She really doesn't wanna throw up on me, he thought with a hidden smile. *I appreciate that, but damn, I can't see it being any worse than what happened to X-ray, back in the day. Spoiled Indabaran lobster is NOT good for the human digestive tract, and even fresh, it doesn't smell that great BE-FORE you eat it. Add projectile vomiting into the mix, and things got bad in a hurry. Ieeuch, what a mess.*

He glanced down at his partner, lying quietly in his grasp, feeling the warmth of her body against his. *Well, she doesn't feel feverish,* he decided. *That's her normal body heat I feel. Hopefully this isn't actually serious, but I'm worried. That damn Glu'g'ik did something to her insides!*

They got to the bottom of the hatch ramp, where the medical team awaited with an antigrav gurney.

"There we go, then," Jig, the medic, remarked. "You must be Agent Echo, and this is Omega?"

"Yes," Echo noted, and Omega merely raised a limp hand in acknowledgement. Echo bit his lip, even more concerned at his partner's abnormal lack of response. *She didn't even raise her head, let alone smile,* he realized.

"Put her on the gurney and let's get her to the medlab," Jig said, compassionate. "Fox already gave us the heads-up, so I have an idea what happened, but I'll want any pertinent observations the two of you have, also. Don't worry. We'll find out what's wrong and see about fixing it."

Echo didn't say what he was thinking: that, if the Glu'g'ik had rearranged Omega's insides down to the molecular structure, there might not be a whole lot of 'fixing' that could be done.

Instead, he eased his partner down onto the antigrav gurney, and the orderlies strapped her down, unlocked the gurney, and headed for the hangar's exit, Omega in tow, Jig on one side, Echo on the other. Abruptly Omega began clawing for the straps.

"No no no," she practically babbled, pushing to a semi-recumbent position, but seeming wobbly. "STOP."

"All halt," Echo ordered immediately. The orderlies kept going. "I said STOP."

"Stop," Jig commanded, and the orderlies halted. "Ink, Vic, this is Alpha One, the premier Alpha Line team. We haven't had an Alpha Line team come through before, so you may not know this: Whenever an Alpha Line team is present, their orders take precedence over anything—except a medical emergency. Understood?"

"Yes, madam," came the dual reply.

"And arguably even that, depending on the nature of the relative emergencies," Echo amended.

"I...see. Now, Omega, what is the problem?" Jig wondered.

"I can't handle this antigrav gurney," Omega murmured, head wobbling a bit in mute testament to her vertigo. "It's too smooth. There's a sensation of movement, but no sensation of WHY I'm moving. I'm just gliding along. It's making the dizziness worse."

"Well, shit," Echo grumbled. "Now what?"

"Omega," Jig asked, "were you all right as long as your partner carried you?"

"Yes, ma'am," Omega agreed. "I could feel Echo's footsteps—you know, the muscle movements of him walking: the thigh movement, the slight arm shifts—so I could anticipate the motion. And he stepped easy, so it wasn't jarring; plus, he had a good grip on me, so I knew I wasn't going anywhere. This thing...I got no cues to anticipate movement. And I feel like I'm gonna roll off it or something."

"I see," Jig said, considering. "Agent Echo, it isn't far to the medlab from here; we brought you in to the emergency entrance upon notice of your code orange. Do you think you can carry her the rest of the way? It is perhaps a hundred yards at most, past the hangar entrance."

"Yeah, I can do that," Echo decided.

"No, Ace. Just let me try to walk."

"I'd rather you did not, until we know what was done to you, Omega," Jig noted. "Ink, run fetch a standard wheelchair, if you would. That will obviate the need for Echo to carry Omega the whole way. Vic, you stay here with us, and be prepared to hand off with Agent Echo, here, in carrying his partner, if we need it."

"Yes, madam," came the replies, and as Ink headed off, Echo bent and scooped his partner back into his arms. Then he turned to follow Jig, and Vic brought up the rear, towing the empty gurney.

Chapter 4

They took Omega in to the London Office medlab's emergency facility, where Jig proceeded to examine Omega very thoroughly, quizzing Alpha One about the attack and determining her focus should be on Omega's hand and forearm, as well as her head and nervous system. But even as they conducted the exam, running Omega through a battery of tests and diagnostics, the female Agent gradually grew better.

"Yes, Agent Echo, Agent Omega," the London medic told them a while later. "That appears to be the nature of the problem. Our testing indicates some sort of molecular disruption in Omega's forearm, likely as a result of the attack. My guess is that the Glu'g'ik used her quantum foam manipulation abilities to try to rearrange the molecular structure of Omega's arm. Had she continued extending it into her body, she might well have managed to kill Omega."

"Damn!" Echo cursed, scowling. "Wait until I get my hands on that bitch!"

"Inadvisable, Agent Echo," Jig noted. "According to what your partner has told me, that is precisely what triggered the attack."

"Yeah, Ace," Omega said, subdued. "Remember, it wasn't until I grabbed her to take her into custody that she attacked. And trust me, it ain't fun at all."

"Okay, baby, but..." Echo began, then turned to the medic. "Is Omega permanently disabled? How bad is her arm messed up? Her nervous system?"

"You are asking for the long-term prognosis?" Jig wondered.

"Exactly."

"The prognosis is actually excellent," Jig said. "She needs food, so her body has fuel for repairs, and some rest, and then the two of you can return to the hunt."

Echo slumped, seeming to go limp briefly, and he raked a hand through his dark hair, disarranging it rather thoroughly.

"Ace?!" Omega exclaimed in alarm, as Jig grabbed a chair for the male Agent.

"No, no," Echo muttered. "I'm okay. Just...relieved. I thought the damage would be permanent."

"Me, too," Omega admitted. "Sit down anyway, Ace, please? For me? You looked...upset just now."

"But...the molecular disruption?" Echo asked, puzzled, accepting the chair and sitting...at his partner's request.

"According to the medical records that Zarnix and Zebra sent, you are already aware of the unique nature of your partner's biology, is that not correct?"

"Yeah..." Echo said, as behind Jig, Omega winced. Echo promptly frowned.

"That same unique physiology is healing the damage right along," Jig noted. "See how much better she is now than when the two of you arrived? No, if we provide her some nutrients and fuel—which you could probably use as well, Echo, just not as badly—I have no doubt she will be fine very shortly."

"How long will you keep her?"

"Oh, perhaps six hours or so. Long enough for a solid meal and a nice long nap."

"But we need to go NOW!" Omega said, distressed. "That's gonna take way too long!"

"You do not have a choice, Omega," Jig said, calm and unswayed. "I am sorry, but if you do NOT do this, then the damage might BECOME permanent. It's a bit dodgy yet, and I want to maximise your healing ability. Your body is evidently capable of some truly unique things, but even it needs fuel and rest to allow it to overcome the disruption and repair itself."

"She's right, baby," Echo urged. "Look, it doesn't have to mean that we lose Gla'd's. While you're eating and resting, I can hit the trail, track her down and try to apprehend her, or at least delay her, until Jig releases you and you can come after me."

"I want you to get a good meal inside before you leave, as well, Echo,"

Jig protested.

"Okay, okay," Echo agreed reluctantly. "Meg and I'll eat, then I'll get back to hunting down the Glu'g'ik that put her here while she rests, and she can catch back up with me later."

"I'm not happy about that plan," Omega grumbled. "I don't think you need to be going after her alone, Ace. I'm feeling a lot better now." Her stomach growled. "Okay, maybe a little hungry."

"Let's see about getting a good hot meal into you both, then," Jig said, turning and leading the way out of the examination room.

* * *

"All right, then, here we are. Let's get some proper food in the two of you," Jig said, leading them into a little cafeteria in the corner of the med-lab, where the other Office medical staff were grabbing a quick bite.

"Um," Omega offered, "you might be surprised how big an appetite Echo and I have got. We, uh, we're pretty active. Alpha Line and all."

"Not to worry," Jig said with a smile. "I understand, and I figured to do you better than a ploughman's lunch. Echo, you're welcome to grab whatever you see that appeals. There's roast meats of all sorts, bangers, meat pies, fish and chips, and all kinds of veg, plus salads. Omega, given how ill you've been, tossing and such like, I'd like to be a bit more sedate in what we select for you to eat, if you don't mind."

"I think that sounds wise," Echo agreed. "Something easy to digest, that's going to sit well on that tummy."

"I've never heard you say 'tummy' before, Ace," Omega said, smile dimpling. Echo decided it was cute.

* * *

"Well, I've never seen you barfing up your pancreas, gall bladder, liver and kidneys, either," he riposted, dark eyes twinkling.

"The kidneys aren't part of the digestive tract, Agent Echo," Jig corrected.

"I know that," he shot back, openly winking at the physician while tilting his head at his partner, to let Jig know he was joking for Omega's benefit, "but I still coulda sworn I saw 'em come up."

"Blegh," Omega grumbled.

"Right, then," Jig said, going along with the flow. "Steak and kidney pie is right out."

Echo AND Omega both groaned.

"Off with you, Echo," Jig said, grinning from ear to ear at their reactions. "Go fetch yourself a bite, and make it as substantial as it needs to be. Omega, you and I are going to see about some mild things for that tummy, as your partner put it. I'm thinking a shepherd's pie, which our kitchen makes in an oversized Yorkshire pudding to soak up the broth. The veg used will be mostly roots—carrots, tatties, nips, and such like—and easy to digest. Lamb also tends to be an inoffensive meat, and the broth will be nourishing as well. It's really quite scrummy—uh, yummy, I think you Yanks put it. Does that appeal, or are you still too off to eat? We can make a protein and fruit smoothie if need be, for now."

"No, that actually sounds pretty good," Omega admitted. "It sounds a lot like a casserole that Echo makes sometimes, and which I practically inhale every time he does. Though I think he uses beef."

"Ah. That turns it into a cottage pie," Jig noted, intrigued. "Interesting, that your partner makes such dishes."

"Not really. That's 'cause Dad had Celtic roots," Echo's voice floated from somewhere nearby. "Several of my casseroles are family recipes, handed down on his side of the family. I've noticed the similarities to shepherd's and cottage pies, too. Of course, the corn pudding Meg snarfs down was Mom's recipe."

"Right," Omega murmured. "That one's nummy. Anyway, that shepherd's pie sounds really good right now. I guess I ought to eat kinda slow, too, huh?"

"It would probably be advisable," Jig agreed. "I know you're likely quite hungry after chundering so much, but the last thing we need is for you to bolt your food right now."

Soon Alpha One was sitting down with Jig at a table; Echo's tray was laden with a salad, roast pork, several vegetables, and a monster serving of sticky toffee pudding, with a large coffee to drink. Omega's plate had a goodly-sized shepherd's pie on it, along with a small fruit salad with cottage cheese and a light drizzle of French dressing. She also had a large bottle of water, being advised by Jig to replenish her lost fluids.

"And if you finish all that and you're still hungry, I believe a basic bread pudding, or perhaps a bit of sponge cake—or better yet, blancmange—might do for dessert," Jig told her.

"Aren't you going to join us?" Omega wondered, looking at Jig's lone cup of coffee with cream and sugar.

"No, no; it isn't my mealtime yet," Jig explained. "I find my blood sugar gets peckish if I deviate too much from my schedule. The coffee will do for now. I just want to make sure you don't bolt your food or the like, and make yourself sick again."

"No, trust me, I'm not gonna risk that again," Omega declared.

"Good. Eat up, both of you," Jig said. "Then Omega is for bed, and Echo for whatever he can figure out to do with your mission, I suppose."

* * *

Not quite an hour later, the duo was finished with their meal.

"I really don't like this, Ace," Omega protested, as Jig turned down a hospital bed for her. "I got a real not-good feeling, like it needs to be both of us or neither."

"I'll be careful, baby, I swear," Echo promised. "I won't confront her unless I have to. But I need to stay on her tail and at least TRY to beat her to the next piece."

"You said Australia, right? You know where it is?"

"Yeah, Down Under is next. And I got a pretty good idea where in Oz, yeah. Remember, Houdini fanboy here." He offered her a grin, apparently trying to raise her spirits.

"Right. Well...yeah. Be careful and stay in touch."

"You know it, baby. You just stay here and rest and get better, okay?"

"Okay. Later, Ace."

"Later, Meg."

And he was off.

A mildly-glum Omega kicked off her shoes, removed her jacket, tie, and all three holsters, loosened her trousers belt, and clambered into the bed.

* * *

Echo climbed aboard the airskimmer, glad to know that Omega was being properly tended and that, should something happen, some unexpected aftermath of the attack, she was where the matter could be immediately spotted and handled...assuming, of course, that it could be handled at all. Meanwhile he would go after Ke'ri Gla'd's himself, and Meg could catch up to him when she was able.

Waitaminit, he thought, bringing himself up short before he reached the pilot seat. *I can fly pretty much anything. But Meg's still learning. And this is HER airskimmer. If I take this, she's probably gonna be stuck here, and then not only can she not meet me, I'm on my own with this Gla'd's person... who already did a number on Meg. I'd have no backup, even remotely. At all. Unless I could reach Fox and have him scare something up. Big maybe on it, too, especially given the season and all the off-world tourists. That... would NOT be good. Nope. I gotta do something else.*

He debarked again, and headed for the hangar master's office to put in a specific request...with Alpha Line priority.

* * *

Moments later, he was headed for the single-passenger spacecraft area of the vehicle hangar. *After all,* he thought, *I already know that the next whatsis is across the planet in Australia. And, given my knowledge of Houdini, I bet I know just where. Or roughly where, anyway.* He grinned to himself. *I just gotta be careful not to go exo, is all. What with that space plane launch coming up in...*he glanced at his wrist chronometer, *oh. Just a few hours now. But I can stay upper-atmosphere and still get there plenty fast in this baby. And nobody will know the difference from a standard high-altitude aircraft flight, if I'm careful.*

Then he pulled his cell phone, texted to his tired partner to explain what he was doing, and boarded the small spacecraft.

Within minutes, his craft shot upward and disappeared into the evening sky, headed east.

* * *

Behind him, a slight distortion in the air, like a heat wave, rose from the roof of a nearby building. It hovered some hundred meters above the roof, then shot off in the wake of Echo's spacecraft...

90

...Faster than the prevailing winds.

* * *

Echo knew that Houdini's great claim to fame in Australia was the fact that he had been among the first to ever fly a powered aircraft there. For many decades he was believed to have been the first, and some still did credit him with that; but in more recent decades, that distinction had been officially awarded to another aviator.

Nevertheless, as the Agent interpreted Ho'd'ni's poem, the site of this feat was the second location to find the...whatever it was that everyone was trying to find. And that site lay near Melbourne, the capitol of Victoria state.

The question was...where, exactly, was that site?

Echo set his destination for Melbourne, engaged the auto-pilot, and activated the global web search function on the flight computer.

Damn, I wish I had Meg here to do this, he thought, wistful. *She'd have the information pulled up in about five minutes, I bet. She is DAMN good at researching.*

But she wasn't there, so he was on his own. And he was no slouch at research, himself.

He set to work.

* * *

It took some time, and far too many tabs open on his search engine—at least, in Echo's opinion, as he went back and forth between them, corre-lating information—but eventually he was able to determine that the flight occurred in a little village outside Melbourne proper, a former way stop en route to the gold fields called Digger's Rest. More, he was able to ascertain that it occurred near a greyhound racecourse facility that had been known as Plimpton's Paddocks, about a mile west of the tiny township proper. So he pulled up an online map, located Digger's Rest, then switched to a satellite view and scanned the area just west of the village, looking for any clue as to where it might once have been.

"Aw, damn, you're kidding me!" he exclaimed in delight, as a particu-lar feature caught his eye.

For lo and behold, it seemed the facility still existed; a perfect oval racetrack, complete with buildings, paddocks, and other support structures, lay exactly where the online sources had indicated.

Echo adjusted his course for the little village.

* * *

Behind him, a shimmering heat wave likewise shifted its course.

* * *

Petey, the boy who tended the dogs, had just come out of the shed with a bag of dry food when the man in the black Suit walked up.

"G'day, mate," the man offered with a smile.

"G'day!" Petey replied, startled. "Holy-dooly! Where'd you come from?!"

"Back o' Burke, mate," the man answered, in a perfect Sydney-sider Aussie dialect. "Up and over th' Top End, around an' down again."

"What d' ye want?"

"I'm a bit of a magician," Echo—for Echo it was; he had hidden the spacecraft in a copse of trees on the far side of the main highway—told the boy. "An' also an historian an' whatnot."

"Oh, ye'll be here about Houdini, then," Petey said, giving a knowing nod. "C'mon while I feed th' dogs an' I kin most likely answer yer questions. If I can't, I'll call me da."

"Ta much. So this is the site where he flew 'is aeroplane?"

"Yup," Petey agreed, moving to the first paddock and dumping kibble into the dishes. Several sleek greyhounds ran out of a small shed and straight to the food bowls, where they happily gobbled kibble, whimpering with excitement and demanding to be petted. Petey set the feed bag on the ground and pointed; the other hand scruffed several dogs with absentminded affection. "See th' racetrack, over there?"

"Yeah?"

"When I weren't nothin' but a wee tad, me great-grandda used t' tell me as how Houdini took off down th' middle o' th' oval. Seen it hisself, when HE was a boy, he said." Petey shrugged, then hefted the feed bag again. "I dunno as it's true, but it's what 'e said. Makes sense ta me, 'cause th' track 'd keep 'im in line, like a runway."

"Sounds dead set t' me," Echo decided. He followed the teen to the next dog paddock and watched as the feeding process was repeated.

"Yeah. I'm givin' ya th' fair dinkum, least as I knows it," Petey averred. "I never had no reason t' doubt me great-grandda."

"No reason ya should, mate," Echo said, voice quiet. "Good, honest men 're hard t' come by. It's good when we're kin to 'em."

"It is," Petey agreed. "An' me great-grandda was one a' those, sure. Sounds like yours was, too."

"Yup; a real ridgie-didge, he was. So...did Houdini leave 'is aeroplane here? Nobody seems ta know what 'e did with..."

"Nah, 'e didn' leave it here," Petey said, shaking his head. "Not th' aeroplane, anyhow."

"But 'e did leave somethin' 'ere?"

"Well, supposin' as how 'e did, but nobody seems ta know what, an' nobody kin find it."

"How ya know that?"

"We got a shed over behind th' old rabbit hutches," Petey explained. "It used t' hold feed f'r the rabbits. But we ain't used 'em for chasin' in the race in a long time—not since well afore I was born, I reckon—special since they got t' be sich pests in th' wild an' all. 'En the govvie gave 'em th' wog, an' it got among th' farm-raised, an' Bob's your uncle. It all went t' hell in a hurry, but th' buildin's are still there."

"Bloody hell, mate!"

"Yeah. Anyways, Houdini leased th' shed from me great-great-grand-da, in what Da calls a 'contract in perpetuity.' Every year somebody in th' Houdini family wires us th' payment; I dunno who, or nuthin'. We keep it maintained an' all, but we ain't never seen nuthin' in it. Just th' four walls an' bare floor. We got no idea what they want it for."

"Anybody else ever ask about it?"

"Nah. Soon's they find out we know the plane ain't here, they lose interest. Why d' ye ask?"

"Oh, I got me notions of writin' a book on Houdini. But lotsa folk have done that. I'd like ta have somethin' new t' throw in it."

"Ah. That makes sense, I guess."

"Mind if I have a look-see at this shed?"

Petey scanned Echo up and down.

"I reckon I better tell Da first," he decided. "Ya look a right fair dinkum mate, but looks 're deceiving, an' all."

"Right, then," Echo said. "Let's go see yer Da."

* * *

"I don't see why ya be wantin' t' look," protested Petey's father, who happened to be the current owner of the racing facility, one James Wilson Plimpton. Echo had produced enough 'documentation'—using his *carte noir* and some fast sleight of hand that would have impressed Houdini himself—to convince the man he was who and what he claimed. "There's nothing in there but dust and cobwebs. Though we try to keep that to a minimum. Still and all, we 'arve a facility to run, and dogs to care for. The building's in good shape, for we see to that; but we don't 'arve time to be dustin' and whatnot."

"A lot of Houdini's life is a mystery, Mr. Plimpton," Echo explained. "Some things, we just don't know about. An' as Houdini was what could be called a 'consummate showman,' sometimes what he told people was what he wanted 'em t' think, not what was th' actual case. In my capacity as an historian of his life and art—I was tellin' your son I hope to write a book one day—if he had to do with your shed, then I'd like to see it. Who knows? I might be able to figure out why he leased it in perpetuity, and solve the riddle of why he needed it t' begin with."

"Well, ya might, at that," Plimpton decided. "C'mon, then. Let's go 'arve a look-see. But I'll 'arve t' leave ya to look about it on yer own. It ain't like there's anythin' in it t' go walkabout in any event, an' me an' me boy has the dogs t' attend. There's a race this weekend."

* * *

The shed in question was surprisingly substantial, being comprised of a combination of stone and brick masonry, with an old concrete slab foundation, one tiny window not even a foot square, and a small slate roof. By the look, it had indeed been there a good while, and the male Agent had no problems believing it was over a hundred years old; there was even a small amount of moss on some of the brick and stone, especially next to the external water spigot. But, as the senior Plimpton had declared, it was indeed well-maintained, and showed no sign of deterioration.

Echo put on a show for the Plimptons, wandering about with a rapt look on his face, exploring despite the forewarned cobwebs and dust. But when they finally left him alone in the small space, he moved to the door and watched them surreptitiously. Once he ascertained that they were not going to come back and surprise him, he pulled his spectral imaging scanner from a pocket and began searching the small structure.

* * *

A translucent, almost ghost-like figure watched through the tiny window, from the shade of the shed. Ke'ri Gla'd's, dressed in matte black even as she had been at the Hippodrome in London, had phased herself halfway out; this enabled her to remain and watch, but made her much harder to see, which was why Alpha One had had difficulties spotting her.

And, given the age of the glass in the window, and the dirt which dusted it, it would have been difficult in any event. Echo, knowing that the Plimptons had departed, and with no inkling anyone else was nearby, focused on locating signs of Glu'gu'ik within the confines of the structure itself.

Which was just the way Gla'd's wanted it.

* * *

It didn't take long, for the shed wasn't that big; an old Glu'gu'ik signature read from very nearly the center of the slab foundation. Echo located the exact spot, then the hurgir came out of his pocket once more. In seconds, it had revealed another small, perfectly spherical cavity deep inside the thick concrete slab. Echo double-checked the scanner for traps, then reached in and pulled out...

...A gold pocket watch.

"Hm," he murmured, turning it over in his fingers. "German make, by the look, and REALLY old, according to the style." He pressed the button on the stem, and the front popped open; he looked inside and found a maker's stamp. "Interesting. Hamburg. I wonder..."

Without thinking, he tapped the stem button a second time...and the back popped open as well.

Inside was another metallic object, similar to the one he and Omega had found in the Hippodrome, but resembling more a traditional flat jigsaw

95

puzzle piece, this time.

"Once again, I thank you," came a familiar voice, before he could reach in and extract the object. "F'al on'cik, la'la'da ge nu!"

Echo spun with a muttered curse as the 'puzzle piece' inside the watch faded and vanished. Absently, he shoved the pocket watch into his own trousers pocket, and confronted the owner of that voice.

"How the hell did you get here?" he demanded of Ke'ri Gla'd's.

"It is quite simple. You led me here." Gla'd's glanced around briefly before returning her attention to the male Agent.

"You FOLLOWED me?! From London?"

"Of course. It was child's play, having once encountered you, to follow your quantum pattern across the planet. I never even had to get close enough for your sensors to discover my ship." Gla'd's spared another look around the small shed; Echo decided she was curious about the structure, and opted to use her apparent distraction to his advantage.

"I think I've had about enough of you," he said, and reached for his primary blaster with lightning speed.

But for the first time in his life, it wasn't fast enough.

In a blink, Gla'd's was there, reaching for his hand, grabbing it by the wrist, holding it away from his holster with surprising strength. Then, to his horror, and before he could react, she shifted her hold, her hands and arms seeming to blur.

As her hands firmly grasped his forearm, he froze, expecting the same excruciating pain he had seen Omega suffer. Instead, he grew dizzy and disoriented, as the room about them blurred, then faded away to nothingness.

* * *

When awareness returned along with his vision, he could see nothing except a brilliant white light. Echo found himself on his hands and knees; some gritty, powdery substance was under his hands, as a hot, arid breeze briefly parched the skin of his face.

He raised his head, blinking violently, his eyes tearing profusely in the intense, nearly blinding light. He squinted hard, dragging the jacket sleeve of one forearm across his face to mop away tears, and eventually his vision resolved.

I'm outside, he realized. *In...damn, this looks like the Outback in... generally speaking, Western Australia, I'd say. Well, shit. That's what she did—she teleported me into the middle of nowhere.*

With that bleak thought, the Agent clambered to his feet, donned his goggle glasses to dim the light to marginally more tolerable levels, and looked around. There was nothing but orange sand, dark rocks of various sizes from pebble to small boulder, and the odd squat, gray-green shrub, for as far as Echo could see in every direction—a veritable Mars-scape. And Echo had been to Mars, so he knew from Martian landscapes.

But Ke'ri Gla'd's was nowhere to be seen.

Yep. Middle of nowhere, all right, he decided with a sigh. *And then she popped back out again. That damn Glu'g'ik moves faster than a body can think, what with that ability to dematerialize and then pop in someplace else. Dammit. And now this is gonna be one hell of a long, hot hike. Emphasis on hell, by the feel. At least it's not full-on summer here, or I really would be in trouble. But it still feels like we got a heat wave going.*

One special pocket held a lone bottle of water for emergencies, and without doubt, this was at least a minor emergency; but he needed to see how far he had to walk to get out before he rushed diving into it. And that also meant trying to conserve the water already in his body, rather than sweating it all out. So he removed his Suit jacket; undid his tie, letting it hang down his chest; and unfastened his shirt collar several buttons down, before rolling up his sleeves.

He pulled his cell phone and activated the decidedly non-standard navigational positioning system, followed by the special Agency mapping application. Then he studied the resulting display.

"Well...HELL," he said with feeling, as he located his position. "Correction: I'm in South Australia state, not Western Australia...but just barely. Far northwest corner of the state, it looks like. And she couldn't have dumped me much farther away from civilization. I'm clear out by—oh shit! Where IS that...?! Search, search, search...Um, lessee...Emu Field, yeah... and the other one was...um...Maralinga! That's it!"

Echo entered several queries into the mapping app, and waited impatiently, glancing around himself in some disquiet. Finally several more locations popped up on the map, far distant from his current location. He sighed in relief.

"Well, that's something, I guess. At least she didn't dump me in the middle of the old nuclear testing grounds. THAT would cause me problems! Probably only because she didn't know they were out here, though. But damn. She had this planned, the bitch. And she has got to be one more highly-trained agent; it's not like I've never encountered Glu'gu'ik before, but I never had THIS kinda trouble with 'em. Gla'd's knows how to use her abilities to maximize offensive and defensive actions, and do it in less than a heartbeat. She— oh!" he exclaimed, as comprehension struck. "That must have been...she didn't ATTACK Meg, at least not directly, I'll bet; she just tried to blink her out of the room. Dump my partner someplace where Meg wouldn't cause the hellion any problems, then come back and finish up her task. I'm sure if Meg had died trying to get out of wherever she got dumped, Gla'd's wouldn't have shed any tears over it. And dumping her, way outside of London in the middle of a peat bog or something like that, would about be the equivalent of what she just did to me; both are potentially fatal, if we aren't on our game...but will still take a long time to get out of, even if we survive it. Only...for some reason, Gla'd's couldn't pop Meg out. And that's what screwed up Meg's arm...disrupted it. Something about what Slug did to Meg when he modified her must have kept the Glu'g'ik from being able to do it. That's...strange. I wonder why...and how. And...is it a good thing, or a bad thing, in the long run?"

Echo sighed and shrugged; he had no answers to any of those questions.

"Well, time for me to start walking," he decided. He consulted the map again, then turned. "Looks like the nearest approximation of civilization is this way. Coober Pedy, here I come. Oh well. As long as I'm in the area, maybe I can grab a bit of an opal souvenir for Meg while I'm there. A necklace, maybe, or some earrings. I bet she'd like that."

He set off.

* * *

As Gla'd's returned to her hidden craft, a thought occurred to her.

Where was the PGLEIA agent's partner, this time? she wondered. *The one of which I tried to rid myself, back in that performance building? I did not see her in the racing facility. She was formidable, and could well have resisted me—she DID resist me. This could cause me problems. How did she do it, and is she perhaps lying in wait for me, somewhere?*

More, is she angry that I have unburdened myself of him? They were certainly close; they may have a special affinity of some sort. In which case, she may well be angry at what I have done.

Hm. It might behoove me to create a few...distractions...to keep her busy. If I do so, at the very least, it will be some time before she can rescue her partner...and by then, I shall be on and done.

I have, after all, finally managed to find the reference material on this planet that I need for what are apparently Ari's historical clues. Though it is rather a good bit to go through, in an effort to find the locations in his clues. Gla'd's shook her head. *But Ari never even bothered to change his name. He must have wanted us to find the F'al. Perhaps, unlike his father, he was a sympathizer.*

At any rate, I do think it is high time for a distraction.

So instead of lifting off in her craft to head to the next site, she phased out again.

* * *

A short, squat, gray form with a bulbous head and huge black eyes materialized in the shadows at the base of a long, winding scenic bridge that paralleled the coast of New South Wales. She scanned the nearest pylon with a knowledgeable eye, then nodded to herself.

"Yes, I think I can do this," she murmured. "It will take me several trips, but I can do it."

She walked over to the pylon and laid both hands on it.

A huge chunk of its concrete masonry grew translucent.

* * *

Ten minutes later, the same short gray figure blended into the gray bluffs overlooking the Sea Cliff Bridge, watching as one of its pylons, chiseled down to no more than a quarter of its width with the removed portions dumped in the nearby ocean, collapsed into the sea.

Seconds later, a substantial part of two spans of the bridge followed.

Several small, brightly-colored vehicles, which happened to be traversing it at the time of the collapse, plunged downward, bouncing off rocks beneath before coming to rest, partly in the surf.

The gray figure cackled in glee.

"Well, there is a good start," she decided...

...And faded away.

* * *

Echo had been walking—slogging, really—through the sand and scree for just over an hour already when he saw it: A dark line on the horizon ahead. *And,* he decided, *it looks like it's moving.* He stopped for a few moments and just watched it. In that time, it grew noticeably thicker...and ruddier. He frowned, and looked about himself, turning in a slow circle.

The light breeze he had felt earlier had died, but now it was replaced by erratic gusts which stirred the sand. A dust devil spun up some hundred yards or so to his right. It swirled dust and dirt around before dying out moments later; a good fifty yards or better past that, another spun up, raced across the desert landscape, and dissipated.

A sudden strong gust of wind hit him, and Echo glanced back at the horizon in front of him.

The dark line had swollen into a massive, dense, reddish-brown cloud that stretched from the distant ground high into the sky.

"SHIT!" he cried. "It's a dust storm!"

* * *

Echo stopped where he was and looked about for some sort of shelter. But there was nothing around except sand, scree, a boulder or small outcrop here and there, and the occasional tuft of outback plant life, usually in the form of scrawny, scraggly shrubs.

"Well, let's see how big it is," he decided, activating another app on his cell phone. "Maybe a wet kerchief, my goggle glasses, and more hiking will do the trick, to get me through to the other side. Then again," he murmured, studying the readout, "maybe not. This is a big one. And heavy, by the look of the satellite image. Given the direction it's coming from, it might just result in bringing at least part of one of the nuclear test sites to me. And inhaling any of that radioactive shit would NOT be good, especially in the long run. I'm gonna have to make the dome impermeable, and that means...yeah. This one's gonna be bad."

So he activated the emergency locator beacon instead, then texted his partner.

Meg, he thought, *I sure hope you feel better, baby, 'cause you were right, and I really need your help, now...*

* * *

Omega woke when the emergency signal on her cell phone went off, where it lay on the bedside table in her hospital room. Seconds later, the text alert went off as well. She promptly sat up in bed, grabbed her phone, and checked out the situation.

"Oh, shit," she whispered. "A haboob?! He's in the OUTBACK?! How the HELL did he get there? I thought he was going to Melbourne! Aw damn, it doesn't matter now. Ace is in trouble. I TOLD him he should wait!"

Just then, an emergency call came in...from Fox. She answered it.

"Hey, Fox, Omega here. I see it," she murmured before Fox could say anything. Jig entered just then, having heard the loud emergency alert from outside Omega's room.

* * *

"I got the emergency signal from Echo's phone as well, yung froy," Fox noted from his office. "The emergency beacon is designed to notify the partner AND the Director."

"Oh, okay. Didn't know that," came Omega's response. "It's a good system, though."

"Yes, it is," Fox agreed. He had been seated at his desk, doing another batch of the interminable paperwork his job required, but upon receipt of Echo's signal, he had grabbed his cell, risen, and paced the floor while he waited for Omega to answer. Now he stood at his desk, looking across the office, unseeing, as he spoke. "You aren't with him yet?"

"Not yet, Fox," Omega replied. "I only just woke up. The London Office medlab insisted I stay here and recover after that attack."

"Do I need to send someone after Echo, then?" Fox moved to the bay window overlooking the Core, and tried to see if there was another Alpha

Line team in the conference room he'd assigned to them.

"No, I—"

"Yes, Fox," Jig's voice cut in. "I have not yet released Agent Omega."

"You have now," Omega's firm voice came through to Fox, albeit at a distance, and he realized the London physician had commandeered Omega's phone. "I'm well, I'm Alpha Line, my partner has an emergency situation, and I'm overriding your medical authority."

"I don't think so," Jig's voice replied, and Fox raised a displeased eyebrow. "I want to run a few more tests to ascertain your medical condition."

"Agent Jig," Fox interrupted, voice as stern as he could make it—which was frighteningly stern—as he addressed the British medic, "you are overruled. She IS Alpha Line, and there IS an emergency, and she is in the best position to respond to that emergency. If you refuse to recognize her authority, I'm sure you'll recognize mine. She is officially released from your care. Give Omega back her phone."

"Ah...yes, Director," Jig said, her tone a combination of irked and meek. Fox heard a scuffling sound, then Omega's voice came back on the connection.

"I'm here, Fox."

"Good. Is your cell in speaker mode?"

"Um, no..."

"Excellent. I can speak freely, then."

"Oh. Yes sir, you can. Do you have any particular orders or advice? Anything...classified or confidential?"

"No, Omega, I don't. But...I can call the Sydney Office to provide backup if you still feel weak. Are you well enough to do this by yourself? Just a yes or no will suffice."

"Um, okay, I get it. Yes. That won't be a problem, Fox."

"You're feeling well, then?"

"I sure am. But keep that other thing in your hip pocket, just in case. Only not for that reason, if you follow me."

"Roger that, Omega, and I do follow you—you're healthy and alert and capable, but may still require backup due to other causes. I'll put Alpha Two on alert, and round up a few of the Alpha Line departmental candidates as well. All you have to do is hit your own emergency beacon and I'll send the lot out."

"Good deal, Fox. Thanks," Omega replied.

"Just be aware that, with the space plane launch in only a few hours, I won't be able to send them via the fastest route, which would be a sub-orbital spacecraft hop. I simply don't dare; all eyes are going to be on the skies, especially including the media eyes, if you follow me. And given all that, you'll still get there first, no matter what other transport I use. I'm going to see about getting some faster help from the regional Offices, and then all you have to do is rendezvous with them, once they have your partner."

"That sounds...really good, Fox. I appreciate it," Omega said, and Fox heard the gratitude...and anxiety...in her voice.

"Omega?" he queried, before she could hang up.

"Yes sir?"

"Are you..." he broke off, tried again, "you sound...worried."

"I've never known Echo to actually call for help like this before, Fox," Omega admitted. "Let alone put in an emergency call. At least, on his own behalf. Have you? You've known him a lot longer."

"Not like this, no—although X-ray did, a couple of times when the pair of 'em got in a situation. Then again, Echo is possessed of an extraordinary amount of common sense, and a large dust storm, when one is alone and in the middle of nowhere, is not a thing to be taken lightly."

"Yeah, I know. And he's plenty smart—I mean, I've never found a topic that he couldn't grasp, even if he didn't know it to begin with—so I'm sure he knows the danger. That said, Fox, I can't imagine that he doesn't have the equipment an' junk to get through this. Which makes me wonder, you know? I'm..." It was her turn to break off, and Fox waited patiently, suspecting she was searching for words to express herself. "After what the Glu'g'ik did to me? And then he goes after her solo?"

"He went after her SOLO?!"

"Yeah. I didn't really want him to, but he promised he wouldn't confront her if he could help it, not without backup. It was more a case of not letting the trail go cold and all."

"Ah. Well, then, that is wiser. But still, drek happens."

"Yeah. And it sounds like the drek DID happen. But, so that's what bothers me. What did she do to him, and how the HELL did he even end up in a place to get hit by a haboob? And how bad is this haboob, that he doesn't have a good way to ride it out? So...yeah, it...worries me. A whole bunch."

"You think a lot of Echo, don't you?"

"Well, I do. Are you familiar with Southern expressions, Fox?"

"After so many years with your partner as one of my oldest, closest friends? I should think so."

"Have you ever heard the expression, 'Ah love 'im to pieces'?"

"I have—though not from Echo. However, as I understand it, it is an expression of intense affection and high esteem."

"Yeah, it is. He's the best friend I've ever had, Fox. Probably the best I ever WILL have. I dunno what I'd do if...if..."

"Understood. Then go fetch him, young one, and call me if you need assistance in the doing. I'll come along myself if need be. And I'll keep my communications lines clear of everything else except any other emergencies; call me if you need ANYTHING."

"I'm gone, Fox."

And the connection broke.

Fox sat for a long time, looking at his cell phone, deep in thought.

I wonder, he pondered. *I'm seeing something there, something that I'm not sure either of them realizes is happening. And in this line of work, I think it's a GOOD thing, all other things taken in the balance. And certainly they've both earned something like that, given their respective histories. But it could get damned complicated before it gets to the good part.*

Although, the Director considered, *judging by the guarded sound of her voice just now, a certain newly-assigned department chief's assistant may already be aware of it. Though I think said department chief is, oddly enough, NOT. Especially given the number of Freudian slips that department chief has been making of late with respect to his partner...and doesn't even seem to notice, half the time. Then again, after all that he went through with Chase, maybe it isn't surprising after all. I'll keep an eye on things, and if I can help grease the skids, so much the better.*

He paused, considering the more immediate problem. *I only hope that we can time this rescue right. If the NASA launch has problems, it could hold us up. And without a space-based route, I can't get anyone who's here to Echo's location any faster than Omega can get there. Maybe I should contact the Ennead for permission to risk it, just in case.*

Then he put Alpha Two on high alert, and called for his own assistants, so they could pop an urgent message to the Galactic Council heads, lock down the Director's communications, and begin rounding up additional backup for Alpha One, if needed.

* * *

Jig still tried to convince Omega to remain where she was and be treated, but the Alpha Line Agent ignored the physician's entreaties as she rose and prepared herself. Jig even tried to grab Omega's holsters before the Agent could reach them, but Omega was much too quick for the determined healer. When a worried Jig tried to bar the door, Omega stopped and stared at her.

"Jig, I appreciate the wonderful care you've given me, and I thank you. I do feel much better, and having some good food in me really helps. And I understand your concern. But my partner—the Alpha Line department chief—is in danger and has issued a mayday. I AM going to find him and provide backup. Please stand aside."

"Omega," Jig began, earnest, "we need to make sure—"

"MOVE, Jig," Omega ordered, voice cold and firm. All indication of entreaty left the blue eyes, which became ice-hard. "That is a direct order from an Alpha One Agent, the Department Chief's assistant. Don't make me move you."

"You wouldn't..."

"You don't know me very well, or you'd know better. Echo called for help. I AM answering that call." Omega held up her right hand, palm flat, facing the physician, forearm parallel with the floor. She stepped toward the physician with her left foot.

Abruptly Jig found herself sprawled on the floor in the corridor, without ever being aware of how she got there; she was out of breath, and her solar plexus region was mildly sore. A black-Suited back, silver-blonde braid hanging down it, disappeared down the corridor in the distance, moving at a dead run.

* * *

In the hangar, Omega briefly checked in with the hangar manager before she strode aboard the airskimmer and strapped into the pilot's seat. She pulled up Echo's emergency homing beacon on the skimmer's instruments, then she read Echo's text message in more detail, in order to determine how best to proceed.

"Hm. He's gonna use a force dome for shelter," she murmured aloud. "And it looks like he's gonna...because WHAT?! Nuclear test site?! Aw, dammit! I didn't even know they did that, down there! Yeah, so it has to be impermeable to keep out any fallout particles that are still hot, so...I get it. And that's gonna be the limiting factor. How big will determine...yeah. I need to know that."

So she popped off a reply.

Ace, how big is the force dome?

Moments later the reply arrived.

Mm, bout 3.5ft, Id say. Not big, but big enough.
Hurry. Air is gonna b a problem.

"Oh geez, he knows," Omega murmured, feeling her gut tighten, then she texted again.

U in it yet?

Not yet. Holding off as long as I can.
Ill ping U right b4.

"Shit shit SHIT!" Omega exclaimed. "I gotta haul ass..."
She immediately notified the hangar master of her imminent departure and its emergency nature.

106

Moments later, she had received approval for departure. She lifted the airskimmer from the tarmac, eased it through the hangar doors into London's early evening, then slammed it into maximum thrust as she activated the passive cloaking.

In seconds she was leaving London behind, crossing over the dark English Channel, headed east.

* * *

"What the hell do you mean, 'No,'?" Fox demanded.

He was on the comm with the head of the Sydney Office, trying to set up some backup for Alpha One which was closer than Omega's position, just departing London. Yoke's face appeared, larger than life, on one of the large wall screens in the Director's office. Unfortunately, Fox was getting the one answer he did NOT want to hear.

"Look, mate, I'm sorrier than I can say," Yoke said, tone and expression apologetic. "But that bloody damn alien sheila what Echo was chasin' has got us all cactus along the whole bleedin' east coast, from th' Top End o' Queensland right down to Tasmania! Her ability to manipulate the quantum foam apparently means she can teleport in someplace, wreak havoc, an' teleport someplace else before me mates can even get there! We got Buckley's chance against that, Fox. An' me people aren't no bludgers, I swear. But we gotta have a fair go! We can't be in two places at once, let alone more! ALL of my field agents are out on calls up and down the coast—Brisbane, Sydney, Canberra, Melbourne, Hobart, even as far west as Adelaide—ALL of 'em, Fox! And half are hunting bunyip, and the other half are flat gone walkabout! I reckon as how she's done much the same to them as she did to Echo."

"Well, call some of 'em in, and send 'em to help Echo."

"I would if I could, mate. But like I said, I can't raise some of 'em, and the others...well, this sheila's doin' damage, Fox. They're all up to their eyes in rescue efforts. She flat took out some of the supports in the Sea Cliff Bridge, and we've had a major collapse. We've got injuries, Fox! We may have fatalities! Near as we can make out, she just...phased out big ol' chunks o' the support pylons! She's damaged the House of Parliament, the Cape Byron Lighthouse, Story Bridge, several skyscrapers from Melbourne to Brisbane...we're trying to handle nearly one and a half million square kilometers, all apparently under attack by one berserk Glu'g'ik with some serious skills."

"Tsu aldi rukhes," Fox cursed bitterly.

"Whatever ya just said, judging by the tone, I'm in agreement, mate. Truth is, Fox," Yoke admitted, "I was gettin' ready to call YOU to ask for backup. We're in a world o' worries Down Under."

"Damnation," Fox grumbled. "This is nothing but a diversion, while Echo dies and Ke'ri Gla'd's gets away with...whatever the hell tchotchka the meshugge klafte is there to get."

"I know. But it's one helluva diversion. Sorry, mate." Yoke's image onscreen shook his head. "If I get some field agents back in the next couple of hours, I'll be happy to send 'em after Echo, an' helpin' Omega and such like. But we have our hands full, tryin' to cover up the fact that parts of buildings and other kinds of brick shithouses around about just flat went missing. That's...kind of telling, ya know, mate? Never mind all the injuries an' people in danger."

"Yes, I know," Fox sighed. "All right. Let me see what I can do from this end, Yoke. Keep me informed, and if you have ANY agents you can spare for the search for my Alpha Line chief—"

"I'll ping ya right off," Yoke agreed immediately. "And thanks heaps, mate."

"Fox out."

"Yoke out."

As the screen went dark, Fox sighed and held the bridge of his nose between his thumb and index finger, grimacing.

"Oy gevalt. And that means," he said aloud to the empty office, "that I'm going to have to send in all available agents from the other field offices nearby—Hong Kong and Tokyo, both. Hell, maybe I should send some agents up from McMurdo, too, by the sound. Which means I have NO one left close by to send after Echo. Dammit to hell and back, ten times over."

Then he hit the intercom to his assistants' office. The answer was nigh-instantaneous.

"Bravo here, Fox."

"Bravo, we have a situation in Australia."

"Yes sir, I know. We have a saucer ready to do a hop, and we're rounding up backup for Alpha One as quick as we can. I'm handling the rank and file field agents, and Lima is going down through the list of Alpha Line candidates, looking for volunteers."

"No, not that situation. Though it is related."

"Oh? That doesn't sound good, sir."

"No, Bravo, it's nowhere close to good. Let me explain, and then I'm afraid I have yet another task for you and Lima..."

* * *

Omega was anything but idle as she flew the airskimmer hell-bent for leather. She had immediately set a great-circle course, terminating roughly at Echo's locator beacon position, but that was still nearly nine thousand miles, and would take some twelve hours to fly the distance, at the airskimmer's maximum speed.

So she had programmed the course, set the digital auto-pilot—or DAP, as she was wont to call it, her old NASA habits dying hard—and immediately launched into a series of calculations.

"First I gotta figure out how big a volume that force dome encloses," she decided. "Then I gotta calculate how much actual oxygen it'll hold, THEN I gotta determine when the O2 levels get too low for Echo to survive. And how long that'll take," she added to herself, raking a distracted hand across her silvery braid, dislodging several platinum strands of hair as she did so.

It took a bit of doing, as well as performing several detailed searches on her special Agency global internet connection, but well inside an hour, Omega had gathered all the data she needed at last, and started to run the calculations that would give her what she needed to know. Said calculations were fairly simple in themselves, and did not require anything more advanced than some basic knowledge of geometry, physical chemistry, and algebra. It was merely data about the initial—and potentially final—conditions that could be difficult to determine.

"Okay," she muttered to herself. "A hemisphere of that radius is gonna be about ninety cubic feet in volume. Less the approximate volume for

Ace's body...at his height and build, that gives...mm. Then percentage of oxygen...oh. Well, maybe this isn't SO bad. That's around twelve hours of oxygen! I'll be cuttin' it fine, but I can get there. Oh no, wait, the lungs can't suck that out indefinitely, not to mention the carbon dioxide an' junk building up. What's the limit for the lungs?" She resumed her searches for data. "Ooo. That's in terms of altitude, so I'll have to figure this in the form of partial pressures. So the partial pressure would start out at...lessee...mm... done. Okay, I can see that. But I need to run that backwards now, to figure out how much volume that is, so I can compare it with my previous calculations. So...um, yeah, like this..." Several minutes later, she had the numbers she needed to evaluate the situation.

She paled as she looked at her results.

"Oh damn," she breathed. "Ace only has about nine, MAYBE nine and a half, hours inside the force dome before this turns from 'search and rescue' to 'search and recovery.' And my flight time is twelve hours! No, no, no! Only...he'll go unconscious probably before that, and start suffering from hypoxia way before THAT. So what are those thresholds..." She bent back over her calculations for several more moments, then raised her head and shook it, lips pressed into a grim line. Then she reached for the onboard computer controls, bringing up the Division One satellite imagery of the haboob that threatened her partner.

"Mm, all right, let's see," she murmured. "Just how fast is that thing movin'...?" A few more keystrokes gave her a small readout label next to the image of the dust storm, and she chewed her lip in concern.

"Well...damn it. Too damn slow, and too damn slow. Neither me, nor the stupid dust storm is movin' fast enough to actually make this halfway easy. There's just no way under God's blue sky I am gonna get there before he passes out. And he IS gonna pass out, 'cause the haboob is pokin' along too much, and is way too big at that speed. But maybe I can get there before he asphyxiates. At least he hasn't activated the thing yet. The farther I can go before he has to, the better our chances get."

Immediately she set about tinkering with the settings on the airskimmer, attempting to eke out a bit more speed...any way she could.

* * *

Echo pondered his limited options as he watched the dense haboob grow steadily closer. It was not moving very fast as yet, and the rusty-shaded dust cloud was still quite thick and opaque, so he adjudged that the triggering weather system was relatively close, and probably still fairly recently-developed, otherwise the gust front would have accelerated the dust storm toward him...and spread it out more.

Disorientation and severe respiratory distress—and disease—due to particulate inhalation were the major dangers. Add to that, the possibility that some of those particulates could be radioactive, and the matter became quite serious. Acute silicosis was nothing with which to trifle—let alone, long-term radiation exposure, for it was difficult, even with the Agency's advanced technology, to remove such particulates from the lungs. But it was the disorientation which was of more immediate concern. For it meant that he would certainly get lost if he tried to navigate through the haboob, and then have to deal with the heat and lack of water, once the dust storm finally subsided.

And Echo was lost enough as it was. *If the damn Glu'g'ik had thought to try to leave my Suit behind, with all its pockets and their equipment,* he realized, *I'd be in really deep shit right now, even without the damn dust storm. Not to mention, sunburned in places no guy wants to get sunburned. I doubt even Shiitsooyee was tanned THERE.*

However, the storm was approaching more or less from the direction he needed to go, and it did him no favors to hurry its onset, so he sat down on a large rock and watched its slow but inexorable approach.

The longer it takes, he thought, *the more time it gives Meg to travel. 'Cause I got the feeling I'm gonna be cuttin' it pretty close on this one, unless she manages some interesting things with the skimmer. I'm gonna have to make the dome settings gas-impermeable, just to keep the fine, radioactive dust out, or it's pointless to use the damn thing.*

The seasoned Agent had a definite plan in mind, as he had already told his partner; and thanks to his tendency to keep all kinds of potentially-useful items stashed in his more specialized pockets, he also had the equipment necessary to pull it off.

But, he realized, *that doesn't mean it's gonna be any kind of fun. Espe-*

cially if anything delays Meg getting here.

So he waited and watched, maintaining a calm outward demeanor for nearly an hour and a half as the storm crept ever nearer; his insides were not nearly as calm as his exterior, however—for the last time he'd had to deal with a heavy dust storm, it had nearly taken out both himself and X-ray, his first partner. Admittedly, that had been about five or six years earlier on Neken, in the WASP-43 system, but the conditions in this instance were similar. So Echo knew, all too well, the potential danger inherent in his current situation. And that was without the possibility of irradiation.

The gusty winds that periodically buffeted him were hot and dry, parching his already-hot skin, so it was something of an equivocal relief when the shadow of the orange dust cloud finally fell across him, hiding the sun and reducing the ambient temperatures around him.

Once the cloud loomed overhead, the wind rose to a howl, and the first wisps of dust reached him, Echo rose and moved to an open space, sitting and folding his legs. He pulled a small silver device from one pocket, and his cell phone from another pocket, then sent off an update message.

Meg, Fox:
Haboob here. Initiating plan. Will take refuge in force dome.
Meg en route?

Seconds later his phone dinged.

Coming as fast as I can, Ace.

"Good girl," he murmured. He coughed briefly, as a swirl of dust inadvertently entered his open mouth. Then another message came in, this one from Fox.

B/ U prepared just in case, old friend.
Will get em 2 U asap if needed.

So he texted,

> *Thanks guys.*
> *Entering dome now.*

He hit <send> and replaced the cell in his pocket, stooped his shoulders and hunched down, placed the small silver device right in front of his crotch—in the hollow created by his folded legs—and activated it. Immediately a compact, pale yellow dome formed around him, just barely tall enough for him to sit inside in his hunched position, but wide enough to lie down when he got tired...as he knew he would, soon enough. *After all,* he considered, *a low oxygen supply tends to do that.*

A soft pecking sound made itself heard as the just-arriving sand and silt bounced off the force shield. Within moments the sound increased, until it sounded like a combination of hard rain mixed with sleet, as the wind-blown sand and dust impacted the outside of the field. Simultaneously the light levels diminished to a dusky burnt sienna, as thick clouds surged about just outside his force dome. Directly overhead, the sky brightened a bit, to a lighter, peachy shade, with occasional swirls of mustard yellow. From time to time the deep brick surrounding him dimmed to a dark dun color, before returning to the more reddish hue.

And that's that, he thought, attempting to school his respiration down from its adrenaline-fueled levels, and pulling out the bottle of water to sip, as slowly as he could. *I'm protected from the dust storm now. But will Meg get to me before the air in here runs out?*

* * *

Omega stared at the text message on her phone, then looked down at the calculations she'd just finished refining.

He's in there NOW, she thought, gut clenching tight. *The countdown has started. He's got nine hours, max, from right this minute. And by my calculations, it's still gonna take me a good 'nother ten and a half hours to reach his vicinity from where I am right now. And THEN I gotta FIND him. And that assumes the dust storm has moved past by the time I get there. Echo ain't gonna make it unless I do something. And that...*She stopped, biting her lip. A sense of nausea swirled in her stomach, which seemed twisted in hard knots, and she fought it down. *I couldn't stand that. Not the way I feel about him. And,* she decided, *I guess I'm left in no doubt now about how I DO feel about him.*

Okay, time to get some help, here; there's no way I can do this on my own. Not like this. I can't let him down. I just can't. Not for his sake, and not for mine...not that mine means much, at this point. I'm just not lettin' this happen, if there's ANYthing I can do. But I need a miracle. And I think I know where to find it.

She keyed the comm, and patched through a communique straight to Fox. The Director answered immediately.

"Fox here, Omega."

"Uh...how'd you know it was me...?"

"The transponder code in your comm identified your airskimmer, my dear."

"Oh, duh. I'm sorry, Fox; I'm not thinkin'. My head's wrapped around a little problem..."

"Don't worry, meyn teyere; as Echo might say, 'You're thinking, all right, just not about that.' So. What might that problem be, which IS occupying your thoughts?"

"Well, according to my calculations, Echo doesn't have enough air in that little force dome to survive until I get there."

"That's troubling, but once the dust storm passes by, he can drop the dome, surely."

"That's the other half of the problem, Fox. See, it's a small dome, only about three and a half feet radius, according to what he texted me—so my calcs show he'll go hypoxic in a few hours, and pass out shortly thereafter. And by the look of the storm on the satellite, it's really big, but it's not moving very fast, so it's gonna take several hours longer than THAT for the thing to go by and things to clear enough for him TO drop the dome. Which means he'll be unconscious BEFORE the storm dissipates in his area, and it becomes safe for him to come out."

"Farkakt! THAT is a problem. What's your current ETA?"

"I've tweaked a couple things that I figured out, and managed to shave off thirty, maybe forty-five, minutes of my travel time. But he's got nine hours, pretty much from right now, before he's...gone. Only it's still gonna take me closer to ten and a half, eleven hours to get there. And that's assuming I go straight to him, and don't have to look around for him...which I probably will, because I'd expect dust to drift over the dome, form a dune, and kinda camouflage it. Listen, can you maybe get someone from the Sydney Office over there to find him?"

"I'm afraid I already looked into that, Omega," Fox admitted, sounding rueful. "It seems our quarry anticipated such, as well as the possibility that we'd send agents from that Office to intercept her, and thus she has been rather...proactive. So much so, that I have had to send in agents from other Offices to help, ah, contain the situation." Fox sighed. "There have been casualties, Omega. No fatalities that I am aware of...not yet, anyway. But I fear that's coming; at least one major bridge has collapsed, and several skyscrapers are threatened. If we lose a skyscraper, we'll have hundreds, possibly thousands, of casualties; think the Twin Towers on 9-11 for scale. And there are at least FIVE that are threatening collapse! I've been getting reports from Sydney, and...it's bad. But I have another idea to help you and Echo; I just haven't had a chance to follow up on it yet. Let me see what I can do and I'll get back to you as soon as I can."

"Roger that," Omega agreed.

Chapter 5

"...That's the second 'no' I've heard in the last hour, that I didn't want to hear," Fox grumbled.

"I'm very sorry, Agent Fox," said Edudighin, an Ererot from the Delta Antliae system, whose homeworld was known to its inhabitants as Eospen. Edudighin was the current head of the Ennead, though he had announced he would step down in just a few months. He had been the logical candidate when Fox's old friend Pulgey Entiyti stepped down several years earlier. But he was getting up in years even for Ererot, and desired to retire to his homeworld and enjoy several generations of offspring.

"I appreciate your sorrow, Lord Edudighin," Fox said, bitter, "but the fact remains that my top agent may well die if you do not lift the restrictions on accidental sightings, or at least make an emergency exception."

"And you and I both know that we cannot risk the revelation of the Agency as yet, Fox," Edudighin responded. "It is not so very long since the Klydonian invasion. And you know how THAT played out."

"Yes, I know," Fox sighed. "It was an absolute nightmare, in many senses of the word. And the 'cleanup' was...difficult."

"Quite. So, no, I am afraid the Ennead cannot allow it, no matter how dire matters are with your agent. It is a dreadful thing, to hold the lives of beings in our hands, but that is why you and I are in the positions we hold, Fox."

"Is there anything I can do to convince you to change your mind?"

"No," Edudighin said. The statement was simple, firm...and unswerving. "I already polled the other members of the Ennead, when first I was informed of the situation by your assistants. Several have expressed extreme concern and regret over Agent Echo's position, but the decision is unanimous. We cannot risk Earth as a whole finding out, until the general population is more disposed to the notion of a galactic civilization. That is our final word. Now, if the civilian launch goes off as planned, and things settle down such that all eyes are not looking skyward, you are, of course, free to use your spacecraft."

"Too late though that may be. Very well. Fox out."

"Edudighin out."

* * *

As soon as the comm link was broken, Fox pinged his assistants.

"Lima here, Boss. Whatcha need?"

"What's the word from the Cape?" Fox wanted to know. "Is the launch still on? Or has it, hopefully, gone off already?"

"No sir. Not only has it not gone off, they've got a problem on the pad. We're in a launch hold."

"They haven't scrubbed it, have they? That might be good for us... they'd have to recycle the whole thing for tomorrow or the next day, or even stand down a few days while they troubleshoot...wait, what did that launch window look like..."

"No sir, I'm afraid they haven't scrubbed the launch today. They anticipate a launch later this evening."

"Geh kibinimat!" he shouted, and punched off the comm. Fox slammed his fist onto the desk hard enough to send writing implements flying off, hither and yon. Then he slumped in his chair.

A deeply disturbed Fox sat in his office, staring into the air, seeing nothing, for long moments.

Finally he reached for the external comm.

* * *

"Well, shit," Omega fussed at Fox's news, her anxiety heightening. "On a bunch of levels. I was really hoping you could get someone else there faster. That's the primary reason I called you."

"I know, Omega, and I would if I could. I already have Alpha Two headed to a maglev, but it won't beat you there, by a long shot, because there isn't a direct route. I assume you're flying a great circle course?"

"Affirmative."

"Right, then—and you started off closer, to begin with. And they'll still be coming into the Sydney Office, then have to traverse to wherever Echo got himself dumped, whereas my telemetry data is showing your

117

flight terminus will be somewhere in his close vicinity. You're his best hope right now."

"Yeah, I know. Dammit. But like I said earlier, I managed to shave off a little bit of transit time with some basic tweaks, it's just that I don't know this craft well enough yet to know how far I can push it."

"Aha. And I do, is what you're saying. That's the secondary reason you called me."

"Yup, it is. If anybody would have that knowledge, at least that I've got access to right now, it'd be you, hon. Echo's told me a few tales of your, um, hot-rodding exploits with spacecraft. And you know the model this skimmer is based on, right?"

"I do, junge leute. All right. Tell me what you've already done, pop me your calculations, and let me think for a moment while I pull up some schematics on my computer screen..."

* * *

"...So you've already pulled in the force shields tight to the skin to increase the aerodynamics, and you've pushed the settings on the magnetic drive to the max specs," Fox verified a few minutes later.

"Right. I figure I can push 'em past, 'cause I know a margin of error will be built in, but I'm not knowledgeable enough yet to know how FAR past."

"Good girl, as Echo would say. Yes, this particular craft has a good bit of margin. And there are actually several more tricks I can help you with."

"I'm listening, Fox."

"I know. All right, for starters, what's your altitude?"

"Nominal cruising."

"Did you and Echo load anything into stowage other than the standard equipment?"

"No sir."

"How handy are you with a magnetic spanner and an acoustic turn-screw?"

"Fairly decent. I haven't had near as long as you guys to work with 'em, but I'm a quick study."

"Good," Fox noted. "Here's what I want you to do. First off, can you arrange for vid comm? I want to be able to see what you're doing if need be."

"Stand by..." Omega hit a few switches on the console, and a holographic image of Fox's head and shoulders shimmered to life. "There we go. How's that? Can you see me clearly?"

"I can indeed. Very good. All right, my telemetry shows me that you're over...mm, looks like maybe you're approaching Bialystok, Poland?"

"Um, I'm not entirely sure, Fox. I've been busy running the numbers. But that sounds about right, yeah."

"Okay, here's what I want you to do first. You should have a compression suit in there."

"Oh?!"

"Yes. Aft stowage, to port. And the skimmer isn't very big, so it won't be hard to find. Get it and put it on, as fast as you can. Then ascend to twice the maximum altitude in the specs. I'll see to it that your airspace is clear."

"On it," Omega said, grabbing the tiny camera, unstrapping, and heading aft, even as Fox directed his attention at something just out of the hologram; when Omega heard a soft pecking sound, she decided he was on his computer, issuing orders to clear her airspace. "I assume you want to minimize atmospheric drag?"

"Right. Then you're going to find the antigrav platform, load everything on it except your and Echo's bags, the tool kit, a little food, the potable water, and the contents of the medical cabinet. Maybe keep a bedroll, too, so he can lie down while you treat him. Everything else goes on the platform. Strap it all down tight, initiate the beacon on the platform, shove the lot into the airlock, then cycle the airlock and eject it..."

* * *

Once Omega had donned her pressure garment for safety's sake, she substantially increased the airskimmer's altitude; a double-check of her instrumentation already verified Fox's assertion that the airspace was clear.

"I'm up at SR-71 cruising altitudes now," she observed. "Wow. I hope nobody manages to pick me up on radar, or visual, or somethin'. I'd hate to pull a Gary Powers. Or worse yet, a Rudolf Anderson, I guess. That'd take out me AND Echo..."

119

"Not to worry, Omega. All the local leaders in Eastern Europe know better than to try to shoot at anything emitting the particular identification our crafts' beacons put out," Fox averred. "So you're good in that airspace—or any other, for that matter, and for the same reason. Now go dump the excess weight. I'll see to it the Vienna Station sends someone by to pick it up right away, so it doesn't create an air traffic hazard on down the line."

Getting the antigrav platform to the hatch took a bit of doing; just because the platform negated gravity's effects on its contents didn't do away with their inertia. Omega had to put her shoulders and back into it. Maneuvering it into the tiny airlock proved even more daunting, but after a few minutes of shoving it around, it finally slid in and the inner hatch closed. Then she moved to the pilot's seat, and prepared to execute a negative twenty-degree starboard roll maneuver.

Moments later, several hundred pounds of equipment went overboard, decelerating and hovering at altitude in the wake of the airskimmer. Omega felt the small craft accelerate with the lessened weight as she brought it back to nominal orientation.

"Good," Fox's image said just then, with his voice. "Very good. I saw you adjust your posture for the acceleration, so that must have helped considerably."

Omega glanced at the readouts on the control console.

"Yeah," she agreed, "but not nearly enough."

"Every little bit helps. Now let's see about juicing up under the hood, young lady. Go get the tool kit."

"You know," Omega mulled, as she headed for the stowage again, "if this works, I think I know what I wanna call this thing. Assuming it survives all we're putting it through."

"What? You mean naming the airskimmer?"

"Yeah."

"What do you have in mind?"

"How does *SchmaltzBlitz* sound to you?"

Fox laughed.

"Someone's been practicing her Yiddish," he noted.

"I work for a master of the language. It stands to reason." She grinned.

He returned the expression.

"Der *SchmaltzBlitz* it is, then," he said, and reached for his keyboard to log it.

* * *

"...So the concept is to tighten the onboard magnetic field, thus effectively making it more powerful," Fox explained as Omega worked, her hands deep in the guts of the airskimmer, even as it flew. She lay on the decking, a large panel of which had been removed and laid to one side, exposing the innermost workings of the airskimmer—most notably, the magnetic induction propulsion system, which was the object of this particular exercise in exceeding specifications.

"I get it," Omega responded as she tinkered. "We want to increase the magnetic flux density in the propulsion unit, thereby generating a stronger interaction relative to the Earth's magnetic field."

"Exactly. The higher the flux density, the stronger the 'field.' The stronger the 'field,' the more force is generated. Be careful, mayn khaverte. The farkakt thing is running while you work on it."

"Don't I know it," Omega murmured. "My hair is all standing on end, or trying to—even the little hairs on my arms, from where this thing is inducing charge in ME, to boot. If my hair wasn't braided up and inside the pressure suit helmet, I'd probably look like a wild woman. And I gotta tell ya, it tickles something fierce, even WITH the compression suit."

Fox snorted despite himself. "Then it's a good thing it's—" He broke off quickly, and Omega grinned.

"It's a good thing it isn't somebody else of our mutual acquaintance, doing this job?" she queried, cheeky. Fox immediately adopted an innocent air.

"Why, Omega, I don't know what you're talking about," he said, more disingenuous than Omega had ever seen him.

"Nah, not a clue," she teased. "I'm not blind, Fox. And I'm not stupid."

"No, you are most certainly not, maydele," he declared. "Neither blind NOR stupid. Does he know? I mean, that you know?"

"Nope. Not gonna tell him, either. Or anybody else, for that matter.

121

I get that it's his little secret...and I understand why. And I'm not gonna embarrass him by letting on that I know. Don't YOU give me away, now."

"Good girl; I won't. He has a truly excellent friend in you, my dear."

"I try."

"I know. And you succeed. So you were saying...?"

"Oh yeah, the induced charge an' how it tickles. And then if I forget and touch something metal, I get zapped. Theoretically the skimmer ain't grounded, at least this high in the atmosphere. I guess the voltage drop between me and the frame must be substantial anyhow."

"Most likely," Fox agreed. "I always had similar issues whenever I was working on a prop system of this type—"

"Umph!" Omega grunted, as a hard, shuddering bump went through the craft. "What the hell...?"

"Oh, now THAT was a good sign. Let me see what you've got so far. Move the camera closer, please."

"Hang on, lemme discharge, or I'll zap the camera and fry it," Omega said, laying aside the acoustic turnscrew and giving the magnetic spanner one last adjustment. Then she put it aside as well, slapped her hand on the metal decking with a cry of, "OOO!" as it sparked, and grabbed the tiny camera on its equally tiny antigrav platform. She shoved it into the opening in the deck, lens pointed into the guts of the propulsion system, and waited for Fox's holographic head, nearby, to react.

"Oh, that's very good," Fox said after only a moment, peering this way and that. "Can you check to see what our current airspeed is now?"

"Yeah, hold on a sec," Omega said, pushing up off the deck and getting to her feet. She leaned over the control console and studied the readouts. "Oh, NICE! Velocity gauge shows we're a little over—get this—a thousand miles per hour! Say...one thousand sixty-four miles an hour? Give or take a couple. At this altitude, that oughta be about Mach one-point-fi— THAT'S what that hard bump was! We broke the sound barrier!"

"That's what I suspected at the time, mayn khaverte."

"That's great! That'd put me...lessee, where are we...Fox, that might just do it! That puts me in Echo's vicinity in about eight and a half hours from the time he went into the force dome!"

"Excellent, maydele!" Fox exclaimed. "Very good indeed! Shall we see if we can eke out a kleyn bisel mer?"

"A little bit more? Do you think we can?"

"We might, we might. Not much, but maybe a little. Maybe nudge your speed up a little over one thousand sixty-five; I doubt we can reach a thousand seventy, but every bit helps. Let me look..."

* * *

The air in the force dome was going to deplete of usable oxygen rather sooner than Echo had hoped, it appeared; it was already starting to seem stuffy and humid inside it. The tension he felt was not helping matters; it was undoubtedly increasing his metabolism, causing him to use oxygen faster than he ought. But he knew the maximum speed on Omega's airskimmer, and he knew that, unless she managed some slick tricks or Fox sent someone from nearby, chances were, Echo wouldn't make it.

So he shifted position, being careful not to hit the force field generator, and curled on his side on the floor of the force dome. *Got to relax,* he thought, *and get my respiration rate to go back to normal. Or even slower, if I can.*

He closed his eyes and tried to envision his partner in the airskimmer, zooming through the atmosphere toward him at breakneck speeds. In his mind's eye, her platinum braid shone in the sun; her blue eyes glinted in amusement as she smiled at him. Her skilled piloting of the skimmer was superb.

Yeah, he decided with a smile, starting to relax. *I got the cherry on top of the cream of the crop, when I got her assigned to me.*

After a few more moments, Echo dozed off.

His dreams were filled with sparkling blue eyes, shining platinum hair, and a mischievous, infectious smile.

* * *

He woke with a start, some while later. *Damn,* he thought, *I didn't mean to doze off like that. But it probably reduced my oxygen consumption, at least a little bit. What time is it?* He checked his wrist chronometer. *Shit! I've been asleep a solid hour and a half. I wonder where Meg is. Damn, I wish I had some way of tracking her. It would give me something to focus*

123

on, instead of sitting here staring at...nothing.

A ruddy miasma lay outside the force dome—the dust storm showed no sign of letting up any time soon. Echo decided, when he got back to Headquarters, to put in a recommendation for some sort of partner-tracking app, for just such circumstances as this one.

And it would probably help Meg to find me, once she gets here, he decided. *Well, I got the emergency beacon, I suppose. But unless they've upgraded the thing since X-ray used it last, it isn't gonna give her a very high-resolution picture of my location. Yeah, I'm puttin' in that recommendation when I get home. Assuming she gets here in time; airskimmers don't fly that fast, after all. Nah, Echo, she's never once yet let you down. She'll find a way. And Fox knows. He'll help. If nothing else, he's probably got the Sydney Office on alert. Not to mention, it wouldn't surprise me to find out that the airskimmer doesn't even LOOK like an airskimmer by the time the two of them get done with it.*

Meanwhile, Echo was stuck there, unable to go anywhere, and with little to nothing to do to keep himself occupied. He read for a while from the ebook app on his cell phone, but the lighting was odd and the flickering reflections made it difficult to see the screen properly. Likewise the two simple game apps he kept on the device for a similar purpose were next to unreadable in the low light levels.

He glanced at his wrist chronometer again. *Shit,* he thought. *Ten minutes later than the last time I checked. It's gonna be a long wait for Meg. And at least this part of it is damn boring. But chances are, I won't know when she gets here anyhow, 'cause I'll be unconscious from lack of oxygen. Unless I can figure out something...*

Echo thought back to his youth, when his mother's father—his Apache grandfather—had taught him the things that tradition said an Apache brave should know. This had come partly in response to a serious staph infection he'd developed from a cut in his leg as a small boy, one which threatened to leave him crippled for life, but which, with diligent care from both the pediatrician and his grandfather—who happened to be a diyin, a 'shaman' or more properly, medicine man—had resolved itself in a few weeks. His shiwóyé hastiin—'maternal grandfather' in Apache, less formally his Shiitsooyee—had helped take young Alex in hand, putting him through exercises and traditional teachings to build back the boy's strength; he had been very sick for many weeks.

But it worked, Echo remembered. *It only left a small scar, and not only did I get back to where I'd been, I got even stronger. I don't think Shiitsooyee ever expected me to get as tall as he was, though. Let alone taller AND broader.* He glanced about himself, then chuckled softly. *And I think he'd find this one helluva strange wickiup. But hey, as long as it works.*

If nothing else, he decided, *I can probably use some of the techniques he taught me for aerobic conditioning to eke out my air supply, maybe. Shiitsooyee, if you're still around playing guardian angel, I could probably use a bit of a reminder.*

Just then, and completely unexpectedly, Echo recalled his accidental encounter with the First Envoy. At the same time, he remembered his grandfather's words, *"Ik aa'ye iidenka ashii nadndaal. Ei nanlwogo aniile shiiyii'ii."*

*Hm. 'Run to the mountain and back. It will make you strong, my son.' Only...it wasn't a literal mountain I ended up scaling. Now that...*he realized. *Yeah. That just might be it.*

So he let his thoughts drift back in time.

* * *

Alexander Ian Bryant, best known to his friends by his nickname, 'Echo,' for his skilled and excellent mimicry abilities, had just turned 17 the month before, and graduated high school—a year early—the month before that. But he was the man of the house now. Echo was an only child, and his father James Robert Bryant had died in a horseback riding accident nearly two years before. His mother, Nalin Iyaaye Bryant, had loved her husband very much, and was still grieving him—as in truth, Echo was as well.

But grief or no, the ranch had to be tended, the cattle looked after, and the oil and gas wells that tapped into the Yates oil field, whose mineral rights brought in a substantial supplement to the family income, paid all due heed—a leak would spoil what pasturage there was around the well, if it was left alone too long. And in this part of Texas, the pasturage was limited, too. Not to mention the loss of the precious petroleum commodity.

125

Fortunately, the ranch was close enough to the Pecos River that watering the cattle was not an issue; the main house had a well into the aquifer, and a water purifier and softener, into the bargain.

Then there was a little matter of illegal aliens.

* * *

The Bryant ranchero went back very nearly a century and a half in the family, an offshoot of the same clan that had founded Bryant Station over in east central Texas. The latter was now a ghost town, but the ranch farther west had more success in the long run, though there had been problems with Indians who resented the white intrusion in its early years.

It had been dubbed Meteor Mountain Ranch by Elijah 'Lije' Samuel Bryant, Echo's great-great-great grandfather, about the same time Crockett County was formally founded in 1875. This name was, according to family legend, because of the rather large mound near one corner of the property, at the northeastern base of which was a shallow, elliptical, wet-weather lake. Echo's grandfather, Samuel Robert, told the lad that 'Grandfather Lije' had spoken to the grandson of the Apache who had seen the meteor impact, gouging the lake and pushing up the 'mountain.'

Calling it a mountain was at best embellishment, and at worst outright fantasy; the highest point in the entire county was only 627 feet above the surrounding land, and that was Southwest Mesa, not Meteor Mountain, which was at best some 250 or 260 feet in height, depending upon who surveyed it. Echo didn't know if any of the family legend was true or not; he only knew that his compass generally went haywire any time he went near it.

And he had gone near it a lot in his childhood. In fact, he knew every inch of it; it was one of the tallest natural structures in the area, and Shi-itsooyee, as Echo had known his mother's father, had been very prone to telling him to run to its top and back—if he got underfoot or in the way, if he was bored, or if he became "too full of himself," as his father was wont to term it.

Young Echo knew he would get into trouble with both parents if he disobeyed the elder, and so he did...though his earliest memories of the 'mountain' had seemed considerably closer, and not nearly so high. As a teen, Echo finally realized that the wise old man had built up the boy's endurance over time; the 'mountain' he had climbed in his earliest recollections had been a berm his father built to redirect water runoff, not too far from the main house and just outside the fenced yard.

Consequently, by the time Grandfather's health had started to fail and he had returned to the Lipan reservation, his grandson had become extremely fleet of foot.

* * *

On this particular day, however, more than fleetness of foot was needed; word had come from the sheriff that several groups of illegal aliens had been seen crossing Crockett County, well outside Ozona, in the general direction of Meteor Mountain; most likely they constituted one or more smuggling rings, using Meteor Mountain as a landmark. These gangs had become more common in the area in recent years, and usually their cargo was illicit drugs or similar contraband. Now and again the cargo was simply more illegal aliens, bound for a population center and jobs.

Echo had discussed it with his mother, and they had decided that it warranted running the fence lines; such a band of smugglers would not hesitate to cut private fences in order to take the most direct route to their desired destination. And that could be disastrous for the little family's herd.

So Echo had saddled his strong little buckskin quarter horse Spirit early that morning, having risen well before daybreak, throwing saddlebags and packs on the gelding which contained a hammer, nails, staples, rolls of wire, pliers, wire cutters, and other fence-mending essentials. Then he loaded a shotgun and rifle into saddle-slung holsters, added his father's semi-automatic pistol thrust into the rear waistband of his jeans, as well as plenty of ammo to go around...and swung into the saddle.

"Be careful, my son," his mother told him.

"I will be, Ma," he replied, leaning down from the saddle to kiss her cheek. "Now go inside, fetch the other rifle and Granddad's revolver, hunker down, and have some beefalo stew ready when I come home, okay?"

His mother laughed, then sobered.

"I will, Alex," she murmured, "because I know you love it. But...be careful. There are more predators out there than humans, though none quite so dangerous."

"I know, Ma. I'll do my best."

"I know you will. Go now, though; you may make it home before dark if you do."

"And if the fences are in good shape," the boy added.

Young Echo turned his horse's nose toward the open gate, and set off at a gentle lope, toward the far side of the pasture.

* * *

Omega sat in the pilot's seat, having strapped back in; behind her, the decking panel over the main drive was closed once more. Her instrumentation showed the *SchmaltzBlitz* was traveling smoothly on auto-pilot at about Mach 1.58, and would arrive near Echo's location some four hours earlier than its nominal-speed arrival time.

That at least gives me about an hour max to try to find him, she concluded. *With any luck, and Somebody Upstairs helping, I can do this. I can keep Ace alive. Provided everything is going according to plan on his end. Maybe I better check.*

She pulled out her cell phone and hit the code for Echo's speed dial.

* * *

Just then, Echo's cell phone bleated with a loud incoming-call alert; it was the ringtone assigned to Omega. He jerked into an approximation of alertness, pushing up on one arm, then ducking as he remembered where he was, narrowly avoiding slamming his head into the side of the force dome. *Shit,* he thought, *that woulda taken off some scalp. Pay attention, boy.*

He slapped at his shirt pocket, and managed to get his smart phone out of it.

"Hey Meg," a somewhat-groggy Echo said into the phone. "What's up?"

"I am, I guess, Ace," came the reply, laden with dry humor. "Fox has been helping me soup up the airskimmer, and I'm movin' at speed now. We'll still be cuttin' it fine, but I should get there in plenty of time now, to fish you out of that mess. Provided, that is, that things are goin' as planned on YOUR end. So I thought I'd call and find out."

"Um. Well, they're going, I guess," Echo decided, trying to gather his wits and bring them back to the present. "Not as well as I'd like, to be honest, but I'll manage."

"Why?! What's wrong??" Omega replied, and he could hear the sudden anxiety in her voice.

"Calm down, baby," he told her, softening his voice. "It's actually pretty simple, and I'm working on recalling some techniques to fix it. It's just that, well, I've gotten used to a dangerous scenario being something I have to fight my way out of, so in this situation, the adrenaline's up, and..."

"Oh," Omega said, understanding in her tone. "So your respiration rate and junk are elevated, but you got limited air."

"Right. I gotta NOT fight."

"Well...shit."

"No sweat, baby. Like I said, I know the techniques I need to get through this, I'm just trying to remember all the little tricks and then implement 'em. I've already implemented some, and it's helping, I think."

"And here I went and interrupted you."

"No, that's fine. Probably better if you do ping me once in a while. I already know I'm gonna pass out before you get here no matter what I do, and if you ping me on something approximating a regular schedule, you'll have a lot better idea of when that happens."

"True. How heavy is the sandstorm now? Has it let up any?"

Echo glanced upward, then out the side of the dome.

"Nope, 'fraid not. I can barely see the sky overhead, sort of, only it's yellow-orange, not blue. And I can't see ANYthing in a horizontal direction. It's just a reddish-black...mess. Even if I brought down the force dome, I couldn't breathe in all that." He glanced at his wrist chronometer, but it was too dark to read; he hit the button to illumine the face, then did a double-take. "Meg, confirm the time for me."

"Okay, stand by. It's...oh, hell, I got not a clue one what time zone I'm in at the moment. Will a kind of mission elapsed time do?"

"Yeah. That's actually what I wanna know anyway. How long have I been in the dome, can you tell?"

"Uh-huh, I got that. You been in there...lessee, you texted at...I need to set up a countdown clock anyhow...there. Yeah, it's been about two hours and...um, about fifteen, maybe twenty, minutes since you initiated the dome. That's with an estimated error bar of plus or minus a couple minutes. I just flew over Tashkent in Uzbekistan, if that helps."

Dammit, Echo thought. *Not good.* "That explains it," he said aloud. He coughed a couple of times, then cleared his throat.

"Explains what?"

"Don't get alarmed, baby, but I'm a little bit fuzzy-headed and sleepy. That's a good indication that the air's getting stuffy in here. I'm also sweating a little, though that's not surprising; I was sweating before I put up the dome. It's HOT in this damn Hollywood substitute for Mars."

"Shit dammit to hell crap crap crap—"

"Hey!" Echo exclaimed, amused. "I said don't get alarmed."

"That wasn't alarmed. That was annoyed to Proxima Centauri and back."

Echo snorted.

"Hey, Ace, look. You can tell me not to be worried, but it ain't gonna work. I AM worried. You're my partner, and...well, it's like this. I already talked to Fox about sending somebody to get you from the Sydney Office or, well, anywhere closer than London, 'cause it was gonna take me half a DAY to get to you..."

"I hear a 'but' in all that," Echo noted.

"Yeah. It seems our perp ensured that the Agency would be twelve kinds of busy, fixing what she's messed up, so nobody has a chance to come after her."

"Oh, damn. What-all has she done?"

"Well, I don't know everything; Fox and I didn't take the time for him to run down the list. But there's some famous coastal bridge that's fallen down, and a few navigational lighthouses damaged, and several high-rises in danger of collapse. Stuff like that. It's...bad."

"Mm. She probably did the same thing to some structural components as what she did to me, and what I now suspect is what she was trying to do to you—phased it out and teleported it elsewhere."

"Oh." There was a silence on the other end of the line. "Yeah, that makes a certain sense, I guess. I wonder why she couldn't do it to me."

"Dunno. Maybe we can figure it out later. Anyway, I take it the only cavalry ridin' to my rescue is you?"

"I'm afraid so, Ace. We can—well, we ARE—bringin' in some Alpha Line backup, but they're gonna be comin' from even farther away, so it doesn't help us any, time-wise. Fox cussed a blue streak when I brought up the notion of bringing someone in from Sydney, so he wasn't happy, but as it is, he's havin' to call in agents from all the other offices in the region, just to help the Sydney Office. And from what I understand, some of their agents are probably having the same thing happen to them as happened to you, 'cause a bunch have gone communications-silent. But trust me, I'm flyin' high—rather than low, considering the altitude I'm at—to get to you as quick as I can. I'm doin' better than a Mach and a half as it is."

"Wow. You and Fox really DID soup that thing up."

"Yeah. But it's all on me to get to you, so...I'm worried."

"I know, baby. But I trust you. It's gonna be okay. You'll get to me in time. I just probably won't know when you arrive, that's all."

"Yeah, I kinda figured as much."

"Where are you, roughly?"

"Um, lessee..." she was quiet for several moments, and Echo knew she was checking her charts. "By my course, I just passed over Tashkent about ten, fifteen minutes ago or so."

"Uzbekistan?"

"Yeah. Headin' into the Himalayas. Um, over 'em, rather."

"You're making good time."

"Trying to. Listen, like you said, you're gonna be out by the time I get there. So make sure, whatever you do, that you leave your cell phone on, with as much battery power as you can eke out. And to that end—and also to conserving your oxygen—I'm gonna get off the horn for now. I'll ping you by text from now on. I just wanted..."

"I know. It's always good to hear the voice on the other end, when you're worried about somebody," Echo acknowledged, feeling the warmth of affection—received, and given—within. "Same here. Later, baby."

"You know it, Ace."

And the connection broke.

Echo turned off everything on his phone that he could in the way of apps and activities, except the emergency locator beacon and incoming text and calls, then he laid back down inside the force dome, placing the cell phone near his head to ensure he heard the text alert when she pinged him next time. Then, practicing the same breath control his grandfather had taught him, and aided by various alien biofeedback techniques he'd learned since, he allowed himself to slip back into the half-asleep, altered-consciousness state of reminiscence in which he'd been before Omega's call.

* * *

Omega stared at the cell phone, gnawing her lower lip.

That ain't good, she thought. *That ain't good AT ALL. He's anxious. ECHO is anxious. And so he's burning up the oxygen faster. And already showing mild signs of hypoxia—he didn't even remember that I already told him I was overflying Tashkent. That's not like him. And the hypoxia will, in turn, tend to increase heart and respiration rate even further. Damn. I hope I DO get there in time. I hope he's not anxious 'cause he doesn't think I'll make it. I GOTTA make it.*

She tried to rake an agitated hand through her hair, but it hit the helmet of the compression suit, and she huffed in frustration.

"Okay," she declared into the air, bringing up a heads-up navigational display. "Let's pull some updated coordinates on Echo from that transmission and see about fine-tuning my course. Every little bit is gonna count on this one."

* * *

Suddenly the comm clicked on, denoting a beamed transmission.

"Gilgit tower namaloom tayyarah behri jahaaz. Gilgit tower na-maloom tayyarah bardaar behri jahaaz. Ekhtataam."

"What the hell was that?" Omega wondered.

"Jasoos tayyaray, yeh hai Gilgit tower. Aap aa rahay hain ke zariye mutanazia zameen. Baat karte hain maqsad, ya goli maar di jaye. Tum ne suna? Ekhtataam."

"Their tone of voice doesn't sound too friendly. Where the blazes is that translator?" A harried Omega searched the communications portion of the console. Finally she found what she thought was the right button, and a loose echo sounded behind the incoming voice.

"Spy plane, this is Gilgit tower. You are coming by means of the controversial land. State purpose, or be shot down. Do you hear? End."

"Oh, shit, I'm over that mess that Pakistan, India, and China are fighting over!" Omega whispered, realizing, then she hunted frantically for a way to send an outbound message. She entered several commands, then keyed the external comm mic. "Gilgit tower, this is the *SchmaltzBlitz*, code D-One Alpha-One Omega Red. I am flying at altitude, but I am not a spy craft. Do you copy? Over."

While she waited for an answer, she scrambled to bring up an interactive map display and locate the disputed territories.

"Yep, there it is, sure enough. Gilgit-Baltistan, Jammu & Kashmir, Aksai Chin, Tibet, Nepal, Arunachal Pradesh. The whole lot. And for all intents and purposes, I'll be over-flying all of it. Hell. Just you watch all THREE countries decide I'm hostile. That code Fox gave me better work, or I could be in deep trouble. I don't got much in the way of offensive and defensive—"

Another transmission cut her off.

"Jasoos tayyaray, yeh hai Gilgit tower. Aap muwasilat toot; barah meharbani dohrayen," was rendered by the translator, "Spy plane, this is Gilgit tower. Your communication breaks up; please repeat."

"Dammit. Like I need this right now. Aaand it's only gonna get worse, I bet. I'm only just now making it well into the region." She raked a hand over the helmet in lieu of her hair, then keyed the mic again. "Gilgit tower, this is the *SchmaltzBlitz*, relaying international emergency code D-One Alpha-One Omega Red. I am not a spy craft. I am engaged in emergency transport for rescue operations. Repeat, international emergency code D-One Alpha-One Omega Red..."

* * *

There were many miles of fencing surrounding Meteor Mountain Ranch, but it hadn't been that long since Echo and their part-time ranch hand had ridden them, repairing the damage from the previous winter, so Echo found they were generally in good shape. That said, cattle tended to

133

use fences as scratching posts, and they sometimes tried to lean over the wire to get to fodder on the other side. Consequently, the teen found a few places that wanted mending, and one fence post that had grown downright wobbly; he made a mental note where it was, so he could come back out with the pickup truck and some cement, and shore it up properly. Meanwhile, he scavenged fist-sized rocks from the area and shoved them into the ground alongside the post; he decided that would hold it until he could come back with the cement.

From time to time he passed through, or alongside, clumps of cattle, with the soft crunching sounds of their grazing, and the faint whiffs like new-mown grass that the breeze bore to him. He smiled and eased Spirit down from his lope to a walk, to enjoy the sunshine and the general ambiance for a few moments. A contented cow on the far side of the small herd lowed softly; Echo mimicked it. This set several others off, and for a couple of minutes he found himself in the midst of a chatty mass of cattle. *I wonder what I just said in 'cow,'* he pondered in amusement.

He grinned to himself, realizing just how much he loved this ranch, this way of life. It was beautiful; it was challenging. It kept him strong mentally and physically, and he thrived in the 'wide open spaces' much ballyhooed in song...but nevertheless true.

The ranchero made a good, comfortable living, and his father had fully expected him to settle down on it, raise a family, and pass the ranch to succeeding generations. And this was exactly what Echo intended to do, once he came home in four years from attending the University of Texas at Austin on the football scholarship he had been promised, likely double-majoring in Linguistics, and possibly Petroleum Geophysics Engineering. He had already started some online coursework with Texas A & M, which would end up giving him at least the equivalent of a minor in Agribusiness.

And he had his eye on a girl in Ozona, Linda Martinez, a cute little brunette Chicano a couple of years behind him in school, who had been on the cheerleading squad the previous year. *Yeah, I think maybe I could stand to spend my life with her,* he considered, complacent. They'd already gone on several informal dates, and when he had indicated a desire to 'go together,' she had agreed.

So, as Echo dismounted to tighten up a section of wire on which a cow had leaned rather too heavily, he considered his future to be settled, and he was happy about it.

That was all about to change.

* * *

As Echo approached Meteor Mountain, Spirit started to spook rather badly, and he had to rein in his mount and work hard to keep control as the gelding shied and sidestepped and bucked. For that matter, young Echo found his own gut oddly disquieted, but he pushed through it. *After all,* he considered, *if there ARE smugglers around, I gotta be ready.*

But when Spirit finally balked and refused to go farther, pinning his ears, rolling his eyes, and threatening to bolt, Echo decided to trust the horse's instincts. He turned the horse, taking it farther away from the hillock, back in the direction they'd come, until the horse calmed once more, and his own respiration and pulse relaxed into normal bounds. He dismounted, slipped halter and lead over the bridle, and tied the gelding to a convenient fence post.

Then he slid the rifle out of its holster, slung it across his back from its strap, and pulled the shotgun.

Echo dropped into Apache stalking mode as he slipped up toward the southwestern side of Meteor Mountain.

* * *

As he approached the excuse for a mountain, the boy felt a kind of free-form anxiety grip him again. *It's like something's about to happen, and my subconscious knows it,* he decided. *So I better be ready for anything. I can't just walk away and let this go; I have to find out what the damn smugglers have done, otherwise we'll be losing cattle, and the well pumps will get vandalized, and all kinds of shit. Never mind what they might do to Ma when I'm away. Especially after I leave for college this fall. We may need to bite the bullet and bring on some full-time hands.*

So Echo practiced every technique his Shiitsooyee had ever taught him for calm and endurance, even as he also practiced the Apache warrior's stealth.

And he kept going.

* * *

And there are the details of the techniques I need to remember. Time to practice 'em, I guess, Agent Echo considered, as he lay quietly inside the force dome, reminiscing even as he put the meditative biofeedback techniques into use.

And it was along about there where Fox and the others first noticed me creeping up on 'em, even if I didn't have a clue at the time. He chuckled to himself. *At least Oboe was thoughtful enough, in her later years, to let me see the video records. It wasn't like I REALLY had a need to know, but I guess she considered I was part of that whole situation, so I deserved to know all sides of what was going on. I'm not sure to this day but what Lord Entiyti didn't issue an order for her to do it, but either way, it works. And she sure didn't seem to have a problem with it, which may mean that she suggested it. Or else Fox did.*

He let his thoughts drift back to the video record, interspersing it with his personal memories, allowing himself to be immersed in the whole milieu.

* * *

Franz Levy, chief bodyguard for the galactic Ennead chair-being Pulgey Entiyti of Emdali, sat beside his superior—on said superior's orders—at the round conference table in the rear of the saucer. Nearby sat several other humans, all dressed in dark suits; a Bastian, black of fur, tail twitching behind, gazing unblinkingly at the others with her yellow-green eyes; several Skulians, intelligent seaworms from the Kusheer system, clad in very specialized environment suits—one of the two rockets standing outside was a shuttle from their mothership, intended to allow them to rest in their natural habitat. There were also two Tethanoids of Flibitz, crablike decapodal crustaceans from a Jovian-type world—the other rocket was theirs, for the same reason; and a Dendroid. Around the walls of the room sat, stood, or reclined an entire cadre of retinue and security for this first-contact meeting.

The leader of the Earth contingent, a woman code-named Oboe, had just leaned forward to propose a trade agreement for exporting bacon from Earth to other galactic systems, when the door opened and one of Levy's security team slipped in. He was a Reptoid, though not a Draconan like Entiyti; Levy was, in fact, the only human in Entiyti's entire contingent. Suud, the other bodyguard, came straight to Levy, bent and murmured, "Boss, we have a situation."

Levy raised an eyebrow in inquiry.

"Intruder," came the response. "Not sure what to make of this one. You're human, so you stand a better chance of figuring out what he's up to than any of us."

Levy nodded, then leaned over to Entiyti.

"Gotta go check something out, Pul. Back soon."

Entiyti nodded, and Levy slipped out with Suud.

* * *

"Oh, now THAT is interesting," Levy said, watching the surveillance cameras as they depicted a teenage human male slipping from boulder to bush to outcrop, ever nearer their hidden outpost.

"Yes, it is," Suud noted. "It appears to be a young human, yet it walks right through our warding field."

"Well, in all honesty, the warding shield is only a pulsed energy screen, designed to unnerve most warm-blooded life forms," Levy pointed out, still intently watching the figure on the video monitor. "It can be overcome."

"Precisely. Which argues that the life form there," Suud gestured at the monitor, "is really a highly-trained agent in disguise. I'm concerned for milord's safety."

"No, not necessarily," Levy noted, eyeing the being onscreen with a practiced, knowing gaze. "No, that's a human teenaged boy if ever I saw one. And I should know; I was one! Suud, I need to get back to Pul. Keep a close eye on this situation," he waved a hand at the monitor, "and let me know how far he gets."

"Yes, sir," Suud affirmed, as Levy turned and headed back to the embassage.

* * *

Hidden behind a large limestone outcrop, Echo stared in surprise at the scene before him: In the dry lake bed that might or might not be an impact crater sat four vehicles such as the teen had never seen before...

137

except perhaps in science fiction films. One was a relatively large silver saucer; two were short, squat versions of the classic vertical-landing 1950s-era rocket ships; the fourth was a sleek, black, aerodynamic, not-quite-jet transport. Two Humvees, a Jeep, and a crew-cab pickup truck were parked close by as well, between himself and the various more exotic craft.

What the hell?! the boy thought, stunned. *Either I've found the camp for the smugglers comin' across the border, there's an unauthorized film crew on the ranch, or something weird is goin' on. And based on those... they look like spaceships...I'd lay money on the 'something weird' right about now. But I think I better find out what, either way.*

The standard four-wheeled vehicles were obviously empty. The jet-thing did not have a recognizable entrance, but from his slightly elevated position on the rim of the crater, he could tell there was no one in the cock-pit. Ladders led down from hatches on the rocket ships, and an open ramp led into the flying saucer. But there was no sign of activity, let alone life, that Echo could see.

He checked to see that the magazines of all his weapons were loaded, with rounds in the chambers, and flipped off the safeties on shotgun and rifle, leaving the safety on the pistol tucked into his jeans; that one could be flipped off with his thumb as he drew. Then he returned the rifle to an easily-reached sling position, hefted the shotgun, and eased forward.

* * *

Shiitsooyee had taught the boy early on how to walk, and even run, without making a sound or leaving a mark, though leaving little imprint was a bit harder while wearing his cowboy boots. And his Dad had always insisted on the boots for stirrup safety when riding horseback; the stacked heels tended to help prevent one's foot from sliding too deep into the stirrup and getting hung, in the event of coming out of the saddle. But Echo had worked hard to hone his proficiency on his Shiitsooyee's methods, seeing the strategy behind the ability, and even with the boots now on his feet, he left little to no discernible footprints on the cracked, dry mud of the crater lake.

As he crept silently across the crater, Echo checked out each truck in turn, but found little of import. All were locked; two—both of the Hum-

138

vees—were rentals, judging by the papers on the dashboards. The Jeep and the pickup both had license plates from out of state, he noticed; both showed significant evidence of wear. There was no sign of weaponry in any of them, though there were some opened suitcases containing clothing and toiletries in the back seats, visible through the windows. He was careful to touch nothing.

The jet-like conveyance was next in his exploration, but he could see no means of ingress, so he moved on to the VTOL rockets. But he pulled his deerskin work gloves from his hip pocket and donned them before hooking the strap of the shotgun over the shoulder opposite the rifle, and silently climbed the ladder of the first rocket up to the hatch. The hatch was sealed, with some sort of keypad next to it, but Echo refused to touch it, realizing that it could trigger an alarm. Frustrated, he climbed back down and tried the other rocket, eliciting a similar result.

He turned to the ramp leading to the saucer hatch, and pulled his shotgun from his shoulder.

* * *

Suud stayed glued to the security monitor, watching as the being outside crept from craft to craft, peering in, checking latches but never attempting to force locks. He noticed, as well, that the being slipping through their encampment kept watching anxiously over his shoulder, as if afraid of being followed. And despite the inherent grace of what was an obviously trained athlete, there was still a certain gangly awkwardness to his movements, too, the Reptoid thought; it put him in mind of a hatchling, shortly before it reached maturity...and suddenly he understood.

"Levy was right. This IS a young human," he decided, "and he is as frightened as any other. He has simply learned to master his fears, and do what he feels is needful for his task. The question is...is that task working for someone else?"

When the lad turned for the ramp to the saucer hatch, Suud summoned another guard, and sent her to fetch Levy once more.

* * *

The saucer was some thirty feet in diameter, with a ten-foot-long ramp leading to a hatch that was much the size of a standard door such as Echo used every day at home...though perhaps a couple of feet taller. He crept up the ramp toward the darkened door; as he did, he saw a faint light from somewhere inside. The boy snugged the butt of the shotgun into his hip and readied himself, then stepped across the threshold and through the double doors of what appeared to be an airlock.

As soon as he passed through the inner door and entered the ship proper, he stopped, gaping.

The craft was far bigger on the inside than it had been on the outside; Echo was strongly reminded of a certain British science fiction television show of long history, and which the boy happened to enjoy...when he could find time, and satellite TV reception, to watch it. But unlike that series' craft, which was ancient and often appeared worn and battered, this space-ship—for such it had to be, judging by the airlock and a few other details within view of the entrance hatch—appeared sparkling, pristine and new... or at least, very well-maintained.

Holy shit, he thought, feeling his heart begin to pound. *This is REAL. What the hell IS this, and what am I going to find in here?! Stay calm, Echo, stay calm. You're armed. Just pay attention and find out what's up, and why. Then leave, make tracks for the house, and call the sheriff.*

He paused for a moment, practicing all the techniques his grandfather had taught him for maintaining his cool, and twelve kinds of thankful to the Maker that his grandfather had seen fit to teach him. After a few seconds, he nodded to himself.

Echo laid his finger alongside the shotgun's trigger guard and eased forward, down the dim corridor before him, toward the light in the distance.

* * *

"So," Levy noted, watching the monitor, which now depicted the human youth in the entry corridor of the saucer, "he made it the whole way."

"He did, sir," Suud averred. "He has skills, that one. He is—or should be—an agent. The question becomes, who taught him?"

"You might be surprised, Suud," Levy said, still eyeing the figure on the screen. "Well, get a couple of the team, grab some weaponry, and come on. We have to catch him before he gets too far. I'd rather he didn't interrupt Pulgey in the negotiations if we can help it; they're kind of getting to some sticking points, and it'll annoy Pul. Oh, and lock down all the doors. We don't need him seeing any more than we can help. He's already seen way too much."

"On it," one of the security team murmured, turning to the control console. "All right, sir. Doors locked."

"Good."

"Blasters, sir?" Suud queried.

"Oy! No! That's meshuginah, Suud! He's a boy! Of COURSE we're not using blasters. Everyone grab a stun beam and let's go. Quietly—extra careful on the quiet, in fact. If the boy has had the kind of training I think he has, he'll hear us coming a light year away otherwise."

* * *

Most of the doors inside the flying saucer didn't seem to have knobs or latches that he could detect, and unlike certain science-fiction TV shows of which Echo was familiar, they didn't open automatically for him. So Echo was striking out royally when it came to exploring the strange space-craft. He worked his way down the corridor, toward a door at the end; it was partly open, and not only did a light emanate through it, he thought he could hear voices. *And maybe if I peep through, I can find out what's going on,* he decided.

Suddenly, however, a voice much closer at hand said, "Take your finger off the trigger and put your weapons down, son. I'm afraid you're going to have to come with us."

Echo froze, his heart leaping into his throat; the voice came from BE-HIND him. *Shit shit SHIT,* he thought. *How did they get past me? How did I not HEAR 'em?! Shiitsooyee is gonna be so pissed at me if I get myself killed. Dad wouldn't be too happy, either. And I'll have to face HIM, like immediately.* He stayed still, just as he was, for a couple of seconds, using the mental techniques of his grandfather to slow his respiration and heart—which latter had leaped into his throat.

"Did you hear me, son?" came the voice again; young Echo tried to place the accent, but it was not one with which he was familiar.

It's not Texan, though, he concluded. *Of course, it isn't any kind of Spanish I've ever heard, either. It's almost...it sounds a little like the Nazis in those World War II movies Dad used to like to watch. But not quite. Some sorta German dialect, I guess, maybe. But with something else overlaid.*

"I heard you," Echo replied then, without turning around. "I was just cussing myself out for lettin' you get the drop on me." He laid the shotgun on the floor; unslung the rifle and laid it beside the shotgun.

"The pistol, too. I see it in your waistband."

Echo sighed, a silent, disappointed sibilance, perfectly expressing his feelings about how badly he had screwed up this encounter. He removed the semi-automatic from the back of his jeans, laying it beside the other two weapons.

"Now spread 'em and let's see what else you have."

"Nothing," Echo lied; he had a large hunting knife in the top of his right cowboy boot.

"I doubt that, son. You came prepared. Now spread 'em." There was a pause; Echo refused to budge. "Don't make me have to use MY weapons, son."

Deciding discretion might be the best part of valor in this instance, Echo finally obeyed, shuffling his feet shoulder-width apart and holding his arms out straight from his shoulders. Hands patted him down from behind. They also found his hunting knife AND pocket knife, pulling them from their hiding places in boot and jeans pocket.

"Hey!" he cried, as the pocket knife was removed. "That was the last Christmas present my dad ever gave me!"

"Calm down, son. Once we get this sorted, you'll get it back."

"Who are you, and what are you doing here?" Echo demanded, hoping that they couldn't hear his heart slamming against his rib cage.

"I was going to ask the same of you," the voice replied.

"My name is Alex Bryant, and this is my ranch," Echo declared.

"YOUR ranch? Aren't you a little young to own a ranch?"

"Nope. My dad died 'bout two years back, an' he left the ranch to me an' my ma. It's MY ranch. And Ma's. But I take care of it."

"I see. And no one asked your permission, or your mother's, for our little...gathering?"

"Not hardly," Echo shot back. "The sheriff DID tell me about your little illegal smuggling band, though, cutting across people's property."

"Aha. This explains much. I'm afraid we aren't quite who you expected to see, Alex." The speaker finally stepped in front of Echo, and to his surprise—given the interior of the spacecraft—he was looking at a human. Not only a human, but a human who didn't appear to be a Mexican smuggler. At all.

The man standing in front of Echo looked to be around thirty, give or take, though something about his bearing spoke 'older' to the teen. He had hazel eyes, which at that moment were trained on Echo with an affable, not hostile, gaze...almost a smile, the boy thought. Almost. There was a certain twinkle in them to which the boy instinctively warmed, though Echo steeled himself against the feeling. The man's hair was dark, his nose slightly hooked, almost aquiline; his skin was quite pale, and the thin lips curved up at the corners, ever so slightly, as if he wanted to smile but wasn't allowed to, in the situation. His body was clad in some strange uniform consisting of dark red, not-quite-burgundy trousers and tunic, decorated with elaborate braiding. The material of which the uniform was made had a sheen to it, almost like silk, but more metallic; it was like nothing Echo had ever seen. Shiny black boots shod his feet.

"Hello there, Alex," the man said then. "My name is Franz Levy."

"I don't talk to smugglers," Echo almost snarled. The twinkle left the man's eyes.

"And as I said, I'm not a smuggler."

"Prove it."

"Suud, come stand by me, please."

A body brushed past Echo, and as it moved to Levy's side, the lad felt his knees all but buckle. The giant reptile-like being was nearly as tall as Echo, but far bulkier—and Echo, a star football player, was not exactly skinny. The creature had greenish-brown scales and a flat, lizard-like face with vertical-slit pupils and baleful, bulging yellow eyes. The legs were short and thick, almost stubby, relative to the torso, but the arms were long, hanging halfway down the creature's thighs, and the hands were possessed of only four clawed fingers—one of which was an opposable thumb. This Suud creature was clad in a uniform very similar to Levy's, but without quite so much decorative braiding. Levy addressed Echo once more.

"Alex, this is my friend and colleague, Suud Guurn. Suud, meet Alex Bryant, the owner of the property on which we landed. Now, Alex, does Suud look like a Mexican drug smuggler to you?"

Suud gave Echo a toothy smile. A...VERY...toothy...smile. Were the being mammalian, Echo would have called it wolfish. The boy closed his eyes for a split-second, taking a surreptitious deep breath, then opened his eyes and nodded.

"Uh, no. I guess you're NOT the group I thought you were. Pleased to meet you, Suud," he said, starting to offer a tentative hand, then thinking better of it. "Um...do you shake hands?"

"We do," Suud allowed, "but not with prisoners."

"Now wait just a damned minute, here! This is MY land you're on, WITHOUT permission, let me add, and—"

"Shake his hand, Suud," Levy ordered.

"Franz, we do not yet know for whom he works—"

"You may not, but I do. Shake his hand. And be nice. The boy—"

"Hey! I'm not a kid!"

"Oh, excuse me, Alex. You are correct; you're not a boy, you're a young man. And when I say that, I am not being patronizing. I simply mean an adult male who happens to be on the young side. Is that better?"

"Yeah, it'll do."

"Good. You'll have to overlook little things like that with me, I'm afraid. After a certain point, everyone younger than a particular age tends to get labeled as 'young' to me."

"C'mon now," Echo remonstrated. "There you go again. Quit puttin' down my age, already. You're not much more 'n ten years older than I am!"

"Oh, do you think so?" Levy wondered; the twinkle was back. "At any rate, Suud, the young man here is quite correct. We ARE on HIS land, and we apparently do NOT have permission. I'll need to speak to Pul about that. I thought that would have been arranged already. We'll have to fix the matter. Don't worry, son, I'll see you're done right by, as much as in me lies. Suud? The handshake, if you please, meyn khaver."

Suud stuck out his hand, curling the last joint of each finger into his palm. Echo stared at it in puzzlement, not sure how to grasp it to shake hands. Levy noticed.

"Oh, it's okay, son. Grab it and shake it like you normally would," Levy explained. "His claws don't retract, so when Reptoids and other members of their genus—like the Draconans—shake hands, they curl their fingertips under, and tuck their claws into their own palms to avoid scratching the other being. It's a mark of courtesy."

"Oh, I get it now. I guess I wouldn't have thought other planets even shook hands," Echo said. "I was actually expecting him to say no when I asked, or not know what I meant. I just...didn't...know what..."

"Ah, I see. Yes, variants thereon are found on most planets on which bipeds live, throughout the galaxy. It seems to be a typical kind of instinctive greeting between non-family bipeds. It's not universal by any means, but it's surprisingly common."

"Okay, I see," Echo said, grasping the proffered hand somewhat gingerly and shaking. Suud offered him another toothy grin, and Echo returned it, somewhat uncertainly. "Now, about this 'prisoner' shit..."

"Well, you are, but you aren't," Levy said, somewhat cryptic. "You're part Native American, aren't you, lad?"

"Yeah," Echo confirmed. "Half Apache on Ma's side. How'd you know? Most people think I take after Dad."

"Oh, it wasn't so much your looks, though the cheekbones, black hair, and brown eyes are suggestive. And you tan quite well. No, it was your bearing and movements that told me you likely had American Indian somewhere in your background."

"Why'd you wanna know, then?"

"Has someone in your family taught you the traditional ways of that tribe?"

"Uh-huh. That'd be my Shiitsooyee," Echo explained. "Uh, my grandfather. Ma's dad. He's full blood. So is Ma."

"Yes, I suspected as much. You learned to control your responses, school your emotions, and channel them into a warrior mentality, didn't you?"

"Well...yeah. How'd you know? Are you Indian?"

"No, I'm Jewish. But...well, let's just say that I have a lot more experience with all kinds of people than you might think, from looking at me."

"Oh-kaaaay..." Echo pondered the conversation, deciding to open up a bit and see where the conversation went. *After all, this Levy hombre,* he considered, *has already told me a buncha stuff about himself that he didn't have to. Not that I trust him yet, but let's just see what happens.*

"Don't worry about my age for now, son. It's enough to know that I've been around the block several times. You learned pretty well at your grandfather's knee, didn't you?"

"I did my best," Echo said, not having to try hard to seem earnest about that subject. "I think Shiitsooyee was pleased. It was hard to tell, sometimes."

"I understand. But you loved him. And he loved you."

"Oh, yeah. He could be tough, though."

"Has he...passed on?"

"No. But his health kinda went down last year, after Dad was killed—he's gettin' on up in years—an' he and Ma decided it would be better if he went back to her side of the family, on the reservation. The doctor access was easier, and he could get traditional herbal treatments, too. Sometimes," Echo made a face, "if the, uh, the 'wrong doctor' was in the office in Ozona, he wouldn't see Shiitsooyee."

"I see. Because he's an Indian?"

"Yeah." Echo scowled despite himself.

"Did he ever do that to you or your mother? The doctor?"

"No. When Dad was alive, he wouldn't 'a stood for it. And I don't take to it much, either."

"And you are not a small young man. I understand. So it is just you and your mother on the ranch now?"

"Mostly. We got a couple hands that help out, on a part-time basis. I was thinkin' about hirin' some on full-time, once I headed off to college this fall. Somebody trustworthy, who'd help Ma out while I was gone, and not cause problems, and look after her for me. What about y'all? If you're not the smugglers—and you're obviously not," Echo added, glancing at Suud, who grinned that toothy grin back, "who ARE you, and why are y'all here?

You're obviously," he looked over his shoulder and saw several more of the Reptoids flanking him, "um, not from around here. At least," he added, looking back at Levy, "not most of you."

Levy laughed, a deep, booming, mirthful sound.

"No, Alex, son, they're not from around here—nowhere even close. And depending on how you define 'around here,' even I am not from 'around here.' And even if you define it as the entire planet, I haven't been 'around here' for a very long time. Come with me. There are some people you need to meet, who are going to ask your pardon, and for permission to meet on your ranch."

Chapter 6

As the adult Echo lay, still and silent in his tiny force dome, while the haboob swirled and raged around him, his cell phone bleated with the incoming text alert. Without fully rousing from his altered state, he picked up the device, swiped a finger across its screen to activate it, and studied the message from his partner that displayed on the screen.

Hey Ace.
You there? Still awake?

His index finger spelled out a response.

Yeah baby. Im still here.
Tired. But here.

Moments later a reply came in.

Tireder than you oughta be?

He pondered that for a while, then sent,

Yeah, probably. Air not great.
But techniques working ok so far.

Ok Ace. Coming as fast as I can.
You hang in there for me. Im not gonna lose you.
You hear me? Hang in there.

Hanging.

There was no other reply, so he laid down the phone, closed his eyes, and returned to memory.

* * *

"What?!" Lord Pulgey Entiyti, chair-being of the Ennead, the Galactic ruling Council of Nine, exclaimed, staring at Echo. "And this was never approved? Or even passed forward?" He turned his fierce glare on the leader of the human contingent at the table. Agent Oboe never so much as flinched.

The Bryant lad, however, while standing his ground, still made that ground about a step behind, if to one side, of Franz Levy, the chief bodyguard privately noted. Which wasn't surprising; Entiyti was a Draconan, and as such was several feet taller than even the very tall Alex Bryant. Entiyti also had an even toothier smile than Suud—only he wasn't smiling just now—with horns and wings to boot. And said wings were now fully unfurled in Entiyti's wrath. The orange gaze of the Draconan, formidable even when calm, seemed like open flames at the moment. If Levy didn't know Entiyti as well as he did, he probably would have considered taking a step backward himself, just to ensure there was sufficient time to react... to anything. As it was, he held his left arm out, down, and slightly behind himself, fingers spread, palm facing the boy, in a subtle 'stay put' gesture. The faintest hum of acknowledgement told him that Bryant had seen it and was content to obey it.

"We made the usual overtures to the family patriarch," Oboe replied, calm. Levy noted, however, that her shoulders were a wee bit hunched; she was not quite as confident as she wished to appear, in the face of this formidable being.

"Which were never received, apparently!" Entiyti bellowed.

"That's as it should be; James Robertson Bryant was the specific contact, and no other. We had no idea the man had died."

"And did not bother to check! TWO YEARS! He has been dead for nearly two full years, and you did not know! And now see what we have! His son, the rightful owner of the land, has walked squarely in on our negotiations!"

That seemed to moderately deflate Oboe. She sighed, and her shoulders dropped in something that was not quite a shrug.

149

"I'm sorry, Lord Entiyti. I hate like hell to admit this, but...well, we're rather woefully understaffed, I'm afraid. After all, there isn't an actual source of funding from which we can develop a budget," Oboe explained, seeming a bit shame-faced. "Only what we can hide in the line items in the federal budget. And each nation's hidden agency is the same. From time to time, when the budgets get cut, our funding sources can be eliminated. And we just had a new administration come in last year, so..."

"Ah. Now matters begin to make sense. So you lack the beingpower to maintain all of your lines of intelligence," Entiyti finished for her, calming. "How many do you have, just on this continent?"

"North America? Less than a hundred—seventy-four agents, all told," Oboe noted. "For the entire continent, from the Arctic all the way down to the Panama Canal. Well more than a hundred thousand square miles per agent; nearly 7 million people per agent to be overseen. And we're currently without any real headquarters, because of some of the political machinations that tend to go on, whenever Washington swaps up administrations." She shrugged. "And of all the various nations, our agency is in the best shape. We take the lead on most of the activity, around the planet. Which," she added, "only increases the strain on our agents. At this point, pretty much everyone except those you see here," she waved her hand around the room, "aren't even full-time agents. They have to hold down regular jobs to make ends meet, and do the agency's work in and around that. And doing that while maintaining our secrecy...gets awkward."

"Yes, that is a definite problem, and one which must be resolved. So you require our active participation in order for your operations to continue," Entiyti deduced. "To help you guide your civilization into the galactic community without panic, chaos or failure of government..."

"—Or finances," Oboe agreed with a nod. "I had hoped...that perhaps our trade negotiations would enable us to fund our own activities in some fashion, so as not to unduly tax the galactic government..."

"I see. This is why you have been pushing hard to develop contacts with us, in recent years, then?"

"It's been one of the main drivers, yes. We're not inept or incompetent," Oboe defended her people, "just badly under-funded, under-staffed, under-equipped, under...everything."

"Well, then. I think perhaps we can do better for you than that. I expect the Galactic Council can furnish you with funding plentiful enough to maintain an annual budget sufficient to keep an adequate staff," an apparently mollified Entiyti responded. "Especially if we re-ratify your galactic territory as a division; given the population of several systems within it, it is likely high time we did, anyway. You would be surprised, Oboe, what a galactic confederation can manage—or what a galactic confederation MUST manage. But...you will learn, soon enough. Meanwhile, we must make things right with this young man." He waved a hand at Echo. "What do you propose to do, to remedy that, Oboe? You know his situation now."

"I do. Let me confer with my colleagues, and try to reach some proposal for appropriate accommodations," Oboe suggested.

"Very well," Entiyti agreed. "I shall, likewise, confer with my people, and perhaps we can make this all work, when everything is said and done."

* * *

Levy turned to the young Echo. "You all right, son?"

"Sure," Echo asserted. "Why wouldn't I be?"

"Oh, I dunno," Levy said, eyes twinkling. "Plenty of aliens around; evidence your dad might have known something he didn't tell you about. Not to mention a pissed-off dragon." He gestured subtly at Entiyti.

"I can deal with it," Echo decided. "I sorta get why Dad didn't say anything, if he was aware of y'all. Even Ma and I woulda thought he was nuts, if he'd tried to tell us..."

"Precisely why this is all being done in secrecy. Your culture—I suppose I should say, OUR culture, worldwide—just isn't quite mature enough as yet. One of the whole points of the human organization that's calling itself the Agency is to keep secret what needs to remain secret for now, while trying to nudge things in the right direction to enable the whole planet to eventually know the truth and become a fully-integrated part of the Pan-Galactic Administration."

"Pan-Galactic...?"

"Yes, son. What you'd probably think of as the galactic government. More of a confederation of systems through the galaxy than anything, though."

"How on Earth—uh, how off it, I guess—do you know all this?"

"That angry dragon that unnerved you?"

"Yeah?"

"He's my boss, and the oldest friend I've got—at least, still living. He's also the being that saved my life, a couple of times over...after I saved his." Levy smiled, his expression warming. "He's the current duly-elected chair-being of the galactic central council, which is formally known as the Ennead. And he's the being who has given me the opportunity to see...most of it."

Echo saw the enthused glow in the older man's eyes, impressed.

"Most of it?"

"The galaxy. At least ninety percent, I'd say." Levy smiled, a far-away look in the hazel eyes.

"But how is that possible? How fast can these ships go...?"

"Pretty damn fast." Levy came back down to Earth and focused on Echo once more. "We do have several varieties of faster-than-light drives."

"Wow. Instantaneous, huh?" Without conscious awareness, Echo took an eager step toward the other man.

"Oh, no. Not THAT fast. We're still working on point-to-point wormhole transitions."

"Then...how long does it take? I mean, how long have you been doing this?"

"About thirty years now, I suppose," Levy mused. "I guess I'd have to go back and do some conversions to be sure, 'cause I stopped thinking in terms of Earth years a long time ago, but that should be pretty close to right."

"Aw, dammit! Don't lie to me!" Echo exclaimed, incensed and backing off. "I was startin' to think you were okay, then you go and do that. You're not even thirty years old!"

"You think? Looks can be deceiving, you know."

"Well, how old ARE you, then?" the boy demanded.

"Would you believe I turned 68 two months ago?"

"Hell, no!" Echo exclaimed. Then he stopped; Echo considered the other man's calmness and general bearing...the things that had spoken to him earlier, telling him that there was much more to this man than it seemed. Levy, seeing the expression on Echo's face, laughed.

"Ah, now you see," he said. "Looks CAN be deceiving. Your instinct, your subconscious tells you I am older, merely because of how I act, in contradiction of the evidence of your eyes." He paused, then offered, "Consider this, Alex. If the spacecraft are so much more advanced than you're used to, what does that say about the medical capabilities?"

"Oh. Damn. You...that'd make you only a few years younger than..."

"Indeed. Than...probably your grandfather, I expect."

"Yeah, that's who I was thinkin' of."

"I expected as much. If it helps any, your grandfather and I would probably have had some very interesting conversations. I'd have liked to know him. I think we'd have gotten on pretty well."

Echo studied Levy, thinking. Finally he remarked, "Yeah, I think you would've. You still might get the chance. I can always take you to the rez and introduce you."

"Well, after all you just heard, do you still think that a wise idea?" Levy asked. Echo saw his gaze shoot past the boy, to something across the room. Levy blinked a couple of times, and rubbed a hand across his cheek, before his gaze returned to Echo, who quickly glanced behind, but saw nothing save a group of aliens in a huddle, the no-longer-pissed Draconan in the midst. "How would you explain me to your grandfather...and the rest of his, and your, family? The discrepancy between my appearance and my true age? Where I've been since I was last seen on Earth?"

"Oh. Yeah, I guess you got a good point there."

"Mm-hm. Your gut says to trust me."

"Yeah. I'm not sure why, but it does."

"You have good instincts."

"Shiitsooyee thought so, too. I'm not sure it's instinct," Echo pondered, "as much as it is just...kinda being aware of things around me, and letting my subconscious point me in the right direction."

"Excellent consideration. I think," Levy said, cocking his head in contemplation, "they probably amount to the same thing, in the end. What do you think?"

"Maybe so," Echo agreed, thinking over the matter.

"Do you trust me sufficiently to come with me immediately, if I were to request it?" Levy asked.

"Huh? Why?" a surprised Echo wanted to know, suddenly wary... though not necessarily of Levy.

"Well...let us merely say, for now," Levy said, "that we have two different groups of beings pondering what to do about your situation. You see, you now know about the galactic government—"

"Aw shit," Echo cursed, careful to keep his voice down. "Yeah, I get it."

"...But I do not know what either group intends. And while Pulgey— the dragon—and I go back a long way, he is the chair-being, not the monarch; he can be overruled, if the Ennead votes against him. And I've rather taken a liking to you, young Alex. I'd like to make sure you get out of this healthy and whole."

"I'd kinda like that, too," Echo agreed. "So would Ma. Yeah, if you need me to come along in a hurry, just say so. I'll come."

"Good." Levy looked up. "Here comes Oboe. Be ready to follow my instructions. As fast as you can."

"Okay."

* * *

"...I think we should simply take him down to the medical lab, use the Cerebellar Holographic Mnemonic Re-Encoding Induction System on him, and return him to his ranch," Stootegon, one of the Tethanoids, recommended.

"No, it is a precedent I do not wish to set, at this point," Entiyti declared. "They do not yet even know of memory re-encoding technology. I am not prepared to give it to them until we are certain they can be trusted with it. And that will take a few orbital revolutions."

"But Pulgey," the Bastian, one Mrrp by name, purred practically into the Draconan's ear membrane, worried the humans would overhear, "you cannot let the humans decide what to do with the young male. What if they conclude it is easier to simply kill the kitten, in order to keep their secret?

154

After all, we all know the planet as a whole is hardly ready to hear of us. It's too soon."

"Mrrp has a point," Vureg, the Dendroid, susurrated, sounding like a breeze in a copse. "It would be a very...improper...way to begin our association with this system. I cannot say how many galactic laws it would break."

"We MUST be prepared to do something," Mrrp pressed.

"I know, my friends," Entiyti murmured, watching the conclave of human agents interact across the room. "I know. And should it come to that, we will. I will not let an innocent youngling be harmed, let alone killed. It would have to be covert, but we will prevent that happening, if it comes to it. But let us be patient in the meanwhile. I would—where is Franz? I would have his opinion. He is, after all, human, and from this very planet. If anyone should know, should be able to read these secret agents, he would."

"He is over with the kitten, Pulgey," Mrrp replied, subtly waving her tail in the direction of Entiyti's chief bodyguard.

"Oh, that is excellent, then," Entiyti decided.

He let out a loud harrumphing cough, then put his index finger to the tip of his snout, raising his horns in a complex pattern. Levy glanced up, saw the slight motions on the part of his employer and friend, then the adult human blinked twice and rubbed his cheek. Entiyti watched as Levy turned to Agent Oboe as she approached the boy, while never leaving the lad's side.

"There," Entiyti decreed. "We have that matter taken care of. Franz will let nothing bad befall the boy now. In the event they determine... wrongly...we will simply take custody of the boy ourselves, mind-wipe him of this incident, and send him off, back to his life...while placing a guardian with him as a ranch hand. This Earth organization need never know. If it should become necessary in order to protect the lad, we can mind-wipe them of the incident, as well." Entiyti glanced around at his small contingent of advisors. "And whatever they do, however they handle it, it will tell us a great deal about their organization as a whole."

"That...is true," Mrrp agreed. "As long as nothing harms the kitten, I can go along with that plan."

"Ah, Mrrp," Entiyti said with a surprisingly soft smile, "that is why

I always insist that you are on my advisory staff. Your mothering instinct always ensures my interactions are gentled."

Mrrp head-butted Entiyti's shoulder in affectionate appreciation.

"And I will be here, as often as you ask, Pulgey," she averred. "Only when my own kits are in need will I ever turn down your request."

"And I understand that, Mrrp, and I would never press the matter," Entiyti said with a nod. "Now, let us see what the human agents are doing. After all, I have a great deal of knowledge of Earth history from Franz, and while he certainly is, I am well aware that not all humans are particularly... admirable."

The small group of mixed alien beings drifted as casually as possible toward the group of humans, who were deep in discussion.

* * *

Oboe approached Echo, stopping when she was just within hand-shaking distance. She offered that appendage, and a cautious Echo took it and shook.

"Hello, Mr. Bryant," she said with a pleasant smile. "Call me Oboe, please, if you would."

"What's your real name?" Echo said, frowning. "I prefer to deal with real names."

"That is my real name, now," she replied with a sigh. "When I became the head of the Agency, my...old life...well, let's just say it went away."

"Oh," was all Echo said. He sensed, rather than saw, Levy move close to his side, and slightly behind.

"So," Oboe tried again. "You're the only son of James and Nalin Bryant."

"Yup."

"You're half-Apache."

"Dunno what that's got to do with it."

"Well, it's my understanding that your Apache grandfather trained you in Apache ways," Oboe explained. "Is that how you got all the way into this spacecraft almost without our being aware of it, using your grandfather's training?"

"Hell, it wasn't hard," Echo declared. "You didn't have any guards posted, and I pretty much just walked right on in."

"Not true," Levy said over his shoulder. "We had guards posted—half a dozen of different species, around the perimeter, all inside cloaking fields. Plus we had an anti-personnel field in place. I noticed you have horsehair on the inside of your jeans legs. Did you ride here?"

"Yeah. So?"

"Did your horse react...oddly...as you got close?"

"Now you mention it, he did," Echo remembered. "He got real skittish and kept spooking. Finally he just plain balked. So I took him back a ways and tied him to a fencepost."

"Ah," Oboe said, nodding. "We'll need to take care of the horse and make sure it gets safely back to its barn."

Echo noted, off to one side, that Lord Entiyti raised a horn, much as a human might have raised an eyebrow. The alien's expression looked pleased...surprised, but pleased.

"Yeah, I can take it back when I go," Echo pointed out. "I'll need to ride 'im back anyhow."

"Well, hear me out, first," Oboe added. "But it's my understanding that your horse most likely spooked when it encountered the anti-personnel field."

"That's right," Levy confirmed. "It should have produced at least some level of anxiety in you, too, Alex."

"Mm. So that's what made my gut do flip-flops," Echo muttered.

"That'd be it, yes," Levy affirmed. "But you pushed through it. Most humans...couldn't. They'd develop an increasingly strong, unreasoning anxiety, then finally panic and bolt, much as your horse tried to do. I take it, you also managed to maintain control of your horse?"

"Well, of course. Spirit's a good horse. I was there when he was foaled, and I helped Dad train him. He's..." Echo shook his head. "He's my horse. Of course I can control him."

Levy, Oboe, and Entiyti exchanged knowing glances.

"Son, there's no 'of course' to it," Levy added. "Your answers are telling us that you have some serious abilities and skills."

"Skills that we would like to use," Oboe agreed. "First of all, my most sincere apologies for the misunderstanding regarding our meeting on your ranch. It was never intended to slight you. We were simply never informed of your father's death...and so our, ah, very specifically targeted communiques never reached their designated recipient. May I ask what happened to him?"

Echo winced as pain, nearly as fresh as the day it had happened, shot through him.

"One of our cows was calving," he explained, "only there was a problem. Near as we could tell, the calf was breech, pretty bad, and Dad couldn't get it straightened out. He left me there in the pasture with the cow, and rode back to fetch the vet. So he was movin' at a pretty fast lope, and...I'm not sure if there was an old prairie dog hole, or a mole run, or what exactly; I never could find the exact place, after. But the horse stumbled, threw a shoe—or maybe it was throwing the shoe that did it—and went down under Dad. Ol' Paint rolled, tryin' to regain 'is feet...with Dad still in the saddle; he didn't have time to bail, it happened so fast. And the saddle horn...it..." Echo broke off, face drawing in grief, and indicated his breastbone, rubbing his fingertips up and down along it. "Dad...never had a chance. He was gone before I could get to him."

"You saw the whole thing, son?" another agent, a man standing near Oboe, asked.

"This is X-ray, Mr. Bryant," Oboe murmured by way of introduction. Echo shrugged.

"Yeah, X-ray, I did. It...wasn't pretty," he admitted after a few moments to find his voice. "Lotta blood an' junk. The wound, out his mouth, his nose..." He turned his face away. "I think...if it hadn't 'a been Dad, if it had been somebody I didn't know, or even one o' the damn smugglers that keep comin' through, it wouldn't have bothered me so much. But Dad...you hadda know him. It just...wasn't right, to see him lyin' there, eyes all blank and staring, and no more life in him..."

* * *

Inside the force dome, the adult Echo lay quietly, but his face drew into a grimace of remembered pain and grief. The slow rhythm of his chest increased in tempo, just slightly.

He sighed...and the cell phone text alert went off.

Good timing, he decided, rousing and reaching for the phone as his mind came back to the present. *I needed a distraction from THAT memory.*

As he expected, it was Omega.

Hey Ace. U there?

Yup. Still here, baby.

Good. Sorry 2 keep bugging U.

No. Thats what needs doing. Keep it up.
Where are U, & what time is it?

Little bit over 3h since U raised the dome. Say 3:04MET.
Im crossing in2 Tibet. Will fly past Kathmandu in ~20m.
Big desert basin off 2 my left. Dunes & stuff.

Mm. Think thats the Taklamakan Desert, in China.
Maybe. Not sure. Have 2 see a map.

Ok. Dont waste battery on maps app.
Can't talk long. Got more incoming comm.
Lay back down & rest.
Im getting closer. Fast as I can go.
And finding ways 2 go faster.

Good. Ill b here waiting.

U better b!

He smiled with a hint of affection, and laid the phone back down. As he returned to the past, he made sure to get past the explanation of his father's death.

* * *

His reactions are slowing down, a lot, Omega thought, staring at the now-quiescent cell phone screen, even as her ship's comm bleated insistently with incoming messages. *It took him way too long to respond, each time. The depleting oxygen is starting to get to him. He's gonna go unconscious soon.*

She glanced at the timer she'd set up, then checked her location; the *SchmaltzBlitz* was, as nearly as she could tell, roughly paralleling the main body of the central Himalayan mountain range, slightly to their north, entering the area that was still known as Tibet, though China now largely ruled it. Absently, she punched a few buttons, cutting off the message alert and initiating a pre-recorded response, piping it through the translator.

"Tower, this is the *SchmaltzBlitz*, relaying international emergency code D-One Alpha-One Omega Red. I am not a spy craft...."

But Omega's mind never left Echo's situation.

Yeah. By my calculations, he's got only around another hour of consciousness left; an hour and a half, max. And that presumes he was able to get himself settled and in a relaxed state. Otherwise, I'd say he's got no more than thirty minutes of consciousness left. That doesn't make me happy at all, and it might cause brain damage in the long run. I just can't get there much faster, no matter what I do. But maybe I can speed things up by a few more minutes.

Omega used the most recent contact with her partner to extract an even better fix from Echo's locator beacon, and adjusted her course accordingly.

Every second counts, she told herself, determined. *And these course corrections are shaving off precious minutes. Minutes that I can maybe use to save him. I dunno what I'll do if I lose him, too. No, girl. Just...no. Don't even think it. You're not losing him. You can't. You WON'T.*

* * *

"...I'm very sorry to hear that, Mr. Bryant," Oboe said softly. Echo shrugged again, then nodded. "I will see to it that the same remuneration which went to your father is deposited into the ranch bank account. Is it the same one?"

"Yeah," Echo confirmed, suddenly understanding why his father had worked with them. More, he abruptly remembered his father making a couple of oblique references to 'the UFO nuts' who wanted to camp on a corner of the ranch from time to time, and look for flying saucers. *I wonder if Dad even believed 'em,* he thought. *Maybe he just figured they were some weird campers, and he used the dry lake bed as a kinda rental camp site, to bring in a little extra cash, now and again.*

"Very good, then. And..." Oboe added, gesturing at X-ray, who pulled a note pad and jotted something down in it. "We have a proposition we'd like to put before you."

"I'm listening," Echo observed.

* * *

"...And you'd be training under X-ray, one of our most experienced agents," Oboe explained. "You'd be one of us, and you'd get to travel all over the world, and..."

"...All over the galaxy, potentially," Levy finished for her, as Entiyti nodded in approval. "In those faster-than-light spaceships I was telling you about."

"You're kidding!" Echo exclaimed. "COOL!"

"You understand the limitations, though, don't you, Alex?" X-ray queried.

"Um, my nickname is Echo, if y'all wanna call me that," Echo offered, seeming to Levy to be suddenly shy, as if his burst of enthusiasm had embarrassed him. Which, he considered, it probably had.

"Echo," Oboe said, and smiled. "That will fit right in with our current code name list, and we don't already have an Echo."

"So you're an agent now, eh?" Entiyti observed, patting the young human gently on the back. "Congratulations. You will be helping to make history."

"How so?"

"You will be one of the first official agents in the new Pan-Galactic Law Enforcement and Immigration Administration, Division One." Entiyti turned to Levy. "As will you, my old friend."

"What?!" Levy exclaimed. "Pulgey—you're ditching me?!"

161

"No, no, Franz, not at all," Entiyti murmured. "Let us face it, my friend, I have kept you away from your homeworld long enough. But I have a specific job in mind for you," he added, then turned to Oboe, "so I want YOU to see to it that he is the diplomatic liaison between your Agency and the Ennead. Most specifically, the liaison between you...and me."

"I...see," Oboe said, almost as startled as Levy. "Well, it makes a great deal of sense. And it provides both of us with certain...advantages."

"It does," Entiyti agreed. "It gives me trusted insight into your operations, and it gives you a direct connection to me. It also gives Franz, here, the opportunity to continue his travels offworld, whenever he wishes." He turned to Levy, who had drawn his brows together in concern. "Franz, my dear old friend. You saved my life, and I saved yours...and gave you the heavens. But now, I give you back your life here on Earth. Find a mate, do good work, keep traveling the galaxy, keep in touch. Though it may not seem like it now, this is my repayment to you for so very many years of highest services rendered...and wonderful friendship."

"I...I understand," Levy said, feeling his throat choke. "I cannot imagine what it will be like, not reporting to you every morning; not discussing the day's events with you over drinks, last thing in the evening."

"We have had a rare friendship, Franz," Entiyti agreed. "It does not end here, rest assured. It merely changes form." The flamelike eyes blinked several times, flexible horns curled; and Levy recognized the sign of the Draconan's emotion. "Now, do you have a recommendation for your successor as my chief bodyguard, as if I did not know?"

"Suud, of course," Levy said with a wobbly chuckle. "He's been my right hand for years."

"As you have been mine. I suspected as much. It will be done." He turned to Oboe. "So. You have your desired organizational support, and two new agents. Let us go hash out the details, as Franz likes to say, then you may send someone to fetch this 'United Nations Secretary-General' person, to sign the treaty."

They wandered back to the negotiations table, and a stunned Levy watched as Echo all but hopped in place with suppressed excitement.

"I'm gonna be an astronaut! I'm gonna explore space!" he exclaimed then. "Just wait'll Ma hears about this!"

"What? Oh, no no, Echo," X-ray said. "We're a secret organization, remember? No one can know about this."

"Well...but—how am I...?"

"We'll set something up for you," X-ray explained. "Your horse will be sent back with a 'broken' lead line; we'll make sure he gets back to the barn safely. And Levy, perhaps you and I can work out some sort of cover for why Echo, here, disappears."

"His code name is Fox," Oboe called. "Comes right after Echo in the phonetic alphabet."

"It's actually 'Foxtrot,'" X-ray corrected.

"I know," Oboe said with a grin. "But the older version of the alphabet, the one that gave me my code name, uses Fox. And he looks more like a desert fox to me than a fancy foxtrot dancer."

Levy and X-ray both laughed; a dismayed Echo merely shook his head.

"Okay then. Fox and I will work something out to explain your disappearance," X-ray continued. "I'm thinking...what kind of big predators do you have around here, Echo?"

"Um, there's more southwest of here, over on the other side of the Pecos River," Echo said, and Levy thought he sounded a lot more subdued than he had moments before.

And downcast, too, the former bodyguard decided. *It's finally setting in what his situation really is. I'd have hoped Pul would use the memory re-encoder on the boy, but I suppose he's not ready to reveal that tech to this new branch of the government, yet. Which is,* Levy added to himself, *probably one of the reasons I'm going to be staying—I can keep an eye on things, and TELL him when they're ready. But this is going to be dreadfully rough on poor Alex. Um, Echo.*

"Well, that's close enough," X-ray decided. "The river isn't far away. What have we got to work with?"

"Well, there's coyotes...lotta them," Echo said. "Pains in the ass, 'cause they attack the cattle. They scavenge a lot, too. Mountain lion—uh, cougar. Every few years, somebody says they saw a jaguar, but they're supposed to be extinct around here. There's always bobcats—pretty widespread, like coyotes."

"Not big enough," X-ray dismissed the local variety of lynx. "Have you ever heard reports of chupacabra in the area?"

"Um, couple times, yeah."

"You thinking fake an attack, X-ray?" Levy—he shook his head slightly; *I'm Fox now,* he reminded himself—asked the other agent.

"That's what I was thinking, yeah. A cougar, maybe even a chupacabra, attacks while Echo, here, is working on the fence. It gets him, but the horse, tied nearby, panics, snaps the line, and runs home. Coyotes come in to scavenge, and there's not much left for anybody to identify."

"Ma's gonna think I got KILLED?! Torn to pieces?!" Echo exclaimed, horrified. "Less 'n two years after Dad...?"

"I'm sorry, son," X-ray murmured, sympathetic. "But look around you. Draconans, Bastians, Reptoids, Skulians, Tethanoids, and Dendroids. Your average human is going to interpret them as dragons, lizard-men, giant cats, sea monsters, giant crabs, and talking trees. You're one of the few humans I've seen, dumped into a situation like this, who hasn't freaked out completely—and even you were unnerved, you just hid it better than most."

"What makes you think that?!"

"Oh, maybe the fact that you stood behind Fox, here, when Lord Entiyti got angry?" X-ray offered with a grin. "Not to mention, you might not have realized it, but your knees were shaking, just a little bit, and you paled so much your lips were even gray. No, son. I'm sorry. We just can't risk it. It's going to be difficult enough to bring Kofi Annan in here for the treaty signing." He shook his head. "You HAVE to disappear."

"But Ma...and the ranch...a-and Linda...my scholarship..."

"Son," X-ray said, his voice low, "look. I know it ain't fun. But every one of us that has gone full-time at this has had to go through this. I'll admit, you're young for this to happen to, but that only makes it easier—there's not nearly as much history to get rid of."

"That's my LIFE you're talking about!" Echo cried.

"I know," X-ray sighed. "Believe me, I know."

Fox laid a gentle hand on Echo's shoulder.

"Let me see what I can work out, Alex," he said.

* * *

"No, Franz. I really am very sorry," Entiyti replied. "I feel for the boy, certainly. But I have told you my reasons. It is planetary security that is at stake here. His life is not in danger, so I must remain firm."

"It depends on your definition of 'life,'" Fox pointed out. "The way of life he's always known, his plans for the future...all of that, it IS at stake, Pul."

"I know." Entiyti sighed. "Could I run time backward and prevent the boy from walking in on things, I would in a heartbeat. In retrospect, Oboe and I should have sent some of her agents with you, instead of my other bodyguards. That way, he might not have seen any non-Terrans, and the technology could be explained away as advanced testing and...perhaps a forced landing due to malfunction, or the like."

"Hindsight is always 20/20." It was Fox's turn to sigh. "So the boy has to lose everything that he loved—his little family, already decimated by his father's loss not so long ago; his ranch; his girlfriend, his university scholarship—his heritage, and his entire future."

"In exchange for another, broader future, yes, I fear so." Entiyti cocked his large head. "He seemed eager and interested enough, initially. What has happened?"

"The ramifications hit home," Fox explained.

"Oh. I see. He realized that the old life was gone, the instant he crossed the hatch threshold."

"Exactly. He apparently hoped, as the Earth saying is, 'to have his cake and eat it, too.' To do the work of the Agency, while still having the life, the home, he was used to."

"Yes. Well, I am very sorry. Perhaps...look, you are working with X-ray to put together a scenario to 'vanish' him?"

"Yes."

"Good. Then...try to leave a few loopholes there, why don't you? That way, once you tell me the Agency is ready for the holographic mnemonic re-encoding system, perhaps we can undo what we have done, and send him home again...if he wishes it. And," another thought occurred to the

Draconan, "let me provide you with some financial information. Create a holding organization, and 'purchase' the ranch from young Bryant's mother—give her an excellent price. Buy it, contents and all, if you can—or as many of the contents as she will let you have. Then we can arrange to hold the ranch, fully operational, in trust for Echo, whenever he should decide to leave the Agency and retire there—be it soon, or late. And the mother will be taken care of from the funds of the sale. Meanwhile, perhaps he will let the Division use it as a safe house for visiting rulers, agents needing a vacation, and whatnot."

"Good idea, all around," Fox murmured. "I'll work with X-ray and see what I can do, without giving away the whole 'memory-wiping technology' bit."

"Very good, my old friend. I wish there were a better way. But at least they were merciful and neither sought to imprison him, nor...worse."

"That's...true."

* * *

So it was done.

Entiyti's personal physician came to Echo and took a small tissue sample, then carried it away to her laboratory. Within a couple of hours, she had cloned several vials of Echo's blood, some small bits of muscle tissue, and several loose bones. All had the young agent's DNA, and all would appear to be part of his nonexistent 'corpse.'

Then X-ray untied Echo's gelding, Spirit, and led him a considerable distance away from the meteor ejecta mound, headed generally south, back toward the ranch house. There, he tied the horse to a nearby fence post, near a loose span of fencing. He pulled out several appropriate tools from the saddlebags, and dropped them here and there near the fence. The horse's lead rope was deliberately frayed, partway between the halter and where it was tied to the post. Levy—Fox, now—even removed the saddle from Spirit and brought it to the well-hidden Reptoids of Entiyti's security detail, all of whom possessed excellent claws, and who put some light, relatively harmless scratches on the seat and fender of the saddle before Fox and X-ray resaddled Spirit.

The Reptoids came out of hiding, waving their arms and growling.

This had the immediate effect of causing Spirit to spook badly, snapping the much-weakened lead rope and sending the horse back toward the barn at an all-out gallop, lathering as it went—though there were covert human agents following, ensuring the horse's safety, to ease poor Echo's wrenched heart; the boy didn't even get to tell the horse goodbye.

More assistance from the Reptoid bodyguards helped set the next stage for this scenario; copious claw marks were made on the dry ground and the post, including one Reptoid who used the post to strop his claws, much as a big cat might.

One batch of the cloned tissue was thoroughly shredded and scattered around the clawed fence post; cloned blood was splattered all about the area. A couple of small hand bones, likewise cloned from the tissue sample Echo had provided, were dropped near the post, as well.

Then Fox filled a handy trash bag with rocks, while X-ray had Echo strip to his shorts; between the male agents and the various bodyguards, he was then clad in a hodgepodge of too-short suit trousers and too-long alien uniform tunic, though one of the Reptoids had a spare pair of boots that fit pretty well.

The boy's clothing was hung from a hook, then ripped up by Suud himself, and more cloned blood liberally adorned it. The cowboy boots and parts of the shredded clothing were given to Fox, who dragged it some distance away to a rock outcrop, atop the bag of rocks, allowing small bits of cloth to catch on shrubs along the way. Then he left some pieces of cloth—a large, blood-stained piece of plaid shirt, part of a jeans leg, a boot—flinging them around the area. Taking a different tack, as if the initial predator had been scared away by a pack of scavenging coyotes, he dragged the bag of rocks into an open area in the pasture. There, he removed the rocks, handing them to various agents and bodyguards, who returned them carefully to their original locations. The now-decrepit bag was wadded up and shoved in his back pocket. The rest of the tattered clothing was scattered over the area, the remaining boot was left, and a couple of cloned ribs and vertebrae were placed in the center, wrapped in what was left of the shirt and jeans, along with another vial of blood splashed liberally over the lot.

Thus Spirit was sent home alone, and just enough carefully-planted evidence provided for an investigation to conclude that Echo had been 'killed' by some sort of large, vicious predator, then the body scavenged by coyotes.

After that, they all laid low, knowing that the local law enforcement would be arriving soon. Fox and Suud jointly ordered maximum security precautions on the encampment, to include a wide-field cloak. A morose Echo stayed in the cabin assigned to him in Entiyti's spacecraft, sitting on the side of the bed, speaking only when someone else spoke to him first. Concerned, X-ray and Fox both stayed close, keeping the despondent young new agent company. From time to time, Entiyti joined them, and he and Fox shared in telling tales of the wonders of the galaxy and the adventures they had had together. This at least kept the boy's attention, though it did not appear to raise his spirits noticeably.

By the end of the second day following, Alexander Ian Bryant, late of Ozona, Texas, was determined to be dead as the result of a probable cougar attack. Agent Echo of the Pan-Galactic Law Enforcement and Immigration Administration, Division One, was born.

* * *

As Echo lay, quiet within the force dome, his cell phone went off once more with an incoming text alert. It was Omega, checking in again. After a moment, the message popped up on the device's screen.

Hey, Ace. Its me. U there?

But Echo did not respond. After several minutes, another text came in.

Echo? R U there? Answer me, hon.

Echo remained lying silently, not acknowledging the cell phone.

* * *

Omega sat at the controls of the *SchmaltzBlitz* as it flew over Bangkok, staring in dismay at her cell phone.

It's been a little more than four and a half hours, she thought. *And he's not responding. Damn. I had really hoped those respiration techniques would have helped the air last longer than this. Then again,* she considered, glancing at the mission elapsed time clock, *he's already pushing an hour past the point I figured he'd pass out. And he went into it hot—I mean, let's face it, that part of the Outback is basically desert—and wired. So I guess maybe he really did pretty good. I was just hoping for even more.*

"I gotta go faster...somehow," she murmured aloud, studying the flight console for any way she could eke out a few more miles per hour of velocity.

* * *

The priority call from the *SchmaltzBlitz* came into Fox' office, and he answered it immediately, putting it on speaker.

"Fox here, Omega. What's up?"

"Echo's unconscious, Fox."

"He's not answering your pings any more?"

"No."

"What's the maximum time it could be since he passed out?"

"It would be...umm...It's been about an hour and a half since I last pinged him, but he was alert and coherent then, though his reaction times were a bit slow. My initial calculations when he first erected the dome estimated that he'd have passed out sometime between four hours and four and a half hours in the dome, probably closer to four. That said, he admitted his adrenaline was up, but he also told me he was using several methods for keeping his respiration rate low and staying calm."

"And how far past your maximum estimated time to unconsciousness is he? Or IS he past it?"

"Yeah, he's past the max time by...about ten or fifteen minutes." There was a pause. "I should have pinged him more frequently, but based on the last time I did, I thought he might even be awake, still. I had a little bit of a problem right after I called him, and then again after I last texted him anyway, and I only just got it all resolved a little while ago...I hope."

"A problem? What happened? Is there something wrong with the skimmer?"

"No, no, nothing like that. It's pretty simple, really...only it's not. Um, well, it's like this, Fox: My great-circle shortest flight time course took me right over the whole damned lot of the disputed territories that Pakistan, India, and China are fighting over...while flying at spy plane altitudes..."

"Oh farkakt," Fox grumbled, realizing the nature of her problem. "Did they call you?"

"Oh HELL yes. All three. From multiple military bases in each country. And threatened twelve kinds of nasty death, every one of 'em. Including surface to air missiles, and scrambling fighters after me. I think Pakistan actually did scramble some jets, but they couldn't catch up to me, because I was already moving at speed, and they had to accelerate to speed, so I was out of their airspace by the time they could reach my altitude...the few aircraft that COULD reach this altitude. I mean, it isn't like they have the latest state of the art. Well, maybe China, but evidently they didn't have anything useful handy. Which is good, because while it's got the force fields, the airskimmer isn't exactly outfitted for hunting bear. Or, really, defending against one. Or more."

"We'll fix that when you get back. And I'll go ahead and have the other skimmers retrofitted with offensive and defensive weaponry, starting now. Did you give them the code I told you to?"

"Best I could, considering I don't speak Urdu, Hindi, Chinese, Tibetan, Mongolian..." The line was silent for a moment, then Omega added, "Nepal wasn't very happy either, 'cause I was flying FROM Chinese airspace TO Nepalese. DAMN, did I miss having Ace, through all that mess. He coulda talked to 'em and settled the whole thing in nothing flat."

"What about the onboard translator?"

"I dunno. The settings and controls aren't like I'm used to. I THINK I set it right, but the various control towers still had trouble understanding me. I kept getting reports that my comm was breaking up."

"A brokh! Does your instrumentation show any lock-ons?! Where are you now?"

"No, no. It's cool, everything's cool, Fox. I must've outrun 'em. I just left Bangkok in my rear-view mirror. I'm over ocean now, headed for...mm, Borneo, I think. Lemme check...Yeah. I'll be coming up on the island of Borneo in about an hour and a quarter, hour and a half."

"Hallelujah. And then?"

"Then past Bali 'bout half an hour after that, give or take. I should cross the northwest Aussie coast in...about two and a third, two and a half hours, I'm estimating. Another hour or so past that should put me someplace in Echo's vicinity. Once I cross the Aussie coast, I'm gonna start a gradual descent, and then peel outta this compression suit. It's gonna be hot in the Outback, and I'm already plenty tired of wearing the damn thing."

"Okay, so you made it past the danger zone."

"Yeah, but there's gonna be political problems in the aftermath. Once they realized I only spoke English and not any of their languages—well, I speak other languages, just not any of THEIRS—they recognized my American accent and started accusing the U.S. of getting involved in the dispute and spying on 'em. Well, the Pakistanis and Chinese did, at any rate."

"Mm. All right," Fox decided, in some relief. "When I get off here, I'll call the Hong Kong Office, the Delhi Office, and the Dubai Office, and have 'em read respective riot acts to the appropriate people."

"That's good, 'cause it just might stop a bit of the nastiness, generally," Omega replied.

"Yes. Let us hope, anyway. I'll also have our people look over the skimmer's translator when you get back. Perhaps something about the factory settings were off."

"Yeah, you might have it on the translator. Or maybe I just needed more time to read the user's manual on this one. But in the meantime, I'm still three and a half hours out, minimum, and Echo is unconscious. I was sure hoping you could give me some more tips on how I can speed things up here."

"Oh. Well...no. I'm sorry, Omega, we've already done all I can think of to do. And believe me, I've been racking my brains, too. If I came up with anything, I was going to call you straightaway. I suppose, given all you've been dealing with, it would have been bad timing regardless, though. But, other than trying to keep getting a better fix on Echo's locator beacon— which will improve as you get closer to it—"

"I'm already doing that every chance I get. 'Bout every ten minutes, it feels like."

"Then I'm afraid I have nothing more for you, mayn khaverte. I'm sorry."

A heavy sigh came across the comm.

"All right, Fox. Thanks for all you've done already. I'm just...grasping at straws, I guess."

"...When there are no more straws to be grasped," Fox added, and nodded to himself. "I know. I've been there myself."

"Okay. I'm gonna let you go now, so you can go avert World War Three, over in the Himalayas."

"Very good, yung froy. Hang in there."

"I'm not the one I'm worried about."

"I know. Him, too. Fox out."

"Omega out."

* * *

But Echo was not unconscious, not by the clinical definition, at least.

Instead, he was deep into a meditative state, induced by the combination of breath control and memory. External stimuli had been tuned out, and nothing but memory remained.

* * *

A young Echo had stayed through what little negotiations were left; had seen the then-Secretary General of the United Nations brought to the dry lake bed, where he was filled in and signed the interstellar treaty. This treaty would later be ratified by the entire governing body of the Pan-Galactic Alliance as part of the Sydys Concordat, making the Sol System a duly-approved member of the Alliance...with limitations, set by the fact that the populace as a whole was unaware of the existence of such a government.

"We have to handle it delicately," Entiyti had noted to Kofi Annan. "We are full well aware that the planetary population must be duly and properly represented, while at the same time not overlaying onerous matters such as taxation, about which they will have had no say, as one of your superpowers protested at its founding."

"Agreed, and an excellent consideration, in the circumstances," Annan averred. "That same superpower can wield considerable influence in the Security Council, sometimes for just such reasons. It is always best to keep these things in mind. But I am glad," he added, "that your intent is to bring us, as a planet, to the point where we may fully participate in the galactic administration."

"It was never our intention otherwise," Entiyti replied.

"Nor ours," Oboe added. "We have worked from the beginning, not only to protect Earth, but to help make it ready to take its place within the larger galactic community that we began to realize existed."

"If I may assist, you need only ask," Annan declared. "And I will ensure my successors are...apprised of matters. As, I assume, you will of the respective nations in which you operate, as well."

"We will. But be careful what open invitations you issue," Oboe warned with a smile. "I will take you up on them."

And shortly thereafter, it was all over.

* * *

Fox, formerly Franz Levy, emptied his personal quarters in Entiyti's flagship, packing his things into a surprisingly few number of boxes. He was unusually quiet and solemn as he did so.

Then he and Echo joined the other agents of the new Pan-Galactic Division One Agency on the rim of the old crater, watching as three spacecraft lifted off, one by one, and disappeared into the heavens. Moments later, the odd black 'jet' followed; it had proved a shuttlecraft, made of carbon composite fibers, for the Dendroid.

Echo did note, however, something of the same sentiment in Fox's eyes as he felt himself. He moved to stand beside the other man, who still gazed upward, into the darkening sky. Fox glanced down; Echo simply nodded.

"Yeah, me too," the teen said. Fox raised an eyebrow.

"Yeah," he agreed.

* * *

The next few years had passed in a swift, exciting—though sometimes difficult—blur. Echo had been taken away from Texas, as Fox helped find and establish a headquarters in a borough of New York City. There, the Originals, as they came to be called, settled and began building a true organization, a bureau dedicated to bringing Earth into a galactic government, an Agency suited to the task they had been given.

Echo verified—remotely—that his mother had settled back into her clan at the reservation, her financial needs well provided by the proceeds from the 'sale' of the ranch...which he also verified was in good shape and being maintained properly. The cover story was that the new buyers were turning it into an operational 'dude' ranch, with associated guest housing, which latter was being added. In reality it was a safe house redolent of Western legend for visiting offworld dignitaries, and any agents who needed down time, as well as being held ready for Echo to return one day.

Echo had trained hard in a number of different ways, increasing his gym workouts to add various other forms and types of fitness, getting better with weapons, learning alien fighting techniques, becoming a pilot, and more. Soon X-ray was taking the young agent out on increasingly more difficult missions, at Oboe's orders. There was a small celebration among the Originals when Echo turned 18, and another when he hit 21, but otherwise, he stayed busy with Agency work.

Occasionally the young man saw Fox, who had founded and now ran the Diplomacy department—as well as founding and training the Security department—and who was heavily involved in helping to establish various embassies within Headquarters.

The day came when Fox decided that Earth needed representation at a Galactic Council meeting, and X-ray and Echo were tapped to help provide security for that representation. The young man left Earth for the first time, and was boggled by the sight of interstellar space...as well as the full Galactic Assembly, with its myriads of races and worlds.

"This...is cool," he had told Fox, who merely grinned...and ensured that Echo and X-ray were the designated security escort whenever he or Oboe had to go off-planet.

Several years passed for the young man, seemingly in the blink of an eye, and soon he was a strong, capable Division One agent, deadly when crossed in the performance of his duties, gentle and caring—though reserved—when the situation called for it. The strong sense of morality and right with which his parents had raised him stood him in good stead, marking him in the PGLEIA as an honest, incorruptible agent.

When a branch of PGLEIA University was opened on Earth, Echo applied, giving due consideration regarding what he should study. Consequently, and studying around his mission schedule, he obtained dual degrees—Linguistics, following one of his original loves, though rather decidedly expanded; and Diplomacy, which he had decided would be a wise choice in helping him better deal with all kinds of offworlders, with all kinds of backgrounds.

Then one day, Fox requested a private meeting with him.

When he arrived in the Ennead liaison's office, he discovered that Fox was not alone.

Pulgey Entiyti stood there.

"Echo, zun, we have a proposal to put before you," Fox told him.

* * *

"...Are you sure?" Fox pressed.

"Yeah, I am," Echo averred. "Ma is settled on the rez now. She's comfortable and fairly happy. If I were to come back now, it would only unsettle her all over again. I mean, it's been—what? Four years?"

"Five Earth years," Entiyti corrected. "And then a few satellite cycles."

"Months," Fox supplied.

"Those," Entiyti added with a grin.

"Besides, the job has kinda grown on me," Echo said with an answering grin, which shortly sobered into serious thoughtfulness. "I honestly don't think I COULD go back to 'just' working a ranch, not now. Not and be happy, anyway. Maybe...later in life, when I can't do this job any more, it'll be good. But not right now."

"You still planning to continue on with the Masters degree in Linguistics?" Fox wondered.

"I think so, yeah. It's already proven useful, X-ray declares."

"I can see that. All right. Just remember, the release of this tech hasn't been announced yet," Fox reminded him. "Don't tell anyone. Not even X-ray."

"Right. But surely we aren't gonna have to call the damn things, 'Cerebellar Holographic Mnemonic Re-Encoding Induction System devices' every time?"

"Well, that is the official name," Entiyti pointed out. "Or at least, as it translates to English."

"It isn't gonna be any less awkward in any other Earth language," Echo observed. "An' it'll get worse, in some. And the acronym isn't even pronounceable."

"That is its name," Entiyti repeated. "It cannot be helped."

"Yes, Pul, but we'll probably just give it a nickname," Fox said. "Echo is right, that's a mouthful."

"I'm voting for brain bleach," Echo said with another, more mischievous grin.

"I like it!" Fox said, returning the grin.

* * *

Six Earth months later, when the Ennead sanction for Division One agents to use the new—to them—tech was officially announced, Fox briefed the Agency on the device.

"...And its official name is, 'Cerebellar Holographic Mnemonic Re-Encoding Induction System,'" Fox noted in the huge assembly, which was being sent to other Offices around the planet via ciphered, point-to-point, closed-circuit video. "But," he added, "we're just going to call it 'brain bleach.'"

And he shot a surreptitious grin at the young Echo.

Echo grinned from ear to ear.

But he never told anyone, not even X-ray, why.

* * *

Nothing but blackness was visible outside the force dome. The dust storm had managed to coat it in a considerable layer of sand and silt, blocking out all light. The only illumination within came from the tiny operating light on Echo's cell phone, lying by his head.

Finally, the air inside the dome was depleted to the point where not even his altered state could sustain Echo in anything like a conscious, coherent condition.

The memories drifting past his mind's eye faded, and Echo slipped into unconsciousness.

Chapter 7

Omega's craft boomed across the Australian coast near Derby, Western Australia and continued inland, headed toward the westernmost regions of South Australia state. As soon as she crossed the coast, the auto-pilot began a gradual, programmed descent in altitude, calculated to put her at ground level by the time she arrived near Echo's beacon location. At Fox's texted suggestion, she had taken the recorded emergency identification code she had made earlier, that was unique to Division One's chief Alpha Line team, and put it on continuous broadcast; RAAF Curtin, though in caretaker status, was right outside Derby. More, at her altitude, even as she descended, she would pass within easy detection distance of several more Australian Defence Force bases, and neither she nor Fox wanted a repeat performance of the debacle over the Himalayas, especially with the *SchmaltzBlitz* at altitudes reachable by surface-to-air missiles; Echo simply didn't have enough time left for that, and Fox didn't want both members of Alpha One taken out in one fell swoop.

Half an hour after passing over the coast, Omega crossed into the Northern Territory, angling across the southwestern corner. Eleven minutes later, she crossed into South Australia, and put her flight sensors on maximum to ensure she didn't accidentally encounter any standard aircraft. With some considerable relief, Omega also began peeling out of the pressure suit; the compression garment could get extremely uncomfortable when worn over her regular Suit for long periods, and she wished she had taken the time to strip down before donning it. She also began to hone her fix on Echo's location.

* * *

A very silent Fox sat and stared at two tiny blips on the map that currently displayed on his largest wall screen. One was moving across Australia at a swift clip; the other remained frighteningly stationary and unresponsive, in the northwest corner of South Australia state. His forehead was wrinkled in worry.

But there's nothing I can do except wait, he thought. *Dammit, if she doesn't make it to him in time...*

His comm alerted. He glanced at the display in the corner of the screen; it was Lima. He hit the comm button.

"Yes, Lima?"

"Sorry to disturb you, sir. I know you're busy."

Fox glanced at the stack of paperwork sitting, ignored, on the corner of his desk. Then he stared at the screen containing the two blips, and raised a skeptical—and not a little rueful—eyebrow.

"I wouldn't have put it...quite like that, young man, but that's all right. What do you have for me?"

"I thought you'd want to know that the space plane just had a successful launch down at the Cape. A nominal main engine cut-off occurred about three minutes ago, and it should be in a known orbit within the next five or ten minutes."

"It figures; Omega's over Australia now. How long until the media frenzy dies down?"

"Bravo and I are estimating about two hours past orbit call, Fox."

"All right. Have the fastest saucer we've got close to Headquarters, standing by for a sub-orbital hop, in case we need to get medical aid to the Australian Outback in a hurry. Omega should have found him by then, and we'll know what needs doing. And I just may be going along for the ride." He paused. "Also have...have a recovery team standing by, just in case. I... Omega shouldn't have to bring..." Fox drew a long breath. *If she's starting to feel for her partner what I think she might be, she doesn't need to be the one to bring his body back home, if we're not in time.* But he didn't voice the thought.

"...Understood, Fox. We'll...take care of it."

"Thank you, zun."

"I...hope Echo is okay. For all that I wouldn't want to meet him in a back alley on the wrong side of the law, I think he's a really cool guy."

"You're right on both counts, Lima. And I hope so, too."

"You two go way back, don't you? I mean, you're both Originals and all?"

"Yes, we do. I was the first of what later became the Originals to encounter him, at the First Envoy." Fox paused, and shook his head. "He was still little more than a boy then, but with skills and abilities already an equal to most of the other Originals. And he's only gotten better since then. And wiser with age and maturity. Not that he's that old, now."

"I didn't think so, sir. He's...what? In his early to mid-thirties or so?" Lima asked.

Fox smiled; his assistant, Bravo, was only in his mid-twenties, and Lima even younger, having just graduated from a standard Earth university the year before.

"Thereabouts, yes. I'd have to go back and reckon up the years anymore to tell you just how old he is, but that's about right. But that still gives him close to two decades' worth of experience in this job."

"Is..." The young man's voice broke off.

"Go ahead, Lima," Fox murmured, suspecting what was coming.

"Is Omega going to make it in time, sir?"

"I have hopes, Lima. She's already over Australia, and flying like the proverbial bat out of hell. And Echo should still have some time left on the meter. The real question will be how long it takes her to locate him in all that dirt and rock they call the Outback. Especially with who knows how many pounds of dirt dumped on top of his force dome. At least the damned haboob has moved on, according to satellite imagery. I'd hate to think she had to find him in that mess."

"...Would you mind keeping us posted?" Lima wondered, seeming hesitant. He seldom made requests of his supervisor, and Fox knew something was up. He found out what with Lima's next statement. "I swear to you, every last Alpha Line applicant on the planet has either called or been by here in the last few hours, wanting to know what's up. Especially after we put out the call for backup volunteers."

"Yes, I will be happy to keep you apprised, jung khaver."

"Thank you, sir. And...well, Bravo and I just wanna know, too, to be honest."

"Not a problem, zun. I rather figured as much. Echo...and his partner, for that matter, I suppose...they're the sort of people prone to becoming heroes to others. Speaking of updates, I think I'd best check on Omega. I'll pop you messages through the network to keep you apprised."

"That'd be great, sir. Thank you!"

* * *

Omega was indeed flying over Australia like a bat out of hell. Just then, the comm alerted; Omega had an incoming signal from Fox.

"All right, maydele," his voice spoke as soon as she answered, "what have you got?"

"Not a whole lot yet, Fox," Omega replied. "I'm in the northwest corner of South Australia state, trying to home in on Echo's signal."

"Right. You still haven't heard anything from him, have you?"

"Nope. Not a peep." She gnawed her lower lip. "I'm...worried, Fox."

"I know, meyn teyere. Me, too."

"I kinda figured. It isn't like you to call me on a mission, unless you're worried about something."

"You...know me better than I thought, young lady."

"Well," Omega smiled absently, trying to fine-tune the coordinates she was getting for Echo's location, "I tend to pay attention to two kinds of people: those I like and trust, and people I don't trust any farther than I can throw 'em. Either way, that usually means I end up getting some idea how they think. And, well, let's just say you're NOT in the latter category."

There was silence on the comm for several seconds. Finally Fox's voice murmured, "Thank you, Omega. I'm...honored."

"Aw. I dunno that it's that much to feel honored over, Fox. I'm just a rookie."

"Echo wouldn't agree with you. And I don't, either. Somewhat inexperienced, perhaps, but definitely no rookie. And said experience is relative, anyway—I meant what I said to How and Paris the other day."

"Just the same, I—wait! Stand by one!"

"Standing by!"

Omega worked frantically with the sensor instrumentation, then punched a fist in the air.

"THERE we go!" she cried, then grabbed the stick, turning the craft slightly. "Echo, dead ahead!" She broke off and winced. "Well, not DEAD ahead, if you get me."

"Excellent!" Fox exclaimed, ignoring the addendum. "Would you object to putting me back on holovid, so I can virtually 'come along,' Omega? I don't mean to kibitz..."

"Not at all, Fox," Omega said, punching a couple of buttons, and Fox's head formed over the co-pilot's seat. "You and he go way back, I know."

"Yes, we do. About as far back as it's possible for two Division One agents to go, I suppose. I am giving serious consideration to summoning Zebra to my office, in case you need medical advisement, once you find him."

"I won't argue that call in the least, Fox."

"Stand by for a moment, then, while I contact the medlab."

* * *

"...I'm here, Omega," the breathless voice of the assistant chief of Medical sounded in the background, only a few minutes later. "What's the status?"

"Still on approach," Omega answered somewhat absently, as she worked with the sensor controls. "Gimme a minute. Uh, sorry; that was really bad comm protocol, an' sounded rude, to boot. Stand by one, please."

"Shuttin' up," Zebra said, amused, and the hologram of Fox's head grinned for a moment, then grew sober.

"Yes, Omega," he said, "I see it. The signal is still growing stronger."

"Yeah, but I've slowed way the hell down. I'm practically crawling now. The signal's pretty strong already, and I don't wanna overshoot."

Omega brought up a heads-up display that showed current signal strength as compared to the maximum possible signal, and another graph depicting the signal fluctuation with time. A dashed line across the top of the virtual graph depicted maximum strength. The graph showed the most recent data as a moving dot; it almost, but not quite, overlaid the dashed line. She reached out, pinched the display, and spread her fingers, enlarging it; the graph then showed a small and ever-narrowing gap between the dot and the line.

Abruptly the dot merged into one of the dashes, and an alarm went off on the airskimmer's dashboard. Omega smacked a hand down on it, cutting it off.

"Well, we're here," she noted. "But..."

"Echo isn't," Fox observed.

"Not that I can see," Omega agreed.

* * *

"I just don't see any other way, Zebra," Omega told the physician. "I gotta find him before you can tell me how to treat him."

"But we need to get oxygen to him!"

"Hush, bubeleh," Fox murmured. "She knows what's needed. And she's at least as worried and anxious as you are, probably more. Let her concentrate."

"Thanks for the faith in me, Fox," Omega murmured, working frantically to adjust the sensor settings to a finer resolution. "I only hope it's as well placed as you seem to think. Otherwise, I've lost the best friend I've ever had." *Not to mention the man I've fallen in love with,* she added mentally. *Even if I know he'll probably never feel the same way.*

"I'm sorry," Zebra murmured. "Fox is right, of course. And...I'm not there to see what needs doing, and you are."

"Well, seeing is apparently the operative term," Omega said. "Hang on...there. That should do it."

"Do what?" Zebra wondered. "And where exactly ARE you? All I see is a bunch of red sand and rock."

"I'm in what's called the Great Victoria Desert in the Australian Outback, Zebra. I followed Echo's emergency locator beacon here. Only I can't see any sign of Echo, or his force dome," Omega explained. "Which means it's probably buried in one 'a these little dunes that's all over, especially after the dust storm came through. But I could dig for days and never find his dome. So I gotta play it smart. I just set up an infrared scanner in the sensor suite—"

"Does it have configuration recognition capability?" Zebra interrupted.

"Not really, from what I can tell," Omega said. "The airskimmer is really new to me, though, so it might have it and I just don't know how to access and set it. But what it DOES have is the ability to recognize the SIZE of a target. And since I roughly know Echo's size, I programmed it in."

"You got him?!" Zebra exclaimed.

"...No," Omega murmured, downcast. "I'm gonna have to run a search pattern."

"I'd recommend a spiral from your current location, yung froy," Fox said.

"Good. You just confirmed what I was thinking."

"And don't forget to check for radiation."

"Radiation?!" Zebra squeaked.

"Calm down, bubeleh. That was one of the main reasons Echo decided to use the force dome as a shelter. But we need to determine how badly the area is contaminated, and run a decontamination if necessary, before we extract him."

"I'm already on it, Fox," Omega murmured absently, working with the sensor controls. "If we got rad, though, I dunno how to handle this."

"I do, and I can instruct you from here. It's one reason I wanted to watch over your shoulder."

"Good. You're welcome to do that any time. Especially when I'm in a craft that's new to me, but not to you."

"All right. I'll shut up and watch while you work, mayn khaverte. Speak up if you have questions, or need anything."

"Wilco, Fox."

* * *

Omega set up an automated spiral-pattern search on the auto-pilot, dividing the path into segments and instructing the sensor array to run a sweep of each segment in turn. Then she sat back in the pilot's chair and drummed her fingers on the console while she gnawed at her lips.

"Calm down, mayn teyere," Fox murmured.

"Mm? Oh. What, is Zebra gettin' fidgety back there?" Omega wondered.

"No, I meant you, Omega."

"Me? Oh, I'm tryin', Fox, believe me," Omega replied, her eyes never leaving the virtual sensor display, which now depicted the ground beneath her craft as it appeared in infrared. "I'm actually sittin' still, see. And you have no idea how much effort THAT'S takin'. Unfortunately, the field of view on the IR sensor isn't very big, so this could take a while. Maybe TOO long."

The seconds ticked by into minutes as Omega continued the search for her missing partner. The minutes mounted up surprisingly—and frighteningly—fast.

* * *

"Omega, how long did you say Echo had?" a subdued Zebra wondered, sitting next to Fox in his office and trying not to fidget, when the search reached and surpassed the half-hour mark, and kept going.

"Nine, maybe as much as nine and a half, hours," Omega's voice responded.

"And how long has it been?" Zebra continued.

"Um..." Omega's image glanced at the mission elapsed time counter on the control console. Even in the holovid, they could see her face pale. "About nine hours."

"A brokh!" Fox cursed.

"What he said," Zebra whispered, then continued in a louder voice. "We still have another half an hour, dear."

"I know," Omega said, voice faint. "Max."

"Keep going," Fox ordered. "How much radiation is showing up?"

"Barely any," Omega noted after a quick check. "Maybe one or two percent above background."

"How do you know what the background should be?" Zebra wondered.

"I grabbed some readings over Western Australia and the Northern Territory as I flew over," Omega explained. "As it turns out, my flight path took me right over the Theseus uranium mine just south of Lake Mackay, and I was able to catch some readings there, too."

"And how does it compare?" Zebra asked.

"Well, like I said, here we're only a couple percent over the background readings I got. And the Theseus region had a lot higher background count even than I'm getting here. That said, there's a whole lot of minerals in this entire region, including a LOT of uranium mines, so the background levels are a little higher than they would be back there in New York City."

"Can you pop me the readings?" Zebra wondered.

"Sure. Hang on." Omega hit a couple of keystrokes. "Okay, data away. I have the files labeled so it shouldn't be hard to figure out what's what."

Zebra's holographic head looked down, just as a ding sounded in the background. "Okay, got it," she confirmed. "Opening it up now."

The little long-distance group was silent for a few moments, while Omega watched the sensor readings and Zebra studied the radiation level data, and Fox split his attention between the two. Finally Zebra looked up.

"This looks good," she said. "I'm thinking your assessment is that there's no contamination from the nuclear test sites southeast of your location?"

"I'm not seeing anything significant that would lead me to think otherwise," Omega confirmed. "What do you think, Zebra?"

"I'm in agreement with that," the physician decided. "I don't see any special need for decontamination. I mean, at this point, Echo had been slogging around out there for an hour or so, right? And probably catching whatever was there anyhow."

"Right."

"So nothing unusual to worry about. When we find him, just go dig him out."

"Roger that." Omega sighed. "WHEN seems to be the operative word."

"Indeed," Fox murmured.

* * *

Just then, the sensor suite let out a startlingly loud bleat as the detector alert went off. Omega nearly jumped out of her skin, then slapped at the control to shut off the audio.

There, on the heads-up display, was a large warm object shaped loosely like the letter S, or perhaps an Arabic numeral 2.

"I got him!" Omega exclaimed.

* * *

"You need to dig the dome out first, Omega," Fox said. "Otherwise,

185

when the dome drops, all that dirt and sand will half-bury him."

"On it," Omega said, unstrapping and running to the stowage, where she dug around for a few moments, emerging with a camp shovel. "When I found this during my load-lightening efforts, I made sure NOT to dump it overboard."

"You anticipated this," Fox noted. "Very good."

"Yeah, those geology studies come in handy every once in a while. You want me to grab the camera and bring y'all with?"

"No, we have a decent view out the windscreen," Fox decided. "As long as it isn't right under the airskimmer, we can watch."

"It isn't. I backed up a little bit and set 'er down."

"Good. Then GO."

"Gone."

* * *

Omega emerged at speed from the *SchmaltzBlitz* with the camp shovel, unfolding it as she went. Then she headed straight for the dune she believed held the dome, and thrust the shovel into it. There was an odd, muffled sort of clank, and she nodded to herself, then began scooping sand and dust for all she was worth. A kind of mini dust storm formed around her frantically-shoveling form.

Soon a pale yellowish force dome revealed itself, tinted slightly orange by the residue of dust still lying on it.

Inside, Echo lay, silent and unmoving. His face and hands were pale and slightly bluish.

"Oh, shit," Omega whispered.

She turned and bolted for the airskimmer's hatch.

* * *

"All right, Fox, I'm gonna try to drop the force dome," Omega declared, sitting back down at the pilot's chair without bothering to strap in. "I've never tried to hack it before, so I'll follow the procedure you laid out for me during my flight over. You watch me and make sure I do everything right."

"Of course, meyn teyere."

Omega brought up the computer, tied it into the communications system, and commenced hacking. The force dome was designed to be adjustable, within limits; it could be programmed to be gas-permeable, or to allow nothing in or out save for very narrow bands of electromagnetic frequencies. These bands included visible light and the specific roving-frequency band used by the agents' decidedly non-standard—at least, by terrestrial terms—cell phones. In a pinch, even those openings could be closed, and in such an event, the tiny but powerful force field was proof against even a nuclear blast—though they tended not to survive the blast, since the energies had to be diverted somewhere, and the central unit typically overheated and shorted out.

That was not the case here, however; Echo's force dome had had no problem withstanding the haboob. And he had left the specific electromagnetic windows open, knowing it would be the only way to lower the dome once he lapsed into hypoxic unconsciousness.

So Omega used that transmission window to hack Echo's cell phone, according to specific and HIGHLY classified instructions that Fox had given her, and reserved for just such incidents as this.

It took several minutes, with Fox's hologram looking over her shoulder, but finally she looked up, a grim smile on her face.

"I'm in," she said.

"Good. Now use his phone as a relay station, and send the remote command for the dome to drop," Fox said. "Just like I showed you...however many hours ago it was, now."

"On it."

Moments later, the yellow dome dissolved into nothingness. There was a reddish puff, as its disappearance dislodged the dust that had been on its surface.

"Go get him!" Zebra cried.

Omega sprinted for the hatch.

* * *

Omega dropped to her knees beside the unmoving body of her partner. She snatched up his prized dome controller and his cell phone in one hand, shoving them both into her pocket, while reaching for his carotid artery pulse with the other.

"Where is it, where is it...c'mon, Ace, don't do this to me, honey...c'mon...THERE!" she cried, triumphant. Then she shook her head. "But WOW, is it slow and weak."

She turned toward the cockpit window and gave the watching dual-headed hologram a thumbs-up, then frowned, shook her head, and shrugged.

Then she rolled him fully onto his back, hooked her arms under his shoulders, and began to drag him toward the waiting airskimmer hatch.

* * *

"He's alive," Fox murmured, releasing a pent-up breath he hadn't even realized he had been holding.

"Yeah, but he's not in the greatest shape, according to my experienced eye," Zebra pointed out. "And Omega agrees with me, judging by that sign language."

"Believe it or not, he's been through worse. And still continued his mission. However, I may have to bring him back and put him in your hands, and send Alpha Two out with Omega to finish this mission, though. If we can revive him fairly quickly, do you think he can last long enough for Omega to take the lead and finish the mission, rounding up that damned Glu'g'ik?"

"I dunno yet. I'm not willing to buy off on that until I've got a lot more data, like vital signs, and some indication that the man hasn't suffered hypoxic brain damage," Zebra hedged.

"Fair enough," Fox said.

No brain damage, Fox thought. *Not that. Adonai have mercy.* He crossed his fingers beneath the desk.

* * *

Omega managed to manhandle Echo into the *SchmaltzBlitz* and lay him on the deck. Echo had his Suit jacket in his arms, and they were locked around it, so she didn't even need to go back for anything.

"Get the medscanner and send me vitals and a cardio strip," Zebra ordered.

"Yes, ma'am." Omega grabbed the full shipboard medikit from its stowage container, which she had placed nearby earlier, dropped it on the deck beside Echo, and sat down next to it, cross-legged. She opened it and

188

commenced yanking out equipment, but the medscanner was near the top, and she activated it and ran it over Echo's body, setting it to relay the data through the skimmer's communications console.

"Okay, got the vitals," Zebra noted. "They ain't great, but they'll do for now. Lay the scanner on his chest, then hit the red heart button and leave it there. Oh, and see about loosening his clothing a bit. Take his shoes and socks off, undo his belt, things like that. He's already ditched the tie, and opened collar and shirt cuffs, so that's good. Once I get the EKG strip, go ahead and unbutton the front of his shirt. I want skin showing in case we need to hit him with a shock. And it won't hurt to help him cool down a bit, either."

Omega obeyed, and while the scanner was sending an EKG back to Headquarters, she commenced untying Echo's dress shoes. As soon as she pulled them off, they dumped small piles of sand onto the deck. *I dunno if that's from where he was slogging through the stuff, or from me dragging him over to the skimmer,* she thought in bleak amusement. *Or maybe a little of both. I'll clean it up later.*

She grabbed the toes of his socks and pulled them off his feet, then unbuckled his belt and unfastened the button on his trousers fly...but did not proceed farther on that front.

As soon as the medscanner bleeped its completion of the EKG, she set it aside and swiftly unbuttoned Echo's shirt as well, pulling the tails loose from his trousers and spreading it wide to allow his still-hot body to cool. By that time, Zebra had studied the medical data.

"Look inside the kit and get out one of the pre-loaded pent-ox hypos," she ordered.

Omega dug around inside the kit, located the medication container, and hunted until she found the pent-ox. She held up the osmosive micro-pore hypodermic syringe and looked at it.

"How much?" she asked.

"For Echo, set the dial on 3x," Zebra replied. "Pump it straight into his chest. Left or right side, it doesn't matter. Just not over the heart."

Omega set the dosing dial, then pressed the needle-less flat-tipped syringe against Echo's right breast and hit the plunger button. There was a soft hiss, but otherwise the unconscious man showed no reaction.

"Now fish out a hypo of Anuvia and shoot that into the side of his neck. Five cc's. It'll help alleviate the effects of the anoxia, and it'll be with the pent-ox in the kit."

"Got it." Omega obeyed without question.

"Put the medscanner back on his chest, and hit the heart button again, only hold it down for three seconds," Zebra commanded.

"What does that do?" Omega asked as she followed instructions.

"Gives me a continuous heart monitor. Go back into the medications pack and look for the pre-loaded kelbixlun. Should be close to where the pent-ox compound was. Oh, and if you can find the surgical scissors, grab 'em, in case we need to slice up his trousers to get to the big muscles in his thighs."

"What's kelbixlun?" Omega asked as she went hunting through the pharmaceuticals.

"It's a Kodatin-developed variant on epinephrine that doesn't cause the vessel constriction in the rest of the body," Zebra explained. "That can be damaging to the brain and other organs, such as kidneys and whatnot, because it restricts the oxygen flow to them in favor of the heart, and we do NOT need that here. I only want just enough to give Echo a light kick in the glutes."

"Oh, I get it." Omega nodded, finally coming up with the requested galactic medication. "Here," she said, holding it up. "What do I do with it?"

"Good. Set it for a one-tenth milligram dose, then pull his shirt off his shoulder, and pump it into his arm at the shoulder, into the deltoid."

"One-tenth milligram, into the shoulder...now," Omega said, administering the medication.

"Aaaand THERE we go," Zebra noted. "That just kicked him into gear."

"Was he in arrest, bubeleh? Or fibrillation?" Fox's voice murmured from the background; Zebra had taken over the holovid comm.

"No, but he had ratcheted himself down so low, the pent-ox wasn't doing as much for his blood oxygen as it should have, because it was circulating too slowly."

"Does his heart still look good?" Omega wondered. "I know epinephrine can sometimes cause irregularities, but you said..."

"That's exactly why I had you set the scanner to monitor the heart, and another reason why I wanted to use the kelbixlun," Zebra soothed. "No, he looks fine. Note how his color is warming up? He's gone from white with blue undertones to a warmer pink."

Thank God, Omega thought, fervent. *Now if everything else...like the gray matter in his cranium...is okay...*

* * *

Hallelujah, Fox thought from behind his desk, as he watched his lover and his newest recruit work on one of his oldest friends. *Now if there hasn't been any brain damage, he might just make this.*

* * *

After a few moments, as the color started to return to Echo's face and his respiration rate slowly increased, he stirred, then let out a sound that was a mingled cross between a groan, a moan, and a snort. Then he mumbled something that, given its vaguely annoyed tone, Omega was rather glad to find unintelligible.

I hope he's not mad at me, she thought, biting her lip. *I did the best I could with what I had to work with. So did Fox. Nah. Ace won't be mad. He knew the score going in. I'm just sensitive because...well, just because.*

Finally Echo emitted another grunt. Then he sniffed several times and, without opening his eyes, he murmured, "Meg? That you?"

"Right here, Ace," she told him, laying a soothing—and orienting—hand on his arm and keeping her voice low and soft, in case he proved sensitive to it. "How'd you know?"

"Good," was all he said for a bit. Omega noticed, though, that he was sucking in long, deep breaths, so she figured he was just resting and trying to get his oxygen intake back to something comfortable. Just then, Zebra inquired about that same thing.

"Echo? This is Zebra. I'm on the comm, and I've been advising Omega how best to care for you. I notice your respiration is a little rapid, and anything but shallow, right now. You're sucking air in like you've been running. Do we need to administer a little more of the pent-ox compound?"

"I wouldn' argue," he said, sounding a little breathless. "But I think I'll be okay in a minute."

"Omega, would you—"

"How much?" she asked, picking up the appropriate hypo.

"Take it down to 1x, and we'll do it again if he needs it," Zebra decided. "Into the other side, this time. Take it high and wide to avoid the heart."

Omega pumped the oxygenating medication into Echo's chest, and they waited.

"That's better," Echo declared after a couple of minutes.

"He still sounds breathless, Zebra, just a little," Omega observed.

"Yeah, I agree. Go back to the right side and administer another 1x dose."

Within a couple of minutes, Echo's breathing had stabilized at his normal rhythm. Two minutes after that, he tried to push up to a seated position.

"No ya don't, Ace," Omega said, placing a hand on his upper chest and leaning on him to keep him prone. "Let's just stay right there for a little bit."

"I'm okay, baby," he protested.

"Let me be the judge of that," Zebra countered. "I want to make sure that noggin of yours is all right, after going so long with depleting oxygen. You stay right where Omega put you until I say otherwise. Omega, are there any bedclothes on board? A pillow, at least? Maybe an emergency blanket?"

"There isn't a sleeping cabin or anything; the skimmer's too small for that. It's barely big enough for Echo to lie on the deck. But I think I kept one bedroll for him, if I can remember where I stuck it when I dumped the tea an' junk overboard," Omega decided.

"'Tea and junk'?" Echo wondered, puzzled.

"Omega did her rendition of the Boston Tea Party, Echo," Fox explained, "by way of lightening the skimmer, to increase speed. I had her put everything she could on the antigrav pallet, activate the locator beacon, heave it out the airlock, and sent some agents out to retrieve it. Got the word it was snagged, Omega, about...um, four hours back or so. I meant to tell you, but...things have been busy."

"Good. Thanks, Fox...for everything," she told the Director, before turning to her partner. "You gonna stay put, Ace?"

"Do I have to?" The male Agent looked vaguely sulky.

"YES!" three voices chorused.

"And that's an order," Fox added.

"A MEDICAL order," Zebra appended.

Everyone—including two who were holographic images—looked at Omega. Her eyebrows rose, and she shrugged, throwing her hands in the air.

"I got no authority here," she admitted. "But I'm bettin' right now, if I had to, I could probably make you stay put, given what you just went through. Of course, then I'd have to turn myself in to Fox for insubordination..."

"No, you won't," Fox declared. "Keep him there, Omega. That's an order, too."

Echo pulled a face.

"Then I guess I'll stay put," he capitulated.

* * *

"...Well, based on those analyses, I'd say he likely doesn't have any brain damage from the oxygen deprivation," Zebra concluded. "Though why, I have no idea. Oh, he might have some transitory, minor stuff, like a glitchy memory for a bit, but he seems to be okay. And the medscanner verifies that."

"Good," Omega murmured, sounding immensely relieved, and Echo shot her a glance that managed to be concerned, slightly shamefaced, and sheepish, all at the same time.

"Between some of the stuff my Shiitsooyee—uh, my Apache grandfather—taught me when I was growing up, and some of the techniques I've learned from agents in other Divisions, I was able to kinda crank down the furnace," Echo explained. "It doesn't work indefinitely, but it enabled me to last longer than I might have otherwise, I think. It at least gave Meg, here, a little wiggle room."

"Yeah, it did, that," Omega agreed.

"But I STILL want you reporting to me as soon as you set foot in

Headquarters," Zebra dictated. "I'm going to run a full cerebral scan on you, just to make sure."

"Aw, I—"

"He'll be there, Zebra, I swear," Omega interrupted Echo's comment. Echo shot a glance at her, then another at Zebra's hologram, and apparently decided to shut up. "Now, what do we need to do? Stay here for a while, and then head home, so you can see to him? What do we do about the Glu'g'ik running amok?"

"Well, the reports I'm getting show she's still rumpusing about Australia," Fox began, "though she's slacked off some—"

"Why?" Omega asked.

"No idea. But at the very least," Fox said, "unless Zebra says otherwise, it ensures you have time for Echo to rest and recover a bit."

"And that sounds good to me," Zebra noted. "How long will it take you to get to the Sydney Office from there, Omega?"

"Hang on a sec." Omega rose from the deck and stepped over to the control console, pulling up some readouts without bothering to sit down. "Mm. 'Bout an hour, give or take," she estimated.

"No, baby," Echo corrected. "It's well over a thousand miles to Sydney from these parts. It'll take us several hours at maximum spee..." His voice trailed off as he saw her raise an eyebrow and fold her arms. He glanced at the holographic image and saw Fox do the same thing. "Um, then again..."

"But I want to give Echo a chance to rest in some good, full-oxygen air," Omega continued as if she'd never been interrupted. She shot him a slight grin, however.

"Believe me, I'm already enjoying the opportunity," he told her, returning the grin with interest.

"Fox, how fast can you get ME to the Sydney Office? I'd like to maybe look Echo over in person before letting him back out in the field," Zebra added. "And me going there keeps 'em closer to where the perp is operating, than if I had 'em come back here. AND the Sydney Office will have a full-up medlab, with all the equipment for me to have a proper look-see."

"Umm." Echo and Omega heard a faint, irregular tapping sound, and knew Fox was consulting transport schedules and other such information on his computer desktop. "All right, there. We finally have a space plane in orbit, and the media has generally settled down. We know the orbit, so we can avoid it, which is a good thing over all; it has improved optical cameras, and we don't want to get in its field of view by accident—but all the media will be looking for it in its proper orbit, not in more random places in the sky. So. I've got a suborbital hop scheduled for you, Zebra. You'll have just enough time to fetch your travel kit and your personal medical kit, and get to the Penn Station hangar via tube, bubeleh. Plus I'm scheduling you some extra time on the other end to meet your counterpart and get set up, before you have to check out Alpha One. Echo, son, you're off duty until Zebra says otherwise. Omega, you're not; you have three hours to get Echo rested a bit, fed, hydrated, and to the medlab at the Sydney Office. Zebra will be waiting for Alpha One there."

"Yes, sir," three voices said in unison.

"Meanwhile, Ace," Omega continued, "let me go get that bedroll and get you as comfy as I can. The *SchmaltzBlitz* doesn—"

"The WHAT?!" Echo exclaimed, in patent shock. "Greased Lightning? Tell me you didn't."

Omega, Fox, and Zebra all broke up laughing.

* * *

"But Meg, baby, I'm fine," Echo protested, from his position on the deck, now lying on a foam pallet and draped with a lightweight coverlet made of some silk-like fabric, a couple of pillows under his head—though he tried to push up to a seated posture...until he saw the look of warning in his partner's eyes. He raised his own eyebrows in surprise.

"I believe you, Ace," Omega said, folding her arms again. "But that whole mess still took it out of you. We have time, for once. Why, I don't know, and I'm sorry for Australia, but our perp has all but gone nuts, rampaging around the continent. From the latest report I got from Fox, nobody died...yet...though it was a near thing for a couple people. And they still aren't sure of a few more, that are in critical condition."

"Shit! You're kidding. She must have wondered where you were, and started creating a diversion to try to keep you busy and me in the backside of Australia, while she made off with the goods."

"That sounds probable. She must not have realized how bad she messed me up for a little while, there."

"You're probably right. She doesn't have a read on you."

"Yeah. But in a way I'm glad, 'cause it gives you and me a breather when we most need it. Don't worry. Fox is monitoring the situation out of the Sydney Office pretty closely, and will notify me if it looks like the Glu'g'ik has gone elsewhere."

"You."

"Yeah, me. I'm on duty; you're not. What, after all this, you don't trust me to be capable of handling it?"

"Aw. No, I didn't mean it like that. I...I'm just not quite used to..." Echo broke off and ran a hand through his hair. "No, baby, you're perfectly capable. I guess, in the couple years since we lost X-ray...then we brought Romeo on...then Romeo switched partners and I became the department chief, then we brought you on...well, I kinda got used to being the lead dog. Even when I'm not, always. Be patient with me; it might take me a while to stop doing that." He shrugged. "Okay. I'm off duty; you're in charge."

"Good. But that doesn't mean I might not be asking you for advice or direction, Ace, so don't go feelin' useless or something. You're still the lead dog for the partnership and the department, an' I got no problem with that; but you gotta trust me to take the ball and run once in a while. And we still gotta figure out where the next whatsis will be, anyway, so we can't really get back on the case until we determine where we're going. And that's kinda your job, because Houdini fanboy an' all, which means you need to be rested, with a clear noggin."

"Oh. You got a point there..."

"Right. So. Kick back and rest a bit, and suck in some good air for a change."

"I have been, and I still am," he pointed out. "Besides, I'm not the one who barfed her guts out and needed carrying to the medlab."

"I'm better now," Omega responded, raising a platinum eyebrow in challenge. "I DID have a really good nap, AND good food to replace what I lost. Though I gotta admit that the intervening...what? Ten, eleven hours?

Yeah, that sounds about right. Those might have been just a wee bit stressful."

"All the more reason, then, for—" Echo broke off as Omega held up a quelling hand.

"I know that. Now, I put some substantial snackies there beside you, plenty of calories within easy arm's reach, along with several 1-liter bottles of water for you. Also, as you'll note, I have one of those full-nutrient protein bars and a bottle of water for myself, as well...'cause I'm HUNGRY! So if you'll stay there and rest for a while, and knock back some of those snackies and the water, I might actually go along with you and sit here in the pilot's seat, kick off my shoes, put my feet up in the copilot's seat, and try to take a nap, too."

Echo cocked his head and studied her up and down for a moment, seeing the tautness about the blue eyes, and the way she had to force her shoulders back to keep them straight. *And chances are,* he considered, *she got out of a hospital bed to come chasing after me. So...yeah. I owe her this. And then some.*

Then he reached for a package of candy-coated, chocolate-covered peanuts and a bottle of water, without saying another word.

* * *

Seeing Echo capitulate, Omega sat down in the pilot's chair and allowed herself to slump in relief, truly relaxing for the first time in many hours. She opened the protein bar and her own bottle of water, sipping and nibbling until they were gone, taking her time and not wolfing it down.

In the meanwhile, she watched as Echo, without another word of protest, leaned back against the pillows and tucked away the peanut candies, a bag of chips, two protein bars, and three bottles of water. Two more protein bars, another bag of chips, and two packs of chocolate candies still lay in a little pile beside him, flanked by two more bottles of water. *He can eat those later, if he needs 'em,* she decided.

"You never answered my question," she noted then.

"What question?" Echo wondered, looking up.

"When you first came to, on the deck. You knew it was me without ever opening your eyes. I asked you how you knew. But you never said."

197

"Oh, that. I was so busy sucking in fresh air I completely forgot. It was your perfume."

"Oh! Was it—I bet it was too strong, after your being stuck in that stuffy little dome for hours. I'm sorry."

"No, it wasn't too strong. You don't wear a whole lot, so it isn't gonna be strong. But I'm thinking, judging by where your voice was coming from, you were leaning over me, at least a little."

"Yeah, I was. Zebra and I had been monitoring your vitals and junk. Plus I was pumping hypos into you, in various places on your chest, neck, and shoulders."

"Kinda figured. So I was in a position to get a good whiff of it, and I recognized it. And since I've never smelled anyone else wearing anything like it, I figured it had to be you."

"Oh, okay. Yeah, I have a little fragrance boutique out on the West Coast make me up some special stuff. Been doing it for years."

"But...doesn't that mean they know who...?" Echo wondered, concerned for security.

"Nah." Omega grinned. "After I came on board with the Agency and my birth identity was declared dead, I contacted 'em with a different name, and explained I was 'a friend of Dr. McAllister's, and regretted to inform them,' blah blah. Then I asked if they could make up a perfume SIMILAR TO the one I used to wear, so that 'the new me' could wear it. Because by then, I'd thought of a couple things I wanted to tweak, anyway. The concept was, I was a friend who had enjoyed Megan's fragrance and wanted one similar, especially since she was passed on, to remember her by. So they worked with me, and that's what I use now."

"Cool. And good work on keeping the whole secret identity thing... secret."

"Thanks."

"Can I be curious?"

"About what?"

"What's the name of the stuff? The particular perfume, I mean."

"Only if you promise not to laugh."

"Huh?" Echo wondered, furrowing his brows. "Why is that even a consideration?"

"Because the perfumerie thought it would be cute to name it based on the fact that I was an astronomer and astronaut. So they named it, 'Heavenly Bodies.'"

Echo snorted. "It fits."

"Yeah, which is why I didn't ask 'em to change it. Besides, I think they'd have been...I dunno...offended. So...do you like it?"

"Like what? The name?"

"No. The, um, the perfume."

"Ah." Echo shrugged. "I guess so. I never really thought that much about it. It's kinda...you."

"Oh. Um, okay," she murmured, hiding her disappointment at his lack of enthusiasm. *But I guess it's just a guy thing,* she decided. *I never met a guy who was much interested in perfume. It would have been nice if he'd liked it, though. I mean, at least it might have meant...*She brought herself up short. *Give it up, girl. It's a moot point. Besides, you got business to attend to.* She took a bite of her protein bar, then quickly sipped some water; for some reason, it suddenly tasted like sawdust.

When they were finished eating, Omega gathered up the wrappers and empty bottles and took them to the recycler in the rear of the skimmer. By the time she got back, Echo was standing up, still in his bare feet.

"What do you think you're doing?" she demanded to know, hands on hips.

"Um," he said, face turning a dusky red. "Three liters of water. Eyeballs 're starting to float."

"Oh," she said, grinning slightly. "Okay. Good; I got you rehydrated. Zebra gave me express orders about that, once we got you properly oxygenated. So go dump the excess. But come back here and rest when you're done." She made sure there was no mistaking her tone: it was an order. *To my superior, granted,* she thought. *But again, Fox specified he's on sick leave, I'm on duty, and that duty right now is taking care of him. And damned if I won't.*

"Yes, ma'am," the department chief murmured, uncharacteristically meek, apparently having finally grasped the temporarily-altered chain of command. "You're still gonna rest, too, though, right?"

"Yeah, I was planning on putting my feet up and taking a cat nap as soon as I got sittin' down."

"Okay. Just making sure."

"Why? You worried about me?"

"A little," he admitted. "I didn't really let you finish out your rest in London and all. I...just wanna make sure you're okay, too."

"I was starting to drift up from sleeping when your alert came in," Omega told Echo. "So I wouldn't have been asleep much longer anyway... maybe five minutes, max. And when I did wake up, I felt fine. Jig wanted to keep me, but I flat refused, and Fox backed me up. Alpha Line and all."

"So why are you so tired now?"

"Um, maybe because I've been flyin' hell bent for leather for hours? Not to mention, negotiating with some hotheads around the Himalayas that thought I was a spy plane and wanted to shoot me down."

"Oh. Shit. Well, yeah, fair enough. Okay. Be back in a couple minutes."

"Go hit the head before you explode. I don't wanna have to clean THAT up. Let alone explain to Fox why the *SchmaltzBlitz* reeks like a Bourbon Street alley on Ash Wednesday."

Echo snorted on his way out of the flight deck. Omega grinned in his wake.

* * *

Echo took his time ambling back to the little head—because, though he was loath to admit it, he did still feel a bit limp—where he relieved a protesting bladder. Then he sighed and took a long look at himself in the mirror as he washed his hands.

"Well, you've looked better, I guess, Echo, ol' boy," he decided. "I see why Meg's been worried. I still look too pale, even despite all the sun I caught before the dust storm moved in. I'm really glad I take after Ma's, uh, Mom's side of the family, or I'd look like a lobster. Not to mention the dark circles under my eyes, and the brick-red coating over all. I need a shower." *And she just might be right about needing a nap, too,* he considered, feeling bone-tired weariness wash over him. *Though like hell am I gonna admit it.*

Still, if it gets her to rest while I do, hey.

He dried his hands, then headed back to the flight deck area.

Omega, necktie and collar loosened, slouched deep in the pilot's seat, her sock feet propped in the adjacent copilot's seat; her jacket was draped across the back of that seat. Her shoes were under her chair, apparently dropped wherever they had fallen, since one was turned on its side; her head lolled on a tiny travel pillow she had found somewhere. She was sound asleep.

Echo tiptoed across the deck to his bedroll, where he stretched out, opened another bottle of water and sipped on it briefly, then capped and set it aside, and slid down into his reasonably comfortable excuse for a bed.

Moments later, he, too, was asleep.

* * *

Omega had wisely set an alarm to wake her when it was time to check in with Fox and head out for Sydney. They both woke up as she reached for the switch to kill the alarm, and stretched simultaneously.

"Umm, that's better," Echo decided. "A LOT better."

"Urgh," was all Omega said, rolling her shoulders and twisting her head from side to side.

"Uh-oh," Echo noted, seeing what she was doing. "Pilots' seats are designed for alertness, not sleeping, huh?"

"I've had worse, and I've had better Ace," she murmured. "I'll be okay. I do feel better for the down time, but my neck and back are a little kinked."

"Well, I'm still considered off duty, but I might can do something with your neck," he offered. "You know, rub it a little bit. If I wasn't on Director-mandated medical leave, I'd offer to fly for you."

"Oh. Um, yeah, tell ya what," Omega decided. "Let me get a course plotted and filed, plug it into the auto-pilot and get us into the air, then I'll take you up on that, provided you still feel up to it by that point. The idea of a neck rub sounds pretty good about now."

"I'm feeling essentially back to normal now, baby. How long were we out?"

"I gave us about an hour, after we finished eating," she informed him, already bringing up the location display to determine flight path. "Little bit more, actually; say an hour an' twenty, to allow for unwinding in case we had trouble relaxing. If you're doing good, while I'm plotting this...and I might add, I'm really glad you taught me to fly the T-bird...why don't you grab the mini-vac and clean up the piles of sand on the deck?"

"Okay. I was wondering how those got there, anyway."

"Your shoes," Omega replied, punching in coordinates to the onboard computer. "Zebra wanted 'em off, and when I pulled 'em off, about a sand-bag-full dumped onto the deck, out of each one. I kinda figured it was from where I dragged you on board the *SchmaltzBlitz*. I had my arms under your shoulders, see, so your heels were dragging..."

"Oh, I get it." Echo turned on the tiny vacuum cleaning device and sucked up the sand, then emptied the debris container into the chute that would dump it back outside. "I got a little in there when I was trying to head for Coober Pedy, too. Like about a bucket each. Sorry about that."

"About what? The sand?"

"Well, yeah...but no; I mean I'm not exactly a lightweight, when it comes to moving an unconscious body."

"Meh. I managed. All that gym work, ya know." She waved a dismissive hand. "Make sure all the sand is outta your shoes, shake out your socks, and shove 'em all on, then come strap in. I'm ready to take off."

"Strap in?" Echo said, sticking his sockless feet into his unlaced shoes and sliding into the co-pilot's seat. He grabbed for the five-point harness and buckled himself into the seat.

"Yup," Omega said. "Hang on."

She lifted off the ground and hovered for a few seconds, then pushed the stick forward and took off at speed, accelerating at just over 2 Gs, headed steeply up and toward the east. Echo's eyes widened in surprise, and he gasped, "WHAT did you DO to it?!"

Omega gave him a wicked grin.

"Fox helped," was all she said in answer.

* * *

"Yeah, much to my surprise, all that biofeedback and crap that Echo did worked, and worked well. I see no sign of brain damage, or anything

202

else. Apparently he's just fine," Zebra decided, as Echo shrugged into his shirt. As her partner hadn't had to completely disrobe, Omega sat in a corner of the examination-slash-hospital room in a visitor's chair, and at Zebra's statement, she grabbed a handful of the braid on top of her head, and slumped. Echo and Zebra both saw it, and Zebra cried, "Oh, shit!"

The physician rushed to Omega's side. Echo leaped off the exam table and followed, kneeling on the other side of his partner, shirt still unbuttoned, shirt-tails hanging loose.

"Meg? Baby? You okay?" he asked, as Zebra felt for a pulse. The physician shook her head, snatched the medscanner from the nearby instrument tray, and ran it over Omega.

"Yeh," came the panted response. "Ah'm okay. Jus'...geez, Ace..."

Zebra promptly shoved Omega's head down between her knees.

"Don't you pass out on me," she told the female Agent, voice stern. "I know you agent types think you have to be tougher than anybody else, and YOU, girl, are worse than most, because you were an astronaut and hadda have the 'right stuff' an' all that shit. AND your partner's just as bad if not worse, 'cause he's 'the youngest of the Originals' and all, not to mention chief of the most badass department in the Agency. But DAMN, woman! You bottle it all up, just 'cause you think you can't let anybody see that you actually care a plugged nickel about your partner, only you're really scared shitless. AND you think it'll be your fault if something happens! That. Won't. DO!"

"Meg?" Echo murmured, bending down to try to look into her face. "That true?"

"Sorta," his partner admitted. "We ARE Alpha One, after all."

"Did I scare you that bad?" he wondered. "Don't you trust me to know my stuff?"

"Lemme ask you something, Ace," Omega began, trying to sit up. "When—"

"Uhn-uh," Zebra interrupted, holding the other woman's head down with an effort. "It's your turn for the treatment: You stay put until I'm sure you won't pass out. Echo, hold her there while I run another scan, here."

"Stay here, Meg, baby." Echo put his hand firmly on Omega's back at the base of her neck. That freed Zebra's hands to wield the medscanner again, 'tsking' the whole way. "Hush, Zebra. Go ahead, baby," Echo said softly, letting the pad of his thumb surreptitiously rub his partner's neck, attempting to soothe. "You were gonna ask me something."

"Yeah. When Slug almost took me out, were YOU worried?"

"Well...sure," he admitted. "My old enemy went after my partner. Of course I was worried."

"As I recall, you were blaming yourself for the whole mess, and trying to take responsibility for it."

"Yeah. Like I said, MY old enemy. So?"

"And, at least that first night after he made the telepathic attack, you were so upset you barely said two words."

"Uh..."

"And when Zebra and Company got done jump-starting me after the big fight to take out Slug down in the sub-basement, from what Romeo and Fox told me, you'd about worn a hole in the waiting room floor, pacing. Because you were worried that, even if I survived, there'd be permanent brain damage or something."

"Well..."

"And then you finished by going up on the roof, so you could be by yourself. Which was a place that *I* introduced you to, and where you never went, until I took you up there, stargazing."

"Um..."

Throughout this entire, rather one-sided conversation, Zebra continued scanning Omega's vitals. But she also kept one covert eye on Echo, whose face was turning redder and redder. *Oh, now THIS is interesting,* she thought, not sure whether to be amused, shocked, or captivated. *Echo's partner is nailing Echo to the wall on the very same thing I just nailed her on. Not to mention, letting out some awfully personal reactions, here— about BOTH of 'em. Things are getting...intriguing. Somebody hand me some popcorn. I wanna watch this.*

"...So do you think maybe, someplace in all that, the word 'scared' might sorta-kinda have applied to you, for just a few minutes?" Omega wanted to know.

"Uh...well, maybe...I guess..." A stammering Echo, unsure what to say, ran a distracted hand through his hair, standing it on end briefly.

"Now turn it around," Omega said. "Swap shoes with me. The alien perp that originally attacked ME goes after YOU, and leaves you in a life-threatening situation, with possibly permanent ramifications, like BRAIN DAMAGE..."

Echo's jaw dropped, and his shoulders slumped a bit, as his eyes grew wide.

"...Aw, shit," he finally said, as Zebra motioned him to release Omega. "All right, Meg. Point taken. Yeah, you had as much right to be scared for me as I did for you."

"Thank you," Omega said, sitting up once more, and allowing the single statement to have dual meaning. "That said, you'll both note I did NOT fall apart at any time, and I DID do everything I could find to do, to ensure that the situation had a positive outcome...just like you did with me and Slug."

"Yeah. Fair points on all counts."

"And Zebra," Omega added, turning to the physician, "I do NOT suck it up and 'play tough' because I'm trying to be 'cool' or some such ridiculous shit. I suck it up and AM TOUGH, because THAT'S WHAT I'VE GOTTA DO, TO DO THIS JOB! I flatly can't afford to lose my cool, or to let my emotions affect my performance. If I did, somebody would end up DEAD. And that's an outcome that I categorically find unacceptable all around, but especially when it pertains to my partner." Omega fixed Zebra with an unyielding gaze. "Or any of my other friends in this business, including you. If you don't believe me, ask Fox to assign you as a ride-along sometime. As for being unwilling to admit to it, I think I just did admit to it. I also think you'll find, once you get home and talk to your boyfriend—"

"Damn, does that sound strange, referring to Fox," Echo muttered, then snorted. "Boyfriend."

"...Who also happens to be one of my bosses," Omega continued as if she'd never been interrupted—though she did roll her eyes at Echo's snort, "I think you'll find that I admitted it to him, too, hours ago, while I was busting my ass to find a way to get halfway around the world in only two-thirds the time that it normally took my aircraft to travel it."

Zebra nodded slowly.

"...Okay," the physician acknowledged. "As Echo already said, multiple points taken, and fair enough."

"All right, good," Omega said, voice dropping into a murmur. "Now that we've got that settled..."

"Yeah, baby?" Echo pressed.

"Can somebody gimme an aspirin or something? I got a tension headache fit to split my skull."

"Done," Zebra declared, turning to the pharmaceutical cabinet.

* * *

"Oh, while I'm thinking about it," Zebra noted, handing Omega an analgesic and a cup of water from the sink nearby, "Fox figured you could use a change of clothes after slogging through the desert, Echo. And Omega, he decided you needed one, too. So there are two complete changes of clothing, from the skin up, hanging in the wardrobe over there." She waved at the tall wardrobe in the corner of the room. "There's a shower in the bath right next to it. You two can sluice off and change before you head out. Oh, and a meal would be good for you both, too."

"Our medical personnel seem intent on ensuring that we eat, Meg," Echo observed.

"I noticed that," Omega said, chuckling. "Let me step out, Ace, and you can strip down, shower, and get dressed."

"Okay. Then you can have the room and the shower, and I'll see about finding us some actual food."

"Oh," Zebra said in some surprise, as she listened to the conversation. Both Agents looked up at that.

"What?" they said simultaneously.

"Oh, nothing. I guess...well, I just figured, after all this time working together, that..." she trailed off, not sure how to say what she was thinking without embarrassing them. Omega figured it out first.

"Oh!" the female Agent exclaimed, flushing bright red. "You thought we'd just both, um, and not take turns...I mean..."

"Oh," Echo caught on. His face, too, darkened slightly. "Um, no, Zebra, we don't have that kind of partnership. Meg is the epitome of a modern Southern lady, and I do my dead level best to be a proper Southern gentleman, for her sake."

"I don't think it takes that much effort on your part, Ace," Omega murmured. "You are one, regardless. And I appreciate that."

"It's okay, guys," Zebra tried to soothe. "Stupid assumption on my part. You two seem really close, and I know Alpha Two is, and so I just jumped to conclusions."

Both members of Alpha One waved dismissive hands.

"Look," Zebra added. "If this were my medlab, at this point, I'd just get Omega an adjacent room, and let you clean up and change at the same time. But it isn't my medlab, and more, the guys around here are short-handed on account of your perp, so they can't clean up after..."

"No, Zebra, this is fine," Echo said. "I'm pretty grubby, so y'all shoo, and let me get cleaned up, and then...well, damn, I AM pretty grubby; Meg, maybe you should go first. That way, you have a clean shower an' junk."

"Not to worry, Echo," Zebra said. "The rooms in this medlab have self-cleaning showers; just close the shower door when you're done. An internal sensor will register that it's been used, that it's currently without occupant, and initiate the cleaning cycle. So it'll be spanking clean once Omega comes in to use it. It's the whole disinfecting thing and changing bedsheets an' crap that requires the manpower."

"That'll work," Omega decreed. "Go ahead, Ace. Zebra, let's us clear out and let him get cleaned up. I'm sure he'll feel better for it, after hours hiking through the desert."

"Good point," Zebra agreed.

"Thanks," Echo said, as the two women exited.

* * *

It didn't take long for Alpha One to get cleaned up, dressed in clean Suits, and grab a quick, hot meal with Zebra in the Sydney Office canteen.

Then all three went to the vehicle hangar. There, Zebra found her spacecraft pilot waiting. Having gotten instructions from Fox, Echo handed a laundry bag to the pilot, who nodded.

"I've already heard from Director Fox, sir. I'll get this back to Laundry for you as soon as I touch down," the pilot said, and turned to Zebra. "Ready to go now, Doctor?" she asked.

"Yes, ma'am," a cheerful Zebra replied, then turned to Alpha One. "You two be CAREFUL," she admonished, "and I'll expect to see you both when you get back to Headquarters."

"We'll be there," Omega agreed.

"Both of us," Echo averred.

"Good," Zebra said, and followed the pilot aboard, as Omega and Echo headed for their airskimmer.

Chapter 8

"Gl'ag'gub'it!" Ke'ri Gla'd's cursed, flinging a book across the cabin of her spacecraft. It hit the far bulkhead with a thud, and slid down it to the deck, pages splayed and bent. "These rab'dr'b humans and their fixation on narrative! Where is the ga'd'an'k'n index?! I do not CARE what Ari did on stage, or how they think he performed his tricks!" She slammed her fist down on the desk.

Then she plunked her head into her hands and thought.

"That Division One Agent certainly knew where to go," she considered. "Maybe I should not have dumped him into the wilderness to die, after all. It was useful to be able to trail him and let him find the pieces of the F'al for me. And much easier than trying to tease out the information myself."

She sucked her lower lip, deliberating.

"I never did see his partner," she realized. "Perhaps she was his fail-safe, and he is not dead. That might prove to be...convenient. If I can pick up his quantum signature, perhaps..."

She closed her eyes and concentrated for long moments. The interior of her craft fell silent, save for the soft hums and clicks of the housekeeping functions.

Suddenly the large black eyes snapped open.

"AHH-hahaha!" she cackled. "Well, now! They ARE quite the resourceful pair!" She jumped up and wandered over to her console display, where she briefly watched a local news broadcast, depicting the havoc she had wreaked across a wide swath of Australia. "I think perhaps I should curtail my activities here," she decided, "and wait for things to calm down a little bit. Only then are they likely to leave and resume the search. Then I can sit back and watch while they find the pieces for me, and I have but to swoop in and get them. They do not seem to be especially bright, and none of these agents has a clue how to handle a properly-trained Glu'g'ik operative. I commence to think that it is, indeed, as Kr'b told me before I left on this mission; the Division One should have been based upon Va'du'sha'ā, not Earth." She let out another cackle. "Yes, I believe I will simply let them do the hard work for me, and reap the benefits."

Gla'd's wandered down to the ship's galley to whip up a gourmet snack.

* * *

The *SchmaltzBlitz* still sat in its designated hangar location in the Sydney Office facility, Alpha One aboard her. As they sat in the pilot and copilot seats, discussing what to do next, Omega somewhat absently popped the local news onto the console display.

"Hm," she said. "That's interesting."

"What is?" Echo wondered, leaning over to look.

"Well, it's been at least an hour since anything cropped up that I think could even remotely be attributed to our perp attacking in Australia," she noted. "But there's no word of anything going down elsewhere on the planet, and we haven't heard from Fox, indicating that Gla'd's has left Australia."

"How will he even know she's left, I wonder?" Echo pondered.

"He said something about getting a subspatial tracer on the rental spacecraft she's in, or something like that."

"Oh. I didn't even know he managed to get an agent close enough. Or maybe one of the rental agencies he rounded up did it for him. Good. So... she's still here, she's just gone quiet," Echo murmured, thinking.

"That's how I interpret it, yeah," Omega agreed. She looked at him, and her eyes narrowed. "You thought of something, didn't you, Ace?"

"Maybe, Meg, yeah," he decided, still pondering. "But I'm not sure yet. Can I bounce something off you?"

"Sure."

"Okay, try this on for size. Gla'd's can't go on to the next site given in the clues, because she probably doesn't know how to interpret the clues— she doesn't know anything about Houdini's life on Earth, or where he went, what he did, any of that. I figure she likely has access to Earth documents and books, but she would have to go through them all in detail, in order to begin to find the information she needs...and she won't know what she needs until she runs across it and connects it to the clues..."

"Ooo. You're makin' a lotta sense, hon. Keep going."

"Okay. So she doesn't KNOW where to go next. At all. But I've spent a lifetime accumulating the information on Houdini's life, because fanboy. So I've already got a pretty good idea of where most of the clues reference."

"But she probably thinks you're dead in the Outback," Omega protested, then muttered, "the bitch."

"Maybe not," Echo speculated. "See, she followed me here from London because she didn't know where to go next."

"What?! HOW??"

"Seems that, having encountered us at the Hippodrome, she recognized my 'quantum signature,' or something like that, and just tracked me with it. Apparently she can do that at some little distance. So she may already know that I'm not dead, and she might even know that you're here now. Which would also explain why she's let things get so quiet. There's only two reasons for that: she's waiting for us, or she's already left. And if she'd left, Fox would have notified us." He shrugged. "I think she's waiting."

"So...you think she didn't intend to kill you?"

"I think she didn't care, one way or the other," Echo declared. "And I think she tried to do the same thing to you in London. Just think if she'd dropped you in the middle of a peat bog or something, all by yourself, and me not knowing where you'd got to."

"Shit. But now she cares that you're still alive?"

"Just possibly, yeah. Because now I can be useful to her...or so she thinks. I'm betting she doesn't have a high opinion of humans, and thinks she can outwit us fairly readily; there's been some scuttlebutt among the fringe elements on Va'du'sha'ā about co-opting Division One for themselves."

"REEEally?"

"Oh, hell yeah. Keep an eye on the Aussie news, and maybe we should ping Fox...or the Sydney Office...and find out if she's really gone quiet. I'm betting she has, because she wants to stop distracting us, so we'll lead her to the next thingamajig."

"Hm. So she won't leave Australia until Alpha One does."

"I'm betting not, no."

"Yeah, okay. Let's ping Fox and find out what he's heard."

"I got a better idea. We're already IN the Sydney Office. And we're Alpha One."

"Go find the office chief?"

"Exactly."

"Lead the way, Ace. I'm right beside you." Omega grinned at her partner.

"Just where a good partner is supposed to be." Echo grinned back.

* * *

"No, mate, you're exactly right," Yoke, the Sydney Office chief, told Echo as Alpha One sat in his office. "That sheila appears t' have quieted down a good bit. We were tryin' t' figure out if we needed to be prepared f'r another round. But by your reasoning, it sounds like she's waitin' f'r you an' yer partner t' make a move."

"That's our take, yeah," Echo agreed, as Omega nodded. "We just needed to verify with you that things had actually quieted down. Omega has been keeping up with matters while I recuperated a bit, and that was her impression, but we wanted to make sure."

"Then consider it verified, mates," Yoke declared. "Thank God f'r Fox notifying th' Pacifica regional offices t' send us a bit o' help, too. Pass along my thanks, wouldja?"

"Wilco," Omega murmured.

"Thanks, mates. Now, uh, no offense, but th' sooner Alpha One leaves, the safer Australia's gonna be from that nutter. So...what do I need t' do, t' help speed ya along?"

Omega and Echo exchanged glances.

"Do you have a professional magician handy?" Echo wondered.

* * *

"Well, I can see that," Omega said, as they sat in the *SchmaltzBlitz* once more. "After all, if the magician isn't an agent, then we can't explain any of this, and it's gonna sound really weird."

"I just can't believe they don't have any agents who are at least hobbyists," Echo said, shaking his head. "I'm gonna put a bug in Fox's ear about checking their entry requirements, when we get home. I'm sure they're sufficient, but maybe they could be MORE sufficient, if you get me."

"I do," Omega agreed. "They seem plenty competent; it's just that as average agents go, this Glu'g'ik is MORE competent. Or at least more skilled."

Echo stared at her.

"What?" she wondered.

"Baby, I think you just clued in on something important..."

"WHAT?"

"This Ke'ri Gla'd's isn't just an ordinary Glu'g'ik," Echo declared, reaching for the comm. "She's an AGENT. And that explains a lot, because I've gone up against Glu'gu'ik before and never got caught off guard. We have to get up to speed on Va'du'sha'ān government agents and their techniques and training before we're gonna be able to defeat her. And we need to tell Fox."

* * *

"It surely does, alter khaver," Fox said, after Echo finished explaining. "It makes a helluva lot of sense. So let me see what I can dredge up for you, and I'll pop it to the *SchmaltzBlitz*'s onboard computer as soon as I can."

"That'll be great, Fox. Meanwhile, I need to go back to that greyhound racing facility and tidy up a few loose ends anyway, with Meg's help. And we'll be puzzling on the next location, while we're at it."

"It sounds good," Fox agreed. "Go take care of loose ends. And I'm glad both of you are feeling better, and that Echo is all right." He took in the startled look on both Agents' faces, then grinned. "Zebra got back a little while ago, and came straight here to report in on your conditions."

He didn't tell them she had also noted—off the record, as lover to lover—that she had observed what she took to be a certain affinity developing between the pair. *Which only serves to reinforce my own opinion*, the Director decided. *My bubeleh may just prove an ally in helping me grease the skids for that.* Then he thought about how tightly she had clammed up when he had pressed the matter, citing patient confidentiality. *Then again, maybe not.*

213

Omega and Echo got knowing looks on their faces, and nodded.

"Might have known," Echo decided.

"Yeah," Omega agreed. "That said, at least you've got the official word that we're good."

"True," Fox confirmed. "Now, why don't the two of you brainstorm about any ideas you have for the next clue, while I hunt up all I can find on Zeta Reticulan government undercover agents? And don't forget the loose ends at the dog track."

"Done," Echo said. "We'll wait to hear from you, Fox."

"I'll get back with you as soon as I dig up anything useful. Fox out."

"Alpha One out."

* * *

"There's a couple of things we need to do," Echo pointed out. "We need to go fill in the hole in that shed floor where I found the last whatsis... before the damn Glu'g'ik stole it from me...and I need to go get the saucer I borrowed from the London Office and at least bring it back to the Sydney Office. They can transfer it back to its home spaceport later. Or," he added, "we can leave the airskimmer here for now, and use the saucer to chase down this little scavenger hunt. It will be faster, now the experimental space plane launch is done. We'd just have to make sure we didn't get spotted by the thing."

"True, which is a matter of avoiding line of sight to its orbit," Omega confirmed. "But our perp also knows the configuration of that spacecraft, if she followed you all the way from London while you were in it."

"Ouch. Good point," Echo agreed. "And maybe it's better to slow her down a little bit, anyhow, if she's using us as her finder scope."

"Yeah."

"So...do you want to brainstorm the clues, or go take care of matters at Digger's Rest?"

"Let's go take care of things, then brainstorm. That way, I can focus on the brainstorming, instead of tryin' to figure out how to fix the other stuff."

"Okay."

* * *

When Echo showed up at Plimpton's Paddocks, Petey and his father James both came out of one of the larger greyhound stables, the son with a rifle, the father with a shotgun.

"What do ya think yer doin' back 'ere?" Petey demanded with a scowl. "You're not welcome 'ere."

"As the lad says, ya made a ripper blue when ya came here, ya mongrel, an' we're mad as two cut snakes. What kinda lurk are ya runnin'?"

"I dunno what you're talkin' about, mates," Echo protested, raising his hands in a 'hold on' gesture. "An' what're ya doin' wi' th' long guns?"

"Bloody hell! We found what ya did t' th' floor o' th' shed when ya was fossickin' around in there," Petey declared. "Ruddy damn vandalisin' thief."

"An' we got the due licences f'r protectin' our dogs fr'm th' dingoes," James added, "so don't go tryin' t' hold one over on us."

* * *

Omega had put the passively-cloaked airskimmer down in the same copse of trees that hid Echo's saucer, across the highway from the dog racing facility. As he headed in through the main gate, she snuck around the back way by the side road; he had apprised her of the layout during their flyover.

Now she located the shed, peeped around its corner at Echo, who was facing her as he confronted the irate owner and son, and nodded at him. He raised an eyebrow ever so slightly, and she knew he had seen her. She ducked out of sight again, and produced an electromagnetic lockpick.

As she worked, she tried to send her partner a mental message. *Oh, be careful, Ace. Those guys are pissed. They might just get pissed enough to shoot, and I really don't wanna have to deal with THAT. I had enough nerve-wracking cavalry ridin' to last me for a while, just coming to get you outta the dust storm. So I hope you got something hidden in a pocket to stop a bullet, or buckshot. Or else a mighty golden tongue. Which former you probably do, and latter, you definitely do, I suppose. There,* she thought as the lock clicked softly and opened.

She slipped inside the shed, immediately spotting the square hole in the floor produced by the hurgir. Reaching into her own pocket, she pulled out the urgir, which Echo had given her before they left the airskimmer. She placed it over the hole in the concrete slab and activated it. The urgir hummed for a few moments, and a soft green light emanated from beneath it, then it automatically switched off. When she picked it up, the flooring underneath looked like the rest of the concrete surface. She nodded to herself, slipped the urgir back into her pocket, then exited the shed and locked it firmly behind herself.

Another peep around the corner revealed that Echo was still in one piece, with no holes in him, and he appeared to be talking fast. She raised her left hand; he raised his chin just a little, and she pulled back into the shelter of the shed, then slipped out the way she had come.

* * *

Echo had seen Omega at the shed almost as soon as the Plimptons had arrived with their weapons, and now he saw her signal that matters were handled.

"Whoa, hold on there, mates," he exclaimed. "I dunno what ya think I did t' th' shed, but I swear I didn' do nothin'!"

"Don't be LYIN' t' us, man!" James shouted. "We got a full quid, both of us! We SAW it!"

"Saw what? I ain't figured out yet what ya think I did!"

"Th' hole in th' floor!" Petey yelled. "Perfect square, 'way down in th' slab!"

"What hole? I didn't leave any hole." Echo dared to stroll toward the shed. "Show me."

Omega walked up just then, apparently having decided that Echo might need more obvious backup, given he was facing down two long guns with no obvious way to defend himself against them. *She knows I have the blasters,* he realized, *but I don't wanna use THOSE on these guys. They're just defending their property, after all. And I DID deface it, without having a chance to fix it.*

"Hey, baby," he greeted her, raising an eyebrow and waggling it in a suggestive fashion. This was her cue to act like his girlfriend, which she did, sidling up to him.

"What's up, Ace?" she murmured, letting her thick Southern dialect

216

flow all over the words, even as she slid her hands around his ribcage and leaned into him. He slipped an arm around her shoulders.

"I seem t' have a little misunderstanding wi' these gennelmen," Echo explained. "Gennelmen, this is me lady friend, Meg; she's from th' States. Meg, this is James Plimpton an' 'is son Peter."

"Pleased t' meetcha, ma'am," the senior Plimpton said, and Petey nodded. "But this 's prob'ly not th' best time. Ya need ta be gettin' yer man friend here an' goin' back where ya came from. 'E's not welcome 'ere."

"What? Why on earth not?" Omega wondered, acting shocked.

"They think I vandalised their shed, baby," Echo explained. "I've just bin tellin' 'em I didn't do no such a thing."

"Ya did," Plimpton senior declared. "Ya left a gapin' big-ass hole in th' floor. Pardon my language, ma'am."

"An' I'll say it again," Echo declared. "What hole? I didn't leave any hole."

By this point, the small group was standing in front of the shed, and Petey leaned his rifle against the side of the shed while his father kept the two Agents covered...though he did lower the barrel of his shotgun toward the ground a bit, in deference to the presumed-innocent lady now attendant upon the proceedings. Petey unlocked the door and threw it wide, saying, "Of course ya did, ya smartass; it's right...huh? Where is it? Da, where is it?"

James joined his son as they craned their necks, scanning the inside of the shed, looking for the damage to the slab foundation.

"Told ya I didn't leave no hole," Echo declared. "I wanted t' thank you gennelmen f'r the opportunity o' lookin' at this historic site, an' apologise f'r havin' t' rush off without sayin' so much as by-your-leave th' other day. I got an emergency call on me cellular an' hadda run. But I weren't expectin' no such greeting as all this. I'll haveta think about how much ta put in my book, when I write it up."

"But...didja find out what Houdini wanted with it?" Petey wondered.

"I did," Echo declared, and turned on his heel without saying what. "C'mon, Meg, baby. Let's head back t' th' Office."

"I'm with you, honey," she purred.

Alpha One turned and left the Plimptons standing there, bemused.

* * *

They walked out the front gate, crossed the highway, and Omega headed for the airskimmer while Echo made a beeline for the saucer.

"See ya back at the Sydney spaceport hangar, Ace," she told him.

He tossed off an acknowledging salute, and they boarded their respective craft.

Moments later, two nigh-invisible craft took off from the clump of trees, headed northeast.

* * *

Behind them, a faint atmospheric disturbance rose from a distant field...

...Headed northeast.

* * *

Echo returned the loaned spacecraft to the hangar in Sydney; it would be returned to London's hangar as soon as possible, along with any couriers that needed to go from one city to the other. The paperwork took a little while to fill out, but that was solely because the saucer was being returned to the 'wrong' regional Office. Omega simply waited in the parked airskimmer while he handled matters; she also contacted hangar maintenance, ensuring the *SchmaltzBlitz*'s fuel tank was full.

Some fifteen minutes later, Echo boarded the *SchmaltzBlitz*, sat in the copilot's seat and strapped in.

"Ready when you are, baby," he told his partner. Omega leaned forward and keyed the comm.

"Sydney Hangar master, this is Alpha One in the airskimmer *SchmaltzBlitz*, craft code Alpha One Omega One," she spoke into the comm. "Permission to launch requested."

"*SchmaltzBlitz*, this is Sydney Hangar. Stand by one, please. I need to let some standard civilian craft clear the airspace."

"*SchmaltzBlitz* standing by."

They sat for a few moments, while Omega warmed up the skimmer and prepared for liftoff. Abruptly the comm popped on.

"*SchmaltzBlitz*, this is Sydney Hangar. You are approved for launch...

now."

"Roger that, Sydney Hangar. Launching now."

The *SchmaltzBlitz* shot into the golden sky of late afternoon in an Aussie spring, banked sharply, and headed west-northwest.

* * *

As the *SchmaltzBlitz* passed over the Blue Mountain range and progressed toward the mining district in the western regions of New South Wales, a faint atmospheric distortion rose from somewhere in the western Sydney suburbs, and fell into their wake.

* * *

Per their previous plan, Alpha One headed for a remote region of the Outback—deliberately selected to be near the scene of Echo's little endurance test—where Echo assisted Omega in programming the auto-pilot to orbit the northern periphery of the Mamungari Conservation Park.

As they swept around in the first loop, Echo abruptly pointed to the sensor readout; Omega quickly pulled up a heads-up display. It showed a slight atmospheric distortion approaching from the east-southeast...against the prevailing wind. It slowed to a stop, and hovered in position for a short time—long enough for the airskimmer to orbit the park again—before sinking slowly to the ground and seeming to disappear.

"You were right," she said. "She followed us."

"Good," Echo said with a grin. "Time to mess with a Glu'g'ik's mind, for a change."

"Works for me."

"Kinda thought it might."

"You know, Ace, you're sorta lucky," Omega decided then.

"How so?"

"If she'd dumped you, oh, a hundred, hundred and fifty, miles southeast of where she did, you'd have had to contend with the fallout residue from the nuclear testing they did around here in the 50s."

"Yeah, I thought about that when I realized where I was. It was one of the reasons why, when I saw the dust storm coming—and from the direction it did—I decided I really needed to NOT try to push through the thing, and to set up the force dome. I didn't want to risk a lungful of leftover radioactive dust."

"Smart man."

"I try."

"You do good, then."

"Thanks."

* * *

Just then, the incoming comm alert bleeped. Echo reached over and hit the switch, remarking, "Alpha One here."

"Echo, it's Fox."

"Good evening to you, Fox. Do you have our information?"

"Not yet, not what you asked for, at least. But I do have some information I thought you'd want to know."

"And that is?"

"Well, it seems that Ke'ri Gla'd's' rampage in Australia has stopped, and she's someplace in South Australia state, judging by the tracer beacon..."

"Yup. About a mile or so from our position," Omega interjected.

"What?! How do you know?"

"Because Echo suspected she would follow us," Omega answered. "She figured out, almost too late, that she doesn't know the Earth-based lore about her cousin—the stuff on which Houdini based his clues—and Echo does. She needs Echo to lead her to the next site on this treasure hunt. And we're going to be ready this time. And lead her on a wild goose chase for as long as we can, into the bargain."

"What do you mean?"

"She means we're not going straight for the next site in the poem, once we figure out what it is," Echo explained. "What Ke'ri Gla'd's is doing, per her own admission to me in Digger's Rest, is following me around, based on having met me in London—and I presume Meg, too, though she seems focused on using me for this—and letting Alpha One find these doodads, then popping in and stealing them from us using her quantum manip, phasing out, and then waiting for us to find the next gadget."

"Apparently she doesn't credit us with much in the way of anything but space between the ears," Omega added.

"Right," Echo agreed. "The thing is, she can recognize my quantum signature, even at a little distance...but she can't actually tell what I'm doing. She only knows where I am. She's not telepathic, and she's not telepresent, so once we arrive someplace, she has to physically follow me around to make sure I haven't located one of the thingamajigs she wants."

"Ohhh, I think I see," Fox replied. "So if you don't go to the next REAL site, she doesn't know, and she has to follow you anyway, just to make sure."

"Right. So I've got in mind to lead her to a whole bunch of different places, and make it as difficult as I can—on HER, specifically, so I'm choosing the sites based on that—and as long as I can, before we ever even bother to head to the next location specified in Houdini's poem." Echo shot his partner a devilish grin.

"We're gonna wear her ass slap out," Omega added, grinning back.

"Ooo, nice. Very good, then. So you're planning how to deal with her, using the artifact search as bait, without actually getting to the next artifact until you absolutely have to?"

"Exactly, Fox," Echo said. "Or until she wears out and gives up, whichever comes first. Her innate quantum manipulation abilities, as honed as they apparently are, leave even an Alpha Line team at a disadvantage, since we don't have anything approaching an ability like that. But as Meg said, she's overlooking—even grossly underestimating—our intellects. And neither Meg nor me are exactly stupid."

"Not by a long shot, old friend. Either of you."

"So we're going to use that as OUR advantage," Omega tag-teamed her partner in the explanation. "Plus the fact that there's two of us, and one of her. One can fly the skimmer while the other one sleeps, or eats. SHE has to fly her ship all by herself."

"Right," Echo agreed. "So she doesn't get a meal break, or a chance to sleep. And we already know that she's been stuffing her face, not exercising, and generally kicking back, ever since she arrived on Earth. So if we choose some really challenging terrain, something that's even possibly dangerous, like a volcano..."

"Farkakt! Be careful!"

"We will be, Fox," Echo averred. "You know us better than that. But we need to push her limits as hard as we can. The more we can put her off physically, mentally, and even emotionally, the more we level the playing field, and even tilt it to our advantage, for a change."

"Aha. I think I see."

"So we take all that," Omega said, "and then we...ENHANCE it..."

"I...don't understand that..."

"You will soon, Fox. We're still trying to plan it. We'll need some equipment to help us pull it off, and when we send in our requisitions, it'll make sense," Echo promised.

"I already got some good ideas on it, I think," Omega declared.

"You do, baby. And right now," Echo added, "we're just flying in circles over the desert, near where she initially dumped me, hoping to confuse her a bit. Make her wonder what we're doing, and are we trying to locate clues on what she did, or whatever. At the same time, though, we could leave at any moment, and she knows that. And that means she'll be busy keeping an eye on us so she doesn't lose us—I think she has more trouble spotting my quantum signature past a certain distance, see—and so she can't get into any other trouble."

"VERY good!" Fox exclaimed. "It keeps Australia...and anywhere else she might decide to go...safe from her destructive sprees."

"Precisely," Echo noted. "Because it keeps her attention focused on us."

"And she doesn't dare actually hurt us," Omega pointed out, "because she needs us to find the next site."

"Well, she needs Echo," Fox observed. "Doesn't that leave you in a bit of danger, Omega?"

"I don't think so, Fox," Echo corrected, "because I don't think she's quite sure exactly what the relationship is with us."

"How so?"

"Well, when she caught me out in the shed at the dog track, grabbed me and dumped me in the middle of nowhere, y'all weren't there to see her reaction," Echo said. "She was looking all around as she was doing it, the whole time—looking for Meg, I'm pretty sure."

"But...why?" Omega wondered.

"Baby, look at it from her point of view: She jumped me, and had no problems phasing me out and dumping me in the backside of the Outback," Echo explained. "If she'd wanted to kill me directly and immediately, by, say, rearranging my guts, she could have done, and I couldn't have stopped her."

"Ugh," Omega murmured, paling slightly and making a face.

"What she said," Fox agreed. "We need some sort of defense against that."

"Agreed. But when Gla'd's tried it first on Meg, according to Gla'd's' lights, Meg stopped her cold."

"But it wasn't anything I did," Omega protested. "It was something about what got done, I mean, the way I was changed..."

"Yes, baby, but Gla'd's doesn't know that. All she knows is, she tried to attack you—whether by restructuring your innards, or 'porting you someplace else, it doesn't really matter—and she couldn't do it. She probably now views you as the senior partner, and certainly the more powerful of the two of us."

"Ooo," Omega murmured, furrowing her brows as she considered it.

"And there's also the matter of how much she may know about humans, and the general Agency structure," Echo added. "She could think that you're the senior partner and I'm a rookie; that you're some sort of bodyguard for me, like maybe you're the field agent and I'm a subject-matter expert on Houdini—"

"Which you are, but that's not ALL you are," Omega said.

"Right, but again, she doesn't know that; or she could even think that we're mates of some sort, with you the dominant partner. Because stronger." Echo shrugged. "Whatever. In any event, she was looking out for you, back in Digger's Rest. And in my estimation, her rampage was calculated expressly to keep YOU busy, and all the other agents in the region into the bargain, to keep you from rescuing me and coming after her, while she tried to figure out what to do next."

"Which means," Fox extrapolated, "that Omega may be the one Agent in Division One she's a little afraid of."

"It...sounds like it," Omega admitted. "You're painting me like I'm some sort of über-agent in her mind."

"I can readily see where you might be," Fox agreed.

"How does it feel, baby, to be so badass that you have alien operatives afraid of you?" Echo asked, grinning.

"It feels...weird." Omega shrugged. "Good, I suppose, but...weird."

"Well, this is excellent. I like the sound of your logic, and this entire plan. There's a reason you two are Alpha One, you know," Fox pointed out, "and the pair of you just demonstrated it."

"We aims to please," Omega said with a smile. "So what else ya got for us, Boss?"

"I see Echo's expressions are rubbing off on you, young lady," Fox observed.

"That's a switch," Echo decided. "Usually it's Meg and Romeo that are swapping personal terminology."

"Huh? What did I say?" Omega wondered, expression blank and confused.

"You called Fox 'Boss,' baby."

"Oh. Um, was that a problem?" Omega asked, meek. "I didn't mean to offend, Fox."

"No, no. I've just never heard you refer to me as 'Boss' before, but Echo does it not infrequently."

"Uh, I can stop, if you'd rather," she offered. "Is Echo the only one allowed to do that? Like a nickname?"

"Not an issue, yung froy. It was merely an observation on my part. Don't worry about it. Now, for the news. I worked with Yoke, and we have developed a cover story for Gla'd's' rampage," Fox continued. "It's going to take some work to execute, but it should serve the purpose in the long run, and I thought in the circumstances that Alpha One needed to know what we came up with. You see, there was a 'rare earthquake along the eastern Australian coastline,' and that's what caused all the damage. We'll have to hack all the seismic data and records, and insert faked data for the quake, world-wide, but it's doable, with some code that the Software and Programming department worked out. In fact, we're already executing it."

"Ooo," Omega murmured. "I wanna see that when we get a chance to look."

"I can arrange that, once you get back to Headquarters. Oh, that's right, you have a degree in geology, don't you? Among others, that is."

"Yes sir," Omega confirmed. "And I'd love to see what you did with the seismic data. I mean, the Blue Mountains formed there, so there have to be some old faults in there someplace. It's just that Australia's pretty much in the middle of a plate boundary, and not much is happening there any more."

"Right. Which is why we specified a RARE quake," Fox chuckled. "Now, do you have any additional news for me? Like, perhaps, what we're looking for, or where the next piece might be?"

"Not yet, Fox," Echo said, "but be prepared to hear from us in some out-of-the-way places for a bit. We're planning on leading Gla'd's a merry chase, as Meg likes to put it, for as long as we can get away with doing it."

"I'm looking forward to it. Keep me posted."

"Always."

"Fox out."

"Alpha One out."

* * *

"How did that Glu'gu'ik poem go again, Ace?" Omega wondered, sitting in the pilot's seat as they flew circles over the Outback.

"Hang on, and let me see," Echo said, reaching into his jacket and fishing out his translation of Houdini's clues. As he did, he also brought out the pocket watch inside which he had found the last object, and which he had shoved into his pocket absently, curious about the device that had been concealed within it. "Well, damn, I forgot all about this."

"What is it?"

"The last gizmo I found was in the slab foundation of that old feed shed at the racetrack, only instead of just resting inside the cavity, it was tucked inside THIS, which was inside the cavity. Look."

Echo showed Omega how, if the stem button was hit twice, the back opened up, revealing a tiny storage space inside.

"Wow. It must have been really small and flat."

"It was. That may have been one reason the pocket watch was there, to protect it or something. But..."

"But what?" Omega asked.

"But I can't help thinking it's a clue, too."

He watched as his partner turned the watch over and over in her fingers, studying it carefully. Finally she shrugged and set it aside.

"Maybe if we put it together with the verbal clues, it'll make sense," she concluded. "We finished the first two lines of the poem, and now it's time for the third. What does it say, again?"

"'Third yet first, the place where first I won my wings, the fastness foundation toward the morn,'" Echo read off his notepad. "I've been trying to figure that one out. I keep thinking it was where he was first 'born,' or first successful, except he was purported to have been born in Hungary—of course, we know he wasn't even born on Earth—but he did his first successful shows on the vaudeville circuit in the States. But I don't know WHERE in the States he'd consider his first success."

"Well, if the watch has anything to add to it," Omega said, picking it up and turning it over again, "it's a timepiece, and it was made in Hamburg, Germany, according to the maker's mark. Did Houdini do anything important in Hamburg?"

"Well, he did several European tours, but I don't recall any special escapes or anything that—OH!" The male Agent whacked his forehead with his palm. "Echo, you IDIOT! And right on the heels of the Australian flight clue!"

"What?! You figured it out?"

"Yeah, I think so," Echo said, offering her a sheepish grin. "See, this one is sorta in an inverse order from the previous clue. Hamburg is where he made his first successful airplane flight. It's where he 'earned his wings,' as we say these days."

"'Third yet first,' yeah, that makes sense," Omega noted. "The poem lists it AFTER the Australian flight, but it happened BEFORE the Aussie flight."

"And it's 'the place where first he won his wings,' as it were," Echo added.

"But then there's that whole, 'the fastness foundation toward the morn,'" Omega pointed out.

"Okay, let's break it out grammatically," Echo suggested, pragmatic. "Sometimes that tells you how the thing is meant to be structured, and makes verbal clues like this clearer." He scribbled the line of the poem on a fresh page of his notebook, then began creating a parsing diagram. "'Third yet first' is kind of its own clause, and it's just two subjects and a conjunction. Then we've got 'the place,' a noun and its article. And 'where' denotes a subordinate clause in this case. 'I won wings' is subject-verb-object in that subordinate clause, with some descriptors added..."

"Damn, Ace," Omega murmured, barely above a whisper. "Is there anything about languages you don't know?"

Her partner still heard it. Echo flushed, and paused his work.

"Well, yeah, a lot," he admitted. "But I work hard at it, and I'm still learning, every chance I get, just like you do on your specialties. I always had it in mind to study linguistics, just because I thought it was cool—interesting to me, personally. That whole mimicking thing, you know. Before I ended up in the Agency, though, it was more than half a whim; I never really expected to do a lot with it except maybe improve my Spanish and my Apache." He shrugged. "Once I became an Agent, it suddenly assumed a whole lot more importance, especially when handling off-world communications. So I double-majored in Linguistics and Diplomacy, then did my graduate work in Linguistics. And I use 'em both. Probably I use the linguistics more, for all that, I think."

"Cool. Sorry I interrupted you, though. I meant that to be kind of just a muttered, 'Wow' kinda remark." Omega waved her hand at his notebook. "Go back to that. Forget I said anything."

"Well, thanks for the compliment, though. That sorta...made me feel like I really have done something with it."

"And you have." Then Omega grinned and waggled a finger at the notebook. "Now get back to it."

So, with a wry grin, and a mumbled, "Yes, ma'am," he bent back to work.

"Um, lessee. Okay, we got to 'I won wings.' Then we've got, 'the fastness foundation toward the morn.' Fastness and foundation are both nouns. But it's a translation, and sometimes articles and pronouns and prepositions an' shit are kind of understood to be there, in other languages. So maybe that should be 'the fastness's foundation,' or phrased another way, 'the foundation of the fastness'..."

"What's a fastness?"

"A stronghold—a fortress or the like."

"Oh! Isn't there a castle sorta on the hill in the middle of Hamburg?"

"Now that you mention it, yeah, I think there is. Pull up the global internet a sec and let's look."

Omega activated the onboard computer, initiated the comm to do a database search on the Agency's network, and typed in the search term, 'Hamburg Germany castle.' Then she brought up the results on a heads-up display so Echo could see, too.

"Um...yeah! There! It looks like it's called Bergedorfer Schloss, or something like that," Omega decided. "It's all in German, and my German's rusty."

"So's mine, but I think you're right. Pop it to Fox; he'll nail the German."

"Oh, good idea. Hang on." Omega hit a couple of keystrokes, typed in a quick message, and sent it off to the Agency Director. "All right. While we wait for him to verify, we got one more phrase in that line of the poem."

"Yeah. 'Toward the morn,' though, strikes me as a directional instruction. You know, 'the east side,' or something like that. Pull up a map or a satellite view of the castle."

Omega hit a couple more keys, then reached out and did the pinch-and-pull motion that enlarged the image.

"Yeah, Ace, you're right," she agreed. "On the satellite view it looks like the diagonals of the main building are oriented more or less with the points of the compass."

"Uh-huh; I see that. Which means, I guess, that 'toward the morn' means the eastern corner, probably either down low on the outside, or in or under the cellars someplace."

"So that's our next stop."

"Well...our next OFFICIAL stop," Echo said with a devilish grin.

Omega looked at him, seeing his expression, and then caught on.

"Are you really thinking 'merry chase,' Echo?" she wondered.

"Oh HELL yes, Meg. I think we both owe her one, don't you?"

"I most certainly do," she agreed.

Just then, the incoming comm dinged. Omega flipped the switch.

"*SchmaltzBlitz* here. Omega, Alpha One."

"Omega, this is Fox. I got your message, and you're correct; the Hamburg castle—or rather, the one you're asking about; there's a lot of so-called castles in the Hamburg area, but there's only one still standing that I'd call a true castle of sorts. And that would be the Bergedorfer Schloss, and even it is closer to being a mansion or manor house than what you'd typically think of as a castle. It's not inside the modern city proper; it's a bit southeast, on a hill on the other side of the Elba River, overlooking it. It was probably intended to be able to guard the river passage from there; it dates from the thirteenth century, or at least what I suspect was the core of the structure does. It's a museum these days, so it'll have a lot of tourists roaming around. You should be able to blend in, if you play it right."

"Great," Echo decided.

"Also I've got some more information for you regarding Glu'gu'ik agents. The legitimate government knows this Gla'd's person, and confirms that she is—or rather, was—one of their operatives, gone south. She's now what we'd call a 'kite,' and working for the Imperial faction, like we suspected. They're hoping and waiting for us to ship her back to 'em in force cuffs. But I've got a new file on her abilities, and how they work, that I'm sending you in a ciphered blip...now."

A soft bleep came from the comm console.

"Got it, Fox," Omega said. "We'll take a look and see what sorts of countermeasures we can come up with, in order to take her down and keep her there."

"Good girl. Anything else?"

"Not right now, Fox," Echo considered. "We'll keep you posted, as usual."

"Be careful, you two," Fox admonished. "I want you back here in one piece—well, given there's two of you, in TWO pieces, preferably as high-functioning as when you started, when this is all over."

"On it, Boss, and we will be," Echo said. "Thanks."

"For everything," Omega added.

"No problem, maydele. Go get 'em. Fox out."

"Alpha One out."

* * *

"Okay, Echo," Omega said, "I'm thinking..."

"I thought it was getting smoky in here."

"Aw, shuddup," she said, sticking out her tongue and crossing her eyes into the bargain. Echo let out a sound that might have been a snicker. "I got some ideas, and I want to make sure we're on the same page, and that what we do next makes sense."

"Okay, baby, shoot."

"I really wanna have a look at this file Fox sent, because I have some ideas of my own regarding what I wanna do to that bitch, and what's in there might help me implement 'em. And you have ideas about leading our perp down the street and around the block to get next door."

"Yeah."

"So I'm thinking YOU need to do the flying from here to Hamburg, while I study this file and work on the countermeasures ideas I have."

"Makes perfect sense to me. I was gonna ask if you just wanted me to go ahead and fly, since I have the idea...and the flight plan, what there is of one...in my head."

"Okay. Yeah, go for it."

"So we're about to commence Operation: Wear Out the Glu'g'ik."

"Right. Not to mention put her generally as off-kilter mentally and emotionally as we can get her."

"Yup. I want her practically loopy by the time we actually go for the next artifact. It's like we told Fox...with her innate abilities, and all the training she's had to use 'em, both defensively and offensively, that's really the only way we're gonna gain an advantage over her."

"I'm in agreement there. If I'm correct about what I think I saw in the files Fox sent, even with what I hope to build, we're gonna need that

230

advantage. Frankly, I don't think just exhausting her is gonna be enough. Granted, we can set the DAP, and take turns flying while the other sleeps... and she can't, to either, 'cause she doesn't know where we're going. But..." Omega shook her head. "We need her physically...depleted. Not just tired, but maximally stressed in every possible way. Given her behavior, I'm not averse to injured, sick...or even dead."

"All right. So we're pulling out the stops. Do you need me to stall for time into the bargain, while you analyze those files Fox sent, and work out your proposed countermeasures to her techniques?"

"That might be good, yeah. Take as long as you think you can get away with; the more time I have to work on this, the more I'll be ready to deal with her once we do directly confront her."

"Okay, I can do that. 'Bout ready to start this rodeo?"

"Yeah, I think so. Right now, though, I'm really glad I topped off the fuel for the *SchmaltzBlitz* before we left the Sydney Office."

"Me, too. But we'll have a couple more opportunities to refuel before we're done, so no sweat. Well, swap seats with me, strap in, and let's go. This should be interesting, in more ways than one."

"Ain't it the truth," Omega said, as she and Echo rose and traded seats.

Moments later, they were strapped in and headed outbound from Australia, on a generally north-northwest header.

* * *

Some distance behind them, a certain atmospheric distortion followed in their wake.

* * *

"Okay, Meg," Echo said after a few minutes. "I got the auto-pilot programmed, and I see a certain 'heat wave' in the air coming along right behind us, maybe a few thousand yards back or so..."

"Good," Omega remarked. "She's falling for it."

"Looks like it. Now, are you gonna be able to help me set up for our first destination, or do I need to work on it myself, while you research Fox's file?"

"No, I'd figured on helping you before starting on that. In fact, given your rationale for this particular stop, I thought it might be good to pick your brain on it while we worked. It would give me a better background for when I dive into the file."

"That makes sense," Echo decided. "Okay, let's get out that equipment we picked up before we left the Sydney Office and get to work. The connections can be kind of complicated."

"I bet."

* * *

"...You're good at this," Echo said, a little over an hour later. "The detail on this is awesome. You could have done special effects for the film industry."

Omega smiled, pleased.

"Glad you like it," she said. "When I was in school, I worked on an animated film short for one of my advanced computer science classes— it focused on graphics design. There were...I think there were three of us working on it, but we were all pretty imaginative. Not only did we get A's in the class, the professor had us submit the thing to a local film festival, and it did really well."

"Cool," Echo said, grinning. "I work with an animation expert."

"Oh, well, I wouldn't say THAT."

"I dunno. This is pretty damn good. I'm thinkin' we'll scare the piss AND shit out of her."

"Make sure you're uphill and upwind, then."

Echo snorted in amusement.

"I plan to be," he noted. "But I'm also going to have to be damn careful where I step, too."

"Not so much," Omega said. "I found those force boots you wanted, before we left Sydney. AND I rigged 'em to run thigh-high."

"You did? Great!" He glanced out the windscreen. "Sun's going down. It's getting dark."

"Just the way we want it."

"Exactly. Whenever possible, let Nature provide the special effects."

"Yup."

* * *

An hour later, it was solid dark and the airskimmer was approaching the eastern end of Java, near the strait between that island and Bali. Steam and ash rose from the summit of several mountains clustered in a large, loose oval very near the coast of the strait. The Moon was a thin sliver of a waxing crescent, low on the horizon, and put out just enough light to show the glimmer of a large crater lake, one with an oddly vivid bluish-green hue that seemed almost phosphorescent. On the southeast side of the lake, a great fume of steam and volcanic gases rose, then drifted north, across the lake's surface.

"Is that it?" Omega wondered. "Looks like the photos I've seen."

"Yep, that's the place," Echo confirmed. "We're gonna set down inside the crater, at the foot of the rim on the southeast side."

"And you're sure the area will be clear?"

"Yeah. Got a notification from Fox a bit ago. They put out word among the locals that seismologists were concerned about a possible eruption of the main vent."

"Ew. That would be...bad," Omega decided. "That would not only turn over the lake, releasing poisonous gases, it would flash it into sulfuric acid steam, and kill everyone inside the crater...and possibly overflow onto the surrounding slopes."

"Right. So the local authorities were shutting down all sulfur mining trips, and warning hiking tourists to stay in their camps and not venture up the volcano. And from what I gathered, people were listening."

"Good."

"Yep. So once we put down, I'll gear up and go out, and you stay put and just follow the plan we worked out. Whatever you do, don't lower the force shields except around the hatch long enough to let me in and out; that lake is nearly pure sulfuric acid, and the fumes are various sulfur compounds, too. Poisonous AND corrosive."

"Got it," Omega agreed. "I'm on the curve, Ace."

"I know, baby. You always are."

He switched off the auto-pilot and began a manual descent into the crater.

* * *

Behind them, the atmospheric distortion, barely visible in the dim light, did NOT immediately follow the *SchmaltzBlitz* down to the ground.

Instead, it looped the top of the volcano once, returning to the point where the *SchmaltzBlitz* had begun its descent.

It hovered there for long moments, seeming hesitant, before finally sinking down, inside the main crater.

Chapter 9

Ke'ri Gla'd's stood in the hatch of her cloaked spacecraft and looked about, unnerved. The altitude-thinned, volcano-warmed air fairly reeked of sulfurous stench, with billowing clouds of the stuff drifting and blowing here and there with the slightest breeze. It made her large black eyes sting and her laboring lungs burn—normal sea level pressure on Earth was slightly too thin for Zeta Reticulans, and the air pressure at the crater's altitude, over nine thousand feet up, was something of a hardship for the alien woman.

The nearby crater lake, which her sensors had told her was VERY highly concentrated acid, glowed a faint, preternatural bluish-green.

A large spatter cone near the edge of said crater lake led her eyes upward. It was in active eruption, as the cinder cone belched copious quantities of flaming blue lava skyward, to land on the slopes of the cone, splatter, and flow downward all around. More vapor clouds of sulfur compounds rose from its summit, drifting away in the slight breeze borne of convection in the hot, volcanic gases.

The landscape consisted of little more than black silhouettes of rugged outcrops in the darkness—the planet's moon was setting in the west, hence below the rim of the crater in which she stood. The area around her ship was poorly but eerily lit with that same flickering azure light from the volcano's eruption. Fiery rivulets in shimmering sapphire and cobalt shades trickled hither and thither among the jagged boulders, hissing furiously and disgorging great clouds of vapor whenever one ran into the fluid in the lake. From time to time, the spatter cone vomited a huge blob of molten rock, glowing blue-white as it fountained nearly twenty feet into the air, splashed onto the cone's sides, and then ran down.

Overhead, the stars, unchallenged by any artificial light sources, shone out clear and crisp, their sharp, cold pinpoints nearly the equal of a similar view above the atmosphere.

Gl'ag'gub'it, Gla'd's thought, agitated despite herself. *If ever there were a real hell, this would be it. The ancient clerics must have seen this, or something like it.*

Just then, she spotted the humans' airskimmer some forty or fifty yards away, as the hatch opened, releasing a bright wedge of white light into the hellish wilderness, and the male Agent stepped out into the harsh, dangerous terrain. Without hesitation he turned and headed into the depths of the reeking clouds, apparently aiming for a niche near the base of the cinder cone, though he picked his way carefully, watching the ground in front of his feet for hidden lava pockets. After a moment, he disappeared behind a large outcrop of broken sulfur lava.

Well, gl'ag'a'dr'b, she cursed to herself. *I was hoping to be able to watch from here. But no. The rab'dr'b human has to find one of the few places where I cannot see him. I cannot imagine Ari came HERE, of all places on this or'k'n'pas planet. But nor can I risk it. I MUST have the F'al, and it must be complete and functional. Only then can I claim it as the new Keeper, and make it do my bidding.*

Gingerly, watching her own path closely to ensure that she did not step into any of the lava flows—her ship's instruments had told her it was some nine hundred standard degrees above absolute zero, and not even her quantum manipulation would function fast enough to prevent serious injury from THAT—Gla'd's moved out, into the night.

* * *

When Gla'd's found Echo at last, he was kneeling on a small block of sulfur, hands raised in the air, murmuring something she could not hear.

He appears to be...praying, she decided, as she peeped around another block of sulfur, half as big as the airskimmer and apparently fallen from farther up the cinder cone. *But why in the galaxy is he doing THAT?*

Just then, a swirl formed in the air before the Agent, and a being materialized. Gla'd's immediately recoiled.

AIIIEE! It is the Adversary itself! she thought, near panic. *Creator help me! I thought it was a myth! But there is the dark blue skin, the huge body—it towers over the Agent by half again his height! The four arms! There is nothing to the face except white eyes and a mouth full of silver daggers! And the horns!* She shivered, then settled. *Get control of yourself, Ke'ri. There is no such creature. It is a myth, nothing more. This is a—*

Then Echo started speaking.

"Sha'h'r, thank you for hearing my plea," the human Agent said, tone respectful and grateful.

SHA'H'R?! Gla'd's echoed, shocked. *Has he summoned the GLU'GU'IK adversary so?! By NAME?! No, no, no. Sha'h'r does not exist. This is not real,* Gla'd's decided. *This is a trick. I will look at the quantum field and know how...they...* The alien broke off the train of thought in horror as she read the quantum signatures present before her. *Gl'ag'gub'it! GL'AG'GUB'IT! There are TWO ENTITIES there! And only ONE of them is human!*

Gla'd's spun, putting her back up against the block of sulfur for a moment, then dared to peep around it once more, too unnerved to watch, but too spellbound to look away.

"Greetings, friend Echo," the demon responded, in a deep, harsh, grating voice. "How is your partner?"

"Excellently well, Sha'h'r," Echo declared. "As you promised, she has proven invulnerable. Not even our Glu'g'ik antagonist could harm her."

The partner! she thought in sudden understanding. *No wonder I could not transport her from the performance building!*

"That is good to hear. I am glad to help, but especially glad to know that I aided you against one of that miserable race."

"I knew you would be."

"What would you have me do for you, friend Echo?" Sha'h'r asked.

"I would that you should make me as my partner, Omega," Echo declared. "The Glu'g'ik attacked me and nearly harmed me. I want to be invulnerable, too."

"That is easily done. You would swear fealty to me, as she has done?"

"I will. I have."

"Then let it be done."

Sha'h'r waved all four hands in a complicated pattern, above, before, behind, and around Echo. A silver shimmer sparkled briefly around the Division One Agent's body, then faded. The demon nodded.

"It is done."

"How do I know?" Echo wondered. Sha'h'r pointed.

"Walk through the blue lava. You will be unharmed."

Without hesitation, Echo turned and walked toward a large pool of fiery blue molten rock, fully ten feet across, and of an indeterminable depth. Gla'd's wanted to scream, *NO! STOP! You must not! If you die, I cannot find the F'al!* but she kept quiet, watching in horror as the Agent set his left foot down firmly into the lava. It vanished in the blue glow...

...And Echo kept walking.

His right foot likewise disappeared into the viscous liquid, then his left re-emerged, dripping blue flame, only to sink back into it, as he strode, unharmed, through the deepest portion of the lava pool and emerged unscathed on the other side. He turned and looked down at himself for a long moment, seeming to consider, then he looked up at Sha'h'r and smiled, holding his hands in the air.

"It worked!" he called. "You've made me as invulnerable as Omega!"

"As I promised," Sha'h'r said, nodding sagely. "Now come back to me, and let me lay my blessing upon you. Then I shall send you back to your partner."

Calm and unhurried, Echo returned through the lava, emerging to stand before Sha'h'r once more. The demon raised all four hands to the sky.

"Rab'or a or'k'n'pas, ne ka'r'ki. D'an, der klo'vi," the demon declaimed.

Then, in a swirling glitter of silver dust, the demon dissipated.

Legs trembling, Gla'd's swallowed hard. *'Son of hell, I claim you. Lost, yet you remain.' The ancient blasphemy, spoken...here! On Earth! By Sha'h'r! It was REAL! It was HERE! And they are its followers!*

Even as Echo turned back toward the airskimmer, Gla'd's spun and bolted.

* * *

By the time Echo got back inside the *SchmaltzBlitz* and removed the transparent, full-head rebreather mask—which had effectively been invisible in the dark and noxious air outside—and deactivated his full-leg force boots, Omega was doubled up in the pilot's chair at the command console, laughing so hard she was red-faced. Occasionally she pounded the chair arm with her hand before letting out a fresh howl of mirth.

"I take it, it worked?" he asked, raising an eyebrow as he watched her hilarity. Omega didn't answer immediately, being rather too preoccupied with sucking in enough air around her laughter, but finally she managed a reply.

"In spades!" she chortled. "Modifying the spare brain bleacher and piping it through the hologram feed worked perfectly! Especially in combo with the effects of the gases out there on the Glu'gu'ik nervous system! According to the onboard sensors, she snuck up to within about ten or fifteen feet of you..."

"Behind, and to my right? Beside that big ol' block of sulfur?"

"Exactly," Omega verified. "And watched the whole thing. Once I spotted her in the sensors—she was playing quantum games, and wasn't much visible to the naked eye, though I think I glimpsed her, once or twice—I fine-tuned the sensors for Glu'gu'ik readings, zeroed in, and watched her heart rate shoot through the roof as soon as I activated the hologram movie! I bet I could even tell you when she looked at the quantum foam!"

"I wouldn't be surprised," Echo said with a grin. "Where is she now? Back in her spacecraft?"

"Oh DAMN, Ace! As soon as 'Sha'h'r' faded out, she bolted back to her ship like a scared rabbit! She's already hovering a couple thousand meters up...OUTSIDE the crater!...waiting for us!"

Echo snorted.

"Well, all I can say is, I'm glad I thought to grab the heat-resistant Suit from the Sydney Office supply department," he decided. "Not to mention, your managing to find and modify the force boots for me—which I didn't know you knew how to do, by the way."

"Eh." Omega waved a dismissive hand. "Crash course. Part of that whole countermeasures thing I'm working on."

"Aha, okay. Well, even with all that, those sulfur flames were HOT."

"Yeah, I was a little worried about you walking through that puddle of molten sulfur, and was glad you picked one that wasn't flaming too high," she admitted. "I noticed that you paused on the other side; I figured it was to cool off a little, so I held up on the scripted response until I saw your signal to keep going. How did my voice sound, once I ran it through the synthesizer program we set up?"

"It did NOT sound like you," Echo declared in no uncertain terms, "and if I hadn't already known it WAS you, I think it might have even given ME the creeps, just a little." He shook his head. "Definite Hollywood film award status, baby."

"Great! You wanna get started on Round Two?"

"Yeah, let's do it."

"Okay, I already got the next leg programmed into the autopilot; once we reach altitude, we can engage it. Now, can you do me a favor, before we take off?"

"Sure. Whatcha need?"

"Can you please go change out of that Suit?" she asked, holding her nose. "You reek of rotten eggs. Among other things."

"Yeah, I better go do that," Echo decided. "And use some wet wipes to get the residue off my skin. Wish the *DonnerFurz* had a showe—"

"WHAT?!" Omega fairly shrieked. "'Thunder Fart'?! It's the *SCMALTZBLITZ*! You know, like 'Greased Lightning'?"

"Yeah, I knew it was something like that." Echo smirked from ear to ear. "But I'm never gettin' this smell outta my nose..."

"Thunder farts," Omega grumbled as a chuckling Echo headed aft, pulling the privacy curtain across the opening behind him. "SOMEbody sure smells like thunder farts right now, but it ISN'T my airskimmer."

* * *

The *SchmaltzBlitz* had lifted off once more, headed west. Behind them, a certain atmospheric distortion drifted along their flight path—against the prevailing winds.

"...So your friend told you all about the Glu'gu'ik religions when he came to visit?" Omega wondered.

"Oh yeah," Echo said. "Well, not ALL about 'em, obviously, but quite a good bit. He expressly wanted to visit that very volcano, for that precise reason—he'd seen pictures, and it looked enough like the Zeta Reticulans' idea of hell that he wanted to find out how close it really was. Given that, unlike most planets, the Glu'gu'ik religions are all variants on a theme, the concept of hell was pretty much the same planet-wide."

"And was it? Close, I mean."

"Oh hell yeah—uh, excuse the inadvertent pun!" Echo gave her a sheepish grin. "He said it couldn't have been any closer if the old clerics who set down their holy writings had visited it. And he said that, even though there was a significant atheistic/agnostic movement which arose after the collapse of the imperial government, it was rare to find a Glu'g'ik who wasn't steeped in their theology, and at some level believed it. Which is why I knew it would serve our purpose here, and how I knew what Sha'h'r needed to look like."

"So how close are we gonna follow this whole thing?"

"Oh, I'm gonna play it by ear, now," Echo decided. "We laid the groundwork, but I want to keep her guessing. Not only did we emotionally stress her back there, we physically stressed her, too, because of the altitude and the bad air. I thought I caught a glimpse of her at one point, out of the corner of my eye, and she didn't look to be wearing protective gear at all."

"Not according to the sensors, no. She may not have been aware of the types of geology we have in some areas, and it probably never occurred to her that we'd lead her to a place like this. So she got nice lungfuls of all that noxious goop...complete with all the psychoactive effects it has on the Glu'gu'ik nervous system! And don't they have a slightly higher atmospheric pressure on Va'du'sha'ā, too?"

"Exactly. Normal Earth sea level pressures are a bit low for 'em, and we were up at around Colorado Front Range altitudes, back there. So she got a good, big dose of psychoactive compounds, and probably a light head, into the bargain."

"Ooo. And then we play brain bleacher games."

"Yeah. So what I think I wanna do from here on out is to build on that foundation, and have her thinking we are nigh-unto bulletproof, you and me, between acquiring more and more high tech and petitioning other such 'entities.' Not to mention leave her guessing as to which one of these stops might actually contain another one of those whosiwhatsises we've all been after."

"Okay, that works. And during the flights, I'm gonna be working on those countermeasure ideas I mentioned, for when we finally do confront her."

"That works," Echo agreed. "Hopefully, by the time that confrontation actually occurs, she'll be so off-balance mentally and physically that she'll be considerably off her game."

"Right. Well, damn, let's face it, Ace, from the sound of Fox's report, she's at least the equivalent of a regular Division One agent, PLUS she's got the whole quantum foam manipulation ability, WITH the training on how to use it to maximum effectiveness, offensively AND defensively. That's a hard combo to deal with."

"I know. We can't match her innate abilities, let alone the training she's had in using 'em, so we gotta play this as smart as we can. Which is why I want her as cock-eyed, worn out, and uncertain as we can manage to get her."

"No arguments there. Besides, you're back to being lead dog, hon. You got way more experience."

"Yeah, but you got real technical smarts, there, baby. And you 'get' how to apply them tactically. Your additions to my basic plan...well, lemme put it like this: We brainstorm really well together as a team. I think it's kinda synergistic—the total plan, now, is way better than just the sum of our respective ideas."

"Yeah, I think so, too. We make a good team, you and me."

"We do. So I guess go ahead and set to work on those countermeasure ideas, and yell if I can help, or if you need an extra hand. Otherwise, I'm gonna kick back and rest a bit—and you should, too, when you can, on this whole snipe hunt. I want us both to be fresh—and the perp NOT—when we DO confront her. We got about six more hours before we reach Spain, anyway."

* * *

Hours later, and having chased the evening twilight all the way across Asia and well into Europe, Gla'd's found herself landing her cloaked vessel in a kind of no-man's-land between two large aircraft runways.

The sign on the front of one of the huge, brightly-lit, glass-and-metal

242

buildings lying alongside one of the runways said ZARAGOSA—she had seen it on approach—whatever that meant; she assumed it meant 'aircraft port.' An historical marker of some sort near its front depicted a large, squat space plane of a design Gla'd's considered archaic, for it used chemical rocket engines.

Both runways were moderately active, even at this time of the evening, only a couple of hours past sunset. One had large, mostly-white aircraft, with multiple windows rowed along their fuselages, landing and taking off at a great rate as they shuttled to and from the building with the large sign. The other runway had a mix of small, fast jet aircraft, and large, lumbering cargo craft, all in sometimes-mottled shades of gray and tan. Those moved to and from a different area; some went inside one of several hangar buildings, others remained on the pavement, and their crew emerged and walked inside yet another building.

But the only aircraft Gla'd's really cared about was passively cloaked, some hundred yards from her vehicle. It was a far more sophisticated airskimmer, and it appeared to be waiting for something; no one was emerging.

Some fifteen minutes later, the 'something' arrived, though it, like Gla'd's' vehicle, was cloaked...but she could still sense the shift in the quantum foam as it approached. *Hum. A large saucer spacecraft,* she decided, *based on the size and shape of its quantum presence.*

A hatch opened in the previously-invisible saucer, and two humans in black Suits emerged, each towing an antigrav pallet loaded with small crates. The skimmer's hatch opened, and the two agents entered. Some ten minutes later they exited the skimmer, their pallets empty. The female Agent came to the hatch of the skimmer and waved to the other agents, who nodded, smiled, and waved in return, before entering their own craft. The hatch disappeared into the cloaked vessel, and within minutes Gla'd's sensed it depart into the night sky, headed northeast.

Mm, Gla'd's thought, studying the direction in which it departed. *An emergency equipment and supplies shipment from the Geneva Office, most likely. Interesting. It should not be that far to the Geneva Office, yet they chose to meet here. That argues they were in need, then.* She thought for a moment. *I have no requirement to be in this place; there is obviously noth-*

ing of Ari's here. But I cannot afford to lose them, either—the male is my best lead to finding the other pieces of the F'al. No matter; they will now leave soon, to resume the hunt, and I shall follow.

But the airskimmer did not take off immediately, as she had expected. Instead, it sat on the ground for fully another half-hour. The Glu'g'ik could sense the pair moving around inside the craft, but could not determine, despite her best efforts, what they were doing, save for the fact that they were moving around various metallic devices.

Abruptly the hatch opened again, and one of them—Gla'd's thought it was the male, based on the quantum signature—emerged in a black mechasuit with dark red boots, gauntlets, and helmet, and walked around for a few minutes, apparently testing it and ensuring proper functionality. Then he turned to the front of the skimmer, held up his armored hand, and gave a thumbs-up, presumably to his partner within. A faint light flashed through the dark-tinted windscreen, and the Agent immediately headed for the hatch, entering and closing it behind him.

Several more minutes passed, and a dull red light suddenly flared around the airskimmer, then faded. If Glu'gu'ik had eyebrows, Gla'd's would have raised hers; she had been unable to determine the purpose of whatever the red glow had meant, even by reading the quantum foam.

Five minutes later, the airskimmer lifted off the ground.

Ke'ri Gla'd's slipped her spacecraft into gear, and ascended after it...

...Headed southeast.

* * *

Some two hours later, Gla'd's found herself in a sandy desert plateau landscape surrounded on several sides by a large metropolis, which mostly seemed to sit on the banks of a relatively narrow, somewhat sluggish river. Nearby, looming up through the darkness, were several pyramidal stone structures.

It was around midnight, or perhaps one in the morning, by Cairo time when she and Alpha One landed in the archaeological area. This, she decided, looked rather more like something that would have been around in Ari's time, so she decided to prepare, just in case. She had the good sense to check the sensor readouts of the local atmosphere; her chest still hurt from

244

breathing the fumes of hell, and she coughed occasionally. But the readouts showed normal Earth atmosphere, so when she saw Alpha One debark, she pulled up the hood on her matte black clothing, de-phased slightly, and ventured out of her spaceship.

Alpha One headed straight for the largest pyramid, crossing over a road intended for internal-combustion vehicles; at this time of night, there was no traffic to speak of. Over some dunes to their right, Gla'd's discerned a large statue of some bizarre human-feline hybrid.

Odd, the alien operative thought, somewhat absently. *I was unaware that Bastians and humans could mate. No, wait, I seem to recall...was there not some sort of Earth mythology regarding such a beast—?*

Just then, a life-sized—and LIVING—sphinx, quadrupedal and well over ten feet tall at the shoulder, materialized in front of the couple she trailed in a blast of red fire. Startled, the Glu'g'ik stepped back a pace. Before she could react, however, the sphinx held its front paw over Alpha One—

—And all three vanished in a puff of red, sulfurous smoke.

Shocked, Gla'd's spun, scanning the area's quantum field. Alpha One was nowhere that she could detect; they had vanished as completely as if they had suddenly developed her own quantum transport abilities. She turned toward the airskimmer, verifying they had not beat some sort of hasty retreat, but it was empty. Her own ship she checked likewise, in case they had managed to sneak aboard in an effort to retrieve the F'al on'chu'ik—nothing. Alpha One was gone.

"Gl'ag'gub'it," she cursed in a low tone. "The rab'dr'b humans have flatly vanished. Was that creature with them their version of Sha'h'r, or was it something else? Either way, it appears to have allied with them. NOW how do I find them?"

Gla'd's stood there, perspiring as profusely as Glu'gu'ik could—it was hot in Egypt, even at night; it was a desert, after all—and considered the matter for a while, then finally turned and stalked back to her spacecraft, to wait in relative comfort. *After all,* she considered, *they have to return for their ship at some point. They do not appear to have secured it, so they dare not wait for the system's star to rise, lest the local populace find it.*

* * *

Omega and Echo, carefully hidden among the ruins at the base of the Great Pyramid of Khufu, watched silently as the puzzled and rather unnerved Glu'g'ik studied the area, then finally marched back to her ship in annoyance amounting almost to high dudgeon. Only once she was within the ship, several hundred yards away, did Omega allow herself a snort.

"Boy, did THAT work," she remarked, trying not to laugh.

"It sure did. She doesn't know what to think, any more than she did back at the Kawah Ijen volcano," Echo agreed. "That tech Fox had the Geneva Office gin up and bring us worked like a charm, especially once we added it into the hologram and brain bleach system we already had."

"Well, that didn't surprise me," Omega pointed out. "After all, Geneva's where CERN is based, and where the world-wide web was invented, and a buncha stuff like that. You got some serious brain trust there. And I'm sure the Agency has been all over recruiting from among THOSE guys."

"And you'd be right. Which is why I asked Fox about it."

"Kinda figured." Omega glanced back at where she knew the alien's cloaked vessel was. "It was also a great idea to give her a taste of her own medicine."

"What, you mean making it look like we were phasing in and out?"

"Yeah."

"Uh-huh, I thought it only made sense. She's been underestimating us in a lot of ways, which is a sign of ego and a belief that her culture and race are superior to ours. Which I'd expect from a dedicated royalist in these particular circumstances," Echo added. "Not that I'm sayin' that that's the nature of ANYone who supports an imperial-type government, 'cause in my experience, it's not—there's bunches on Earth, and even more in other planetary systems, and I've got friends all over, so I've got a lot of experience. It's just that she's in the middle of a conspiracy, a key player in said conspiracy, and believes she's in the right and everyone else in the wrong." He glanced around. "Well, are you ready to go 'teleport' back in?"

"Sure. 'Unlock' the *SchmaltzBlitz* with the remote, and let's go."

* * *

Gla'd's sat at the helm, watching the airskimmer across the way.

Suddenly there was a burst of red flame and smoke, and she flinched and blinked.

Alpha One stood there.

"Gl'ag'a'dr'b," she cursed.

* * *

And so it went.

From Cairo it was all the way across the Atlantic, headed west, to the American East Coast.

In Boston, Ke'ri Gla'd's followed the pair of Agents to several venues which Houdini had visited—including the Harvard Bridge and Margery Crandon's house. She watched as they acquired more equipment and hardware, and observed as they visited a certain old house in the Salem suburbs, emerging with several special little charms...but no F'al on'cik.

Back across the Atlantic they flew, and on across Europe, headed east.

Near Budapest, purported birthplace of Harry Houdini, once more Alpha One visited several locations associated with Houdini, including the site of his purported childhood home, but the building was modern...so they came away with nothing of interest to the Glu'g'ik, though they appeared to meet with the Morrighan and the Daghdha at the site of the ancient Celtic—and later Roman—settlement of Aquincum, petitioning for and acquiring certain arcane abilities.

Once more over the Atlantic, only to pause halfway.

In the archipelago of the Azores, they put down inside the crater of the Montanha de Pico volcano, amid a significant dusting of snow. It was cold and windy, and at nearly eight thousand feet above sea level, most of the clouds were below the summit. The Glu'g'ik was very tired; after all, by this point she had been traveling for well more than an Earth day with no rest, let alone having endured the arduous conditions found in some of the sites, as well as the general emotional and mental stress of having to remain alert, combined with encountering more demons than she had previously realized existed in the entire universe. And not only was the Va'du'sha'ān atmosphere denser, its day was shorter. The alien woman's stamina was beginning to fail her.

Nevertheless, Gla'd's, recognizing the mountain's shape as volcanic in nature, checked the atmospheric composition before exiting the space-ship...but in her weary state, did not think to check weather conditions. Consequently as soon as she departed the shelter of her ship, she found herself miserably cold and struggling to breathe at altitude, even as she watched anxiously while Echo and Omega called up yet another Glu'gu'ik demon, the fire dragon K'ur.

By this point, she had scanned the quantum foam so closely for the various metaphysical beings' signatures—and found a different one each time, carefully planned by Echo and Omega, and based on secret data being fed through Fox from the Zeta Reticulan homeworld, by way of assisting the Agency in capturing their rogue agent—that it no longer occurred to her to doubt that the encounters were real.

She also found that she no longer wanted to get too close, lest the mysterious, supernatural entities notice her. *After all, there IS truth in the old Va'du'sha'ān aphorism, 'May you live in interesting times, and attract the attention of important and influential people.' These...beings...are certainly important, as well as powerful and influential. Not to mention those Division One Agents,* she considered, as she watched K'ur appear to bless the couple. *By now, I may have difficulties obtaining the items I want from them. I will have to be crafty, instead of relying merely upon my foam manipulation skills. But or'k'n'pas, I should hate to be them, upon their demise.*

* * *

A couple of hours later, Alpha One—with a certain rogue Va'du'sha'ān close behind—arrived in Stockholm. They followed a storm system inbound, and so when the *SchmaltzBlitz* landed, it was in the midst of an early-season snowstorm; nearly a foot was already on the ground, and more fell in gentle flurries, covering the ground and turning the trees of the Royal Game Park into a delicate black and white lacework. They had chosen to land near the Ugglevikskällan, an ancient holy spring or well that had once been a source of drinking water for the area.

"Ooo!" Omega exclaimed in delight as Alpha One, well bundled in black overcoats and black mufflers and gloves, emerged from the hidden airskimmer into the middle of a snow-covered landscape. "Oh, I LOVE this! I NEVER got to see snow in Houston, and Daddy used to say—pretty accurately—that we only got about one good snow a decade, back home in Huntsville!"

Echo chuckled, watching in affectionate amusement as his partner practically danced in the snow.

"Well, get ready, then, 'cause you'll probably see a lot of it this winter, in New York," he warned. "Especially if we get a nor'easter or two."

"YIPPEE!" she cried, flinging her hands in the air.

Echo snorted, grinning, then turned to survey the area. No sooner did he turn his back to his partner than he felt something cold and wet and semi-solid smack into the back of his head, and slushy snow splattered his shoulders and flew past his face, even as a trickle of cold water ran down his scalp and into his collar.

"SHIT!" he yelled, spinning, to find Omega grinning from ear to ear, and making another snowball. "Damn, Meg! Is this really the time?"

"No, but I couldn't resist," she told him, her grin somehow growing even wider.

"I don't think you wanna go there with me, baby," he told her, removing his muffler and using it as a towel to blot up some of the ice-cold water in his hair. "Remember, I've been in New York plenty long enough to be used to snow, and my throwing arm is still pretty damn good..."

"Oh," she said, promptly dropping the fresh snowball she held. "Um, are you mad?"

"No," he told her, letting a devilish smirk form on his lips, "but that doesn't mean I'll forget."

"Uh-oh."

"Yep. You got that right." He raised an eyebrow, then dropped into their unspoken codes. *Look to your right, about thirty yards out, under the trees. But don't look like you're looking.*

Omega twirled slowly, looking up into the snowstorm, sticking out her tongue to catch snowflakes, rather to Echo's additional amusement.

"Want some sugar with that?" he wondered. She turned to look at him and stuck out her tongue AT him.

"They're fine the way they are, thanks," she told him. "Nice and fresh." Then she, too, dropped into codes. *Yeah, I see it. A nice bowl-shaped depression, with several holes in the snow equidistant around its circumference. Just about what you'd expect if there was a cloaked saucer sitting there with its landing gear down.*

Right, Echo agreed. *So we still have our shadow, just like we wanted. Oh, would ya look at that...*

What? Omega met his gaze, biting her lip, apparently to resist the urge to turn around and look.

I just saw several footprints appear in the snow, coming out from that bowl.

She's here, and she's watching. Standing in the snow. I wonder if she has snow gear, like we got on our last little supply stop in Zaragosa.

By the look, I'd say not, Echo decided. *Looks to me like she's stomping her feet.*

Good. Omega grinned wickedly. *Let's do this, then.*

Okay. Just like we planned, timing and all. Echo looked around, then added aloud, "I'm not seeing our contacts. We must be a little early."

"Wanna build a snowman, while we wait?" Omega wondered.

"Have you ever built one?"

"No. I've only ever seen one before in my life. When I was really little, there was this monster snowstorm that hit the Southeast. The local weather people called it the Blizzard of '93. I dunno if it was really a blizzard, but we did have white-out conditions in places, and when I woke up the next morning, there were, like, four-foot snowdrifts in our back porch, which was drifted level with everything else!"

"Wow!" Echo exclaimed, beginning the process of rolling the snowman's base. "In Alabama?!"

"Yeah. It was a doozy," Omega told him. "Dad built a snowman once it stopped and the weather cleared a little; that's the only one I've ever seen. The next day we tried to get out to go get some stuff at the grocery store...at least, that's what Mom said, but I think Daddy was just wanting to go look at it all...but even his pickup truck didn't have high enough clearance for the snow between the ruts, and we kept dragging bad and slipping and sliding everywhere, so after maybe a quarter of a mile, he turned around and we came back home. Momma was REALLY glad."

"I bet," Echo agreed. "C'mere and let me show you how to do this, 'cause now we need to roll it around and let it pack on layers of snow, to build it in size. And on the next tier, I'll need your help to lift it into place."

"Okay."

* * *

Nearby, a certain half-phased rogue alien agent stood in the snow and watched Alpha One's playful antics in some disgust.

Should I go back inside and watch from there, where it is warm, she wondered, *or should I be more prepared to act? There is, after all, a structure yonder, and it is, according to its quantum field, easily old enough for Ari to have visited it. Perhaps I should remain vigilant, and stay here.*

The feeling was starting to fade in Gla'd's' cold feet as she watched, wondering what in the systems of the Nine Sisters the idiotic agent duo was doing. From time to time, one or the other of them moved near the small structure, so the alien woman did not feel mentally comfortable abandoning her vigil. But she felt not in the least PHYSICALLY comfortable standing in the cold snow with only the standard cloth Glu'gu'ik booties encasing her feet, and nothing heavier than a kind of cardigan wrapping her torso over the traditional Glu'gu'ik unitard.

* * *

Finally, almost an hour later, a half-frozen Gla'd's watched in bemusement as the Agent pair put the finishing touches on their snowman. Echo and Omega used odds and ends cobbled from the stowage in the skimmer for the details—the snowman had blue eyes, consequent to their having been made from the caps of two disposable water bottles, but the mouth was a bright, curving row of candy-coated peanuts; the nose was a bit of cardboard, twisted into a rough cone. A couple of small evergreen branches, culled from one of the nearby trees, formed arms.

* * *

"He's cute!" Omega decided.

"Oh, it's a he, is it?" Echo wondered.

"Of course."

"And you can tell this how?"

"Well, he's bald, and he doesn't have a, um, a bust, or a booty," Omega pointed out. "Besides, it's snowMAN, not snowWOMAN."

"Oh. Uh, yeah, I guess those are all good points. Some, a little more so than others," he added, a rakish eyebrow raised.

"Behave, you!"

"So it's a guy. He got a name?"

"Mm—what's the Swedish for 'bald'?" she wondered with an impish grin.

"Skallig it is, then," Echo said, returning the grin. *And here come our supply teams,* he coded to her, *right on time.*

* * *

Just then, two groups on snowmobiles arrived from opposite directions, each towing cargo sleds with boxes.

"Here we go, Meg," Gla'd's heard the male Agent say. "One set of equipment from a special group at Stockholm University, and another set from the corresponding group at the Royal Institute of Technology."

"Terrific, Ace!" the female Agent replied, as they moved to greet the new arrivals. "The more we have to work with, the better our outcome."

"Exactly. Which is what this is all about, after all."

In short order the new cargo was stored in the airskimmer—Gla'd's wondered where they were finding space to store it all—offers of gratitude were extended, and the humans on the strange snow conveyances departed.

Alpha One went inside the airskimmer, and Gla'd's watched for a moment, then turned in relief to re-enter her own craft—

—When Alpha One emerged again, with metallic objects in hand. A resigned Gla'd's turned back to watch as they shook the objects, and soft chimes sounded through the steadily-falling snow.

The chimes continued, and then the Glu'g'ik realized that the Division One Agents had stopped shaking the bells; this sound was coming from somewhere in the forest. Suddenly a small sled, pulled by a lone deer, emerged from under the trees on the far side of the clearing; a man garbed in brightly-colored furs of dark red, forest green and snow white rode in it. He was stout and rosy of face, with long white hair and beard, and he reined in the deer, bringing the sled to a stop next to the well house, before dismounting. He did not tie up the animal; rather, he laid a gentle hand on its snout and seemed to speak to it. It huffed once, tossed its head, and was still.

A quick scan of the quantum foam in the vicinity of this strange man told Gla'd's that he was much as the other demons, dragons, and supernatural entities which Alpha One had been consulting. But somehow, this one seemed...more benign.

* * *

"Ho! Echo! Omega!" the man boomed, smiling. "You two have surely been good this year! Oh, and what a handsome snowman you've built!"

"His name is Skallig," a mischievous Echo noted, and the newcomer laughed.

"And indeed he is, too!" the man chuckled.

"Santa!" Omega exclaimed with a grin, stepping forward. "It's good to really meet you!"

"Oh, now, you've met me before, young lady, you just don't remember it. You were a wee tot, after all. Echo, how's it going, you old dog?"

"Pretty well, Nick," Echo averred. He offered a hand, but the other male swept him into a big bear hug, then pulled Omega into it as well. "Oof! Damn, Nick, you're as strong as ever."

"I, I, um," Omega stammered, not sure whether to hug back or not. Nicholas 'Santa' Claus winked at her then, and she settled. "You, um, you and Echo are old friends, I take it?"

"Oh yeah, I've worked with Nick before," Echo said, grinning. Then he leaned over and breathed into her ear, "What, you thought he was gonna be a hologram, too? Not hardly. Nick and I go back a ways. He's been here a long time, of course, way before the Agency—or even modern civilization—existed; but then, Wintourns have naturally long lives anyway, and they've been exploring the galaxy for thousands of millennia." He raised his voice. "But some people know him by a different name."

"Oh yes," Claus said then. "It was not of my choosing, you understand. And some of the legends are...a bit off, in places. But I have also been known...as ODIN!" He flung his hands in the air, and thundersnow cracked and boomed.

* * *

A heavy flurry descended, and swirled around the trio, briefly obscuring them from Gla'd's' gaze, though not from her quantum sense. Black eyes, already large, widened further, and she stepped back, under the edge of the saucer, as lightning flashed overhead and the thunder rolled again and again.

"Rab'dr'b," she muttered. "This one may be the most powerful yet."

* * *

"Whoa," Omega murmured, keeping her voice as low as she could; the storm seemed unusually quiet after the first discharge of thunder, but she heard no more after that. "You didn't really do that, did you? Echo, that was something of yours, right?"

"No, Meg, he did it," Echo replied in a normal tone. "And don't worry about talking too loud; the Glu'g'ik can't hear us now. See, Wintourns are natural elementals. Nick is especially gifted with weather manipulation—something about being able to tweak the ionization in the atmosphere, best I could ever understand it. He's also been mistaken for Thor, and a couple of the other Norse gods."

"Well, I'm not sure 'mistaken' is the precise word, Echo," Claus explained. "I'm fairly certain the myths were based on me, before I knew any humans had migrated in, around my place, to watch me."

"How old ARE you?!" a startled Omega nearly shouted, keeping her voice to a reasonable volume only with an effort.

"Near as we've been able to reckon it, Meg," Echo explained, "he arrived on Earth a couple of millennia before the last ice age. He explored the planet—"

"I was a scout for my homeworld of Wintou," Claus interjected.

"—Then decided to stay here and try to start a small colony," Echo continued. "He sent for his wife and family, and they settled in the arctic regions—he could adjust the localized weather patterns to make it comfortable for them, see, while at the same time being isolated from the early human types. His history, unfortunately, would take way longer for me to tell you than we have right now, because SOMEbody is gonna get suspicious if we take too long."

"Well, she's watching right now, so we gotta be careful," Omega realized.

"Not quite," Claus said with a grin. "Look around, Omega."

She glanced about, to discover that they were enveloped in a blinding white-out of swirling snow. Nothing outside a radius of some six or seven feet was visible.

"Oh! That's convenient," she decided.

"Very much so," Claus chuckled.

"And I guess, between the swirling wind and all that snow, she can't hear us, either."

"Right," Claus confirmed. "And I'm making a few, uh, 'sound effects' on the outside, just to make sure. Now, once I drop the snow shield, I'm supposed to wave my hands and pretend to bestow some of my powers on you, right?"

"Exactly," Echo confirmed. "Or at least, to bless us as if you've already done it."

"Are you two willing to follow my lead on something?" Claus grinned mischievously.

"Sure," Echo agreed. "What have you got in mind?"

"Something that'll make this alien witch sure that I really HAVE bestowed powers on you."

"That sounds good," Omega said, matching Claus' wicked grin with one of her own. "Let's rock and roll."

"Let me give you two some instructions first..."

* * *

As a concerned Gla'd's watched and waited, the snow flurry diminished; the winds dropped, and the thunder and lightning ceased. Gradually the trio in the midst of the clearing, near the springhouse, became visible once more.

"There," Claus said as the snow finally died away; even the flurries stopped. "You are properly prepared. Bow before me."

Alpha One crouched low in the snow...and closed their eyes.

"Very good. Let the thing be done...NOW!"

Claus flung his hands into the air once more, and this time, lightning cracked down around them, dancing bright across the surface of the snow,

255

which sizzled and hissed with the heat.

A deafening, instantaneous thunderclap and shockwave bowled the Glu'g'ik over, plumping her backwards into the cold wet snow, blind and nearly deaf for several moments.

* * *

"That did it," Echo breathed, removing the earplugs he'd inserted, even as Omega and Claus did likewise. "Did you see the dent in the snow where she fell over on her ass?"

"Oh hell yes," Omega choked, trying to avoid laughing outright. "That was priceless, Mr. Claus."

"Please, call me Nick, like Echo does," Claus offered. "And we aren't done yet. Her sight should be coming back in a second or two, but her ears will be ringing for a while yet. Put your earplugs back in."

Quickly they shoved their special, high-tech, Royal Institute of Technology-developed earplugs back in place. Then the three watched without appearing to do so, as the snow beside the cloaked spacecraft was disturbed by invisible scrabbling motions, then finally settled. This, they interpreted, was the sign that Ke'ri Gla'd's was now back on her feet and watching them.

So it was time for Act 2.

"Wow!" Omega exclaimed, gazing in awe at Claus. "That was incredible!"

"It was," Echo agreed. "But, Odin, how do we know that we now have the power...?"

"Did you not sense the invulnerability? The lightning struck you directly, you know."

Claus' statement was a huge exaggeration, and arguably an outright lie; he had carefully controlled the strikes so that a circle was formed around the three, but no one had been actually hit—including Gla'd's. It was easily within his ability to do so, even to kill her; but it was against his moral code to harm another being with his powers. This was a matter that he and Echo had discussed when the Agent had contacted him to help.

But with his ability to control the ionization, he had even been able to send the dispersing, grounded charge away from their feet.

256

"It...it did? The lightning struck us?" Omega wondered, wide-eyed. "But...it didn't hurt! I didn't even feel it! We're fine!"

"Of course you are," Claus declared. "I saw to that. You are invulnerable to such things now, as I said you would be. But I understand your concern, so...raise your hands."

"Both, or just one?"

"Whatever it takes for you to command the lightning yourselves."

* * *

Omega raised both hands as if she were about to cast lightning bolts; Echo lifted one hand, palm outward, arm at an angle. An admiring Omega secretly thought it was incredibly dramatic-looking. The fact that his palm faced the area they knew Gla'd's to be standing only added to the effect, in her mind. *Because she's gotta be about to piss her pants, given what she just experienced,* she thought, desperately stifling the urge to laugh. *And now Echo looks to be aiming at her.*

"Now—call the lightning," Claus commanded.

Both Agents brought their hands down and forward in a casting motion, fingers splayed.

Great bolts struck all around the meadow. Once again another Glu'g'ik-buttocks-shaped depression appeared in the snow, and this time Omega could not stifle the giggle that escaped. But it was doubtful Gla'd's could hear it, and it would have seemed appropriate in the circumstances, in any case.

* * *

They waited until the snow churned and stopped once more, then suddenly the trio looked anywhere but at each other—footprints were appearing in the snow, and they were BACKING UP, toward where the saucer's ramp should be.

Oh shit, Echo coded to his partner at last, when he was finally sure he could look at her without bursting into laughter. *Somebody's about had enough.*

I do think so, Omega agreed, biting her lip as the corners of her mouth twitched.

You haven't seen any yellow snow over there, have you?

No...not yet, anyway.

Okay, let's finish this.

Right.

* * *

"So...can we do that all the time, now, too? Throw the lightning?" Omega asked. "That would be so cool!"

"Ah, no, my child. That is a singular ability reserved for myself and my son Thor. This was merely a...how to put it? A guarantee of oath fulfilled, let us say."

"Excellent," Echo said. "We thank you, sir."

He and Omega swept deep bows to Claus, who smiled, beneficent.

"Off with you, now," Claus said mildly, as the snow began to fall again, growing heavier. "You have work to do."

"We do, sir," Omega agreed. "Thank you." Then she leaned forward, her back toward the cloaked saucer, and murmured, "I hope I get to see you again sometime."

"I have no doubt you will," Claus said with another smile, his lips hardly moving with the words. "Especially given who you work with. And tell Fox I said hello."

* * *

Claus watched as Alpha One returned to their hidden airskimmer. They boarded, and moments later, there was a soft hum. The *SchmaltzBlitz* lifted off and shot away, headed southeast.

A soft crunching heralded mysterious footprints appearing rapidly in the snow, in the same area that had been so recently scuffed up, then vanishing into one of the other depressions. Another hum, at a different pitch, made itself known. Within seconds, an atmospheric distortion, much like a heat wave, rose from the snow and shot into the sky, headed southwest along the same heading as the *SchmaltzBlitz*.

Claus watched the two vehicles as best he could, given one was passively cloaked, the other fully so, until they disappeared into the distance. A heavy snow flurry swirled in just then, filling the clearing with a gray-white haze as the daylight dimmed.

"*SchmaltzBlitz*," he murmured with a chuckle. "More fitting, perhaps, than she considered, when she named it. But he's never going to stop teasing her with '*DonnerFurz*.'"

Then he walked over to the snowman, studying it with a discriminating eye.

"Really very nicely done," he decided. "Even if she's never made one before. All the same, we can't leave THESE here. They're not biodegradable."

He waved a hand over the two plastic bottle caps that formed the eyes. When he uncovered them again, they had been replaced by large blue gummy candies; the bottle caps were now in his palm.

He pocketed them and turned to his sled, rubbing the reindeer on the nose as he passed it. The deer—who had remained unfazed throughout the entire pyrotechnic display—grunted at him in a friendly fashion, and tossed its head again. Claus laughed.

"And people wonder why I named you and your sibling what I did," he chuckled. Then he climbed into the sled, picked up the reins and gave them a toss. "On, Donder," he murmured, and the deer started forward effortlessly.

Within moments the sled and its lone occupant had vanished into the snowy forest.

Chapter 10

Once they were well on their way to the next—and final—stop in their efforts to exhaust their Glu'g'ik perpetrator and set her at a disasvantage, Echo decided to place a ciphered call.

"Atlantis Office, this is Alpha One Agent Echo," he said, "using cipher code Alpha-Line-zero-three-zero-niner-four."

"Agent Echo, this is Atlantis Office Dispatch. We read, and are ciphering accordingly. What may we do for you?"

"Get me Klack on the horn, please."

"You mean agent Burbulon Vex?"

"That's correct."

"All right. Please stand by one, Agent Echo."

"Standing by." He threw a knowing look at his partner, who was tinkering with something in her lap, but glanced up to meet his gaze, curiosity apparent in her own eyes.

* * *

"...Yah, mon," the cheerful voice on the other end bubbled, in a distinct kind of Caribbean accent that bordered on Jamaican, to Omega's ear; yet it had a unique quality to it that she couldn't quite place. "I can do dot. Don' worry. We got dis. You got de equipment?"

"Yeah, we're good. And the underwater mods to the airskimmer are already installed," Echo confirmed.

"I be more worried 'bout you den de skimmer. Yo' potnah stayin' in de skimmer?"

"Yes," Omega answered then. "I'm working on some stuff to help us take her down once we finally confront her again."

"Okay," Burbulon decided. "Dat means jus' one ob yous gonna be out here with me. An' dat one is gonna be Echo."

"Right," Echo agreed. "And you know I've been around the Atlantis Office once or twice before."

"Yah. Das good, mon. Yah, we got dis. I was kinda hopin' to meet yo' new potnah, but mebbe next time."

"Yeah, unfortunately we've already had to spend way the hell too long on this snipe hunt as it is, Klack," Echo pointed out. "I'll see if I can't come up with an excuse for Alpha One to swing by the Atlantis Office again at some point—"

"Pref'rably soon," Burbulon interjected in a strong hint.

"Preferably soon," Echo repeated, "and then you two can meet. For now, we gotta just stick with the plan, and get the hell outta Dodge while our perp is off balance."

"Dat makes sense," Burbulon agreed. "Well, Omega, we'll meet one 'a dese days, you an' me."

"We sure will, agent Burbulon," Omega said with a smile.

"Nah. Don' call me dat. Call me what Echo calls me—Klack."

"Okay, Klack, and thank you," Omega capitulated with a shrug and a puzzled frown. "But I'm afraid I'm not gettin' the nickname."

"Aw, ain't nothin'. It jus' sounds more like mah native language."

"I...see," Omega said, giving Echo a look that said, *I don't see.* He just grinned.

I'll explain later, he signaled to her. She shrugged.

"Awright, Echo, bring it on in," Burbulon said. "I'll be waitin' f'r ya, mon. An' I'll handle t'ings on dis end. No worries."

"Great. Looking forward to it, Klack," Echo said. "Alpha One out."

"Atlantis Office out."

* * *

"After that, I kinda wish I was goin' with you, now," Omega said, as Echo initiated certain modifications to the *SchmaltzBlitz*, causing a brief, dull-red flare of light around it, and they descended to the open ocean east of Bermuda. "Promise me you'll bring me back for a visit of some sort."

"I swear I will, as soon as Fox will let us loose," Echo vowed. "Hang on, now. She's gonna buck a little bit once we hit the waves, but it'll steady out as soon as we go below."

"Tighten my straps?"

"It might be good, yeah," Echo said. "Here we go."

261

The *SchmaltzBlitz* hit the water...and sank like a brick.

* * *

A few miles behind, a dreadfully weary Ke'ri Gla'd's, having only just managed to get warm again, saw the Division One airship deliberately down itself in the ocean, then sink straight down, below the surface.

"Gl'ag'gub'it," she cursed. "That was no accident. They are going under deliberately! As much dihydrogen monoxide as they have on this planet, I was afraid I was going to have to do this, sooner or later. DO they ever STOP?!"

With a sigh, she aimed the rented saucer at the ocean surface, and plunged below it, determined to stay close on the heels of the frighteningly bizarre Division One Agents.

* * *

"I guess I just didn't expect there to be a damn amusement park down here," Omega said in bemusement, as Echo flew over the underwater city. "And that's where you're gonna meet Klack, not in the Office itself?"

"Oh, after the hullaballoo our failed candidates created back at Head-quarters? I doubt we could get Ms. Ke'ri Gla'd's within a block of the entrance," Echo pointed out. "No, this will be better. And since I happen to know that there are NO amusement parks on Va'du'sha'ā, I can safely say she has never ridden a roller coaster before in her life. Let alone an under-water version."

Omega let out a peal of laughter.

"Now I REALLY wish I was going along!" she chortled. Echo grinned again.

"Can you stop what you're doing long enough to help me suit up?" he asked, waving a hand at the tools and such which were spread all over the side worktable beside the main console.

"Yeah, I can do that," Omega agreed, putting down her tools, unstrap-ping, and standing.

* * *

The lone occupant of a cloaked spacecraft settled down on the flag-stones of the paved sea bed some thirty yards from the airskimmer, which latter was heavily wrapped in visible force-fielding. The skimmer's tiny airlock hatch opened, and an Agent emerged, clad in the black and red me-cha suit a certain extraterrestrial observer had seen at the Zaragosa airport, which proved to be an under-fluid pressure suit; judging by its height, it was the male again. Ke'ri Gla'd's watched as he walked across the parking lot and into the main building of the Atlantis Office.

"Like or'k'n'pas am I going in THERE," Gla'd's grumbled. "He is probably only going to get more equipment, anyway. Rab'dr'b if I know where they are finding space to store it all. That airship isn't that big. Maybe they have found a way to create space warps that small."

While she waited for him to emerge, she studied the structure and its surrounds.

* * *

The Atlantis Office was constructed alongside the ruins of an ancient city, and of the same building materials—hexagonal, columnar blocks of basalt, swirled in raw colors of dark red and black, and decorated with dark gray limestone; the soft hue of the naturally-pink sand of the area set off the colors of the stone rather attractively, even if artificial underwater light-ing WAS necessary in order to see said colors. As deep as it was, no one had bothered with any attempt at landscaping more sophisticated than the occasional stone sculpture, though extensive clumps and beds of the local varieties of tube worms, spirorbids and sabellids 'planted' as larvae, pro-vided additional brightness and motion as their fronds and tentacles wafted gently in the currents.

The island of the modern state of Bermuda constituted the caldera rim of an extinct volcano. Much of that volcano had been above sea level during the last ice age, forming a large, stable, fertile island, and thus an extensive ancient civilization had been constructed on and around it. Per the inscriptions and documentation found in the ruins by PGLEIA archae-ologists, said civilization had called itself Telemonis, 'The Bearers,' imply-ing that they bore civilization to the world. The etymological link to later names for the ocean area, such as Atlantikos, 'Of Atlas,' the Titan who bore the world, immediately became clear.

It was still debated among galactic scholars the exact nature of this civilization—had they been humans who had seized the opportunity to ad-

263

vance; humanoids from another world, similar enough to humans to pass as humans and perhaps even interbreed; human—or humanoid—time travelers from the future, who came back in time to establish a beachhead on the Earth? No one knew for certain.

But they knew this: When the glaciation period ended and the sea levels rose—rather catastrophically, at one point; likely due to an asteroid impact in the polar ice, according to PGLEIA researchers—the island had been shaken by a violent earthquake, then flooded by a megatsunami. The civilization, which in after ages came to be known as Atlantis, was wiped out.

But the ruins of the capitol city were still there, buried beneath the waves. And it was a popular tourist attraction for off-world visitors from water worlds and other such high-pressure dwellers; between the mystery of its origins and its people, and the fascination of the silent ruins, it garnered much interest. So much so, that not only had the Division One Agency seen fit to establish a field office close by, difficult though that task had been, a certain company known for its entertainment had taken on the daunting task of constructing a suitable resort and theme park there.

And so when Agent Echo emerged from the Atlantis Office half an hour later, still in his mecha suit, instead of returning to the *SchmaltzBlitz* and his waiting partner, he headed straight for the entrance of the Atlantean Wonders theme park.

"Aw, gl'ag'gub'it, you gr'ub rab'or a or'k'n'pas," Gla'd's cursed at the Agent, and scrambled to don her own pressure suit, provided in stowage when she rented the vehicle to 'explore the planet.'

* * *

Echo showed his *carte noir* at the entrance of the theme park, and Security waved him on through. Knowing full well he had a shadow, who was probably struggling to find the appropriate funds to pay for the entrance ticket—assuming she hadn't de-phased and gate-crashed, in which case she was apt to have even more difficulties, including sudden death, as soon as she tried to rematerialize in the water—he dawdled a bit near the entrance, finding a relatively small fossilized Megalodon shark tooth pendant and purchasing it for Omega as a little souvenir of their visit. He stuck it into a pocket, checked out of the corner of his eye to find that, sure enough, Gla'd's—pressure suit slightly askew, and not as well-fitting as it might have been, testament to her rush job in donning it—had caught up and was pretending to window-shop. So he headed on, deeper into the park.

* * *

Echo made straight for the most popular thrill ride in the park—The Vortex.

The Vortex was a powerful, giant whirlpool or gyre created underwater, and kept from reaching the surface by dint of special force fields and multiple layers of thermoclines, technology developed on the water-world of Yuvida and imported to Earth for this very purpose. Open cars were sent spinning through it, filled with excited, screaming riders who loved the rush of water through their gills. In the low-pressure center, the cars would pause, enabling riders who so desired to exit their car and play in the whirlpool—and there were a lot who chose to do so. Eventually the cars would float upward and out of the gyre, along with most of their occupants, though from time to time an over-enthusiastic rider would have to be fetched from the ride and escorted away from it...usually only to get back in line to ride it again.

It was a fun ride, even for humans with the equipment to survive at ocean-bottom depths—provided they, like Echo, had learned to conquer fear long ago. For an alien air-breather whose homeworld was possessed of very little open water, it could be an absolute hell.

But it was not without problems, in any event. Whenever the containment failed—for whatever reason, and said reason was often no accident—and the vortex reached the ocean surface, it affected the buoyancy of the water itself, as well as the air above it. This was the reason for the so-called 'Bermuda Triangle' effects of the region.

This usually happened on spring break when the visiting alien kids slipped in and disabled the containment; the resulting surface breach heavily oxygenated the water in the whirlpool, providing a buzz for all the riders. The extraterrestrial juveniles seemed to care little that the end result for any ordinary Earth craft in the vicinity was destruction for the craft and death for the crew; their attitude apparently was, "So what if we drown a few of the simple natives? They're not even people."

But it was not spring break, and Burbulon had confirmed for Echo en route that the ride equipment had just had its biannual thorough maintenance and inspection, passing with flying colors.

So he nodded politely at the ride attendant—who happened to be a planted PGLEIA agent assigned to the Atlantis Office, just not a human one—sent her a few coded signals to ensure that she knew which of the other 'tourists' got placed in his car...

...And boarded the ride.

* * *

Before she was entirely aware of what was happening, Gla'd's found herself hustled into a seat aboard an open car, several rows behind the human she was keeping under scrutiny. An attendant quickly strapped her into her seat, and suddenly the ride was under way.

As the maelstrom formed in front of their car, Gla'd's pressed back into her padded seat, already-large black eyes widening in horror.

"Gl'ag'gub'it," she cursed under her breath. "Or'k'n'pas bo rab'dr'ib, what has the ga'd'an'k'n gr'ub gotten me into now?"

Just then, the car accelerated forward and to the side, as the whirlpool sucked it in.

"Gl'ag'a'dr'IIIIIB!" she screamed, as the vortex took them.

* * *

Echo felt the acceleration as well, and a huge, boyish grin formed on his face inside his mecha helmet visor. He loved speed, and he had always enjoyed thrill rides. His only regret was that Omega was not in the seat next to him; he had no doubt she would enjoy the ride too, as much alike as they tended to be.

But, he reminded himself, she was doing an essential job back in the airskimmer, prepping some very specialized equipment that, she had promised him, would enable Alpha One to take the rogue Glu'g'ik agent into custody without further problems.

And then he heard a Glu'g'ik voice screaming in fear, somewhere behind him, the frequency distorted by the water.

Echo grinned even wider.

* * *

As usual, The Vortex performed. The ride was swift, dizzying, and powerful. As the car spiraled in toward the center, Echo, himself whooping in delight, still managed to prepare himself for the next part of his mission.

As the car entered the low-pressure center of the whirlpool and slowed dramatically, spinning gently as it settled, the Alpha Line chief unstrapped with the rest of the excited water-breathers and pushed out of the car. But unlike the tourists, instead of swimming into the inner regions of the gyre, he initiated the mecha suit's ballast shift, which allowed him to sink down...

...To the ride-control equipment hidden on the sea bed below.

There, he began looking for a particular panel in the circle of camouflaged equipment.

* * *

Ke'ri Gla'd's was only thankful the ride had stopped; Va'du'sha'ā was not possessed of very much in the way of bodies of water, and she had NEVER heard of such a monstrous...thing...as she had just experienced.

Then she saw her quarry unstrap and leave the ride car, sinking straight down...even as the ride car began to float upward.

Quickly she followed him, taking her time; she dared not de-phase, because when she re-phased, it would include the water that filled in the space where she had been, filling her pressure suit and drowning her.

I will just have to be careful and exercise a more standard stealth, so he does not see me, she thought. *He appears to be paying more attention to his search for something than to his surroundings. I wonder if it is equipment, or some way to contact another demon. Surely this was not here when...well, I suppose the ruins would have been, by the look. But surely Ari did not visit HERE. Not according to what I have read of the local technology at that time.*

A quick, confirming sweep of the quantum field in the area around the human Agent revealed the presence of a Glu'gu'ik signature, much to Gla'd's' surprise.

More, she thought, *that certainly seems like Hou'd'ni, not merely generic Glu'gu'ik. So perhaps Ari did find a way to come here. WE certainly had the technology, even if the humans did not.*

Curious, she crept closer, hiding among the ruins that littered the ocean floor around the ride equipment. Abruptly, something long and black—easily larger than her entire arm—and possessed of singularly vicious teeth darted out of a crevice, straight at her face. Badly startled, she stifled an instinctive scream before it swam off in a swift flurry of fin and tail.

Oh dear Maker, what the or'k'n'pas WAS that?! she thought, working hard to school her pulse back into a normal rhythm, and largely failing. *Well, at least the sound could be taken for a tourist on that damned ride.*

* * *

Echo heard the muffled shriek from the Glu'g'ik, and smiled to himself.

Good, he thought. *Klack had a chance to plant his pet giant dragonfish where she'd find it. This is all going off like clockwork. As for this next part, I really hope Glu'gu'ik don't have heart attacks. Then again, it sure would make it easier to apprehend her and take her in, if she's medically incapacitated.*

He located a certain mark on a panel—a curving row of circles—and very lightly rapped on the metal with his fingertips, before laying the palm of his gauntleted hand flat against the panel. The faintest tapping came back to his touch, and he nodded to himself.

The gizmo's ready, he thought. *Rock and roll.*

Echo pulled out the hurgir from a warp pocket and prepared to affix it to the panel in question...

...When an unpleasantly-familiar voice, distorted by propagation through water—and not a little wobbly, at that—addressed him from behind.

"Thank you once more, gr'ub. I think I shall have what is inside. F'al on'cik, la'la'da ge nu!"

And with that, a small trinket box of Glu'gu'ik make, accompanied by a very LARGE...and MOVING...object materialized in her outstretched hand. Large black eyes grew huge and round in horror; gray skin blanched almost white...before being engulfed.

Echo stifled a snort.

Then he initiated the water jets in his mecha suit, and made his way out of the park, laughing the whole way.

* * *

Gla'd's had scant fractions of a second to register that whatever had just materialized in her hand was BIG and ALIVE before the salmon-pink creature wrapped itself completely around her helmet. Whatever it was had far too many long, writhing tentacles covered in suckers, and its hard, beaked mouth was scant inches in front of Gla'd's' eyes, clacking audibly. Abruptly the beak spoke.

"Tag! You're it!" it cried.

Some things were just too much, even for an agent as highly trained as Gla'd's.

She screamed.

In a surge of heavy, pitch-black ink, Division One agent Burbulon Vex contracted the muscles around his siphons, shooting away into the darkness outside the ride as if propelled by rockets.

Behind him, engulfed in a cloud of inky darkness so deep that she dared not move, Gla'd's just kept screaming.

From somewhere nearby, human laughter sounded, diminishing in the distance.

* * *

Enclosed in his own form of environment suit to give him water to breathe and maintain the higher pressures in which he'd been operating, Burbulon Vex came inside the *SchmaltzBlitz* with Echo, only long enough to meet Echo's partner. The pair had just finished telling her what had happened in the theme park, and when Omega stopped laughing, Echo provided formal introductions, even as Burbulon passed a small package to Omega, one on which she'd filed a formal requisition form, earlier that day.

"...So in case you haven't guessed, Klack, this is my partner Omega."

"Oh, very pleased to meet ya, ma'am," the octopus burbled cheerfully, holding out a tentacle for Omega to shake. Behind him, Echo began the process of removing the mecha suit and stowing it.

"Likewise," Omega said with a smile, shaking the appendage, which was sheathed in an arm of the special suit. "And please, do call me Meg, like my other friends."

269

"She be takin' this pretty well, mon," Burbulon noted to Echo. "Me an octopus and all."

"Oh, no no! I always suspected octopuses were REALLY intelligent," Omega supplied. "And that if we could only figure out how to communicate with you, we'd find out just how much."

"An' you were right, Meg," Burbulon agreed, shifting his skin to a pale lavender to express the pleased amusement his features could not. "One ob dese days, you two gotta come back so we c'n hab a long talk. I'd come ta New York, but dat's a mite chilly for de likes ob me dere."

"Can I ask a question?"

"Sure, mon."

"You sound like a human from Jamaica, or someplace close to it," Omega observed. "Caribbean, generally, I guess. Whatever I figured a talking octopus might sound like, that isn't it."

"He's FROM Jamaica, Meg," Echo answered. "Well, from the waters AROUND Jamaica, anyway."

"Yah, an' I goes back dere eb'ry chance I get, on my time off," Burbulon agreed. "I likes to hang out in de shallows aroun' de island an' unwind. W'en I was younger, I played wif de local kids in de surf, ya know, an' dat's where I learned my English. Dat's where my accent comes from."

"How long does it take to go back home? And do you have family there?"

"I gots fam'ly all ober de place," Burbulon averred. "Dat's an octopus fam'ly for ya. But it depends how I go. I hitch a ride on a saucer, few minutes. I gotta go all my own self, takes 'bout a day ob hard travel, each way. But I'm pow'rful hungry w'en I gets dere."

"I'll bet," Omega said with a smile. "So you sound like you're from Jamaica because the humans you learned from were Jamaican. What does OCTOPUS sound like?"

"Let's just say there's a reason I call him Klack," Echo chuckled.

"Word," Burbulon averred, bouncing gently on his tentacles. "Kkkttk-krlk a klck trtk momom, clk kkk hakrk."

Omega blinked.

"What did he just say?" she wondered. Burbulon looked at Echo with an expectant gaze. Echo grinned.

"He said," the male agent supplied, "'Octopoid speech sounds like clacking to humans, because we have beaks.' Octopus beaks are actually shaped kind of like parrots' beaks, Meg, so there's a certain similarity to the avian languages. But their tongues are different, and the medium—water—doesn't allow for the addition of trills like, say, Ke!endarian might have."

"Ooo," Omega hummed, impressed. Burbulon shot Echo a slight glance, turning a delicate shade of pale rose pink. If Echo saw, he gave no notice of it. "Cool," she continued. "But wow, I really wish I'd been there to see you scare her witless, Klack! There were alarms and alerts going off all over the park, and security running everywhere." She waved her hands at the front windscreen. "And then they escorted her out of the park under guard."

* * *

Echo laughed, and a series of staccato clicks emerged from Burbulon—octopus laughter.

"I'm not surprised," Echo said. "It was priceless."

"Dere should be video, mon," Burbulon told him. "I had a feeling dis gonna be funny, so I set up a portable camera on top ob de nearest ruin. I'll pop you de file w'en I gets back to my quarters dis evening."

"Lookin' forward to it, Klack." Echo snorted. "I just realized this last little incident lends a whole new meaning to the phrase, 'You suck.' Not to mention singing songs like, 'Stuck on You'..."

"Aw, shuddup," Burbulon riposted, turning a light shade of purple, so Echo knew he liked the puns. Omega just sat in the co-pilot's chair, giggling until her face turned red.

"Well, much though I'd like to visit longer, Klack, we need to get going," Echo said with a sigh. "We're a long way from finishing this mission, yet."

"And miles to go before we sleep," Omega paraphrased, finishing with a sigh herself. "At least, in our own beds. I'm looking forward to coming back again soon, though, for that visit. I want to get to know you better!"

"Oh, not to worry, my dear," Burbulon said, reaching out a tentacle to take her hand; a quick nod by the octopus left the impression in both humans that he had bowed over it in a courtly fashion. "Echo's friends are my friends. You will come back, an' we will become de best ob friends, you an' me." He turned to Echo. "You pay 'tention, mon, an' take good care ob her! An' you," he turned back to Omega, "you do de same for him."

"That's what partners do," Echo murmured. "We already have been, and we'll keep it up."

"Right," Omega agreed.

"Awright, den," Burbulon said, studying both of them for a long moment with his big eyes. Then he turned and scuttled toward the hatch. "Get dis airlock workin' like a waterlock an' let me back out. Den you two get gone awready. We all gots de work to do."

* * *

Ten minutes later, the *SchmaltzBlitz* broke the Atlantic surface and rose, dripping, into the air.

"I think she's ready now," Echo decided.

"It sure sounds like it. Worn out, fried, and frazzled."

"Something like that, yeah. On to Hamburg, then?" Echo asked. "Are you ready? Do you have everything you need?"

"I sure do," Omega declared. "I only got a few minutes' more tinkering left to do and it'll ALL be ready."

"Good. I'll start us headed east, then, while you take care of last-minute 'tinkering.' We should be there in under four hours."

"Perfect. Even time for us to take turns napping," Omega said, rising and heading aft with the small package that Burbulon had brought. "And maybe some more laughs, if Klack sends us that video."

The *SchmaltzBlitz* accelerated, headed east, back across the Atlantic.

* * *

Moments later, a large, invisible object broke the water's surface, and copious water streamed off it, briefly outlining a saucer-shaped craft in gleaming, silver liquid.

Then it, too, accelerated, headed eastward, shaking off the last droplets as it went.

* * *

Burbulon Vex was true to his word; halfway across the Atlantic en route to Germany, the compressed file containing his video arrived. It was short, but sweet. By the end of it, Echo was laughing uproariously, and Omega had to unstrap from her seat to double up and pound the chair arms, she was laughing so hard.

"Oh-oh! Ace, I don't know WHEN I've laughed so hard!" she gasped finally. "Ohmigosh! That last glimpse of her face, just before Klack covered her helmet! PRICELESS! Was there anything in her face BUT her eyes?!"

"You should have heard her screaming when the ride car took off into The Vortex," Echo chortled. "Between that, Klack's pet dragonfish, and Klack himself, I expect the rental agency is gonna assess a massive cleaning fee for that pressure suit...assuming she ever gets a chance to return it."

"If all goes according to plan, Ace," Omega said, finally starting to sober, "the Agency will be the ones returning it. But they still should take the fee outta her hide."

"Ain't that the truth," Echo agreed. He glanced at the chronometer on the console. "Just under an hour 'til arrival, baby. You ready?"

"I am now," she told him with a smile. "I needed that laugh! Geez!"

"I'm with ya, there. This is proving to be one damn long mission."

"No shit."

* * *

They took the *SchmaltzBlitz* right over the castle proper; the building in which they were interested was now designated der Museum für Burgedorf und die Vierlande.

"Und die Vierlande," Omega noted. "And the Four Lands. What's that mean?"

"No idea at the moment," Echo said, studying the terrain below. "And I don't have time to think about it right now; I'm trying to find a good spot to set your *DonnerFurz* down. See if there's any notation online, if you're curious enough."

"*SchmaltzBlitz*!" she corrected, and he grinned.

"Look online," he repeated.

"Okay. Oh, there it is," she said, fiddling with her cell phone. "Aha, it's the four original parishes that were united under the area's dukes—of Saxony-Lauenburg, judging by this."

"So just an old medieval historical notation."

"Pretty much, yeah. Wow, did this thing used to have a moat? It's got water pretty much all the way around it, looks like."

"Yeah, I noticed," Echo said. "A double moat, actually, according to what I'm seeing. And that really screws up my original notions of where to land. Either we're gonna have to set down awful damn close to the castle walls and hope nobody trips over the skimmer, or park it a ways away and walk."

"Look over there," Omega said, pointing. "Isn't that a mall? On the other side of the road around the outer moat?"

"Yeah! With a flat roof," Echo added. "That'll work."

* * *

In short order, the pair were striding across the bridge over the double moat, and up to the castle walls. Fox had been right, as usual; the current structure was a castle only in the sense of having been the manor house of the lineage of dukes for the region. It was red brick, roughly square with a central courtyard and high peaked roofs of what appeared to Alpha One to be red tile, surmounted by tall, narrow chimneys. The highest points of the gable ends contained no less than six stories.

Arches and towers with conical roofs, as well as hints at crenellations, added to the 'castle' ambiance; whether or not the crenellations had comprised the original parapet, or were merely there for decoration, was not possible to ascertain without more time and effort than the two Agents had available.

What appeared to be wrought iron torch sconces dotted the walls in strategic places, and there was an overall feeling of age to the structure... indeed, not all of the brick was of the same hue, and lent the distinct impression that, rather than being built at one time, the castle had rather grown over the years, with additions and modifications, as well as repairs, occurring from time to time.

* * *

"I wonder if it was damaged during World War II," Omega wondered, studying the differing shades of brick. "See over there?"

"Mm, I don't think so," Echo considered, "but you could be right.

We can always ask Fox later; he'd know, if anybody would. He was from Germany until the Nazis shipped his family to Majdanek."

"Yeah," Omega murmured, subdued.

"You okay?"

"Yeah. I just hate thinking about what happened to Fox. As a kid, yet."

"Oh. Well, yeah, me too. Best concentrate on work, for now."

"Good point."

* * *

Insofar as they could tell, the proper front of the castle faced northwest, but Alpha One's approach deliberately brought them in from the southwest. They walked quietly along the gravel path around the rear of the castle, playing tourist, pointing at this feature or that, and from time to time pulling out their cell phones to take photographs.

A soft crunching sound—as of light footsteps in gravel—could be heard, some distance behind them, and without turning their heads, they glanced sidelong at one another.

We're being followed, Echo telegraphed, and Omega nodded ever so slightly.

Wanna guess who? she signaled back.

Three guesses, and the first two don't count, Echo told her.

Yup.

They kept walking; the crunching continued, maintaining a steady distance. Echo stopped to take a picture with his phone; the crunching sound stopped. Blue eyes and brown cut around at each other again. *Have a look,* Echo signaled, *but make it subtle.*

Okay, lemme think a minute. Oh, I got it. Stand by.

Standing by.

"This is utterly beautiful," Omega said with enthusiasm, just then. She flung out her arms and spun, gazing with a smile at the castle grounds. "Ace, I really gotta thank you for recruiting me. I get to see SO much that I wouldn't otherwise see, doing this job!"

"I know, baby," he said, offering her a smile. "And I can tell you love it." Then he telegraphed, *Did you see anything?*

Nope, came the nonverbal response. *There's nobody back there. At*

275

least, nobody VISIBLE.

Right. She's exactly where we figured she'd be. And how we figured she'd be.

Yup. Let's do this.

Are you sure?

Oh hell yes. I got a few tricks up my sleeve that I think her cousin would approve of.

All right then. Let's see what we can find.

They headed straight for the eastern corner of the castle.

* * *

"Lookee, lookee," Omega murmured. "A little door in the foundation. Surprise, surprise."

"It looks really new," Echo observed, "but that doesn't mean the DOORWAY hasn't been there a damn long time. And by the look of it," he added, fingering the door frame, "I think it has."

"I got this," Omega told him, pulling out her electronic lock pick. "Just make sure nobody's watching."

Echo turned slowly, his trained eagle eyes seeing nothing...except a slightly scuffed place in the gravel some ten yards back on the path.

"You're good," he told his partner. "Just make it fast."

"Done," she said, and pulled the squat metal door open. "Get low and let's go."

* * *

The floor was several feet below the bottom of what amounted to a half-door; as Alpha One eased themselves through the opening, they found they were able to stand upright. Both Agents extracted cell phones and turned on the flashlight apps, looking around the dark space.

"It's a storeroom," Echo noted, seeing old furniture and other such objects stacked along the walls. "There must be another entrance to this cellar, from inside the main floor."

"Yeah," Omega agreed. "The walls are plenty thick, but I got an idea where this gizmo might be."

"Oh? Lead on," Echo said, as they put away their cell phones. "I got an idea, too, but I'm curious to see if my idea matches yours."

"Ooo, wait, is that a light switch? It is!" She flipped the switch and dim yellow illumination filled the space from an old incandescent bulb overhead.

"Ah! That's better."

"Yup. I'm bettin' there's a nice big ol' cube of rock over here," Omega said, turning left and heading toward the exact corner of the structure. "A cornerstone. And I'll bet our whosiwhatsis is in it."

"My exact idea," Echo agreed. "Let's see what we find."

But there was a heap of discarded furniture stacked in the corner, and the pair had to move several dusty items, including a heavy oaken table, before they could get to the corner proper.

"There better not be spiders in here," Omega grumbled.

"Oh, that's right, you're arachnophobic, aren't you?" Echo teased.

"Not enough to prevent my taking on Charlotte in that damn obstacle course you and Fox ginned up, when I tested for the department," Omega shot back.

"Point," Echo conceded. "And there's the cornerstone, a nice big chunk of...looks like limestone?"

"Hard to tell," Omega decided, running her hands over the surface. "Feels like it, but the lighting in here isn't really good enough for me to tell. But I'd be willing to betcha there's a Glu'gu'ik artifact in there." She tapped it.

"And I wouldn't bet against you," Echo said, digging in his pockets. "Bust out your imaging scanner, and let's have a look-see."

They both scanned the big stone block carefully. Suddenly Echo tapped the scanner's screen.

"Yep," he said, satisfied. "Right there. Hang on while I get out the hurgir."

* * *

Moments later a small shaft opened onto a spherical chamber within the cornerstone; a tiny silver device, looking like nothing so much as a three-dimensional jigsaw puzzle, lay inside.

Alpha One threw surreptitious glances at each other. It was time to confront their perp. And this time, they were ready; it had been no accident that they left the half-door into the cellar ajar. Sure enough, the fish took the bait.

"Once more I thank you, rab'or'ne a or'k'n'pas gru'ub," came the all-too-familiar voice from behind them.

"Oh, I don't think so," Echo declared, spinning, his blasters already in hand and aimed at the weary Glu'g'ik, who had foolishly materialized behind them.

"Not hardly," Omega said, both of her blasters likewise pointed at the alien.

"...You're under arrest," Echo added.

* * *

"On what grounds?" Ke'ri Gla'd's demanded, feeling herself turning a much ashier shade of gray as the Agents confronted her and she found herself staring down the barrels of four blasters.

"Conspiracy and insurrection against the Va'du'sha'ān government, failure to disclose intent during interstellar Customs interrogation, failure to follow international customs regulations, multiple counts of attempted murder, multiple counts of assault with intent to commit murder..."

"Yes, yes, I grasp it," a sullen Gla'd's interrupted Echo. "Now what?"

"I'll get her restrained, Ace," Omega murmured. "You get the gadget."

* * *

Omega, much larger and stronger than the frail-limbed, tiny Zeta Reticulan...and much better rested...caught the alien's wrists in force cuffs—careful not to touch her hands, or any other part of her body—and pinned them firmly behind the Glu'g'ik's back.

"NO, MEG!" Echo exclaimed, as Omega applied and locked the cuffs, then stepped back. "She's a Glu'g'ik! Remember what she did at Headquarters and in London! Don't touch her! The quantum foam manip—"

"HA!" Gla'd's exclaimed in triumph, and faded away...

...into translucence. But did not disappear.

"What in the infernal?!" Gla'd's muttered.

"I...second that," Echo murmured, eyes narrowed, watching.

"Not a problem, Ace," Omega said with a grin. "You know how the force cuffs work, right?"

"Of course," Echo noted. "The housing generates a low-grade, shaped Higgs field with virtual Higgs phasing in and out from the quantum foam on a particular frequency."

"Right. All that studying up we did before she arrived? I went back over the dossier. PLUS the new stuff Fox sent. And YOU figured out what she did to me in London. So I researched all I could on how the Glu'gu'ik manipulate the quantum foam, and I learned a lot. Then I brainstormed how to build a restraint. Turns out all I really had to do was to tinker with my standard-issue force cuffs a little, so that it moves through the phasing frequencies on a random cycle..."

"Aha! So a Glu'g'ik can't adjust to what he or she can't predict," Echo realized.

"Exactly. Trust me. She's not goin' anywhere now."

"You truly have been assisted by other powers." Gla'd's shook her head. "I should not wish to be you on the day of your death."

Omega and Echo exchanged significant glances. The expression of each told the other, *It worked. In spades. All of it.*

"Good job, baby." Echo grinned, returning his weapons to their holsters. "Now, let's see about getting this gizmo."

"Good luck with that," Gla'd's muttered, as Echo reached for the device in its hidden compartment.

But fractions of a second before he laid hands on it, the object let out a soft *ding!* and scooted aside by a few inches; Echo's fingers grasped nothing but air.

"Wha?!" he exclaimed, grabbing for it with his other hand. It blinked out, vanishing in mid-air, and reappearing several feet away, on the table. A sudden lunge on Echo's part, swiping at it with both hands, did no good—it scooted just out of reach, then dematerialized and rematerialized fractions of a second later, back in the alcove in which it had been hidden.

"Aw, shit," Omega grumbled, fishing out another pair of force cuffs. This pair went around Gla'd's' ankles, wrapping around a heavy walnut table leg in the process—even in the unlikely event that the Glu'g'ik managed to phase out the table, she wasn't going anywhere very fast with only a few inches' stride. "Stay. There," the stern Agent told the Zeta Reticulan, "'cause I won't be very happy if I have to chase YOU down, too. And believe me, you've already made me more than unhappy enough. You do NOT want to see what I do when I'm seriously pissed off." Then she moved across the room, where Echo still strove to get a hand on the elusive little alien mechanism.

"Meg, try maneuver Alpha-One-twenty-three," Echo suggested.

"Pincer move? Okay," Omega said, as she approached from the opposite side of the gadget, reasonably effectively blocking its escape route, as Echo came in from his side.

But the apparently semi-intelligent construct shot through the air between them, to the far side of the storage room. Alpha One ran after it, only to find it had returned to its proper alcove.

"You are not going to be able to obtain it," Gla'd's observed. "It is keyed only to Ho'd'ni genetics and—"

"Aw, hell! C'mere, you little bugger!" Omega exclaimed, annoyed.

A soft tone suddenly sounded from somewhere; both Echo and Omega thought it came from the object...which suddenly decided to rise a few inches into the air and hover for several moments. Abruptly it zipped into Omega's hands.

"What the hell?!" Echo exclaimed—just as Gla'd's gave a shocked cry. "Meg, how'd you do that, baby?"

"I...dunno."

"Take it off! TAKE IT OFF!" the Glu'g'ik cried.

"Take what off?" Omega wondered.

"Your human disguise! You are kin! You MUST be!" Ke'ri Gla'd's exclaimed, lunging at Omega and only falling short by dint of her feet cuffed to the table leg. "Only one with Hou'd'ni genetics could have called it!"

* * *

Omega and Echo exchanged glances; Echo saw the pain in his partner's gaze. It took him several seconds to process why—until the explanation hit him.

Well, shit, he thought. *Some of the genetics that Slug spliced in must have been Glu'gu'ik. Worse, he must have got hold of tissue from a member of Clan Hou'd'ni. And now she knows it. Damn.*

"You will help me NOW!" Gla'd's demanded. "You are kin! You are a Ho'd'ni! You MUST help me!"

"I can promise you, I'm not a Ho'd'ni. I'm not even Glu'g'ik," Omega pointed out. "And I'm sure not gonna help you."

Gla'd's scowled. Large black eyes closed, and a high gray forehead creased in concentration, as Omega slipped the little alien device into an inside pocket with a seal, and fastened it in...after producing yet a third set of force cuffs and wrapping both loops around the artifact, thus ensuring it could not dematerialize.

"Somebody was REALLY busy with force cuffs during the flight," Echo decided, watching. "How many you got on you, baby?"

"Several more sets," Omega remarked. "All modified to hold Glu'gu'ik and their tech. See, I— uhng..." She staggered, suddenly clawing at her throat and chest.

"What? What's wrong, Meg?" a concerned Echo wondered, stepping toward her.

"You will obey me, Glu'g'ik, or you will die," Gla'd's declared. "Just because I cannot manipulate myself does not mean I cannot kill you."

"Told...you," Omega gasped, dropping to her knees in pain, clutching at her breastbone, "not...a...Glu'g'ik. Uhn. Stop...that..."

"You ARE. You MUST be. You are Hou'd'ni. The F'al on'cik recognizes your genetics. Only a true Ho'd'ni could call it—as you did. You will do as I say! I am chu'p'ik! You can only be or'd'ot. I am your superior. You will obey me or die!"

Echo drew both blasters again, quick as lightning, leveling both of them at the alien. "Omega is no more a Glu'g'ik than I am," he declared. "She was, however, abducted by a gastropoid criminal as a child and subjected to illegal and unethical genetic experiments."

"Wha-what?" Gla'd's said, surprised. "But..."

"Release your hold on her, or I swear, there won't be enough left of you to send home," Echo growled. "Try actually studying her, rather than just attacking her. Meg, she's trying to manipulate the foam in and around your body. Again."

"I...I gathered that," Omega panted. "Emphasis on trying. But she's eased up for the moment."

"Meaning, while it hurts, she isn't actually damaging your insides?"

"I don't think so, no. It hurt like hell, but...I'm dealing, this time. Consciously...at least to a point."

"Good."

"Gl'ag'a'dr'b!" cursed Gla'd's. "You are indeed invulnerable, by the will of god and demon. That should have scrambled your internal organs. You should be dead."

"Not dead. Not even close. As for you," Omega addressed her prisoner. "Have you finally figured it out yet? What Echo said?"

"Yes. I...your partner is correct," Gla'd's murmured to Omega. "There is...there is Glu'gu'ik genetic material in you, and there is other I do not recognize, as well...but mostly human."

"See?" Echo murmured. "Toldja."

"Yeah, yeah," Omega grumbled, getting to her feet. She walked over to the Zeta Reticulan and got right down in the alien's face. "If you EVER try that again, you will NOT like the consequences."

"And just what do you propose to do about it?" Gla'd's asked, insolent.

Omega reached around to the small of her back, beneath her Suit jacket—as Echo watched AND maintained a bead on the Glu'g'ik's head with both blasters. She produced a shiny silver packet and unfolded it...

...Then shoved the triangular, 'tin-foil' hat down on the alien's head.

Gla'd's let out a shriek of pain and tried to clutch at her head with tightly manacled hands for a moment, then sighed and slumped in on herself.

"You win," she murmured. "I could not attack if I wanted to, now."

"Good," Omega declared. "Now, let's keep it that way. I don't want you damaging that, too, if you were to figure it out."

Reaching around to the small of her back again, Omega produced a series of straps that looked like it had once been a couple of pairs of force leg irons for one of the larger humanoid species. But Omega had repurposed it; it now formed a kind of partial sphere, or at least the framework of one. She moved to the Glu'g'ik, wrapped it around her head, slid one of the straps under what passed for Gla'd's' chin, fastened and activated it. Gla'd's choked for a moment, though Echo could tell that the straps were not too tight; then the alien woman sighed and sank down to the floor, sitting there in mute surrender.

"What did you DO, baby?" Echo wondered, astounded, and unsure whether to lower his weapons or not.

"As soon as I had the mod to my force cuffs figured out, I requisitioned all that stuff from the different Offices. I didn't discover the thing about the aluminum foil until pretty late in the game, so that was what was in the package Klack brought me," Omega gestured at the 'head wrap,' shrugging, "and then I reworked all of it. Once I understood it, I could think of all sorts of ways she could use her ability to manipulate the quantum foam to cause problems, and while I knew I could keep her from getting away with the cuffs, I figured I needed something to keep her under control overall. The brain is the key, so I just...de-phased her brain, I guess you could say. But I needed something that would work even faster, and that would be easier to put on. So I discovered that they don't have aluminum on Va'du'sha'ā..."

"Damn. You mean she doesn't recognize the atomic structure?" Echo wondered.

"More than that," Omega explained. "Near as I can figure, based on the information I had to hand, it's only one step removed from kryptonite to a Zeta Reticulan. Somehow or other—I didn't follow all of the neurological discussion, I'm afraid; that's not one of my specialties—but it seems to completely block their...'quantum sense,' I guess you could call it. She can't get through it. In fact, according to Fox, it may well be the origin of the whole concept of 'tin-foil hats' to protect the mind, among those who encountered a Zeta Reticulan before the Agency was a full-up thing."

"Aw, shit. You're kidding."

"Nope. Then you put the force bands on top of it, and stick a fork in her, she's done."

"So she can't tweak anything at the quantum level now?"

"Not like that, no," Omega averred. "So you can probably go ahead and put away your blasters again."

"Shit, baby. Have I mentioned lately that you make a damn fine partner?"

"No," she threw him a grin, "but you can say it as often as you want to. I sure won't mind."

Echo laughed.

"Okay, we got our conspirator, we got the next clue in the treasure hunt, and we got miles to go before we sleep. So let's get a move on."

"I'm with you," Omega agreed.

* * *

As they headed for their aircraft, escorting their prisoner but prepared to brain bleach any witnesses, several agents from the Geneva Office arrived, meeting them on the roof of the mall across the street.

"Fox contacted us and said you might need some extra hands," the lead, code-named Nordpol, remarked with a grin; he had been one of the agents to provide equipment during their brief Zaragosa visit. "It appears that the two of you did fine, though. Alpha Line and all, I suppose, eh?"

"Yeah, but we DO need you to do a few things," Echo noted. "This is a Glu'g'ik conspirator from the Zeta Reticuli system. Are you familiar with 'em?"

"Are those not the beings that can manipulate the quantum foam?"

"Right. And this one isn't an ordinary Glu'g'ik, she's an undercover operative gone rogue, so she has skills commensurate to her position. See the force cuffs on her feet and hands? They've been modified so she can't use her abilities to dematerialize and get out of 'em. And the headset prevents her using it to attack—which she's already tried a couple of times, on my partner. So under no circumstances remove 'em, not even the aluminum foil liner on the headset," Echo warned. "She's already gotten away from Alpha Line several times, and wreaked havoc in Australia. We need to make sure she stays in custody until we can ship her back home to be tried for sedition and conspiracy. She'll have to answer for charges here on Earth too, including two counts of assault and battery, multiple counts of malicious destruction, a couple hundred counts of battery, and probably as many counts of attempted murder, plus two. We're still waiting to see if some of those turn into actual murder charges—a lot of people were hurt during her rampage in Australia, all in an effort to distract the Agency—but we'll see to that later. For the time being, we need to find the rest of these devices."

"Right. So you need us to take her into custody and hold her?"

"Bingo," Omega answered. "And swing on tight."

"What she said," Echo agreed. "If you need to, call Fox and have him send Alpha Two to fetch her back to Headquarters. I'm betting by now, he's got a holding tank all ready for her."

"Roger that, sir, madam. And there's a team already on the way to handle her rented craft."

"Good," Echo said.

Alpha One handed over custody of the rogue Glu'g'ik to the local agents, and headed for where they knew the rental spacecraft sat.

* * *

A quick hack with a special app of his own design on Echo's phone dropped the cloak on the rental saucer. Another hack unfastened the locked hatch. Omega headed for the hatch, which was now opening, its lower half becoming the boarding ramp. Echo grabbed her arm.

"Wait, baby," he told her. "She may have booby-trapped the thing. The Geneva Office has a team en route to...'decontaminate' the ship, for want of a better word, and return it to the rental agency. All we really want are the pieces that she's already got. Do you think you can call 'em from here?"

"I...can try, I suppose," Omega agreed. "Lemme see...I said, 'C'mere, you little bugger!' and it came to me..."

Her pocket flapped where the object they'd just retrieved rested, and both Agents knew it had responded.

But within seconds, a silvery blur zipped through the open hatch of Gla'd's' spacecraft, and straight to Omega's outstretched hand.

"Wouldja look at that," Echo murmured, studying the lone object. "It isn't two pieces, it's one bigger piece made out of the original two."

Omega stared down at the object in her hand. Then she reached into her pocket and pulled out the third piece, still wrapped in the modified force cuffs.

"Do you suppose...?" she wondered. "They ARE shaped like puzzle pieces, after all..."

"Yeah, I'm betting it would," Echo agreed. "This isn't half a dozen different gizmos we're looking for, it's one, broken into half a dozen different components."

"Shall I try assembling this piece into the whole?"

"Wait until we get on board our ship," Echo advised. "I'll feel marginally better with the hatch closed. I suppose it can still phase through the hull, but..."

"Let's go, then."

"Okay. Hang on."

Echo used his phone to reactivate the cloaking, then they deactivated the solid hologram and boarded their airskimmer.

* * *

Once the hatch was closed, and before they did anything else, Echo helped Omega set up a kind of bounded work area for what she was about to try, using several sets of modified force cuffs, daisy-chained together. Then Omega sat the composite piece in the center, laid the newly-captured piece in its force-cuff prison beside it...and released the new piece.

Both components just lay there, inert.

"Well, it isn't automatic," Echo murmured, watching. "Try telling it to merge or something."

"She called each of them something," Omega noted. "She called 'em, 'F'al on'cik.'"

Suddenly both pieces vibrated.

"Ooo," Omega murmured. "F'al on'cik, merge."

They vibrated again, but nothing happened.

"F'al on'cik, join," she tried again.

This time the pieces rose a couple of inches off the console on which she worked, hovered, then zipped together, spinning rapidly about a common center. There was a soft click, and one object fell to the console surface.

"That did it," Echo crowed. "You did it, baby!"

"Yeah, but it's obviously incomplete," Omega decided. "I...Echo, do you know what the word 'F'al' means in Glu'gu'ik?"

"No, I've never heard of it before."

"What about the word 'on'cik'?"

"That, I do know. It means 'piece,' or 'part.'"

"I had a sneaking feeling that's what it meant," Omega murmured, as she trussed the joined object back up in the jerry-rigged force cuffs. "I think, whatever this thing is, the proper name for it, at least in their language, is F'al."

The object in her hand vibrated in response.

"Wow," she said. "It's almost like...like a dog barking in response to its name, or something. It's programmed to recognize certain words."

"Interesting," Echo decided. "Once we're airborne again, I think I'm going to do some linguistics research and see if I can at least come up with the root and etymology for that word, or name, or...whatever it is. Because I'm betting you're right, and if I can find that, we might actually get an idea what this thing is supposed to be for." He pointed at the device. "Do you think it'll let me handle it, as long as it's in that set of force cuffs?"

"It shouldn't have a choice," Omega said. "Why?"

"There's a safe on board the skimmer, in the back of the stowage, and I was gonna put it inside."

"Okay. But let me carry it back there, just to be on the safe side."

"Deal."

Chapter 11

Once the alien artifact was safely stowed, the Alpha One team headed for the tiny flight deck proper.

Omega sat down in the copilot's seat, careful not to touch anything on the console, then sighed quietly, seeming to collapse in on herself. Echo noticed.

"Hey, what's wrong, baby?" he asked. "We got the whatsis, AND the perp. You should be feeling pretty good about that, since you're the one responsible for both of those. Or are you still feeling bad from her attack? Now that we have her in custody, we can take our time finding the rest of the stuff—at least, provided none of her compatriots show up to grab it, which I guess we need to check with Fox about..."

"No, I forgot to tell you—back when I was flying to fish you out of the Outback, Fox called and told me that the Va'du'sha'āns caught Gla'd's' accomplice before he could get off-planet. And they tightened security at their spaceports. Unless they already had someone on Earth, we got this."

"Well, that's some serious good news. But still, my point is, that's gonna give us a little bit of leeway right now. Do we need to take you to the Geneva Office medlab? Or back to London? Headquarters, even?"

"No, it isn't that," Omega said, voice very low. "She didn't do any damage, this time. I kind of..." She broke off, then shrugged. "I kind of modified my mental block, and, and extended it, I guess you could say. It seemed to work. It still hurt...like, like somebody shoving hard on your chest from the inside out, I guess...but it worked. She couldn't actually rearrange anything."

"What, then? What's wrong?"

"I..." She broke off, then shrugged. "I just suddenly realized that... well, what Slug did to me...there's a whole lotta other repercussions to what he did, that are OUTSIDE me."

"What do you mean?"

"Ace, we just discovered that he spliced Glu'gu'ik genes into me—among other things," Omega pointed out. "And not just any Glu'g'ik—someone from Clan Hou'd'ni specifically. Now, I dunno if he did that deliberately for some reason, or if it was purely coincidental that that's who he got his...pseudopods...on. But I'm not sure it matters that much, 'cause I know what it means."

"What does it mean, then?"

"It means that we need to investigate and find out if there are any cold cases involving a missing or dead member of that family, from around twenty years ago."

"Oh SHIT! You're right," Echo realized, smacking his forehead. "Which also means—"

"Yeah. We need the medlab to try to separate out the various other 'additions' to my...whatever," Omega added, "so we can see if there are any OTHER cold cases, from other planets, that we can close out."

"Good point. Lemme get on the horn to Fox—" Echo reached for the comm, but Omega caught his hand.

"Wait," she murmured. "You need to hear all of it, before you do anything. Because you may change your mind about what you wanna do next."

"All of what? What else is there to discuss?"

"Stuff like this: Whatever Slug did, to get all that genetic material," Omega pointed out, "he almost certainly committed major crimes to do it. Kidnapping at the very least. Maiming, possibly. More probably, outright murder."

"So? That's kinda the point to being able to close out the cold cases, isn't it?"

"Yeah, but Echo, that makes me a kind of accessory to all of those crimes." Omega drew a deep breath. "I need to turn myself in until the whole mess is worked out. And," she let the remaining breath out in another sigh, "that might end up meaning you need another partner. Especially if I'm convicted of being an accessory after the fact."

"Oh HELL no!" a shocked Echo exclaimed, vehement. "I'm not lettin' you do that, baby! Not when you were the VICTIM!"

"You know as well as I do that on some of the worlds out there, that won't hold water, Ace," Omega noted, shoulders drooping farther. "At the very least, I'm a kind of evidence for what Slug did. A, a receiver of stolen goods, or the like."

"No. Just...Meg...don't..." Echo's face was drawn in a kind of mental pain.

"I don't see that I have a choice, Echo. Yes, we need to contact Fox and put this in work, which gives us a chance to see how far along we can get on our current mission before everything all goes down on the cold cases. But I have to tell him that...that I'm turning myself in, once we've established that I AM complicit in whatever cold cases we uncover..." She waved a hand at the comm section of the panel. "Okay. NOW call Fox."

"Damn," Echo grumbled, initiating the call.

* * *

"...Shit, merde, cachu, khro, abdab, and gronk!" Fox's holovid image finally finished cursing in multiple Earth languages, and several offworld ones. "Will that damned gastropoid NEVER stop coming back to haunt us?!"

"Believe me, sir," Omega murmured, "as far as I'm concerned, he never stopped." Fox quieted his tirade at once.

"I know, yung froy," he responded, gentling his voice. "Forgive me. I'm simply tired of being blindsided by additional repercussions. I'll contact Zebra at once and put the analysis at the top of the medlab's priority list; Zebra and Zarnix should have it worked out pretty quickly, since we already have your detailed genetic analysis from when you joined us. They just need to separate out the added components. And then I'll turn around and contact Va'du'sha'ā, to see what we can find out from their law enforcement department; I need to notify them that their prisoner is in custody anyway. While you two were on that crazy jaunt to confuse your perp and wear her out, they sent a contingent to help handle her, and they're already en route to the Geneva Office, to take her home and face the music there. After that, we'll be convening an interstellar tribunal, though it'll probably be on Va'du'sha'ā, because they can handle the bitch better! Anyway, I'll let you know as soon as I hear anything...about the lot of it. And I'll look into whatever else the medlab finds, and try to determine if there are any more cold cases that need looking into."

"Fox?"

"Yes, Omega?"

"I, uh," Omega shot a pained, sidelong glance at Echo, who grimaced and dropped his gaze, "I wanted you to know that...well, as an unwitting accessory to Slug's crimes...as soon as you establish the nature of the crimes under consideration, I'll be returning to turn myself in..."

"What?!"

"The way I figure it, at the very least, I'm a clue, a piece of evidence," Omega explained. "And undoubtedly on some of the planets, I'll be an accessory to murder, or kidnapping, or...or whatever."

"Meg," Echo said, hoarse, "you do understand that, on some of those planets, a piece of evidence is taken apart to see what additional data can be obtained?"

Omega swallowed hard, then nodded once.

"NO," Fox declared, firm. "Just...no. On many levels. I am NOT letting you be vivisected for the sake of some damn investigation, and I am NOT letting you be blamed, let alone convicted, for something you'd have done anything to stop! For one, you were well under legal age when it all occurred, and therefore cannot be held accountable. For another, you yourself were kidnapped, mentally...'raped,' and, from what I understand, physically—and possibly mentally—tortured. No. We're not even going there, maydele. We're not."

Omega winced.

"But—"

"No buts," Fox decreed. "I lived through a concentration camp incarceration, Omega; I KNOW about such things. I saw them firsthand, and was fortunate to avoid them myself. If anyone has a clue what you likely went through, it's me. And that knowledge now informs my decision as Agency Director: We are not going there, and that's final. End of argument. And if anyone offworld tries, I SHALL be involving the Legal department—and probably will anyway—to ensure they can't bring you into this, as ANYTHING other than another victim. I appreciate your willingness to try to help put this right, but that's not your responsibility."

Omega bit her lip, looking down, then nodded once.

"Omega...you do know that you are not at all responsible, right?" Fox pressed, more gentle than she had ever heard him. "You are not to blame for any of it."

She shrugged.

"Meg, baby, don't take on any guilt for what happened to you," Echo soothed. "I mean, I understand you might have some survivor's guilt and all, but Fox is right. None of this was your fault; you're as much a victim as anyone, maybe more. I'm betting you fought like hell when it was happening, right? As hard as you did when your programming tried to shoot me?"

Omega nodded, swallowed again, then opened her mouth to say something. Initially nothing would come out. She closed her mouth and swallowed once more, as both men hid their own winces of sympathetic pain; then she tried again.

"I did," she admitted in a low voice, finally forcing the words out. "The problem was...well, I was outside, and it was the middle of the night. I was stargazing on a hillside on the farm, alone...and he snuck up on me from the other side of the hill. I didn't even know he was there until his saucer was literally overhead...and by then, it was way too late. He already had mental control of my body...and a good chunk of my mind, too, I guess. And I didn't know how to erect a telepathic block back then, anyway," she added. "So it wasn't like I could really fight much."

"No," Echo corrected. "You couldn't fight EFFECTIVELY, baby. I know you better than that—if you say you fought, it means you fought tooth and nail, with everything you had. It's just that...well, you didn't have access to anything to fight WITH." He ran an affectionate hand over her hair, scruffing lightly. "You aren't to blame, just because you were a kid, you got ambushed, and didn't have any weapons handy."

"Right. So let's go forward with it that way," Fox said. "And since you are not an inanimate object, you are a WITNESS, not a piece of evidence."

The two members of Alpha One watched as Fox's holovid image looked Omega up and down. "Echo?"

"Yeah, Fox?"

"I am about to give a very strange order, zun..."

"What?"

"If the two of you were in my office right now, I'd opaque the windows, note that we were on an off-duty break for a few minutes, and give your partner a fatherly hug...because to me, she really looks like she could use one, right about now. But you're NOT here..."

"Ah. Orders received and understood, Fox," Echo said with a slight grin. Then he leaned over, wrapped an arm around his partner's shoulders, and pulled her into his side. "It's okay, baby," he murmured, as she turned into his shoulder for a moment, hiding her face. Her shoulders heaved once, and he tightened his hold. "Shush, now. Don't cry, Meg; you'll just get all stuffed up, and I didn't bring along any of those mint strips of India's that unstuff you. I know you're eighteen and a half kinds of upset over this, and I don't blame you..."

"Nor do I," Fox interjected.

"...But it's gonna be okay, baby, I swear. I promise you this: The Alpha Line department chief's assistant, not to mention half of Alpha One, ain't goin' anywhere without one hell of a damn big fight from us."

"But we WILL get this resolved," Fox amended. "And I personally promise you that. And it was a good call on your part, Omega, that there are likely cold cases out there that we should now be able to close."

Omega nodded...but did not look up.

"Okay, guys," she said in a low voice, muffled by Echo's chest. "Run with it the way you think you ought to. Let me know what you DO need me to do, and I'll do my best."

"We know you will, Meg," Echo said, squeezing her shoulders briefly. "You always do."

"Indeed. You, Omega, like your partner, never give me less than one hundred percent," Fox observed. "Which is why you are Alpha One."

"And why we'll STAY Alpha One," Echo added, giving Fox a meaningful glance. "Both of us."

"Exactly," Fox agreed. "Now..."

"Back on duty?" Echo queried, affectionately and gently scruffing the silver-blonde hair with his free hand again, careful not to mess up Omega's braid.

"If Omega is up for it."

"I...I think so," came her response, still muffled by Echo's shoulder.

"All right. Say when."

Omega drew a deep breath, and let out a sigh that seemed to come from her toes. She was still and silent for a long moment, apparently gathering herself. Then she patted Echo's chest with her palm, and murmured, "When."

"The word is spoken," Fox declared with a fond smile. "Back on duty, Echo. Any ideas where the next device is hidden, you two?"

"Workin' on that, Fox," Omega said, straightening up as Echo released her from the gentle but firm embrace he'd maintained since Fox had suggested it. Her voice was a little hoarse, and pitched lower than usual, but both men were glad to see there were no signs of tear stains on her face, though her cheeks were somewhat paler than usual. "Echo's got some ideas where it is. And I'm thinkin', if I got this whole Ho'd'ni vibe goin', I might be able to make some use of it—especially given how hard it was to get our hands on this last one, otherwise."

"Yeah," Echo agreed. "We never actually managed to get our hands on the first piece, and the second one just seemed kind of...inert...until Gla'd's called it. Then it...it was like it shivered, and, and woke up in my hand... well, in the WATCH in my hand, so I guess I didn't really touch it, either... and then went straight to her. So we were thinking, if these things recognize Meg as part of the family somehow, we need to take that and run with it. Otherwise, we might never manage to finish this mission."

"Good. You have my permission to run with it."

"Running with it, Fox," Echo said with a smile. "C'mon, Meg, let's see what we can figure out, while Fox goes off with the stuff you gave him."

"Right," Omega said, eyes hardening. "Later, Fox. Keep me posted."

"Of course, meyn khaverte. Fox out."

"Alpha One out."

* * *

"Okay, Ace, so what was the next line in that poem?" Omega asked, still sounding a bit hoarse.

"Um, hang on," he said, and fished out his notebook. "All right, here

294

it is. He said, 'Fourth, the place where I was writ larger than life. Ominous framework, no fun at all, it happened here.'"

"You got any idea what it means?"

"Mm, maybe," Echo pondered. "'The place where he was writ larger than life' could only be Hollywood. 'Ominous framework, no fun at all'...I'm less certain of that. Probably one of a handful of films; I'll have to think about it. But 'it happened here' most likely means the soundstage where it was filmed, especially in context with the way the other clues were worded."

"Damn, it sounds grim," Omega murmured.

"What?" Echo said, sitting up straight.

"It sounds grim. 'Ominous framework, no fun at all.' That just sounds—"

"Of course!" Echo exclaimed. "He did a film called *The Grim Game*! It's the set for *The Grim Game*! It has to be! 'Ominous' refers to grim, and 'no fun at all' to game—because a game should be fun. So that identifies the particular movie! And 'framework' has to mean the set!"

"Ooo," Omega hummed. "That's good, Ace! Off to Los Angeles, then?"

"You betcha, baby. Strap in, we're headed out!" Echo told her, reaching for the controls. "Oh, and you might want to ping Fox and ask him to give the L.A. Office a heads-up that we'll be coming through, just in case."

"But do you know where we're going once we get there?" Omega asked, reaching for her cell phone to send the requested text message.

"Oh HELL yes."

* * *

"So about your tinkered-up force cuffs and shit—I knew you were busy with something on the 'merry chase' flight all over," Echo noted, as he took the controls and lifted off. He had decided to change the topic completely, and ensure he got her mind off of the matter of cold cases. He had also decided not to lay the need for alertness on her that piloting would require, and she didn't protest, which told him that she tacitly agreed. "You were so face-down, you weren't even paying attention to the flight."

"Yeah, now I can focus on it," Omega agreed. "I wanted to, earlier, just because we went to some really cool places, but I was afraid I might not get all the modifications done if I didn't really buckle down and work."

"All things considered, I think it's time I loaned you some of my pockets," Echo decided, programming the autopilot. Moments later the course was set on a shortest-distance great circle for Los Angeles, via Iceland, Greenland, and the Hudson Bay.

"Huh? You mean let me stow some of this stuff in your jacket?"

"Well, you can always give me a set of those modified force cuffs, in case she has an accomplice someplace, already here," Echo pointed out, "but no, I meant actually loaning you pockets to put in your own Suit jacket."

"I...don't get it," Omega admitted, a puzzled expression on her face.

"You haven't noticed how I always have all this equipment and shit on me?" he asked.

"Well, hell yeah. You come up with pockets in places I didn't know you could even PUT pockets."

"There's a reason for that. They're called pocket warps."

"Aw, hell. You don't really mean..."

"Yup. At any given time and depending on the mission assignment, I have at least four, and sometimes as many as six or seven, miniature space warps that I tuck into my Suit. Kind of a real-life version of a 'bag of holding' like in D&D, only more high-tech. It's kinda cool, and I can pack all kinds of shit in there."

"What about the weight?"

"Built-in antigrav system."

Omega turned her seat toward her partner, and put her fisted hands on her hips.

"Ace, you been holding out on me."

Echo laughed.

"Not intentionally, I swear. I'm so used to it, I don't even think about it most of the time. I might think about it, say, when I'm getting ready for bed and mentally planning the next day—you know, emptying my pockets and transferring stuff to a clean Suit an' junk —and I think, 'Hell, I meant to show this to Meg.' And then by the time I wake up the next day, I forget about it again. Sorry."

"Well, at least now I know," she said, half-whimsical. "Yeah, if you can, loan me one now, and then when we get home, show me how to requisition some."

"Consider it done," Echo agreed. "Lemme get this thing into a safe spot for unattended flight—I wanna be a little farther out from land, and away from airports an' shit—and then I can shuffle things around and free one or two up for you."

"Much appreciated!"

"Kinda figured..."

* * *

"...Meg," Echo said, some time later, "I gotta say, you are damn good at this whole online research thing, baby. I can't begin to estimate how much time you just saved us."

"Well," Omega said, flushing in pleasure, "it kinda stood to reason. If we needed to find something Houdini left, then we needed to find which buildings were around on the studio lot during the time Houdini was there."

"And I had no idea that the studio had moved when it changed hands and names, let alone that the old lot had been bulldozed for a mall parking lot," Echo admitted. "I'd kind of assumed that the 'old' part of the Paramount lot was the same as the old Lasky lot."

"But it isn't," Omega pointed out. "There's only one building still extant, what they call 'the Barn.' And even that has been through several site moves. It's on the National Register of Historic Places, or I'd have had a hellacious time trying to find it now."

"So it's on North Highland, across from the Bowl?" Echo verified, modifying their flight plan slightly to accommodate the change in destination.

"Right," Omega affirmed. "And we'd better hope that's where Houdini left the F'al on'cik, or we're in trouble."

"What do you...oh shit," Echo mumbled, realizing. "Because if he put it someplace else, it's been destroyed already."

"Yup. Along with the building it was in," Omega finished for him. "And its pieces are now probably part of the asphalt of that mall parking lot. And worse," she added, "even if it IS the right building, the F'al on'cik may still not be there, or be there only in a damaged form; there was a fire in the place back in 1996 or so, and it almost burned down."

"Damn," Echo cursed.

"Exactly," Omega agreed.

* * *

The area in front of the building that was now part of the Hollywood Heritage Museum, aka the Lasky-DeMille Barn, was largely wide-open parking lot. However, behind the 'barn' was a lushly-landscaped area with plenty of trees, and the odd clearing just big enough for an airskimmer.

So Echo landed the *SchmaltzBlitz* in one of those clearings, ensuring the passive cloaking was functioning well, then he and Omega erected a solid hologram cover that made the airship look like merely another part of the shrubbery. Then they emerged, walked the few feet to the sidewalk, and entered the building, paying the admission fee and looking around the museum housed inside, pretending to be tourists...though both had to be careful to avoid becoming lost in the displays, innate curiosities and interests wanting to engage.

"Ace, this is a cool place," Omega murmured, "but I think we got a problem. This is a wood-frame structure, with nothing big enough for a decent-sized cavity like we've seen before. Not without weakening the structural integrity, anyway."

"Yeah, I was thinking the same thing," Echo agreed. "But we have to try, at least. There's a silver lining, though, I think. If you're right about each one of these gizmos being a part of a larger piece—and given you were able to put the third piece into place with the others, I expect you are—and if we can't find it, then we can't reassemble it. BUT, if WE can't put Humpty back together again, neither can any faction of Glu'gu'ik."

"Well, that's true," Omega admitted. "And I guess that puts us back in the safe zone, huh?"

"I'd think so," Echo decided. "I'd want to talk to Fox about it and get his opinion, though. And I'll bet he'll want to run it past the Ennead, in turn. After all, we don't really KNOW what the thing is. SOMEbody among the higher-ups has to know, or there wouldn't be such a big push to get our hands on it first."

"Okay, how do you want to do this?" Omega wondered. "Fortunately the museum isn't very crowded, this time of day..."

"How 'bout this: You jam the security in each room so they can't get a live look, and I'll run quick scans as we go. That will at least tell us if it was ever here, I think. Unless it was in something that got burned in the fire and totally replaced."

"In which case we fall back to, 'We ain't got all the pieces-parts,'" Omega added.

"Right."

"Okay, Ace," Omega murmured, fishing out her cell phone and activating an app, then locating the nearest security camera and standing under it. "Nobody's in here. Let's go."

* * *

It didn't take long; the wooden structure provided far less interference than a metal-and-brick structure would have, or even an old stone-and-brick shed. Soon they had located a thick wooden beam from which the Glu'gu'ik signature emanated. Then it was a matter of zeroing in on the exact location.

"But the museum is about to close," Echo warned.

"Yeah, they're seeing my jamming and think something's wrong with the system, so they're closing early," Omega agreed. "I heard a couple of docents talking."

"We need to get out of sight and wait for them to close, then we can take care of things and be gone before the security people show, and no one will be the wiser. Did you bring some of the equipment from our little diversion jaunt?"

"Yeah, I got it," Omega confirmed. "Hang on a sec, and I'll get it set up."

In no time, Alpha One had set up a combination of holographic imagery in a corner of the museum, running through one of their brain bleachers for maximum effectiveness, and tucked in behind a display of a large film prop. They crouched close together there as the solid hologram formed around them, and to anyone passing through the area, there was nothing visible other than the display itself. The two visitors in the not-quite-so-crisp black Suits had apparently left the building unnoticed a few minutes earlier.

* * *

Echo and Omega, having listened as the on-site manager called the local security firm responsible for the museum's system, watched as the last of the staff left the building, turning off most of the lights as they went. As soon as they heard the key click in the lock, both Agents glanced at their wrist chronometers, timing off fully five minutes.

"There," Echo said, as Omega reached for the compact holographic equipment. "We've got about fifteen minutes from now. Let's go."

"All over it, Ace," Omega asserted.

They rose and moved to the support beam they had identified earlier. It was a column, and the Glu'gu'ik signature came from about two-thirds of the way up.

"Time for the hurgir?" Omega asked.

"No, I don't think so. I see something up there, in the shadows. Hang on and lemme see."

Echo stretched up, activating the flashlight app on his cell phone, and shone it on the area in question.

It was a five-pointed star, burned into the wood and filled with something...pink. In the center was burned the number 75.

"What?!" Omega wondered. "It's some kind of code. What star system is that referencing...? Maybe something from the Draper catalogue? Ooo! Kepler-750?"

"Meg, hold— hold on a second, baby," Echo murmured, thinking fast. "The obvious relation in this instance might not be the one intended." He pulled out his cell phone and performed his own internet search. "Mm. Yeah, I thought he did. And...oh, really? And it happened...yeah. THAT'S it." He looked up. "Meg, Houdini has a star on the Hollywood Walk of Fame, which is made of pink terrazzo...and it was awarded in 1975."

* * *

It was late at night when two maintenance workers, dressed in black coveralls, set up utility construction barricades around the sidewalk on

300

7001 Hollywood Boulevard, across North Orange Drive from Madame Tussaud's. Mesh wind screens went up inside the barricades, and the pair— a big, tall brunet male, and a tall white-blonde female—disappeared inside.

A soft, humming ululation echoed down the street, which was mostly empty at that late hour, even given the tourist trade, and from inside the mesh screens, a faint blue light glowed, low against the pavement of the sidewalk.

Suddenly all was quiet. A couple of flashlights darted hither and yon inside the screens, then a soft, triumphant exclamation sounded in a deep male tone. A female voice murmured something, then there was silence.

Another hum, in a slightly different frequency, drifted down the street, accompanied by a slight greenish glow against the concrete and granite.

Within minutes, the two utility workers emerged, taking down the screens and barricades. The sidewalk where they had been working looked no different than it had when they set up.

Moments later, they were gone.

* * *

"Well, THAT worked okay," Omega decided. "We need to make sure to thank our liaison in the L.A. Office for the loan of the coveralls an' film set barricades an' junk."

"Yep. And we got the gizmo."

"Yeah. It came right to me...again."

"Yeah," Echo agreed. "But I'm bothered by the time frames."

"Oh, you mean the fact that that star wasn't even in existence until 1975?"

"Yeah. And yet it had Glu'gu'ik spectral signatures all over it."

"Maybe it was one of the descendants? You know Houdini's siblings had offspring. Surely, if the clan was the collective caretaker of...whatever this thing is," Omega offered, "SOMEbody in the line of descent knew about it. Or at least, knew its pieces needed to stay hidden."

"Yeah, that's probably it," Echo decided. "But it still raises my hackles. It means there's somebody ELSE out there that we might need to look out for."

"Or maybe they picked up what we're doing through the quantum foam, and are glad to get rid of the thing."

"Maybe." Echo shrugged. "We'll just have to watch each other's sixes until we get this over and done, and the tchotchke, as Fox puts it, tucked away in the Vault."

"Yeah."

They sat in the airskimmer for several moments, thinking in silence. Finally Echo roused himself.

"Okay," he said, waving a hand at his partner. "You go fish out the other assembly and add this piece to it, while I work on that last clue."

"Consider it done," Omega said, extracting the latest F'al on'cik, wrapped firmly in a set of the modified force cuffs, from her new warp pocket, and heading aft.

* * *

"Got it figured out?" Omega asked as she came back forward.

"I think so," Echo informed her, as he set up the autopilot. "You get the new piece integrated?"

"Yup. Not even a moment's hesitation; it clicked right into place. Looks like there's only one piece missing now."

"Good, because we've only got the one more clue."

"How did it go, again?"

"'Fifth, the place they purport, yet I did not. Watch well the time! Bright the days, but how light the nights!'" Echo quoted. "I'm pretty sure it refers to some rumors that persisted for a long time that he did one of his strait jacket escapes hanging from the Eiffel Tower—'the place they purport, yet I did not.'"

"Ooo. Yeah, that would make sense. So then 'bright the days, but how light the nights' probably refers to Paris' reputation as the City of Lights."

"That's how I figure it, yeah."

"What about the business about watching the time?"

"I'm still working on that. I got some ideas, but I need to think through it. I might want Ms. Online-Research to check some stuff out for me while we're en route, though. If she doesn't mind."

"Of course not." Omega offered him a smile. "You KNOW that if you ask me to do something, I'll do my damnedest to get it done."

Echo smiled back, feeling warmed by her trust and friendship.

"You wanna drive this time?" he offered. "This is your skimmer, after all."

"I can, I guess. You got the DAP set up yet? Otherwise I can't fly AND do your web search."

"Yeah, got it...now. Swap seats with me, and let's go. The sooner this whole hunt is over, the better. I don't even wanna think how many thousand miles we've already racked up on this skimmer."

"Tell me about it."

They exchanged seats, Omega taking the pilot's chair as Echo strapped into the co-pilot's seat, and lifted off, headed back toward Europe...again.

* * *

"...So you think that's it?" Omega wondered, looking up from her internet research, as the *SchmaltzBlitz* skimmed back over the north Atlantic.

"Yeah, I'm pretty sure, now," Echo declared, "especially given the period pocket watch in the second hidden site. We need to check out the timing mechanism that causes the lights on the Eiffel Tower to sparkle for 5 minutes every hour on the hour. I'm betting we'll find something there—if not this last F'al on'cik, then a clue to where it is."

"It's gonna be dark by the time we get there."

"So much the better. We won't be noticed, sneaking around on the tower."

"We'll just have to make sure we don't fall off," Omega said with a wry chuckle, "and that we have the timer thing working again by the top of the next hour."

* * *

"Well, those go without saying," Echo agreed. "We'll put down and land under the trees in the park surrounding the tower, then see what we can find." He paused, and eyed her up and down, considering. "You hungry?"

"Huh?"

"Are you hungry, baby?"

"Yeah, I am. What, you wanna get some protein bars out of the galley stowage?"

"No, I was thinking about certain medics telling me you needed to fuel the healing after the Glu'g'ik attacked and nearly scrambled you," Echo responded. "See, there's a couple of really good restaurants in the Eiffel Tower, and frankly, the later we wait to do this, the better chance we have of not being detected. So if we arrive, then have a nice dinner while we wait..."

"Oh! Are you sure we should?" Omega wondered, scrunching her face. "It sounds nice, yeah, but maybe we need to just stay out of sight and concentrate on the mission?"

"I'm actually concentrating on a secondary mission," Echo confessed then. "See, while you were cleaning up and getting changed at the medlab in Sydney, Zebra told me she'd gotten the report from Jig, and gave me specific instructions to make sure you ate occasionally, and preferably healthy stuff."

"Oh. That explains the frequent snack breaks during the whole wild goose chase."

"Exactly. And she told me that she'd discussed it with Fox before departure, and the medical order had the Director's approval and backing, too. And," he added reluctantly, "after my little Outback adventure, it seems they decided to include me in that order."

"So you need to eat, too," Omega said, a considering look on her face.

"Well, I'm supposed to," he admitted...just as his stomach grumbled. He tried not to flush as she eyed his belly, then grinned at him. "Anyway, I dunno if you've ever been to Paris before..."

"I haven't."

"One of those restaurants in the tower is one I think you'd get a kick out of, then. It's called Le Jules Verne."

"Ooo!" Omega actually clapped her hands. Echo grinned.

"I take it, that's a good idea?"

"It sure is!" Omega confirmed with enthusiasm. "But, um..."

"What?"

"My spoken French is okay, but my French reading ability is a little rusty. I, uh, might have some trouble with the menu."

"Hey, linguist here, remember?" he reminded her with a smile. "I got that covered. In fact, if you trust me to have a good idea of your likes and dislikes at this point, I can just order for you. Depending what we get, a certain amount of it is fixed-menu, anyway."

"That works," Omega said without hesitation, and Echo felt something inside grow warm with affection and gratitude at her instant trust.

"You feel like three, five, or six courses?"

"What?!"

"How hungry are you? I dunno about you, but I'm starved."

"I'm...pretty hungry. But...Echo, this sounds expensive."

"So? It isn't like we don't have expense accounts. Fox doesn't expect us to starve while we're on a mission. If we have time to eat, we eat. And in this case, we're ordered to eat. I say we splurge and get either the five-or six-course meal."

"Hey," Omega said, holding up her hands, palms outward, "you evidently know this place. And you know me awful damn well. You make the call. I can promise you, I'll eat it!"

"Okay, hang on a sec," Echo said with a smile, reaching for his cell phone. "I need to make some reservations, or we won't be able to get in."

* * *

By this point, landing and hiding the airskimmer in a copse of trees was routine; the pair debarked in a Parisian twilight and headed straight for the base of the Eiffel Tower.

A not-so-quick, but very delicious, dinner later, and the couple watched the Illuminations show from within the restaurant...several times. After the third time, however, they exited into the relative darkness of the second-floor viewing deck through the restaurant's private door.

The tower's projector lights had been dimmed out of respect for the 'quake damage' in Australia, and Alpha One was able to use this to their advantage, slipping away from the deck and into the superstructure of the tower itself.

"That was wonderful," Omega murmured, as they crept along the girders. "Positively nummy."

"You liked it?" Echo glanced at her, a slight smile on his lips. Omega patted her belly.

"Loved it. The food was delicious and the views were stellar."

"Good. Not too much wine?"

"No. I was careful. And I took a DeTox tab before we ate."

"So did I. Now we have to figure out where to find this last gizmo."

"Well, I've been thinking about that," Omega said in a careful undertone, ensuring their conversation could not carry to any tourists or guards on the tower. "According to what I found online, the projectors are on from sundown to sunup, and controlled by a sensor—as soon as it gets to a certain level of dark outside, they come on, and vice versa. That way, they don't have to be constantly adjusting the timer for the time of year. And they're mostly turned off right now anyway, because of the mess our perp made Down Under."

"Right..."

"The whole sparkly Illuminations thing is computer-controlled. And the computers may not even be on-site."

"Okay."

"That leaves the beacons up top."

"Well, shit. Let's find the elevators, then. We can always pretend to be hitting the champagne bar up there, for a second dessert or something. At least, until the tower closes. Then we'd better be hidden someplace." He checked his wrist chronometer. "It's nearly a quarter past nine. We've got less than two hours."

* * *

The DeTox tabs were still in effect, so they sampled the champagne and pretended they were tourists until the champagne bar closed. Then they slipped out of the bar and into the museum portion, finding a quiet, out-of-the-way corner and repeating the ruse they had used at the Hollywood Heritage Museum. Soon the lights were turned out in the small facility; the sounds of activity died away, and there was a distant thud as the elevators were shut down for the night.

"You realize we'll have to spend the night up here?" Omega noted. "Unless you know of some other way to get down."

"No. The stairs don't go all the way up here. I figured we'd stay up here until the first tour groups start coming through in the morning, then blend in with 'em and go down."

"Eh. At least there's places to sit, and we can both nap sitting upright." Echo snorted.

"Somebody tired?"

"Just ready for this to be over."

"That'd make two of us. Get out your scanner and let's see if we can find it. I'm betting the timing equipment is housed somewhere in the recreation of Eiffel's office. Otherwise, it's up on the open platform. We might have to climb, though I hope not."

* * *

Soon enough, they ascertained the timing mechanism was hidden behind one of the walls; a panel was fastened over it with screws. Omega fished out her Swiss army knife, pulled the screwdriver blade, and had the panel off in moments. Then she and Echo used the scanners again to locate the specific place with a Glu'gu'ik signature.

"Over there," Echo noted, pointing. "Look behind that electronic panel. That's older tech."

"It sure is," Omega agreed, reaching into the designated area and pulling out...an analogue clock timer, carefully wired into the mechanism. "Wow. Brass and everything. This is beautiful work. But...Echo, this is weird..."

"How so, baby?"

"I'm no expert, but I know a few things about clock drives. This manufacture predates Houdini's career." She shook her head. "Look at the electrical wiring. I'm betting this even predates the Eiffel Tower itself."

"Is there a removable screen, or part, or something?" Echo wondered. "That's practically making my scanner go nuts for Glu'gu'ik."

"Um...hang on. Lemme look closer," Omega decided, poking it. "I'd rather not have to take it loose from the timer, if I can help it, 'cause it'll screw up the timings for tomorrow night..."

"Well, at least the attachments appear to have been designed with the ability to pull it out in mind," Echo said, quirking his face. "Kinda like somebody planned for this to be done, maybe?"

"Yeah, I noticed that, too," Omega agreed. "Ace, I'm not seeing any way to get into this one. I wonder if nobody but another Glu'g'ik was supposed to…”

“Huh. Why don't you try calling it directly?”

“I can try, I guess.” Omega said with a shrug. She sat the antique timer on the edge of the cavity in the wall and held out her hand. “F'al on'cik, c'mere, you.”

A small silver object, looking rather like a three-dimensional jigsaw puzzle, materialized in her hand with a soft *ding!*

“Great!” Echo exclaimed. “Did you bring the rest of it?”

“Got it in my warp pocket,” Omega averred, pulling out the rest of the F'al, wrapped in its modified force cuffs. “Want me to put it together and see if it blows us up or something?”

“I doubt it would do THAT,” Echo said. “I suppose it very well could be some sort of doomsday weapon, but I doubt it. I'd expect something like that to have been used to stave OFF the civil war, and with it gone, all hell would have broken loose. Instead, the whole movement fell apart. So… yeah. Put it together and let's see what it does. Gimme your knife and I'll see about putting everything back inside the wall and the wall sealed off, while you get shit ready.”

“Okay.”

Omega handed Echo the Swiss army knife, and he promptly tucked the old brass timer back into place and began replacing the panel hiding the equipment. Meanwhile his partner laid the incomplete pieces on Gustav Eiffel's desk, which sat nearby. Then she addressed the pieces rather sternly.

“All right, you guys. You recognize me, and there are people around who are wanting to misuse you. So you behave and stay put for me, and just do what I tell you, okay?”

Larger and smaller pieces both buzzed quietly. She took that as a *yes*, and as Echo turned to watch, she gingerly unfastened the force cuffs around the larger unit. Omega spared a quick, anxious glance at her partner.

“Here we go,” she told him.

“Do it,” Echo urged.

“F'al on'cik, join,” she commanded.

Once more the pieces rose into the air, spun swiftly, and clicked together. The device fell to the table, one complete unit.

Just then, another voice, male and deep, sounded from behind them.

"F'al, la'la'da ge nu!" it said.

The completed F'al faded out.

Alpha One spun, to see a man of somewhat below-average height, with high forehead, white hair, and gray eyes, clad in a waistcoat and frock coat, standing there looking at them.

"Who the hell are you?" Echo demanded.

"You may call me Jean Eugène Robert-Houdin," the man said. "For the time being, at least; that is reasonably close to the name with which I was born, at any rate. But I do not intend you nor your repugnantly-adulterated accomplice shall live to tell of me."

* * *

"I don't think so," Echo declared, stepping forward, both blasters appearing in his hands. "I am Agent Echo, of the Division One Agency, department Alpha Line, team Alpha One. This is my PARTNER, Agent Omega."

"Then your partner is untrustworthy," Robert-Houdin replied, calm. "She has modified herself genetically, to enable her to access a dangerous artifact for corrupt and treacherous purposes." He shook his head. "I will not allow her to complete her task, even if I have to kill you both to stop her. You cannot trust her, Agent Echo; you cannot see what she has done to herself, but I can."

"No, no, you don't understand," Omega responded, patently upset. "I didn't do it! I didn't WANT it! I've never even been off Earth! I was—"

Echo stepped forward, laying a calming hand on her shoulder. She glanced up at him, and he saw the pain in her eyes, the wet gleam that she was trying hard to control, lest it spill over. He drew a deep, sympathetic breath, then nodded at her.

"I got this," he told her softly. She bobbed her head once in acknowledgement, then let her gaze drop to the floor. Meanwhile, a scowling Robert-Houdin took in the entire exchange in a kind of towering silence. Echo met the other being's gaze, composed.

"We already know she's been genetically modified. But Meg didn't do it to herself," he said, voice calm and authoritative. "We already know all of this, and have proof of it. She was—as I've already told your cousin who tried to snatch this device for her own purposes, and likewise discerned Meg's genetic, uh, 'conundrum'—she was abducted as a child and modified against her will. It was," he broke off, looking away and shaking his head, "as near as I can determine, from what little Meg's been willing...or able...to tell me, not at all pleasant. In fact, I doubt I'm going too far if I say the word 'torture' probably applied."

Omega nodded her head, but said nothing. Robert-Houdin's brows knit.

"But why?" Robert-Houdin asked then.

"It's a long story," Echo murmured.

"I have time if you do."

Echo glanced at his partner. Omega shrugged.

"Yeah, go ahead and tell him," she decided, voice low. "Better that than have to fight him. All things considered, I guess we're gonna need to do this for families of the cold cases, as we uncover 'em, anyway. Just..." She broke off.

"Just what, baby?"

"I don't wanna have to be the one to tell him," she whispered, choking. "It's still...too close. The whole mess with Slug, and, and nearly shooting you, and Zz'r'p recovering the memories, and..." Her voice cracked, and she fell silent for a moment, swallowing hard several times. "Eventually, I guess I'll have to, but...not now. Please. Can you...?"

"Yeah. I can do it this time," Echo told her. "And as far as explaining to any of the cold case investigators and families, I'll sic Fox on that, so you don't have to do it. You're as much a victim as any of the families, so the onus shouldn't have to fall on you."

"Thanks, Ace..."

"No need for thanks, Meg. I'll always have your back on it, and everything else. Just pay attention, and correct me if I miss the mark on something. So, Mr. Houdin," Echo began, "this all started about twenty Earth years ago, when a Snail assassin was sent to Earth..."

* * *

When Echo finished the tale, there was a long silence.

"Dear Lord," Robert-Houdin finally murmured. "I see it in the quantum field about her, now. Though it is complex; it takes more than a cursory glance at the field to ascertain it. Child, please forgive my assumption. I was wrong. You are, indeed, a victim. And I should be selfishly glad of it, for it sounds as if you have now saved my birth world an horrific blood bath, because of it."

Echo looked at Omega, and saw her jaw tighten; he realized she was unable to speak. So did Robert-Houdin, who shot a glance at Echo.

"That's our take, too, sir," he replied for himself and his partner. "Alpha One—and Director Fox—believe that, if Ke'ri Gla'd's had gained control of this...F'al...that civil war on Va'du'sha'ā would have been the inevitable result, and that it would probably have spilled over to other worlds, most likely including Earth."

"Very well, then. We are in accord." Robert-Houdin nodded. "As you might say, what is the next step?"

"How about telling us about yourself?" Echo decided.

"There is surprisingly little to tell of any significance," Robert-Houdin noted. "I am, as you have no doubt guessed, Glu'g'ik. I was the first of my people to discover Earth, for I was an explorer and engineer. But more, I am Hou'd'ni; the story of my hyphenating my name and my wife's is false, though I was married...to a fellow Glu'g'ik. When I discovered Earth, I fell in love with it and its people, and decided to settle here among them— among you—and sent for my wife. I devised a false family history, and put my engineering skills to use in a somewhat whimsical fashion that would not draw attention, as a clock- and watchmaker. That was my work you were admiring earlier; the timing device was of my creation, and it does indeed predate both Houdini and the Eiffel Tower itself. Then I discovered illusionists, and realized I could have a bit of fun with my quantum foam abilities." He shrugged. "It is as simple as that." Abruptly he morphed into the figure of a true Zeta Reticulan. "This is my real form. When they fled Va'du'sha'ā, the Hou'd'ni came here, in part because they knew my family was here already, and hoped for assistance, which we provided to the best of our ability."

"What about your family, then?" Echo wondered. Robert-Houdin shook his head.

"I have, by a quirk of fate, outlived them all," he said with a sigh. "One son died in battle; one died of old age, as did his son, his wife, and my wife. But all save my son U'je'n still lived at the time of May'r's arrival." Robert-Houdin cocked his head. "May I now ask a question?"

"Of course," Echo murmured.

"Now that you have found the F'al and assembled it, what would you intend to do with it?"

"Guard it," Omega declared; it was the first thing she'd said in some little time, and her voice was hoarse. "We'd take it back to Director Fox, and he would make disposition, in all likelihood storing it safely in a very hidden and very secure and secret location."

"Aha. The Vault," Robert-Houdin said with a knowing nod; Alpha One looked startled. He laughed grimly. "No, no. Remember, I have been here since long before your Agency, and I am aware of many things. But understand: while I know OF your Vault, I do not know its whereabouts. Nor do I wish to do so. It is merely...mm, I suppose one might term it an 'urban legend' among those of us who were born on other worlds than this. No, I think this an excellent idea. And have no fear; I shall not give away the secret that the Vault is real."

"That...works," Echo decided. "And thank you for guarding the F'al all this time."

"Yes," Omega agreed. "And...thank you for understanding, as well. About...many things."

"Of course, child," Robert-Houdin replied, voice soft. "I must admit, I had help. My thanks to you and your partner for your role in its safety, as well." He cocked his head to one side. "Do you know what it is, what it does?"

"No sir, we don't," Omega said.

"Just that it's important, that it's something the Hou'd'ni brought with them, and the impending civil war fell apart when it left the planet," Echo added. "And a lot of that is just deduced from the sequence of events."

"Well deduced," Robert-Houdin noted. "The F'al is the great invention of the ancestor of the Hou'd'ni. It is a device which is capable of identifying what you call the imperial bloodlines of my people."

"Whoa," Echo murmured.

"What he said," Omega breathed. "How?"

"Even as it apparently recognized your genetics, it reads the genetic makeup of all of the candidates presented to it, factors in mutations and genetic drift, and determines which of the lot is the closest to the royal lineage. It will also reject any candidate with damaging genetic mutations in favor of the next closest candidate, ensuring a healthy—and sane—monarch and continued lineage."

"That...is a pretty serious gadget," Echo decided.

"It is," Robert-Houdin agreed. "And because of it, my clan has been designated the Royal Stewards for very many of your millennia."

"I'll bet," Omega averred. "I guess I just don't understand why taking it AWAY stopped an impending civil war. It looks to me like that's the sure way to CAUSE one, in a situation like that."

"The F'al is not infallible," Robert-Houdin explained. "It can be 'gamed,' as your people put it. According to Ari, who brought it to me decades ago and petitioned my help in concealing it, there were plots involved by the various factions, to use it to set their own candidate on the throne of Va'du'sha'ā."

"How?" Echo wondered. "I have to agree with Omega, here—I'm just not seein' it."

"It is really quite simple," Robert-Houdin said with a rueful smile. "It selects the closest candidate...OF ALL THOSE PRESENTED TO IT. If the F'al and the chief steward are kidnapped, and ONLY the particular faction's chosen candidate is presented to it..."

"It forces the device's hand," Omega realized. "It only has the one choice, so it picks that choice."

"Precisely," Robert-Houdin said. "And according to my cousin Ari, several factions were out to attempt exactly that. It was simply a matter of which was able to get their hands upon Ari's father May'r first. For this reason, the F'al was carried by one or another of Ari and his brothers, apart from their father, for several years. They hoped, by keeping the two separate, to hinder the various plots. Only the chief steward, the one true Keeper of the F'al, can utilize the F'al, you see. Others of the clan may CALL it, as you have seen—as you have DONE, yourself. But only the Keeper can activate it and command it to perform its intended task."

"Ah," Echo murmured, thoughtful. "I'd assume, then, that when the factions figured out what the Hou'd'ni were doing, things got tighter..."

"Correct. Several of Ari's siblings were killed before ever the family left Va'du'sha'ā. And eventually the entire family would be in danger of being wiped out...for certainly cousin May'r would have been killed after the F'al was fraudulently used."

"So, with the F'al gone," Omega reasoned, "all of the plots fell apart, because there was no longer any way to 'prove' ANY candidate was of the royal lineage."

"You have the way of it." Robert-Houdin smiled. "You are quite bright, young one."

"Yep," Echo agreed. "I got one helluva smart partner in her." Omega blushed and tucked her head, embarrassed.

"Yes, I think she will do." Robert-Houdin held out his hand. "Give me your palm, youngling."

Puzzled, Omega held out her hand, palm up.

Robert-Houdin placed his hand on hers, palm down. As he slowly lifted his hand away from hers, something materialized between their hands.

It was the F'al, complete and functional.

"It will remain with you now, youngling, for so I have instructed it. Take it and go at once," Robert-Houdin murmured. "There may be others coming in the morning; I have sensed some disturbance in various places upon the planet. Go now, before anyone else can come upon you. Be safe."

"Wait," Echo said. "We have to get down. The stairs don't go this far, and the elevators—"

"Did you not think of that before?" Robert-Houdin asked in some amusement. "Look about you."

Alpha One did so, only to find they were on the ground, under the trees near their airskimmer.

"Whoa," Echo whispered. "I didn't even feel that one."

"Thank you, sir," Omega murmured, as Robert-Houdin's form faded and vanished.

'You are welcome, youngling,' came the faintest echo of the ancient Glu'g'ik's voice.

Alpha One turned toward the airskimmer.

* * *

Inside the *SchmaltzBlitz*, a very quiet Omega deposited the F'al into a special container she had cobbled together on the way to France, and which was based on the modified force cuff technology, then she put it into locked stowage.

"Home?" Omega wondered then, strapping into the pilot's seat.

"HOME," Echo declared in no uncertain terms. "Finally. And thank the good Lord."

"Amen," Omega averred, voice soft, and reached for the controls.

Chapter 12

"...And that's that, Fox," Echo explained, setting the small but VERY high-tech metal container on the Director's desk. "Here it is."

"Damnation, what a ride," Fox grumbled, staring at the container in annoyance, "for such a small tchotchke."

"Small, but incredibly powerful," Omega pointed out. "But as Echo says, it's done. And glad we are of it."

"No shit," Echo agreed, then shot a glance at Omega. "Um. By the way, Boss, how are things progressing with the search to close cold cases?"

"Pretty well, actually," Fox answered, turning his face to Echo, but watching Omega out of the corner of his eye. "It was all right there, ready to be identified, it seems—at least in the main. Once anyone thought to look, that is. Zebra was able to identify quite a few individual sets of genetic input to Omega's original DNA, though she said she suspects there are a few more they're still working to isolate. Of those, only seven proved to be, uh, anything that we needed to concern ourselves with."

He tap-danced around what Zebra had actually found out; his paramour had explicitly told him to let HER explain some of the less-savory details, in private. *'No one else needs to know this,'* Zebra had said. *'The ONLY reason I told you as much as I did is because you're the Director, and need to know what some of the ramifications might be.'* And given what he now knew, coupled with what he'd been able to infer from what Zebra had NOT said, Fox was quite content not to explain; he rather wished he didn't have a need to know at all.

It will hurt Omega, quite badly, I expect, if what I suspect to be the case proves true, he considered. *It may be as well that I feign even more ignorance of the matter than I already have, for her sake.*

"That sounds decent," Echo offered, as Omega remained silent, merely listening. "And of those seven?"

"We have already been able to match up five with cold cases, around the galaxy," Fox continued. "The other two, we're still working on. But we've contacted the appropriate Divisions, and they've opened the cases back up. Four have been resolved already, and the fifth is in work, expected to be resolved within another Division day or two."

"How bad?" Omega wondered, voice low. "What were the results?"

"Three missing persons, now presumed dead, with searches ongoing for the remains, in the vicinity of Slug's known whereabouts on the given homeworld; two outright, known murders," Fox replied, making sure to keep his tone gentle. "If remains are found, identified, and mode of death determined in the three missing persons cases, those will also most likely change to murders. No jurisdictions have asked for your additional involvement, Omega. Everything is fine. I brought in the Legal and Diplomacy departments to help me make the overtures, and all the pertinent agencies have come back and declared that, as an additional victim, there's no need to hurt you further. The scientific data has been provided, as well as a history of your victimization—unambiguously emphasizing that you were a juvenile at the time of the occurrence, not even having reached adolescence—and that's all they need from us to help them close the cases. The knowledge that the perpetrator is dead, at your and your partner's hands, was the last detail needed to seal the deal regarding your complete lack of complicity."

"What about...about the families of the, the victims?"

"I'm working on a letter of condolence now," Fox explained. "I haven't finished it, let alone sent it yet, because I didn't know if you'd want to be involved in that."

"I...I guess I should," Omega said with a sigh.

"You don't have to, my young friend," Fox soothed. "You aren't required, and you aren't even obligated. I just wanted your opinion before I finished it, because I didn't know if you might have a message for the families, or not."

"Meg," Echo murmured, "why don't you just let Fox handle it?"

"Um, okay," she agreed. "But...well, yeah, I kinda do have a message for the families, I guess."

"What would that be, meyn teyere?"

"Um, just that, that I'm sorry for what happened. I'd have stopped it all if I could have. And that I understand how they feel, because Slug killed my family, too, in order to further his plan," Omega decided. "Um, you can pretty up the wording if you want to. I'm not sure how to say it right, anyway."

"I think you did fine, Meg," Echo said.

"Well, but I dunno the tone of the letter, or the tense, or anything," Omega pointed out. "Fox needs to make it fit in."

"How about this," Fox suggested, having scribbled notes as she spoke. "'Agent Omega asked me to give you a message. She says, "I'm sorry about what happened. I'd have stopped it all if I could have. And I understand how you feel, because Slug killed my family, too, in order to further his plan." It is worth noting that she lost her mother, father, and grandmother to the perpetrator, so she truly does grasp the loss you feel. Let me add that, when one of the genetic components forced on her was unexpectedly identified in the course of her most recent case, it was her idea that what had happened to her might result in our ability to close the cold case on your loved one.' Will that work, Omega? I only tweaked your wording slightly, to avoid the appearance that you're shouldering blame; I don't want any of the families blaming you OR Echo for the heinous machinations of an insane gastropoid."

"That works for me, Boss," Echo averred.

"Yeah, I can see that," Omega said. "And I don't want 'em holding grudges against Echo, or Division One, either. Yeah. I'm good with it, Fox."

Fox glanced at Echo, barely raising an eyebrow. Echo tilted his head a bit, allowing the barest hint of frustration to show: Both men had noted that Omega did not seem to care about grudges held against herself.

"All right, then. That concludes what I had for Alpha One. Do the two of you have anything more for me?" Fox asked.

"Not me," Echo decided. "Meg, baby?"

"No, that's all I can think of, right now. If I think of anything else, I guess it can wait til tomorrow, anyway."

"Good. You both look tired. Omega, I need for you to run by the med-lab and see Zebra before you go off-duty; she's requested a private medical conference as soon as possible, to discuss this latest genetics analysis with you. No need for a post-mission exam for either of you until you both get some rest, she said. Echo, would you mind putting in a preliminary report for Alpha One, while your partner does that? Just sketch out the barest bones, and don't worry about the rest for tonight. You can compile a detailed report together in the morning. After you both finish all that, I want you to go home and crash. It's been a rough, long, hard mission, and you both had some close calls, there. I'm less worried about getting the reports logged quickly than I am in seeing my two top Agents get the rest they've earned. If you need to call in late tomorrow because you're dragging, do it. You did great work on this mission, both of you."

"Okay. Thanks, Fox," Omega murmured.

"What she said," Echo agreed. "C'mon, baby, let's go. You head for the medlab while I knock out that bare-bones report, then we can go home. We've been through a helluva lotta time zones in recent days. I'm starved, and I'm wiped."

"Me, too."

Alpha One rose together and left Fox's office, heading across the Core.

* * *

"Hey, Ace?" Omega asked a bit hesitantly, coming to a private decision as they strode together across the large room.

"Yeah, Meg?"

"You gonna wait in the Alpha Line room for me, or go on home when you get done with the prelim report?"

Echo pondered that for a moment, then shrugged.

"Doesn't matter to me. Which had you rather I do?" he asked.

"Oh, I dunno. I guess...go on home. Don't wait on me," Omega decided. "No telling how long this will take."

"I'll wait dinner on you, though," Echo determined. "It doesn't seem right for me to go ahead and chow down if you haven't even gotten home yet."

"I'll leave that call up to you," she concluded. "I know you're hungry."

"So are you. I heard your stomach growling in Fox's office."

"Well, yeah, but Medical and all."

"Yeah."

"Listen, though..."

"What?"

"Um, I kinda wanted to talk to you about something, after we ate and junk."

"Okay. Something important?"

"I, um, I dunno," she hedged. "Maybe, maybe not." *If you go for the idea, it'll mean a HUGE difference in the partnership,* she thought. *And make me really happy. If you don't, it could break up the partnership. And make me miserable. So I think it probably IS important, but maybe not from your perspective. I just dunno.*

"Okay. I'll keep the evening clear for a chat. Heart to heart, or just something you wanna brainstorm?"

"Um...maybe a little of both? I dunno," she waffled again. He raised an eyebrow.

"Huh. Something's on your mind, and you're really uncertain of it, huh, baby?"

"Yeah, kinda," Omega admitted. "Okay, a lot, yeah."

"All right. How about this: You run on to the medlab, and I'll slap down a report that hits the highlights and shoot it to Fox. Then I'll go home and pop in one of those casseroles you like..."

"The cottage pie thing?"

"Yeah."

"Num!"

"Thought you'd like that. But it'll also work well for keeping warm, however long it takes you in the medlab, then we can eat, and yak afterward. I can put on some music and we'll talk until we're too worn out to talk."

"Which probably won't take long, after this scavenger hunt of a mission we just did."

"Amen to that. But maybe we can at least thrash out whatever's on your mind."

"Maybe so," Omega agreed, hoping it would be a positive resolution—that either Echo would like the idea of a more intimate relationship, or that he at least wouldn't be offended by her interest. Just then, they arrived at the door of the conference room, and she looked up. "Oh, wow! Echo, look!"

* * *

The large conference table that had been the big room's focus had been removed, and multiple rows of small college-classroom-style desks had replaced it. In the back corners and taking up about a quarter of the room were two full-sized, U-shaped computer desks, back to back, facing opposite side walls. Upholstered executive chairs stood inside them, and the wall space between contained a wide, low bookshelf. Above it on the right side was a small safe, and on the left side was an emergency medical kit.

But centered on the back wall, flanking the bookshelf and above it, were two large logos.

One, the Division One Agency logo, was composed of a large black circle on a white field. Inscribed within the circle was an equal-armed, black cross. Together, the circle and cross represented the centuries-old astronomical and alchemical symbol of Earth. But superscribed over that was a large, bright red, Arabic numeral 1.

To its right was another logo, newer and more subtle. It, too, consisted of a large black circle on a white field. But within it was imprinted a horizontal black line. Atop this, and centered upon it, was a black Greek capital letter lambda; when combined with the horizontal line, it also formed a capital alpha. It was the formal logo for Alpha Line.

"Nice," Echo decided, surveying the room. "Fox got a lot done while we were gone. I didn't expect all that. At least, not so soon."

"Wait, Ace. The best you can do is 'nice'? Nuh-uh. That is damn cool, is what that is," Omega declared. Echo grinned.

"Yeah, Meg, okay. You're right. It IS cool."

The two turned and shot thumbs-up gestures at the bay window, seeing the figure standing in it.

* * *

"Okay, baby, you run on to the medlab; I'll get the report going," Echo noted. "It's only gonna be a skeleton, but it'll give Fox something to start on in the morning. And while he's looking it over, we'll use it as a framework to flesh out a full report."

"All right, Echo," Omega decided. "See you at home."

Echo entered the Alpha Line conference-room-cum-office, and Omega turned toward the corridor to Medical.

* * *

Fox rose and moved to his bay window to watch them go. He saw when they spotted the room's new layout, and smiled to himself at their pleased reactions.

As Echo disappeared through the briefing room door and Omega took the corridor toward the medlab, he made a slight hand gesture, and the windows opaqued.

Then he moved to the far wall of his office and pressed his hand against a hidden panel. A green light grid appeared on his face, as a retinal scan was performed. Suddenly a small door formed in the wall, popping ajar.

Fox opened the door wide, revealing a hidden safe; several odds and ends lay within, including strange little objects and mysterious file folders. He fetched the container holding the F'al from his desk, placed it inside the safe, and closed the door.

The outline of the door promptly vanished back into the wall.

Fox sighed, and ran a hand through his hair.

"Speaking of going home for the day..." he decided, heading for his office door.

* * *

When Omega arrived at the medlab, Zebra was waiting; the Alpha Line member noted that a quick look was exchanged between Zebra and Zarnix, the department head, who happened to be passing through the waiting room. The physician showed the Agent into her private office and closed the door.

"Have a seat, hon," Zebra said, gesturing to the visitor chair, as she moved behind her desk and took a seat. "I don't think this will take very long, unless you have a lot of questions."

"Okay," Omega said. "Knowing me, I might, but I'll try to hold off on anything that isn't important. It's late, and I'm coming off a damn long mission and, frankly, I'm wiped."

"I know; Fox is going to be waiting dinner on me, and probably Echo on you, too, huh? Normally I'd have waited until in the morning to do this," Zebra admitted. "But I rather thought you'd want to see the files as soon as possible. Here." She passed a folder across the desk to Omega. "It's the results, to date, of the genetics breakout that Zarnix and I did on you, at your and Fox's request."

Omega felt her gut clench tight in apprehension as she accepted the folder and opened it. As she scanned down through the printouts, she noted the seven different identities that comprised the cold cases—five of which, she recalled, had been more or less solved; handwritten check marks were beside those. And, she observed, one of those was, indeed, from clan Hou'd'ni. Two more still had penciled-in question marks; these were the two that Fox was still working to identify, though the particular race and planet was known in each case.

But in addition to those, there were five more creatures whose genetics had been identified as being inside Omega.

And as the Alpha Line Agent stared at those, she felt her face blanch and her head spin.

"No," she whispered. "I have to be mistaken. I must not be remembering right..."

"No, honey," Zebra said, her voice very quiet, "you're probably correct."

Omega looked up at the medic, horrified.

"B-but, but," she stammered, "these other five...they, they aren't..."

"They aren't sapients," Zebra confirmed.

"The bastard spliced ANIMAL genes into me?!" Omega wailed.

* * *

Zebra winced at the raw agony on her patient's face, and in her voice. *Times like these,* she decided, *I'm awful glad for the soundproof walls policy.*

"Yes, honey, I'm afraid he did," she said, as gently as she knew how. "So far we've counted seven intelligent species, and five of what we humans would call animals, whose DNA was mined and incorporated into yours. And there may be more...of both," she added. "There are a few anomalies here and there that Zarnix and I are still trying to figure out. Those might be nothing—mutations of your own normal human genetics, some probably ordinary, some possibly induced by what was done to you— or we may be able to identify additional species the gastropoid used." She paused; then, seeing Omega was just staring at her in shock, appended, "If we find any more sentients, we'll notify Fox and help him start the process of identifying additional cold cases. It'll be handled just like the ones he's already closed."

Omega nodded mutely.

"What...effects has it had?" she finally wondered, voice so low Zebra had to lean forward to hear.

"We're not a hundred percent sure about any of it," the medic replied. "But Zarnix hypothesizes that at least some of the, um, non-sapient genetic material may have been intended to express as increased speed, endurance, strength, and the like. It would be subtle, but would have an effect, by bring-ing you near, if not outrightly into, the top percentile in each attribute."

Omega nodded again, but remained silent for a long time. Zebra wait-ed patiently, understanding that the other woman was in shock and trying desperately to gather her wits. Eventually Omega spoke again.

"I...I'm sorry. I'm sitting here, not saying anything, wasting your time. But I...don't even know...what questions to ask..."

"No, it's okay, Omega. I understand," Zebra said, rising and coming around the desk to crouch beside her patient's chair. She eased a comfort-ing arm around Omega. "This is why I had you come down here, alone. I thought it would be a little easier...as if it's gonna be easy in any sense. But at least it would be less embarrassing, just us two."

"Who else knows?" a miserable Omega asked.

* * *

"Nobody, except you, me, and Zarnix," Zebra said. "Fox knows only the bare minimum, as required by his position as Director."

"What is 'bare minimum,' then? Does he know about the animal...?" Omega wondered, trying not to cringe.

"I didn't tell him that," Zebra said, and her gaze was clear and straight-forward. "What I DID tell him was that we'd found about a dozen identified individual species, and I gave him the seven that pertained to his search for cold cases. That said," she added, "Fox is damn smart, hon. Never underestimate his gray matter. He probably was able to extrapolate some information based on what I told him. But he doesn't KNOW, because he didn't ask—and probably won't—and I didn't tell. And I won't. It's confidential patient information, and only you have the authority to order the release of that info."

"O-okay," Omega murmured. *So Fox probably suspects,* she thought. *But he won't pursue it. But Echo doesn't know at all, though if he stops to think about what Fox said in his office...no. It didn't register on him, because it didn't register on me, and it was ABOUT me. Besides, I saw his eyes, and there wasn't any sudden realization there—he's tired, and it went right past him as a result. Otherwise, he'd probably have picked up on it, too.*

So he doesn't know, at all. And I think I wanna keep it that way, if I can. I don't think I could stand to see the look in his eyes if he found out. There's really only two possible reactions he might have—pity, and shocked horror. And I don't wanna see either one in his eyes when he looks at me.

"So...do you WANT me to tell him?" Zebra wondered. "And what about Echo? Do you want him to know?"

"NO!" Omega blurted. "No, Zebra! I don't want anybody to know! I— oh, God help me," she groaned, fighting back tears of humiliation, horror, and confusion. "What am I? Zebra, does this make me an ani—?"

"No, honey, no!" Zebra exclaimed, shocked. "The percentages are actually very, very small. They're just...in specific locations in the genome. The crazy git obviously intended each one to do very precise things to your developing adult form, to accommodate his own ends." She shook her head. "I hope you don't take offense at this, because I'm not condoning what he did, at all—nobody in this medlab would, ever. But Zarnix and I both had to admit, the science he worked out is nothing short of brilliant. In a very perverted, immoral kind of way."

"Mengele," Omega murmured.

"Exactly. And Wirths, and Heim, and..."

"Yeah." Omega drew a deep breath. "Are you sure this doesn't make me...? I mean, at what point does...?"

"Omega, I know you have degrees in several pertinent sciences, and I think one of them is biology, if memory serves; but perhaps you didn't specialize in genetic studies?"

"Yes I do, but no, I didn't dabble in genetics. I was more interested in things like how microgravity affected the musculoskeletal structure, stuff like that."

"And given your original life's plans, that makes sense. Okay, then you may not know that *Homo sapiens* shares anywhere from ninety-five to ninety-nine percent of its genetics with the great apes?"

"They...they do?"

* * *

Aw damn, Zebra thought, listening to Omega and hiding a wince with effort. *Not, 'WE do,' but, 'THEY do.' She no longer considers herself human. I wonder how long THAT thought has been in her head.*

"Yes, WE do," Zebra replied, emphasizing the pronoun. "You, me, Fox, Echo, Romeo, India...every human born on this planet. Do you consider any of the rest of us to be animals?"

"N-no..."

"So when you have far less of a variance in your DNA as a result of the manipulations, than the rest of us have differences from a chimp, yet we're still considered human, why would anyone consider you anything other than human?"

"Well, because humans ARE considered a separate species from chimps, Zebra. From all the apes, for that matter."

"Because there is anywhere from an entire percentage point to up to FIVE percentage points difference, Omega. As opposed to your...something like a tenth of a percent. Honey, the differences are, at most, comparable to what the typical mutation rate might produce, and at least, an order of magnitude or two less. So let me ask again, why would anyone consider you anything other than human?"

"Maybe because no less than two Glu'gu'ik picked up on those differences..."

"Well, but they were looking for Glu'gu'ik genetics, too, because of what they saw you do, from what Fox told me. And found them, because they ARE there. Not a lot, but they're there. What about the rest of the added DNA?"

"They saw that, too. But they didn't recognize it as anything except genetic tinkering. And that, only after Echo told them."

"So neither recognized other specific species?"

"No."

"Which, from what I've seen of Glu'gu'ik, says a lot. If they didn't recognize it, there wasn't enough there for them TO recognize."

"O-okay," Omega agreed, raising her head. "That makes me feel better. But I still don't want anybody to know, if I can help it."

"And I comprehend that, and will abide by it to the best of my ability," Zebra swore. "You do understand, however, that in an emergency situation, I might HAVE to tell either Fox or Echo, in order to get the information or permission to treat you, if you're unconscious?"

Omega slumped.

"Only in extremis," Zebra added. "If there's no other way."

"I'd almost rather die than have them find out," Omega whispered.

"No, girl, don't you dare talk like that," Zebra chastised. "It isn't about quality of life, and it isn't about survival. It's just a quirk of your particular biochemistry." She paused, thinking, then offered, "I could try to downplay it, so they might not recognize the significance, if that would make you feel better. They're both awful damn smart, and I might not succeed—hell, I got my doubts but that Fox hasn't already figured out some of it already—but I'll try, if you just say the word now."

"The word is said, then," Omega declared. "I get that they might figure it out. But they won't KNOW, and if you, Zarnix, and I don't confirm it, they never will know for sure."

"True. Okay, that's the way we'll play it, if it should ever become necessary," Zebra agreed. "I'll drill it into Zarnix. He can get absent-minded about such things when he gets into an emergency situation. I don't want him to slip up and say something off-handed that gives away your secret.

And here's another alternative I just thought of: Since India is a physician, I can bring her in on this, so she knows and can tend to things in the field, but she has to keep it quiet even from Romeo, which she knows to do anyway, because patient confidentiality..."

"I hate to do that to her and Romeo." Omega chewed her lip in thought.

"Well, but she does that sort of stuff anyway," Zebra pointed out. "I bet you didn't know she's already been read in on your medical records, Echo's, Romeo's, the agents Echo has approved to join Alpha Line..."

"Really?"

"Really. Because she needs to know about specifics, in case something happens in the field and she ends up treating one or more of you. She is your department's field medic, with all that entails. And Romeo understands the nature of her job in that regard. He doesn't ask questions. In fact, she says he's quite sweet about it."

"Um, okay, that might work, then. Lemme...lemme think about it. I work with her, after all, and I'm not sure..."

"Take all the time you need, dear. I'm not going to rush you."

"Can...can you tell me...what she thinks of, of me? I mean, with the genetic splicing, and all..."

"You're her friend, Omega. Insofar as I know, it makes her angry what was done to you—and she doesn't make a secret of that. But I don't think she views you differently because of it. And she may well have considered something like this already; she's quite up on her medical research, and she's smart and savvy—or she wouldn't be in Alpha Line. I don't think you have to worry that the news will change her opinion of you."

"Um, okay. Yeah, that's what I needed to know. All right, lemme think about it."

"Like I said, no rush."

Omega grabbed Zebra's hands in hers.

"THANK you," she whispered, intense.

"Omega?" Zebra decided to ask the question she'd been thinking for the last ten minutes. *The most she can do is tell me it's none of my damn business,* she considered. *Which she might. But all things considered, she's more than earned the right to do that. But her answer, regardless, is going to tell me a lot about her mental state.*

"Huh?"

"Why does it scare you so much, that Fox or Echo would find out?" Omega sighed.

"It's like this, Zebra. It's bad enough to deal with the knowledge and, and the memories," she tried to explain. "Then you look up and you see this expression on your partner's face. Who also happens to be your boss, by the way. And then you glance over and see the same expression on HIS boss's face." She shook her head. "I don't want pity. But I don't want to be looked at as a monster, either...even if I am, and I'm still not sure I'm not. Especially when I remember those moments where my programming was trying to make me kill Echo."

"Oh, I see," Zebra said, realizing. "And you think this knowledge would make those reactions they have worse, stronger."

"I KNOW they would," Omega asserted. "And I can barely stand it now. Sometimes, I glance at Echo when we're discussing it, or when we're having to explain it...and it's all I can do to keep from crying, just on account of the look on his face. He's trying to be sympathetic, I know, but..." She shrugged.

"All right. As your partner and I both said in Sydney, 'Fair 'nuff,' girlfriend."

They both drew deep breaths.

"So. Any other questions or instructions for me?" Zebra asked. Omega thought for a minute.

"Not that I can think of, at the moment," she admitted. "I'll probably come up with some later on, though. I'm just too...too flustered to think straight, right now. And too tired to get my wits together."

"Well, you know where to find me. I'll make sure my nursing assistant knows to put you at the top of the priority list, second only to a flat-out emergency, if you need to contact me about it all. I want to make sure you have all the information you need to be as comfortable as you can about this."

"I'm not sure 'comfortable' is a word to associate with the situation, hon," Omega said, expression wry. "But I understand, and I appreciate it."

"All right, dear. Head on home and grab something good and substantial to eat."

"Wilco."

* * *

Echo noticed that, when Omega finally got back to their joint quarters, her appetite didn't seem as hearty as he'd expected, and she was much quieter than usual. *But I suppose, if I'd thought about it,* he considered, *I'd have realized that that whole genetic thing was gonna take her mood down a couple pegs. And she was already tired, so she didn't really need the stress, on top of everything else. But it really was something they needed to go ahead and discuss, I guess.*

Still, she ate reasonably well, and tucked away a substantial portion of the cottage casserole, though not as much as he'd thought she would. Even so, between them, there wasn't much in the way of leftovers.

After dinner, which they ate at his dining table, she rose and wandered toward the 'back door' between their quarters, seeming absent-minded. Surprised, he paused his task of loading his stereo with soft, soothing background music, which he'd intended to help take the edge off her mood and enable them to talk about whatever she'd wanted to discuss.

Instead, he followed her silently into her den, watched her sit down in the armchair, and slipped past her to take the near end of the couch; she didn't seem to notice. That disturbed him on several levels, some of which he didn't quite understand. He finally decided he wasn't used to his partner ignoring him. She just sat there, staring off into space, her mind apparently many thousands of light years away. When she showed no sign of even recognizing his presence, let alone speaking, he finally tried to get her attention.

"Meg?"

She startled badly.

"Huh-what?! Echo?! What are you...?"

"Baby, are you all right?"

"Um, oh, uh well, yeah, I guess so. I just...got a lot on my mind."

"This whole thing with the cold cases has really bothered you, hasn't it?"

She stared at him, an odd expression in the blue eyes.

"Uh, yeah, you could sure say that."

* * *

BOY, could you say that, Omega thought, hiding a wry wince. *And then some.*

"Okay, so tell me about it," Echo offered.

"What?!" Omega blurted. "About what?"

"About what Zebra told you, or whatever it is that's bothering you. You told me, before you met with her, that you wanted us to have a talk tonight. So I'm here, baby. What is it you wanted to talk about?"

"Oh," Omega said, her voice sounding flat even to herself. "I, um, well." She paused and drew a deep breath, trying to settle herself, while a patient, concerned Echo sat close by and watched her. "To tell the truth, Echo, what I wanted to talk to you about...well, it's sorta been OBE."

"Overcome by events?"

"Um, yeah. It's pretty much a moot point now." *Is it ever,* she added mentally, as a wave of pain washed through her being. *There's no way on this big blue marble...or any other...that I can ask him if he'd like to take our relationship any farther, given what Zebra just told me a while ago. Not without being honest and telling him about it. And that would probably blow the whole thing up in my face. And even if it didn't blow it up, is it really fair to him?*

"Are you sure? You seem awfully bothered by something. Is it what Zebra told you about the whole alien genetics thing, with the cold cases and all?"

"Um, yeah, that's pretty much it," Omega sidestepped, though everything she said was true. "It's...well Ace, it's one thing when...when the whole spliced genes thing is the memory of an unwanted medical procedure. It's another when you start attaching other beings to the various 'gene grafts,' I guess you could call it. Specific other beings, no less."

"Ooo," Echo murmured, thoughtful. "I hadn't thought about it like that. You've even got names and images on some of 'em now, don't you?"

"Yeah," Omega said; several of the files in the folder Zebra had given her had brief dossiers on the cold cases, complete with photos of the vic-

331

tims, and the Alpha Line Agent had found those as disturbing in their own way as the discovery of animal genes in her makeup. *And at least I can talk to him about THOSE,* she thought. *Maybe...eventually...I can dredge up the courage to talk to him about all the rest too, including our relationship...IF he's okay with the whole other mess. But...not now. Not tonight. I need time to deal with it myself, before I have to deal with the reactions of the man I've come to love.*

"Do you wanna talk about that?" Echo wondered. "I'm here, and I'm set to listen and talk. And you know I got a good shoulder, if you need one."

"Yeah, I know, Ace," she said, offering him what she knew was a wan smile, but unable to make it cheerful. "I suppose it might be good to talk about the, uh, the people I've got in me, I suppose you could say." She watched as Echo pulled a face, apparently not liking her mode of expression.

"Baby, I hate like hell to hear you talk like that," he admitted then. "You put yourself down over this whole thing, when you were a VICTIM. Just as much as those people from whom Slug forcibly took that genetic material, you were a victim who was forced to accept that genetic material."

"I know," she sighed. "It's just...sometimes I think, if I'd been stronger, if I'd been paying more attention...if I'd listened to Momma and not gone out at all, that night..." She shook her head.

"Woulda, shoulda, coulda," Echo said. "Like Fox is fond of saying, hindsight is always 20/20, baby. You aren't a mind reader; you didn't know he was coming. From what you've told me, you had every reason to think you were safe on your family's property. You said your mom didn't want you to go out. What about your dad?"

"He thought I would be safe."

"And was he a good man, a good father?"

"Oh, yeah." Omega smiled, her mind drifting back to her childhood for a moment.

"Then if you're going to blame yourself, you should blame him, too. Don't you see? And so, if it wasn't his fault, it wasn't yours, either."

Omega sighed. *I don't know how to make him understand,* she thought.

* * *

But Echo had heard the sigh, seen the frustrated expression, and read her thoughts from them, to a limited extent.

Okay, he decided. *That's something we'll have to work on, I guess. She can't hear it yet. Not the way I'm trying to say it, at least. I'll keep after it, though, trying different ways to express it, because I really want to get her out of blaming herself for any of it. But she's had enough for now. Time to shift the subject.*

"All right, never mind, baby. We can talk about that some other time, when we're both less tired, and you haven't had upsetting info dumped in your lap."

"Thanks, Ace. I appreciate that."

"So...you wanna talk about the people in the cold cases? Do you remember any of the names?"

"Yeah, I do remember a couple. I'd need to go back and study the files a bit more to remember 'em all. But I think I might do that, just for the sake of honoring their memories."

"Good. I think that's a great idea. Let me know if I can help with that..."

* * *

The next morning, Fox headed for his office, bright and early. Alpha One could already be seen in the Alpha Line briefing room, hard at work on their detailed mission report. Echo looked rested and alert; Omega, slightly less so, but that was understandable—Zebra's glum mood upon arriving home the night before had told the Director how hard Omega had taken the information she'd imparted, without any words being spoken. So he smiled and waved as he went by, and they looked up and waved back. Echo's expression was chipper and friendly; Omega's was friendly enough, but to Fox's knowledgeable eye, troubled and rather downcast.

Uh-oh, Fox suddenly realized, as he headed for the ramp to his office door. *The relationship between them. And the information Zebra gave her last night. I'd lay money Omega has suddenly realized the ramifications of said information on any deeper relationship they might develop. Oh, my poor girl; you're hurting. No wonder you still look tired. Tsu aldi rukhes.*

He shrugged mentally; there was little he could do at this stage of things in any event. So he entered his office and closed the door, heading straight for the wall containing the safe; the bay window was still opaqued from the previous night. In moments it was open, and a certain container extracted. He closed the safe and moved to his desk chair, setting the container in front of him. Then he pulled up the preliminary report Echo had submitted the night before and reviewed it. When he finished, he sat back in his chair, thoughtful.

"Mm," Fox hummed, as he stared at the container on his desk. "You've been a problem, little nudnik..."

Inside the container was, of course, the F'al, the special artifact of Va'du'sha'ā, the one instrument which could identify the rightful monarch of an entire planet, the device which had been in the keeping of the Hou'd'ni for so many millennia.

Now it was in the hands of the Agency, and Fox had to decide what to do with it. Sending it back to Va'du'sha'ā was out of the question, as he already knew; the best he could hope for in such an event would be a temporary destabilization of that planet's government. The worst—and most likely—was a complete overthrow of the government, followed by a civil war, and a return to what had always been a despotic rule under control of some member or another of the royal family. *And by the time you factor in all of the offworld alliances,* Fox considered, *it quickly ends up being interstellar war. And I've had more than enough of THAT in recent years.*

"Perhaps I can help," a faint voice drifted into Fox's consciousness.

"Huh-wha? Who's there?" Fox exclaimed, spinning about to look into all crannies of the room. He slipped one hand surreptitiously into a pocket, fingering one of several lethal weapons always kept hidden on his person. *Who the hell got in here?* he wondered, his other hand drifting toward the hidden button that initiated an emergency summons to Security. *And how did they get in?*

"You need not fear." This time the voice was localized to the volume in front of his desk, as a shimmering shape slowly formed. "I am a friend, and I am here to help."

The being solidified; it was a Gray, a Glu'g'ik from the Zeta Reticuli system.

"Oy! Who the hell are you?" Fox demanded. The Gray smiled, then its features shifted into those of a human—short, with dark wavy hair parted in the middle, and intense blue eyes.

"Perhaps you recognize me now," the alien offered. "I am Ari Ho'd'ni."

* * *

"...You're kidding," Fox said after several moments of intense interrogation.

"No, not at all. I simply got tired of the fame and attention—in addition to realizing that I put my family at risk, should the word of my shows get off Earth and back to Va'du'sha'ā—and thus staged my own death, becoming Bess. Easy enough to pull off for someone of my talents and abilities. Then, many years later, I staged my 'wife's' death, as well. And every year, disguised, I attend the gathering of fans at my supposed 'grave site'—out of nostalgia, I suppose."

"How is it you're still alive? You've far exceeded the normal lifespan of your species."

"That is a long story," Houdini smiled. "You are aware of my, ah, predecessor, Jean Eugène Robert-Houdin, as some make his name?"

"I've heard about him, yes. Supposedly that's where you derived your stage name, except of course in the Agency we know that it's really an Anglicization of your true clan name."

"Precisely. As was Houdin's."

"He was a Glu'g'ik too, then? I know that my top team of agents encountered him recently...but I don't have all the details yet."

"He is, and he is a kinsman. But he desired to be an explorer, and he left Va'du'sha'ā centuries ago in order to explore the galaxy. And it seems that, at some point, he heard of a small planet orbiting a fairly ordinary star, a planet with a primitive culture, but one with great promise. He came to Earth, fell in love with it and its people, and stayed."

"And I suppose you found him when you and your family landed in Europe? But wait—he shouldn't have still been alive either!"

"Precisely, and yes. You see, in the course of his explorations, he learned many things. Among these things were ways in which those able to manipulate the quantum foam could combat certain degenerative diseases, such as what you know as cancer. J'ēn, once on Earth and in the absence of the distractions and stresses of the royalty, and upon the development of his 'stage magic show'—really Glu'g'ik quantum manipulation—he began to practice these techniques and, well, he found some additional abilities developing. One of these was an ability to extend his own life."

"How?"

"By continually modifying the quantum foam within our own bodies, to counter the aging process. It is a difficult technique to develop, but it is effective."

"So it appears. And he taught it to you?"

"Indeed. He secretly mentored me upon my arrival. He is currently the curator for the museum that has been made of his old home, if you can believe it! He finds it amusing. And I suppose it is."

"So you're both immortal?"

"Oh, no, far from it. We are simply considerably more long-lived than our brethren."

"But you could teach other Glu'gu'ik the technique."

"No," Houdini murmured, seeming thoughtful. "It would appear not. J'ēn tried to teach his wife and children, but they were unable to master the technique. In turn, I tried to teach my brother Ar'd'n—you would know him as Theodore; I called him 'Dash'—but he could not learn it, either. Oh, he assimilated a few rudimentary things, sufficient to enable us to perform some very sophisticated stage illusions. But he never learned the ability to repair the body, to extend its life. He seemed...uninterested. As did, I might add, the rest of my family, despite my best efforts."

"So...you became the caretaker of the F'al by default. When the rest of your family...passed."

"More or less, yes. And once that came to pass, J'ēn helped considerably, of course. He understood its importance. He was not himself in the direct lineage of caretakers as was I, but he was certainly aware of it, merely by dint of being Hou'd'ni." Houdini drew a deep breath. "But it has been... difficult. When a man is supposed to be dead, it can be hard for him to maintain care of such things over decades, over centuries."

"I expect so."

"And so I believe that the Agency is the best place for the F'al now," Houdini continued. "But it requires a Ho'd'ni in order to control it."

"And that's a problem," Fox agreed. "If we let your homeworld know we have it, the whole political destabilization comes to pass anyway."

"Entirely true. And that is why I am here."

"You're volunteering to work with us?"

"Not exactly." Houdini grinned. "You do not need me."

"Of course we do! We don't have a Ho'd'ni to control the thing!"

"But you do," Houdini pressed. "For word has filtered back to me that there is now a...how shall I put this? An adjunct Ho'd'ni, on Earth."

"I...don't understand."

"Director, would you be so kind as to summon Agent Omega to your office, in private?"

Fox's eyes went wide.

* * *

"What the...? You mean me?" Omega asked, astounded.

"I certainly do," Houdini declared. "I can sense the Hou'd'ni genetics in you from here."

"Fox, how do we even know he's the real deal?" Omega demanded.

"Because I've had him under clandestine surveillance since he arrived, Omega," Fox explained. "And not only have my systems identified him without doubt as a living Glu'g'ik, they've also pegged him as Hou'd'ni...with a considerable amount of upstream genetic drift."

"Meaning this is an OLD Hou'd'ni," Omega verified.

"Right," Fox confirmed. "A REALLY old Hou'd'ni."

Houdini chuckled.

"Older than you know," he said. "For I am several decades older than even my purported Earth birth date."

"Okay, look—I want Echo in here," Omega said.

"He is not involved in the matter," Houdini replied.

"The hell he's not! He's my PARTNER, he's the head of Alpha Line, the department to which I'm assigned, and if you want me to do this thing, then he HAS to be involved! Besides—Fox, if that's really Houdini, and you do NOT call Echo in here to meet him, he'll never forgive you," Omega ended her rant with a grin.

"She has a point there," Fox agreed, matching her grin. "Several, actually. I think we really do need Echo here, if for no other reason than he's her department chief, and we need his approval."

"Oh, very well," Houdini agreed.

"Let me get him," Fox said, reaching for his cell phone.

* * *

"You're kidding," Echo declared, folding his arms, his expression skeptical in the extreme.

"No, zun, we aren't," Fox replied. "Here. Have a look at my sensor data."

Echo and Omega bent over the virtual readout embedded in Fox's desktop. Omega pointed at several entries; Echo met her glance, querying, and she nodded.

"Satisfied?" Fox wondered, as Houdini waited patiently in one of the visitor chairs.

"I...guess so," Echo finally gave in. "If y'all are sure."

"We're sure," Omega vouched.

"This is him, and that's the current plan. Are you game for it?" Fox asked.

"Well, that's not the real issue, is it?" Echo responded. "This isn't about me, though I appreciate the chance to meet Mr. Houdini. Meg, baby, are you up for this?" Then he added, swiftly using their secret codes, *As upset as you were about the whole genetic cold case stuff last night, are you sure you want to involve yourself in this, in addition to?*

"Yeah, I think so, Ace. Provided I got your backup, should anything go sideways," Omega decided. "I'm not sure I really have a choice, anyway—SOMEBODY has to do it. But I believe, once we get the thing suitably stowed in...what was it y'all called it? The Vault? Then there's not gonna be a whole lot more to be done. Oh, maybe check on it once in a while. But if I understood Mr. Ho'd'ni correctly, it's pretty much self-sustaining, so it'll just...BE there."

"Correct," Houdini averred. "You will be the caretaker. That is all. You need not activate it or otherwise interact with it, other than to ensure it remains where you put it, unharmed and undamaged."

"Which it will, in the Vault," Fox agreed.

"What happens when I..." Omega began, then broke off.

"When you what?" Fox wondered.

"Okay, guys, let's face it," Omega elaborated with a sigh. "I'm not immortal, and ours is a dangerous business. And I'm in Alpha Line, the department that takes on the toughest assignments. ASSUMING I live to retirement, eventually I AM gonna retire...and kick the bucket sometime thereafter. And then who takes care of the F'al?" Unseen by his partner, but not his director, Echo winced.

"That is surprisingly easy to handle," Houdini said. "It merely involves something I had intended to do in any case, once our current little, ah, 'treasure hunt,' I believe you put it, was at an end. I am the current caretaker. You and I will perform the ceremony of caretaker transferal... and then we will perform an additional ceremony which will permanently modify the F'al. I had been 'talking' to it, you see, over the years. It seems the makers always expected Va'du'sha'ā to develop a representative form of government, sooner rather than later; the ruling family proved uncommonly steadfast and stubborn, so the Imperial authority lasted many of your millennia longer than anticipated. But there is a program hidden in the F'al, and when we perform the additional ceremony to activate that program, it will designate you as The Last Keeper. When you cease, it will..."

"Die?" Omega finished for him, seeming sad. "I've kind of gathered that it's alive."

"It is, and it is not," Houdini said. "But when you are no more, it will detect the cessation of your quantum pattern, no matter where in the Universe you are; that is part of the ceremony we will perform, so that it forms a quantum entanglement with you. Upon your demise, then its primary function—the identification of the ruling family of Va'du'sha'ā—will also cease. You can perform a ritual to deactivate it earlier, if you so choose; I will teach it to you, as well. Then it becomes nothing more than a small computer. It is ancient, and it is tired; it will likely shut down when you do, and willingly."

"Why didn't anybody do that before?" Fox demanded.

"Because no one had the lifetime to develop the kind of relationship with it that I have done. No one else—save its creator—could 'talk' to it. I can, and have."

"So nobody knew, huh?" Echo asked.

"Precisely. That knowledge was lost to the Hou'd'ni clan..." Houdini shrugged, "millennia ago. Likely during Kre'd'ta's Coup; unfortunately, my clan split and took sides in the revolt. We were nearly wiped out."

"Ouch," Omega murmured.

"Exactly. This is why, when an even worse political situation began to form during my youth, my family chose to flee, rather than stay around for the blood-letting."

"Is this ceremony stuff something y'all need my help on?" Echo asked.

"No, Agent Echo," Houdini informed him. "It must be done by Omega and myself. No one else must even be present. Well," he addressed Omega, "a trusted spouse may be present. None other. But I have gathered...?"

"No, I'm not married, espoused, or otherwise mated, or even engaged; nor likely to be," Omega noted, and Echo briefly wondered why she said it in such a weary tone. In his concern for his partner, he missed the narrow-eyed, thoughtful glance that Fox gave both members of Alpha One. "So it's just you and me, Mr. Ho'd'ni."

"Then what do you need me for?" Echo wondered.

"For one thing, I knew you'd love to meet him," Omega said, shooting her partner a tired smile. "Especially after that whole treasure hunt thing we just did."

"Thanks." Echo smiled back. "You were right."

"But for another, we really DO need your okay, Ace," Omega continued, growing sober. "You're my partner, so anything I'd need to do, you'd likely be involved with, to some degree or other. AND you're ALSO my department chief—which means this whole thing needs your buy-off, or it won't fly."

"Well...in all honesty, Fox CAN override me," Echo pointed out. "He's the Director, after all."

"I've tried never to throw my weight around if I don't have to, Echo," Fox said. "And I don't want to start now. You're her department chief; the normal order is, you have to sign off on such a long-term assignment before I even get the chance."

"Okay, then. I'm good with it," Echo concluded. "You got paper-work?"

"Electronic, but yes. Here." Fox brought it up on his desktop display, then shifted his chair to one side, to permit access. "Use my virtual key-board and do your thing, Alpha Line chief. Then I'll approve your autho-rization."

Within moments, the matter was done.

* * *

"...Wow. So you learned how to partly counter aging," Echo noted, some time later, as the three Agents—Alpha One and the Director—contin-ued a conversation with Houdini, largely driven by curiosity and a desire to understand. "That's...pretty cool."

"So does that explain why we found one of the F'al pieces in your star on the Hollywood Walk of Fame?" Omega asked. "In a much newer cavity?"

"Oh yes, and that is readily explainable," Houdini said. "I did indeed have it in a different building on the old Lasky lot, where my films were originally made...though we did a fair amount of what is termed 'location shooting,' so in no wise was the entirety of any one film made on the lot. But when it seemed that this 'barn' was the only structure which would sur-vive the transition to the new studios, I moved the on'cik into it. I was never happy with that as a hiding place, however; in a wooden structure, I did not feel it was as safe as those I hid in stone or concrete or the like." Houdini shrugged. "Then, after some few decades, I heard that I was about to be awarded that star, and in some amusement—and, I must admit, a certain amount of performer's ego and pride—I decided to go in disguise to watch the ceremony...which was to be on the anniversary of my purported death, adding to the humor, at least from my perspective. And of course, at the time, this barn was once again in danger of demolition, its future in doubt. It was then that I realized that a cavity created in the sidewalk beneath the star would be the perfect hiding place, because it, as opposed to the barn building, was unlikely to be going anywhere. So I moved the on'cik, and left the clue leading to it."

"That...makes good sense," Echo decided. "What about the séance? I take it that was you, partly 'phased in,' I guess you could say?"

"Indeed," Houdini confirmed. "It was surprisingly easy to fool my cousin. She is still very young, for all her training, and I am very old for a Glu'g'ik, with skills commensurate with my age...for I have continued to learn and develop my abilities over my entire life. It was child's play to remain on the outskirts, essentially invisible even without my innate powers; a good illusionist learns to do these kinds of things, as I am sure you all know in your own fashion. I knew the Agency had a presence there, for I saw you lot mingling in the crowds, though no one else noticed—not even Gla'd's. I had long planned for how to manage in the event someone from Va'du'sha'ā came looking, and wrote and memorized the poem years ago. I fully expected that one or another of you Agents would know the lore that has sprung up about me, but I knew that someone from the homeworld would have no idea! So I couched my clues in a kind of coded wording that alluded to my career on Earth and the traditions and legends that sprang up around it. In that way, I was assured that any emissary from Va'du'sha'ā could not find the parts, but only a member of the Division One Agency, who knew the truth about me and my family, could do so."

"Nice touch," Echo determined.

"Yep," Omega averred. "And explains a lot."

"I thought so," Houdini agreed.

* * *

Houdini remained several more days, performing the rituals designed to make Omega The Last Keeper of the F'al of Va'du'sha'ā. He also spent a good deal of time teaching Omega how to handle the F'al, as well as familiarizing the F'al with her. By the time he was done, the F'al recognized Omega as its only and last Keeper, and Houdini indicated to her that it was glad its long life was at last ending.

Houdini also spent time helping Fox proof Headquarters against rogue Glu'gu'ik who might have abilities such as his own...which, he demonstrated, even eclipsed the capabilities of Ke'ri Gla'd's and her compatriots, after well more than a century to develop them.

342

While Omega learned those details essential to keeping the F'al, Echo took the opportunity of having an expert—and possibly THE expert—teacher; he added a few more sleight of hand moves to his repertoire, pointing out to his partner that such things often came in handy in the course of a mission.

"Because it's kinda useful to be able to suddenly produce a pair of force cuffs, or even a weapon," Echo declared. "Tends to throw off the perp, see."

"Yeah, yeah," Omega grinned, as an amused Houdini watched the interaction. "You're just using it as an excuse to be able to say that the great Houdini taught 'em to you."

"That too," Echo agreed without a moment's hesitation. "Wouldn't you?"

"She already has been," Houdini interjected just then, and Omega flushed.

"Aha! Gotcha!" Echo crowed.

"Yeah, well, maybe a little," she acknowledged, grinning sheepishly.

* * *

Once Houdini declared Omega ready, Alpha One, accompanied by Houdini and Fox, carried the F'al to the Vault. Its location was so secret that only special computer-guided transportation could take them there, and none of them knew where it was, once they'd arrived.

The special maglev train deposited them in front of a large, relatively simple, metal door—but all of the Agents present knew that this was a special alloy of tungsten, titanium, and several offworld metals, and was nearly impenetrable. It had had to be cast in one giant form, because it was too hard to machine.

To one side of the door, set into a wall of similar material, was a control panel. Fox and Omega offered retinal scans and voice prints to identify themselves; seconds later, there was a soft click, and actuators slowly opened the massive door, allowing the small group access to the Vault. Once they had entered, the door closed...rather more swiftly than it had opened. It latched with a loud clang.

Before them lay a maze.

"All right, Echo, you stay here with Ho'd'ni, guarding the door, and I'll escort Omega through the maze to the lockbox for the F'al," Fox ordered.

"On it, Boss."

"Let's go, Omega."

* * *

The two headed deep into the maze, which was largely composed of solid, opaque force fields. Fox made sure that his companion was adequately tracking her route through the maze, the container with the F'al in hand.

"It's not a short route, is it?" Omega noted, after a good ten minutes of working their way far into the maze.

"No, but that's as it should be," Fox agreed. "We've got another twenty or thirty minutes before we're at the lockbox I assigned for this tchotchke."

"Oy, as you like to say."

"Just so, maydele."

* * *

Twenty-four minutes later, Fox came to a stop, and Omega stopped beside him.

"This is the place?" Omega asked.

"It is. Do it like I showed you."

Omega waved her hands in a specific series of motions; a soft hiss sounded, and a small door opened in the force wall.

"Put it in there, then press your hand on the inside of the door," Fox instructed.

"But I don't have fingerprints."

"You don't need 'em. Your hand still has a distinct shape, and will leave a unique pressure pattern for the computer to recognize."

"...Which no normal organizations on Earth know how to utilize, anyway," Omega realized. "Right."

She followed instructions, and moments later, the ancient artificial semi-intelligence known as the F'al was sealed away in a high-tech tomb.

They turned to retrace their steps out.

* * *

"How was it?" Houdini asked, when the pair reappeared.

"It felt...content," Omega decided. "It understood, and it was satisfied. And maybe tired. Glad of the rest."

"Waitaminit," Echo said. "It thinks? I mean, really? I thought you were just sort of drawing analogies, that day in Fox's office. And you heard it?"

"Sort of, I believe," Omega said, thoughtful. "I think it's got a kind of low-level sentience. That's why it responded to my induced genetics, and why it would run from anyone without Hou'd'ni bloodlines."

"She is correct," Houdini declared. "One of the things I made certain to do, as I was teaching your partner how to handle it, was to impress upon it that it could be misused, and that anyone but myself, J'ēn, or Omega, here, was not to be trusted, even if that person had Hou'd'ni genetics."

"That way," Omega added, "nobody else can fetch the thing out but us."

"Except YOU. Though I think it would not mind if I came by to say hello with you, from time to time. It also informed me that it approved of your partner, so if he were with you during a visit, it would be accepting. And once we three—you, me, and J'ēn—are at long last departed to the Beyond, it effectively becomes inert," Houdini finished. "No one else will ever be able to access it, because it will not allow it. And in all likelihood, as I said at our earlier discussion, it will choose to deactivate itself. It can and does become lonely, and it has often been tucked away for many decades at a time. An eternity locked away from the universe will not appeal to it."

"An excellent resolution," Fox said. "All of that."

"Ace? You okay?" Omega asked. "You got a funny expression, there..."

"He simply does not like to think of your death," Houdini explained, as Fox unlocked the outside door and they exited.

"Yeah, he's right," Echo agreed with a sigh. "After losing X-ray a couple years ago, then almost losing you to Slug, it's not something I'm especially enthusiastic about considering, these days."

"Aw," Omega said with a smile, leaning into him and hooking her arm through his. "Thanks. I appreciate that. For what it's worth," she added, growing serious, "the feeling's mutual."

"Good," Fox interjected. "Then you'll keep each other alive on these missions I have to send you on."

"Yup," Alpha One said in unison, as the four boarded the maglev to return to Headquarters.

* * *

"And what is done is done," Houdini told Fox, over drinks from the secret stash in his office, much later that day. "May I compliment you on the quality of your agents, Fox? I am most impressed with the integrity of the Last Keeper of the Fa'l. And her partner."

"Me, too," Fox agreed, then sipped his Balvenie thoughtfully. "I suppose Omega told you a little of her history?"

"She did. She has been through much, that one, and come out the other side."

"Yes. Though I rather think my choice of partner for her...if it really was a choice, given the machinations to get her here...played a significant factor in that."

"Without doubt. Echo is her bulwark. And I suspect she is his, as well."

"They go together pretty damn well."

"They do, indeed. I wonder..." Houdini sipped his own drink thoughtfully.

"Yes, I've wondered that, too," Fox agreed, reading the other man's facial expression, despite the fact that Houdini was currently maintaining an appearance halfway between Glu'g'ik and human; it was something, Houdini had told him, he learned to do many decades earlier, in order to speed up his 'metamorphoses' between roles. "But, while I know they think VERY highly of each other, and I've heard Omega call Echo her best friend, and other agents have reported similar remarks, I have no idea whether or not their relationship goes, or even could go, past friendship to...more."

"Interesting."

"Isn't it? I do know that Echo insisted, a few months back while she was...'gone'...that a special provision be put in for their partnership, assuming she came back. But it wasn't in the nature of a life partnership or anything."

"How so?"

Fox shrugged. "Bureaucratic stuff, mostly. But it did necessitate the establishment of a new category of partnerships. Just not a life partnership, though by the sound of it, this one will run until they're both dead and gone."

"A life partnership...that is how your Division One designates spouses?"

"Right. When the Ennead worked up and approved our charter, no one thought to add provision for formal marriages. It was a helluva big oversight, but so far it hasn't been one that the Council considered important enough to amend the charter. So we got around it by designating this thing we call a 'life partnership.' The couple can have a ceremony if they wish, or not, but the paperwork designates 'em as a spousal partnership."

"But that is not what they have."

"No."

"Pity. I think they make an excellent couple."

"Don't say that to them. I'm not sure HOW they'd react."

Houdini laughed.

"Never fear, friend Fox; I will say nothing. But that does not mean I may not watch from a distance," he warned with a grin.

"Not a problem. Come by and visit once in a while, now that we know you—and J'ēn—are still here."

"I may do just that. Though not openly. And now, my friend," Houdini said, draining the last of his Scotch, "it is time for me to go. You know how to find me if you need me..."

"I do."

"Give the very special lady Omega, and her equally special partner Echo, my best wishes, and my goodbyes until the time comes when we may meet again, would you?"

"Of course, Houdini. It has been a pleasure, sir."

"Likewise, Fox, likewise."

The Glu'g'ik became translucent, then faded away; nothing was left to show he had ever been there except the empty old-fashioned glass, a few half-melted ice cubes in it.

Fox took a long breath and let it out in a sigh. He swirled the drink in his glass, mixing the ice water into the last remnants of his Balvenie, then he knocked it all back and drained the glass.

Fox rose, picked up the two glasses, and slid them into the recycling chute. He moved to the door of his office, turned out the lights, closed and locked the door behind himself as he exited.

Then he headed for his quarters, where a certain off-duty physician awaited with dinner...and satin and lace for dessert.

Author Notes

First of all, there are the usual suspects to thank: My parents, Steve and Colene Gannaway, and my husband, Darrell Osborn. They are always supportive and helpful, and Darrell is great for brainstorming, not to mention cover art.

But speaking of brainstorming, there are a few other people to thank—my beta readers, Dr. James K. Woosley, Larry Bauer, and Evelyn Hively. Much brainstorming with them on this entire series is making for a lotta fun. (And yes, this series is a delight and a romp to write.) An additional brainstormer includes Susan Powers of Lady Osborn's Pub group on Facebook, and the entire group called 'Stephanie Osborn's Fan Club,' who helped me determine a name for Burbulon Vex, aka Klack! Specific kudos go to Christopher MacArthur for the name, but everyone threw in suggestions. It was a lot of fun.

Charlie Martin was a wonderful help with some German and Yiddish tidbits; I am not a Germanic scholar by any means. (Romance languages, I do okay. Germanic ones, not so much. But Yiddish—Germanic mixed with Hebrew and a smattering of other languages, too? I'm lost.) Specifically, he helped me work out the name of Omega's airskimmer, *SchmultzBlitz*, which translates to—you may have guessed it—Greased Lightning! (After all, it IS a souped-up hot rod!) And yes, Echo's jesting, rather disparaging nickname for it, *DonnerFurz*, translates to...Thunder Fart.

You also may or may not recognize my reference to Zaragosa, Spain, during the, er, 'snipe hunt' sequence, and the fictional historical marker featuring an 'archaic' space plane craft. Zaragosa has a huge runway and, back when I worked as a payload flight controller for the Shuttle program, Zaragosa was one of a couple of emergency landing sites for the Shuttle, in the event of a TAL Abort, aka Trans-Atlantic Landing Abort. (If you paid close attention during Shuttle launches, you sometimes heard the references, such as, "Single Engine Zaragosa," which specific call meant the

Shuttle could reach Zaragosa for a TAL abort on one engine.) I thought it would be a fun site to throw in there.

Also, in my defense, my husband, in addition to being a fantastic graphic artist, is also an award-winning magician, and so I am well aware of all of the lore and legend—true and otherwise—surrounding Houdini (though, like Echo, I make no claims to being an expert). This means I'm aware of the current unkempt state of the Machpelah Cemetery, as well as the fact that some years back, the cemetery administration started closing the cemetery on Halloween after someone vandalized Houdini's grave, chopping off and making away with the bust of Houdini. For the purposes of my story, I chose to go on as if the cemetery were NOT closed; given the tendency for the gate to remain unlocked most of the time per reports, this seems not improbable to me. (If you have heartburn about it, consider the entire universe in which I'm writing, and realize that it may well be an alternate reality in any event.)

I hope no one takes my story as in any way disrespecting Houdini or his family; I am myself in awe of what I have seen and read of his abilities. I wanted to write a story loosely revolving around Halloween; and his untimely death on that date, coupled with a bit of creative license, played perfectly for the story.

~Stephanie Osborn

Huntsville, AL

January 2017

About the Author

Stephanie Osborn is a former payload flight controller, a veteran of over twenty years of working in the civilian space program, as well as various military space defense programs. She has worked on numerous Space Shuttle flights and the International Space Station, and counts the training of astronauts on her resumé. Of those astronauts she trained, one was Kalpana Chawla, a member of the crew lost in the Columbia disaster.

She holds graduate and undergraduate degrees in four sciences: Astronomy, Physics, Chemistry, and Mathematics, and she is "fluent" in several more, including Geology and Anatomy. She obtained her various degrees from Austin Peay State University in Clarksville, TN and Vanderbilt University in Nashville, TN.

Stephanie is currently retired from space work. She now happily "passes it forward," teaching math and science via numerous media including radio, podcasting, and public speaking, as well as working with SIGMA, the science fiction think tank, while writing science fiction mysteries based on her knowledge, experience, and travels.

For more, go to http://www.stephanie-osborn.com/.

A sneak peek at *A Very UnCONventional Christmas*, Book 3 of the Division One series, by Stephanie Osborn!

"All right," Fox summarized, after the Alpha teams had debriefed to Fox about their respective excursions, "so we have the connection between the toys and the movie. A Dabanoran going by the name of Michael Smithers is feeding information to the toy designer, AND developing the script for the movie. The cartoon is a promo spinoff."

"Looks that way," India confirmed.

"Good job, India. Between that information and what Romeo and Echo brought back from the film shoot, we've got our connection," Fox commended.

"Uh, Fox, it was partly Meg's idea," India volunteerered. Fox ignored her and continued.

"I'll have Smithers taken into custody. And Echo, great idea about using the science fiction convention as cover for the diplomatic visit. I'll set that up right away."

"Will you still want Alpha Line to work the diplomatic detail, Fox?" Echo asked him.

"Probably...or at least, those of you who aren't already on assignment. I'll let you know. Call it a day and get some rest for now. Dismissed. And Romeo, goth eyeliner is not an acceptable part of the male Agent attire. We want to blend in, not stand out."

Romeo and India both looked chagrined as India muttered, "Oh, hell, I thought I got it all."

* * *

The four exited Fox's office, and the door closed behind them.

"What gives?" Romeo asked, confused and worried, as they walked across the Core toward the Alpha Line room. "I saw four of us in there, but it looked to me like Fox only saw three."

"You noticed that, huh?" Omega noted, wry. A silent Echo watched Omega, concerned.

"Looks like you were right, girlfriend. I wonder what's wrong?" India pondered.

"I don't know." Omega shrugged and tried to act nonchalant. "I guess I'll find out soon enough."

* * *

Zero Days—Eight Days

Omega was almost ready to report to work the next morning, and was reaching for her Suit jacket, when the cell phone rang.

"Omega here. Oh, hi, Fox..."

She listened for a long time. Halfway through the call, she went white to the lips.

"Yes...but I...well, no! Of course not! Surely you don't think...but... oh...yes...all- all right. I...understand, Fox."

She slowly closed the cell phone, staring at it in shock.

"No," she whispered. "It can't be...after everything, this was the only place I...had left..." Finally she threw her head back, closed her eyes, and fairly howled. "NOOOOOOOooo...!" It was a cry of despair.

A despondent Omega sank slowly to her knees, arms dangling in front of her, shoulders bowed, head hanging dejectedly, utterly hopeless. She still unconsciously clutched the cell phone.

* * *

An alarmed Echo, in sock feet and shirt sleeves, cuffs undone, tie loose, slammed through the bedroom door scant seconds later and hit his knees in front of her, grabbing her shoulders.

"What's wrong?! Meg??"

She raised her head and looked at him, so white he thought she would pass out.

"It all makes sense now, Echo. Fox... has confined me to quarters. They think...Echo, they think I'M the mole."

353

Don't miss any of these highly entertaining SF/F books by Stephanie Osborn!

Burnout: The mystery of Space Shuttle STS-281 (ISBN: 1-60619-200-0) by Stephanie Osborn

How do you react when you discover the next shuttle disaster has happened...right on schedule?

Burnout is a SF mystery about a Space Shuttle disaster that turns out to be no accident. As the true scope of the disaster is uncovered by the principle investigators, "Crash" Murphy and Dr. Mike Anders, they find themselves running for their lives as friends, lovers and coworkers involved in the investigation perish around them.

* * *

Sherlock Holmes: Gentleman Aegis series by Stephanie Osborn:
Sherlock Holmes and the Mummy's Curse

Sherlock Holmes and the Mummy's Curse (ISBN: 1-51888-312-5) by Stephanie Osborn

Holmes and Watson. Two names linked by mystery and danger from the beginning.

Within the first year of their friendship and while both are young men, Holmes and Watson are still finding their way in the world, with all the troubles that such young men usually have: Financial straits, troubles of the female persuasion, hazings, misunderstandings between friends, and more. Watson's Afghan wounds are still tender, his health not yet fully recovered, and there can be no consideration of his beginning a new practice as yet. Holmes, in his turn, is still struggling to found the new profession of consulting detective. Not yet truly established in London, let alone with the reputations they will one day possess, they are between cases and at loose ends when Holmes' old professor of archaeology contacts him.

Professor Willingham Whitesell makes an appeal to Holmes' unusual skill set and a request. Holmes is to bring Watson to serve as the dig team's physician and come to Egypt at once to translate hieroglyphics for his prestigious archaeological dig. There in the wilds of the Egyptian desert, plagued by heat, dust, drought and cobras, the team hopes to find the very first Pharaoh. Instead, they find something very different... (First book in the Gentleman Aegis series)

Sherlock Holmes and the Mummy's Curse is a Silver Falchion Award winner.

* * *

Displaced Detective series by Stephanie Osborn:
The Case of the Displaced Detective: The Arrival
The Case of the Displaced Detective: At Speed
The Case of the Cosmological Killer: The Rendlesham Incident
The Case of the Cosmological Killer: Endings and Beginnings
A Case of Spontaneous Combustion
Fear in the French Quarter

The Case of the Displaced Detective: The Arrival (ISBN: 1-60619-189-7) by Stephanie Osborn is a SF mystery in which brilliant hyperspatial physicist, Dr. Skye Chadwick, discovers there are alternate realities, often populated by those we consider only literary characters. Can Chadwick help Holmes come up to speed in modern investigative techniques in time to stop the spies? Will Holmes be able to thrive in our modern world? Is Chadwick now Holmes' new "Watson" — or more?

And what happens next?   [First book in the *Displaced Detective* series]

The Case of the Displaced Detective: At Speed (ISBN: 1-60619-191-0) by Stephanie Osborn

Having foiled sabotage of Project: Tesseract by an unknown spy ring, Sherlock Holmes and Dr. Skye Chadwick face the next challenge. How do they find the members of this diabolical spy ring when they do not even know what the ring is trying to accomplish? And how can they do it when Skye is recovering from no less than two nigh-fatal wounds?

Can they work out the intricacies of their relationship? Can they determine the reason the spy ring is after the tesseract? And — most importantly — can they stop it? [Second book in the *Displaced Detective* series]

The Case of the Cosmological Killer: The Rendlesham Incident (ISBN: 1-60619-193-4) by Stephanie Osborn

In 1980, RAF Bentwaters and Woodbridge were plagued by UFO sightings that were never solved. Now, McFarlane, a resident of Suffolk has died of fright during a new UFO encounter. On holiday in London, Sherlock Holmes and Skye Chadwick-Holmes are called upon by Her Majesty's Secret Service to investigate the death.

What is the UFO? Why does Skye find it familiar? Who — or what — killed McFarlane?

And how can the pair do what even Her Majesty's Secret Service could not? [Third book in the *Displaced Detective* series]

The Case of the Cosmological Killer: Endings and Beginnings (ISBN: 1-60619-195-0) by Stephanie Osborn

After the revelations in *The Rendlesham Incident*, Holmes and Skye find they have not one, but two, very serious problems facing them. Not only did their "UFO victim" most emphatically NOT die from a close encounter, he was dying twice over — from completely unrelated causes. Holmes must now find the murderers before they find the secret of the McFarlane farm. And to add to their problems, another continuum — containing another Skye and Holmes — has approached Skye for help to stop the collapse of their own spacetime, a collapse that could take Skye with it, should she happen to be in their tesseract core when it occurs. [Fourth book in the *Displaced Detective* series]

A Case of Spontaneous Combustion (ISBN: 1-60619-197-7) by Stephanie Osborn

When an entire village west of London is wiped out in an apparent case of mass spontaneous combustion, Her Majesty's Secret Service contacts The Holmes Agency to investigate. Once in London, Holmes looks into the horror that is now Stonegrange. His investigations take him into a dangerous undercover assignment in search of a possible terror ring, though he cannot determine how a human agency could have caused the disaster. Meanwhile, alone in Colorado, Skye is forced to battle raging wildfires and tame a wild mustang stallion, all while believing that her husband has abandoned her. Who — or what — caused the horror in Stonegrange? Will Holmes find his way safely through the metaphorical minefield that is modern Middle Eastern politics? Will this predicament seriously damage — even destroy — the couple's relationship? And can Holmes stop the terrorists before they unleash their outré weapon again? [Fifth book in the *Displaced Detective* series]

Fear in the French Quarter (ISBN: 1-60619-202-7) by Stephanie Osborn revolves around a jaunt by no less than Sherlock Holmes himself — brought to the modern day from an alternate universe's Victorian era by his continuum parallel, who is now his wife, Dr. Skye Chadwick-Holmes — to famed New Orleans for both business and pleasure. There, the detective couple investigates ghostly apparitions, strange disappearances, mystic phenomena, and challenge threats to the very universe they call home.

It was supposed to be a working holiday for Skye and Sherlock, along with their friend, the modern day version of Doctor Watson — some federal training that also gave them the chance to explore New Orleans, as the ghosts of the French Quarter become exponentially more active. When the couple uncovers an imminently catastrophic cause, whose epicenter lies squarely in the middle of Le Vieux Carré, they must race against time to stop it before the whole thing breaks wide open — and more than one universe is destroyed. [Sixth book in the *Displaced Detective* series]